Fool Me Once . . .

"First salvo away," Commander Maguire reported tensely. "Impact in twenty-five seconds."

Hannah grunted, watching her display narrowly. *You bastards are dead. You should've known better than to send tin-cans through without support. Were you that sure you could sucker me again?*

"Sir!" It was her communications officer. "I'm receiving an emergency hail!"

Hannah nodded. The Thebans had already demonstrated their ability to masquerade as Terrans over the com, and if they could confuse the defenders, even if only long enough to complete their scans and send back courier drones with exact data on the defenses, the advantage for their follow-on echelons would be incalculable.

"What sort of hail?" she asked almost incuriously.

"They say they're Terrans, sir. It's from a Captain Meuller."

"What?!" Hannah leapt from her command chair and vaulted Maguire's console like a champion low-hurdler. She landed beside the com officer, grabbing his small screen and wrenching it around to stare at the face of her best friend from the Academy.

Baen Books by David Weber

Honor Harrington
On Basilisk Station
The Honor of the Queen
The Short Victorious War
Field of Dishonor
Flag in Exile
Honor Among Enemies
In Enemy Hands
Echoes of Honor
(forthcoming)
More Than Honor
(editor)

Oath of Swords
The War God's Own

Mutineers' Moon
The Armageddon Inheritance
Heirs of Empire

Path of the Fury

Insurrection
(with Steve White)
Crusade
(with Steve White)
In Death Ground
(with Steve White)

DAVID WEBER
STEVE WHITE

CRUSADE

This is a work of fiction. All the characters and events portrayed in this book are fictional, and any resemblance to real people
or events is purely coincidental.

A Baen Books Original

Baen Publishing Enterprises
P.O. Box 1403
Riverdale NY 10471

ISBN: 0-671-72111-9

Cover art by Paul Alexander

First printing, March 1992
Third printing, July 1998

Distributed by Simon & Schuster
1230 Avenue of the Americas
New York, NY 10020

Printed in the United States of America

TABLE OF CONTENTS

CHAPTER ONE
Exiles' Return

"Is the *zeget* to your liking?"

Twenty-Sixth Least Claw of the Khan Khardanish'zarthan, Lord Talphon, combed his claws suavely through his luxuriant whiskers, and his slit-pupiled eyes glinted across the table at his liaison officer.

"Yes, thank you, Captain. And it's quite well cooked, too."

Khardanish noted Lieutenant Johansen's teeth-hidden smile with approval, for Humans often forgot that bared teeth were a challenge among his people. He knew Johansen had studied the *Zheeerlikou'valkhannaieee* carefully in preparation for this assignment, yet it was still gratifying to see such awareness of proper behavior. Not that he was quite prepared to stop teasing his guest just yet.

"I am glad," he said, "and I apologize for how long the cooks took to grasp that you would truly prefer it cooked."

"Not necessary, Captain. I console myself with the

thought that a TFN chef would find it just as hard to believe *you* would truly prefer it raw."

Khardanish allowed himself the snarling purr of a chuckle. It was remarkable how well he and Johansen had learned to read one another's nuances, particularly since neither had the proper vocal apparatus to speak the other's language. Khardanish suspected he had drawn the Lorelei Patrol at least partly because he understood Terran Standard English. There was much talk of new translating software, but the current generation remained crude and imprecise . . . and used too much memory for a lowly destroyer, anyway.

The least claw had been less than enthusiastic when he heard about his new post. It was flattering for a least claw to serve, in effect, as a small claw with his own squadron, but the Tenth Destroyer Squadron's four old ships hardly constituted the Navy's cutting edge, nor did the Lorelei System qualify as a critical sector. It was one of the very few systems the Khanate had succeeded in wresting from the Federation in the First Interstellar War of two Orion centuries before, but the thoroughly useless star was hopelessly indefensible (as the Terrans had proved in ISW-2), which, he suspected, was probably why the Federation had permitted his people to keep it. Lorelei had no habitable planets, and only one of its six warp points led to Orion territory; four led to Terran space, and the sixth led only to death, for no survey ship had ever returned from its far terminus. His *Znamae* and her sisters were here purely to "show the flag," as the Terrans put it.

Yet Khardanish had come to realize his duty held an importance too few of his fellows could appreciate. Most agreed that when the Federation and Khanate allied against the Rigelians in the Third Interstellar War, the Treaty of Valkha's assignment of liaison officers to all border patrols had made sense as a means of defusing potential incidents. Far fewer would admit that the contact those liaison assignments engendered remained equally desirable as a means of nurturing the still slow-growing mutual respect of the star nations' warriors.

Khardanish himself was surprised by how genuinely fond of the lieutenant he had become. He would never find Humans attractive. Their faces were flat; their ears were small, round, and set far too low; they lacked any hint of a decent pelt; and the absence of the whiskers which were an Orion's pride made it difficult to take them seriously. Even their males had only a soft, cub-like fuzz, but it was even worse in the lieutenant's case. She was a female, and the long hair which framed her face only emphasized its total, disgusting bareness. And if the Human custom of wearing body-shrouding clothing at all times was less aesthetically objectionable—at least it hid their naked skins!—it still seemed . . . odd.

But Samantha Johansen had many qualities he admired. She was observant, intelligent, and keenly sensitive to the inevitable differences between their cultures, and her military credentials were impressive. The lieutenant was only fifty-three—twenty-eight, by her people's reckoning—but she had seen the *zeget*. Her mess tunic bore the ribbon of the Federation's Military Cross, the *Valkhaanair's* equivalent, which must have been hard to come by in the fifty Terran years of peace since ISW-3. Perhaps, he speculated idly, she had been chosen for this duty by her superiors just as carefully as he was coming to believe First Fang Lokarnah had chosen him?

"Ah, Saahmaantha!" he said now. "At times, you are too much like one of my own for comfort."

"I take that as a compliment, Captain," Johansen said, chewing another slice of *zeget* appreciatively. In fact, she found it overly gamy, but it was a warrior's dish. The bear-like *zeget* was four furry meters of raw fury, the most feared predator of the original Orion homeworld, and Least Claw Khardanish had done her great honor by ordering it served.

"Do you?" Khardanish poured more wine. The Terran vintage was overly dry for his palate, but it had been Johansen's gift, and he drank it with the pleasure she deserved of him. He tilted his glass, admiring the play of light in the ruby liquid. "Then I will tell you something, Lieutenant. Do you know what we *Zheeerlikou'valkhannaieee* call our two wars with you?"

"Yes, Captain," Johansen said softly. "'The Wars of Shame.'"

"Precisely." He sipped delicately. "I find that apt even though we are now allies. We had twice the systems, ten times the population, and a navy, and you had—what? A few dozen lightly-armed survey vessels? Should not any warrior feel shame for losing to an enemy so much weaker than he?"

Johansen met his eyes calmly, and the least claw approved. Even among his own people, many would have sought to hide their discomfort with some polite nothing; this Human merely waited.

"But you were not weaker where it mattered most, Saahmaantha," he said seriously. "For your people, war was a matter for planning and discipline; for mine, it was a chance to win honor by individual bravery. Your First Fang Anderson lured us into traps, ambushed us, and massed his fire to burn us down as we charged against him, and to the *Zheeerlikou'valkhannaieee* those were coward's tactics. My grandsire, the first Lord Talphon, fought in both Wars of Shame. He was an intelligent officer, one of Varnik'sheerino's proteges, but even he thought your people's way of war fit only for *chofaki*."

Johansen still said nothing, though her eyes flickered. Literally, the term meant "dirt-eaters"; figuratively, it implied beings so lost to courage and honor they could not even recognize them as concepts.

"Yet I have read his journal many times, Saahmaantha, and he learned better." Khardanish watched his guest relax. "He was not at Aklumar, but his ship was the sole survivor of the First Battle of Ophiuchi Junction, and he fought in every major engagement of the Junction Campaign. By the end, he had learned what your Federation Navy taught us so well; that the duty of a warrior must be to *win*, not to count coup. So if you are like one of us, perhaps that is in part because my people have grown more like *yours*."

"And is that a good thing, Captain?" Johansen asked.

"Yes, Saahmaantha." He refilled her empty glass and raised his own to her in the Terran manner. "We owe you much for teaching us there is no cowardice in forethought. Some might argue that point even now—they remember only the shame of defeat and prefer still to think of Humans as *chofaki*—but my grandsire died defending Tanama against the Rigelian First Fleet with a single Alliance task group, and his Terran units died with him. None fled, and the names of their commanders are inscribed among my clan's fathers and mothers in honor." He regarded Johansen levelly. "I believe he would approve of you."

"Your words do me honor, litter master," Johansen said quietly.

"True honor is in the heart which understands them, cubling," Khardanish returned the formality, then twitched his tufted ears in humor. "But listen to us! We grow too grave, Lieutenant."

"Perhaps." Samantha sipped her own wine, leaning back from the low table on the cushions which served Orions in lieu of chairs, then grinned wryly. "But if we're growing more like one another, we've paid enough along the way, sir. This very system's history is proof of that."

Khardanish nodded. A hundred and fifty Orion years before, a Terran fleet in Lorelei had cut off and trapped a third of the Khanate's battle-line. Forty years before that, an Orion flotilla had penetrated the Terran frontier undetected during ISW-1 and surprised an entire Human colony fleet here. There had been no survivors.

"Perhaps," he suggested dryly, "that is because we have *always* been alike in at least one regard, Saahmaantha." His liaison officer raised an eyebrow in the Human expression of interrogation, and he gave another chuckle. "Both of us are incredibly stubborn," he said simply.

A gentle vibration quivered through the superdreadnought *Alois Saint-Just* as Engineering ran her final drive test, and her captain watched his read-outs with profound satisfaction. There was honor in commanding even the smallest unit of Task Force One, but to command the flagship—!

He turned his eyes to the tactical display. Only *Saint-Just's* squadron mates *Helen Borkman* and *Wu Hsin* lay close alongside, but the dots of other ships dusted the three-dimensional sphere with a thick coating of data codes, and the nav beacons marking the warp point pulsed amid the minefields and asteroid fortresses. A thrill of pride ran through him, and he forced himself to settle back, watching the chronometer tick off the last few hours.

"Captain to the bridge. Captain to the bridge."

The computer recording was both calm and unhurried; the wail of alarms was neither, and Least Claw Khardanish erupted from his quarters, still sealing his vac suit. A luckless maintenance rating bounced off a bulkhead as his captain ran right over him and bounded into the central access shaft, cursing softly but with feeling. He loved *Znamae*, old as she was, but her accommodations had been designed by eight-thumbed *zarkotga*. Destroyers had no mass to waste on intraship cars, and his quarters were the full length of the hull from her bridge. It was bad enough to take so long to reach his station, but the unseemly haste it forced upon him could not be reassuring to his crew.

He slowed abruptly as he spied the bridge hatch. By the time he reached it, he was moving with a warrior's measured, purposeful stride.

Son of the Khan Yahaarnow'ziltakan, *Znamae's* exec, looked up with obvious relief as Khardanish dropped into his command chair and racked his helmet. He was, he noted sourly, the last to arrive. Even Johansen, whose cabin was almost as inconveniently placed as his, had beaten him this time.

"Report!" he said crisply.

"Unknown drive fields, sir." Observer First Hinarou'-

frikish-ahn's experience showed in her precisely enunciated report. "Bearing oh-seven-two level by oh-three-three vertical. Range approximately three-point-two light-minutes. Estimated base course two-four-nine by oh-oh-three. Data are still rough, sir, but data base does not recognize them."

"Are you certain of that bearing, Observer?" Khardanish demanded.

"Positive, sir."

The least claw darted a quick look at Yahaarnow and Lieutenant Johansen and saw his own surprise on both faces.

"Astrogation, back-plot Observation's estimated base course."

"Aye, sir. Computing now." There was a moment of silence, and when the astrogator spoke again he sounded startled. "Sir, assuming Observation's course and bearing are correct, it looks like they came from warp point six!"

Khardanish's tufted ears flicked in quick acknowledgment, but he was deeply puzzled. Point six was the warp point Lorelei's Human discoverers had named Charon's Ferry, and if no survey ship had ever gone into it and lived, how in Valkha's name could anything come *out* of it?

"Unknowns are now at two-point-nine-five light-minutes, sir. Coming up in the outer zone of your tactical display—now."

Khardanish glanced into his holo tank. Human designers preferred a more compact, flat-screen display, but Orion eyes had problems with such systems. Now he watched drifting lights blink alive, glowing the steady yellow of unidentified vessels. They blinked again, and suddenly each bore a small light code denoting its estimated tonnage.

There were twelve of them, he noted digging his extended claws into the padded armrests of his command chair. Most were no larger than his own destroyers, but the largest was a heavy cruiser.

"Come to Status One," he ordered. "Prep and download courier drones." He waited for the acknowledgments, then made himself lean back. "All right, Communications—standard Alliance challenge."

"Aye, sir."

The range was still two and a half light-minutes—thirty minutes' travel for *Znamae* under full drive—and the five-minute wait seemed eternal.

"They are responding, sir. I do not recognize—wait! Coming up from data base now." The com officer paused, then continued flatly, "Captain, they appear to be using pre-Alliance Terran communication protocols."

Khardanish looked up sharply. Pre-Alliance? That would make them at least fifty Terran years out of date!

"Com Central confirms, sir. Their protocols match those used by the Terran Federation Navy at the time of the First War of Shame."

"Lieutenant?" Khardanish looked at his liaison officer, and Johansen raised her palms in the Human gesture of helpless ignorance. Which, he thought sourly, was a great deal of help just now.

"Can you unscramble, Communications?"

"Affirmative, sir. We have no visual, but audio is coming up now."

The com link was none too clear, and there was a hiss of static under the voice, but the distorted words were recognizable.

"Unknown vessels, this is the Terran cruiser *Kepler*. Identify yourselves."

"*Khhepaahlaar*?" Khardanish's tongue twisted on the word and he frowned at Johansen. "I do not recognize the name, Lieutenant. Do you?"

"No, sir." She punched keys at her console, calling up the TFN navy list. "No ship of that name is listed in my files, either, sir."

"I see." Khardanish combed his whiskers for a moment. There might, of course, be one explanation, for one could never be certain one had located all the warp points in any system. "Closed" warp points were undetectable; they could be located only by passing through from a normal warp point at the far end. It was possible a Federation survey flotilla had done just that—that they were coming not from Charon's Ferry but from a new-found closed point on the same approximate bearing. But that would not explain unknown drive frequencies or archaic communication codes. Or why this *Kepler* was not in Johansen's data base.

He pondered a moment longer, but there was only one way to find out.

"Identify us and ask if we can render any assistance, Communications."

"Aye, sir."

"Maneuvering, slow to thirty percent." There was no point closing too rapidly. The range was less than two light-minutes now, and his old destroyers were slow; if he should have to run he wanted all the start he could get. There was another frustrating wait as the signals crossed, and then—

"You are in Terran space, *Znamae!*" the voice from the speaker snapped, and Khardanish growled under his breath. This was becoming ridiculous!

"Sir!" Observer First Hinarou's voice was sharper. "Additional drive sources detected. Two new formations. Designate them Groups Two and Three. Group Two bears one-six-four by oh-three-three, range three-point-two light-minutes; Group Three bears oh-two-eight by oh-three-two, range three-point-one light-minutes. Both are on converging interception courses!"

Khardanish's eyes slitted. That sort of spread suggested only one thing: an attack formation. The first group must have been an advanced screen, and the others had spread out behind their scouts, maneuvering beyond scanner range to position themselves to run down his squadron whatever he did.

But *why*? If they were truly Terrans, they were *allies*, and if they were *not* Terrans, how could they have known to use Terran com protocols—even ones so sadly out of date? It made no sense! Unless . . .

No one had ever come back from Charon's Ferry, but

Fleet records suggested that at least some of the Terran colony fleet annihilated here had fled *down* it in a desperate bid to escape. Was it possible they had survived?

It seemed fantastic, but it might be an explanation. After all, more than ninety Terran years had passed since then. Survivors might have managed to cling to their technology. But how could colony ships survive what survey ships could not? And how could they have produced sufficient population to build this many ships? And why wait this long to return? If—

"We have tentative classifications on Group Two, sir," Hinarou said tensely. "Coming up on your display."

Khardanish looked back down and tightened internally. At least seven of those ships were capital units; three were superdreadnoughts.

"Maneuvering, come about one-eight-oh degrees. Maximum power." *Znamae* swerved in a course change so radical it could be felt even through the drive field, and Khardanish turned to Johansen. "Observations, Lieutenant?"

"Sir, they may claim to be Terran, but they don't match anything in my records. I don't know *what* they are."

"Could they be survivors of the colony fleet of 2206?"

Johansen blinked, then frowned. "I suppose it's possible, sir, but if they are, where have they been all this time?"

"I do not know, but if that *is* the case, they cannot know what has transpired since. They may even believe we are still at war."

"Sir," Observer Hinarou broke in, "we are picking up additional sensor emissions. Battle Comp estimates they are targeting systems."

"Acknowledged, Observation."

Their pursuers were far outside weapon range, but that would change. The capital ships were gaining only slowly as they cut the angle on the squadron's course, but their escorts were twenty percent faster than his ships. They would reach missile range in little over two hours, and the first group was far closer. *They* would have the range in less than eighty minutes, and it was thirty hours to the nearest warp point.

Khardanish beckoned, and Johansen crossed to his side. He leaned close to her, speaking softly.

"Either those ships truly are Terran, however and wherever they have come from, or they are not. In either case, we cannot outrun them. If they attack, we will undoubtedly be destroyed, and the consequences to the Alliance may prove disastrous."

"I understand, sir," the lieutenant said when he paused.

"But perhaps we can avoid that eventuality. So far we have used only our own com techs, and they are *Zheeerlikou'valkhannaieee*. You are Human. You must speak for us and convince them of the true state of affairs."

"I'll try, sir."

"I know you will, Saahmaantha." He waved her back to her console, then turned to his com officer. "Patch the lieutenant into your link."

"At once, sir." The communications officer touched a key, then flicked his ears to Johansen, and she drew a deep breath.

"*Kepler*," she said slowly and distinctly, "this is Lieutenant Samantha Johansen, Terran Federation Navy, aboard the Orion destroyer *Znamae*. You are *not* in Terran space. This system was ceded to the Khanate under the Treaty of Tycho. The Federation is not—I repeat, *not*—at war with the Khanate. We are allies. I say again, the Terran Federation and the Khanate of Orion are *allies*. Please acknowledge my transmission."

Lieutenant Johansen's words winged across space to the cruiser *Kepler*, and a stunned com officer relayed them to the superdreadnought *Saint-Just*.

"*What* did she say?!" The admiral commanding Task Force One stared at his flag captain in disbelief.

"That the Federation and the Orions are allies," the captain repeated shakenly.

"Holy Terra!" the admiral murmured. "It's worse than we feared possible!"

The captain nodded silently, trying to grapple with the blasphemous possibility, then shook himself.

"Shall we reply, sir?"

"Wait," his admiral commanded, rubbing his prominent nose as he thought. He was silent for several seconds, then looked back up with cold eyes. "Instruct *Kepler* to reply, Captain. Emphasize that we've been out of contact for many years. Tell this Lieutenant Johansen"—the name was an epithet in his mouth—"we must investigate her claims. Request, politely, that the Orion ships halt and permit the screen to close with them."

"Aye, sir." The captain's voice was flat with disapproval, and his admiral's eyes flickered with cold amusement.

"If the infidel agrees, we'll halt the remainder of the task force while the screen closes, and then . . ."

The long delay between Johansen's transmission and the response was agonizing, but it finally came, and all eyes on *Znamae*'s bridge turned unobtrusively to the least claw.

"Comments, Saahmaantha?" he asked quietly.

"I don't like it, Captain," she said flatly. "They don't *feel* right, but they've got the speed to catch us if we run."

"I share the lieutenant's suspicion, sir, and I must point out that if they close to such a short range, their weapons would—"

"I know, Yahaarnow," Khardanish said, "but we have small choice, and the Alliance serves both our Khan and the Federation well. If we risk our lives to preserve it, we do no more than our duty." He held the exec's eyes until his ears twitched agreement, then looked at Johansen.

"Very well, Lieutenant, inform them we will comply."
He turned back to the exec. "Maintain Status One, but
I want no active targeting systems."

The Orion Tenth Destroyer Squadron hung motionless, watching a handful of scanner dots close with
it. The remainder of the "Terran" fleet had halted well
beyond attack range, and Khardanish hoped that was a
good sign, yet uneasiness simmered in his blood, and it
was hard to keep his claws from twitching. The faceless
com link had refused further communication until rendezvous was made, and its silence bit at his nerves.

He watched *Kepler's* light dot. The heavy cruiser was
now at eight light-seconds and closing at a leisurely two
percent of light-speed with two light cruisers and three
of her brood of destroyers. The other six destroyers had
halted at ten light-seconds, just within standard missile
range. It *looked* as if the other side was doing exactly as
agreed.

"Range six light-seconds, sir," Observer Hinarou reported.

"Lieutenant, request that they come no closer until we
have established visual communications."

"Aye, sir." Johansen activated her com once more.
"*Kepler*, this is Lieutenant Johansen. Our commander
requests that you come no closer until visual communications have b—"

"Incoming fire!" Yahaarnow snapped, and the display
was suddenly alive with missile traces.

"Return fire!" Khardanish slammed his clawed fist
against his armrest. "Enemy flagship is primary target!"

"Aye, sir, opening fire now!"

The Tenth Squadron belched homing missiles, but the
reply was pitiful beside the holocaust racing for it, and
the enemy drive fields peaked as they charged in for the
kill.

"Evasive action!" Khardanish commanded, and his
ships, too, leapt to full power. They swerved in frantic
evasion maneuvers, and *Znamae* lurched as the first warhead burst against her shields. The energy gunners had

required a moment to activate their targeting systems, but now the force beams opened up, slamming at the enemy with electromagnetic fists.

"Launch courier drones," Khardanish said softly, and his bridge crew knew their commander had already written off his entire squadron.

"There," *Kepler*'s captain said coldly. "That one's done all the talking. That's the one we want."

Courier drones spilled from the embattled destroyers, racing for the warp point beacons as nuclear flame boiled on their mother ships' shields. The squadron's overloaded point defense stations could stop only a handful of the incoming missiles, but Khardanish's own missiles were striking home, and he watched explosions crawl over the heavy cruiser's shields. The invisible blows of his force beams savaged them as well, and they were going down.

But so were his, and the light code of the destroyer *Tramad* flickered as her last shield died and the first missile impacted on her drive field.

"Target's shields are weakening," Yahaarnow reported. "One enemy destroyer streaming atmosphere. We—"

His voice broke off as a savage burst of energy swept past *Znamae*'s shields and slashed into her bows, and Khardanish's eyes went wide in shock.

"Forward armor destroyed. Life Support Three inactive. Shield Compartment Two no longer responds. Heavy casualties in Missile One."

Khardanish slewed around towards Hinarou, and the observer first's ears were flat to her skull in disbelief.

"That was an x-ray laser, Captain!"

The least claw turned back to his display, but his brain raced. That surpassed anything the Khanate or Federation could do. It took a bomb-pumped laser to produce a weapon-grade beam of x-rays at such a range, and though independently deployed bomb-pumped lasers were feasible for static defenses, they were far too cumbersome for deep-space use against targets capable of radical maneuvers at ten percent of light-speed. And how could anyone use a bomb-pumped laser *on board* a ship, anyway?! Carbon lasers were retained there because their neutrally-charged photons could pierce a ship's electromagnetic shields, but none of them could do damage like that at *this* range!

His display wrenched his mind from its thoughts as *Tramad*'s light code suddenly vanished. Now he commanded only three destroyers—and then *Honarhae* followed *Tramad* into destruction.

"Shields down!" Yahaarnow reported as *Znamae*'s defenses crumbled under the enemy's pounding, but no fresh missiles darted in to take advantage of her nakedness. They were tearing his ships to pieces, but aside from that single laser hit, *Znamae* had taken no damage at all! Why?

"Enemy cruisers launching capital missiles!" Hinarou snapped, and Khardanish gripped his chair's armrests in fingers of steel. Capital missiles from cruisers? Ridiculous! And why wait this long and then launch extended range weapons at such close quarters?

"*Sonasha* is gone, sir," Yahaarnow said flatly. The least claw merely nodded. *Znamae* was alone, but there was no time even for grief; she would be joining her sisters soon enough.

The bridge lighting flickered as fresh energy stabbed his ship. Her shields were down, baring her to the enemy's needle beams, and the close-range precision weapons struck viciously. They ripped through her weapon bays, mangling her force beams and crippling her point defense, and the capital missiles screamed in to complete her destruction.

But they never struck. An explosion trembled through the hull, then another and another, but they were too weak for warheads. They were—

"Captain!" Yahaarnow whirled from his useless weapon console. "Those missiles were some sort of vehicles! Their crews are blowing holes in the hull and *boarding* us!"

Khardanish stared at his exec. *Board* a starship under way? How could they even penetrate the drive field?!

"Intruders on deck eight!" a voice shouted over the intercom. "Deck seven!" "Deck five!" Pressure loss tell-tales burned crimson, and a sick wave of understanding swept the least claw. He had no idea how it had been done, but he knew why. They wanted his ship . . . and her data base.

More explosions bit breaches in the hull, and vac-suited boarders swarmed through them like demons, armed with automatic weapons and grenades. Destroyers carried no Marines, and *Znamae*'s pitiful stock of small arms was locked in the armory. Her officers were armed, but only with the edged steel of their *defargaie*, the honor dirks of the Khanate.

Yet *Znamae*'s crew were Orions, and they turned on their enemies with clawed fists and feet and improvised bludgeons. They were cut down by bullets, slaughtered as grenades burst in the confines of steel passages, but they did not die quite alone. A few captured enemy weapons, turning them upon their foes before they, too, went down on the blood-slick decks and the tide of combat swept over them.

A tractor beam dragged *Znamae* toward *Kepler*, and Least Claw Khardanish rose, reaching for his own *defargo* as a thunderous explosion blew the sealed bridge hatch open and hurled Yahaarnow and two of his ratings to the deck in bloody gruel. Chattering gunfire cut down still more of his bridge crew, and then the first invader leapt through the hatch.

Khardanish's eyes were slits of fury, but even through his rage he realized it had all been a lie. Whatever their attackers were, they were not Terrans! The squat-bodied invader was too stocky, his arms too long and his legs too short. The least claw's mind recorded it all as the alien's thundering autorifle swept the bridge.

Observer First Hinarou vaulted her console, *defargo* drawn, but the invader cut her down and swung his weapon towards Khardanish. The entire bridge lay between them, and even as the least claw charged, he knew he would never reach his killer.

The rifle spoke, and Khardanish went to his knees in agony, dropping his *defargo*, as slugs mangled his right shoulder and side.

The invader took fresh aim, but before he could fire, Samantha Johansen was upon him with a *zeget*'s scream, and the fallen observer's *defargo* flashed in her hand. She drove it deep, twisting her wrist savagely, and the alien went down. The lieutenant kicked the body aside, snatched up the fallen rifle, and threw herself on her belly in her enemy's blood. The weapon's function was easy enough to grasp, and she emptied its extended magazine down the passage in a single, endless burst that piled the rest of the assault team on the deck.

The silence was deafening as she stopped firing, and Khardanish heard a click of metal as she jerked a fresh magazine from the alien's body and reloaded. Blood pumped from his wounds, and he felt Death's claws grope for him, yet his mind was cold and clear as he dragged himself across the deck. Only he and Samantha remained, and more boarders would be here soon. She could never stand them off alone, and she did not know the proper codes. He must reach the engineering station before he died.

He heaved to his feet with a kitten's mewl of pain and clung drunkenly to the console. His strength was going fast, but the visual display showed what he had hoped for. *Kepler*'s tractor had drawn *Znamae* close aboard.

Fresh thunder bellowed as Samantha fired down the passage yet again. Return fire whined off the bulkheads, but she was protected by the ruins of the hatch. She could hold a moment longer.

He flipped up the plastic shield and entered the code slowly and carefully. The single red-tabbed switch was cool under his claws, and he looked at Samantha one last time. Her round-pupilled, Human eyes met his, and he saw her agreement.

"Together, clan sister!" he gasped, and pressed it home.

CHAPTER TWO
A Decision of State

The Honorable Francis Mulrooney, Terran Ambassador to the Khanate of Orion, leaned against one side of the deep window and watched the light of a sun very like Sol stream across an oddly blue lawn of "grass" whose like Terra had never imagined. The "trees" beyond the courtyard wall were feathery spires, caparisoned in the orange and yellow and fire-red blossoms of spring, and wispy creatures flapped lacy wings above them.

To Mulrooney, *Valkha'zeeranda* had always seemed a fairy wonderland. On the surface, it was hardly the proper capital world for a warrior race, yet there was a subtle undercurrent of rightness to it. He'd often wondered what "New Valkha's" first colonists had thought and felt as they left the ships which had borne them here from the world their Wars of Unification had reduced to ruin. How must they have felt to leave their breath masks and chemical detectors and radiation counters behind forever?

He stroked the deeply incised shield and crossed

swords of the Khanate, graven a centimeter deep in the windowsill, then swept his gaze over the magnificent white spires and minarets of the imperial compound and knew he saw the answer. Mulrooney was one of the very few Terrans who had visited Old Valkha and seen the cyclopean fortresses which dominated pre-stellar Orion architecture like expressions of a warrior ethos in stone and mortar. New Valkha did not boast their like. As a fortress, the imperial compound equaled any planetary defense center in the Federation, yet it hid its teeth like an Orion smile. An almost tangible sense of peace hovered over its elfin beauty, perfected by the background of the Khanate's mailed fist.

And that, he told himself, was how the *Zheeerlikou'valkhannaieee* saw their imperial capital. It was flowers and cold steel, the jewel in the Khan's iron crown, an eye of tranquillity in a hurricane's heart.

He sighed and turned from the window, pacing slowly back and forth. The summons had come from the *kholokhanzir*, the grand vizier, himself, and it was unusual to be kept waiting so long. Mulrooney had many contacts in the Orion bureaucracy, and he knew some major crisis had blown up with absolutely no warning. He could uncover no clue as to what it was, but the whispers of rumored disaster made an ominous counterpoint to this unprecedented delay.

The sharp rap of wood on stone interrupted his thoughts, and he turned, reminding himself just in time to avoid any quick movement which might suggest impatience. The *kholokhanzir's* personal herald met his eyes, gripping the elaborately carved haft of his gemmed pike of office. There was more than a little white in the Orion's tawny felinoid pelt, but his spine was straight and he bowed with limber dignity. Then he straightened and beckoned politely for Mulrooney to follow.

The herald led him down a sunny hall fringed by balconies with balustrades entwined in nodding tendrils of ornamental vines. It wasn't a long walk, but Mulrooney's heart was beating fast when the herald knocked at the door at its end. Two statue-still guards flanked it, armed not with ornamental, palace-duty weapons but with businesslike needle rifles and side arms. Then the herald opened the door and bowed him through.

Mulrooney entered with a crisp stride, then stopped dead. He'd expected the *kholokhanzir*, but it seemed he'd been summoned to meet another.

He recovered and moved forward once more towards the ancient Orion seated on the cushion-strewn dais in the center of the room. He was bent with age, but his silvered pelt still showed the midnight black of the noblest Orion bloodlines.

Mulrooney stopped a precise three meters from the dais and pressed his clenched right hand to his chest as he performed his most graceful bow. Then he straightened and stood silently, giving no sign of his racing thoughts, as he met the old, knowing eyes of Liharnow'hirtalkin, *Khan'a'khanaaeee* of all the Orions.

"Greetings, Ambassador," the Khan said, and Mulrooney swallowed. Orions guarded their khan's person fanatically, yet he and Liharnow were alone. It was unheard of for any person not sworn to *hirikolus* or *hirikrinzi*—much less an alien—to be allowed into the Khan's presence unguarded, and there was no protocol to guide him in modes of address, for the Khan *never* spoke directly to a foreign envoy.

"Greetings, *Hia'khan*." He hoped it was an appropriate response.

"I have asked you here to discuss a most urgent matter," Liharnow came to the point with typical Orion brevity. "It is vital that there be no misunderstanding, so I ask you to forego the courtesies of diplomacy. I shall speak my mind fully and frankly, and I wish you to do the same."

"Of course, *Hia'khan*," Mulrooney replied. He had no choice but to accept whatever ground rules the Khan chose to set.

"Thank you." Liharnow settled more comfortably into his cushions, combing his shoulder-wide whiskers, and his ears inclined forward as if to underscore his serious mood.

"Two weeks ago, the Tenth Destroyer Squadron, commanded by Lord Talphon and stationed in the Lorelei System, was treacherously attacked." Mulrooney stiffened. There could be only one Orion response to an attack they labeled "treacherous."

"The attackers apparently entered the system through its sixth warp point, the one which your astrographers call 'Chaaraahn's Ferry,' and enticed Lord Talphon into attack range with a false parley offer. The frequencies of their drive fields matched none in our Navy's data base, but they identified themselves"—the Khan's eyes locked with the ambassador's—"as Terrans."

Despite himself, Mulrooney gasped, and the Khan shifted his ears slowly, as if obscurely satisfied.

"Lord Talphon's courier drones bore our equivalent of your Code Omega. They were dispatched very early in the engagement, as it was obvious his ships could not survive. Their messages were transmitted to *Valkha'zeeranda* by the warp point relay net and reached here five days ago. During those five days, our intelligence service has analyzed Lord Talphon's report and reached certain conclusions.

"First, the attackers did employ Terran Federation Navy communication protocols, although they were of an obsolete nature. Second, the single ship name provided by the enemy was *Kepahlar*"—Liharnow did much better with the Terran name than Khardanish had managed—"and our xenologists have identified this as the name of an ancient Terran scientist. Third, all communications from the enemy were in Terran Standard English. From these findings, a board of inquiry has judged that the attackers were in fact a Terran survey force."

Mulrooney's face was white.

"There are, however, several points which puzzle me," the Khan went on levelly. "The odd drive frequencies are one such point, as also are the peculiar communications protocols employed. In addition, our intelligence arm has observed no re-deployment of additional Federation units, nor is the Lorelei System of great military value. Finally, I have reviewed Lord Talphon's last report, and I am at least partially inclined to accept his hypothesis as to his attackers' identity. I do not believe the Federation attacked the Tenth Squadron," Mulrooney's shoulders relaxed, only to tighten afresh as Liharnow finished, "but I suspect its attackers *were* Terrans."

"*Hia'khan,*" the ambassador began, "I—"

"A moment, if you please," the Khan said softly, and Mulrooney closed his mouth. "Lord Talphon concluded that these unknown 'Terrans' might be descended from survivors of the Terran colonization fleet attacked in Lorelei by the Eighty-First Flotilla in 2206, who fled down 'Chaaraahn's Ferry.' If this is indeed the case, the Federation Navy and Assembly cannot, of course, have ordered the attack, yet it was still the work of Terrans.

"I make this point," Liharnow said very carefully and distinctly, "because a majority of the Strategy Board have officially advised the *Khan'a'khanaaeee* that they reject Lord Talphon's hypothesis and that, even if he were correct, that fact could not in their judgment absolve Terra of responsibility. They recommend"—he met Mulrooney's eyes once more—"that the Treaty of Valkha be immediately repudiated as the first step in a renewed war with the Federation."

"*Hia'khan,*" Mulrooney chose his words as carefully as the Khan, "this is the first I have heard of any of these events. My government will be as shocked by them as your own, but I implore you to proceed with restraint. If the Khanate attacks the Federation, we will have no choice but to defend ourselves, and the consequences for both our peoples will be terrible."

"That," Liharnow said quietly, "is why I have summoned you in this irregular fashion. I have over-ruled the Strategy Board"—Mulrooney breathed in thankfully—"so far, and First Fang Lokarnah has supported my decision, but our courses of action are limited.

"First, we may accede to the demands of the Strategy

Board. Second, we may punish these Terrans ourselves, as honor demands. Third, we may require the Federation to punish them. Should we accept the Strategy Board's recommendations, the result will certainly be general war. Should we punish them ourselves, we embark upon an almost equally dangerous road, for I cannot believe the Assembly would permit the Federation Navy to stand idle while we kill Terrans, regardless of their origin, for attacking the ships of a navy with whom they may believe themselves to be still at war. But, Ambassador, should we adopt the third option, the Federation may still find itself in a most unenviable position.

"You know our honor code. My warriors' blood has been shed by *shirnowmakaie*, oath-breakers who have violated their own sworn offer to parley in peace. There must be *khiinarma*, scale-balancing. I could not deny that even if I wished to, and Ambassador"—the Khan's eyes were cold—"I do not wish to. There is one and only one way in which the Federation may intercede between the *Zheeerlikou'valkhannaieee* and those who have attacked us."

"And that way is, *Hia'khan*?" It was a question, but Mulrooney's tone said he already knew the answer.

"The Federation must become *khimhok ia' Zheeerli- kou'valkhannaieee*," the Khan said softly, and Mulrooney swallowed. The term had no precise Terran equivalent, but it translated roughly as "scale-bearer to the Orions." In effect, the Terran Federation must step into the Khanate's place, assuming the duty to punish those who had offended. Yet it was far more complex than that, and his brain raced as he tried to envision all the implications.

The Federation would have a free hand but no Orion assistance. From the moment Terra accepted the "scale-bearer" role, the Khanate would stand totally aloof, and the Alliance's mutual assistance clauses could not be invoked. Worse, in a way, the final resolution must be acceptable to the Khanate. The Federation might choose to be merciful or harsh, but if the Orions did not perceive the ultimate solution as one which satisfied their own honor, the *Federation* would assume the guilt which the Khan had now assigned solely to those beings who had attacked his ships, and the consequences of that did not bear thinking upon.

"*Hia'khan*," the ambassador said finally, "I will transmit your words to my government, yet I must tell you that I foresee grave difficulties. If, indeed, those who attacked you are Terrans, then the people of the Federation will find it most difficult to demand blood balance of them."

"I understand," Liharnow said gravely, "for we would find it difficult to demand *vilknarma* of *Zheeerlikou'valkhannaieee* who had been lost for two of our centuries and attacked Terran warships in ignorance of the truth. Indeed, I understand too well, and that is one reason I would prefer to place the matter in Human hands. Honor demands punishment for treachery, yet if these Terrans truly believe we are still at war, then they did well to defend their own people, however dishonorable the manner in which they did so.

"Moreover," he continued even more seriously, "I have spent my life teaching my people the Galaxy can belong neither to he who is too cowardly to fight nor to he who is too stupid to know when *not* to fight. It has not been easy, and suspicion of other races remains strong, but I do not wish to see the Treaty of Valkha torn up and lost while our peoples destroy one another. And so I make this offer not just as Liharnow but as *Khan'a'khanaaeee*.

"We have no colonies between Lorelei and our own fortifications. Should the Federation become *khimhok ia' Zheeerlikou'valkhannaieee*, the Khanate will cede the Lorelei System to the Federation and withdraw all units from its borders. We will regard the affair as an internal problem of the Federation, to be settled by the Federation, and we will renounce *vilknarma* and accept reparations and *shirnowkashaik*, acknowledgment of guilt by the offenders. My people will find this difficult to bear, for we do not equate reparations with restitution as yours do, but if *I* accept in their name I sacrifice only my own honor, and they will abide by my pledged oath. This I will give in the cause of peace."

Mulrooney drew a very deep breath. The Khan's offer was an enormous concession, and the ambassador allowed himself to feel cautiously hopeful for the first time since the interview had begun.

"I thank you, *Hia'khan*," he said with utmost sincerity, "and I will immediately transmit your generous offer to Old Terra."

"My heart is not generous," Liharnow said flatly. "It cries out for *vilknarma* from the *chofaki* who have done this thing. Were they not Terrans, I would crush them into dust, but I cannot heed my heart in this. It is a decision of state, and so I must decide it, so hear my oath, Ambassador. I do not hold your government responsible, and I swear upon the honor of my clan fathers and of Valkha, shield-bearer to Hiranow'khanark, that I will sheathe my claws. Whoever these *chofaki* and wherever they spring from, I declare that I will accept the Federation as *khimhok*, to act in my stead and the stead of all my people. I have spoken."

The aged Khan lowered his ears and raised one hand in dismissal, and Ambassador Francis Mulrooney turned silently to leave.

CHAPTER THREE
The Peace Fleet

Howard Anderson was in a grumpy mood as he walked through Federation Hall's huge doors onto the Chamber's marble floor. He supposed change was inevitable, but in *his* day, the Legislative Assembly had simply called its meeting place the Assembly Chamber, and the new, highfaluting title irritated him immensely. *"Chamber of Worlds"* indeed! It was all part of the damned imperial trappings—and so was the revolting deference everyone insisted on paying *him*. He suppressed an urge to kick the lictor who escorted him almost reverently to his seat, then sat and listened to the rustling mutter as the Chamber filled.

"Hello, Howard."

Anderson looked up and smiled as a small, uniformed figure paused beside him.

"What's an honest sailor doing in this whorehouse, Chien-lu?"

"I admire the effort you put into perfecting your curmudgeonly image, Howard, but you might consider the virtue of an occasional courteous word."

26

"Damn it, man, I'm a hundred and fifty years old! If I can't be a cranky, difficult son-of-a-bitch, who can?"

"Given how many people feel you *are* the Federation, I might suggest a proper decorum is in order," Admiral Li Chien-lu said with gentle malice.

"Do that and I'll drop kick your scrawny Oriental ass clear to the speaker's podium!" Anderson snorted, and the admiral laughed.

"Very well, Howard. Play your silly game if it amuses you."

"Damn straight it does." Anderson thumped the chair beside him with the gnarled walking stick he affected. "Sit down, Chien-lu." His grumpy tone had become serious. "I want to talk to you." Li hesitated, and Anderson's blue eyes hardened. "*Now*, Admiral," he said softly, and Li sat with a small shrug.

"You take unfair advantage of our relationship, you know," he said mildly. "A fleet admiral is no longer an ensign on your HQ staff."

"Granted. But we've known each other longer than either of us wants to remember, and I want to know what the hell Sakanami thinks he's doing."

"Precisely what he's said." Admiral Li shrugged again. "I won't say I'd do it the same way myself, but he hasn't slipped me any secret orders, if that's what you mean."

"I wouldn't put it past Sakanami—or that vulture Waldeck—but that wasn't what I meant. I suppose I should have asked what you and the CNO think *you're* doing?"

"Howard," Admiral Li said plaintively, "why is that when *you* were President 'cheerful and willing obedience to the lawful commands of civilian superiors' was a virtue?"

"When *I* was President, you insubordinate young sprout, your civilian superiors knew what they were doing. This bunch of fuck-ups wouldn't know a sane military policy if it shot them in the ass, and you know it!"

"You know a serving officer has no right to admit that. Besides, you're far more eloquent than I. And you carry a bigger stick."

Anderson grunted and folded his hands over the head of his cane. Despite the lightness of his earlier words, he knew Li was right. Commander Anderson had won the first battle of ISW-1, and Admiral of the Fleet Anderson had ended it as chief of naval operations, a post he'd retained throughout ISW-2. In a very real sense, the Terran Federation Navy had been his personal creation, and then he'd stepped over into politics. By the time of the Third Interstellar War, he'd been serving his second term as President Anderson. Even now, when he was all but retired, he commanded a unique respect.

Unfortunately, respect and power weren't the same thing.

There'd been intrigues enough within the Fleet, but at least responsibility and the chain of command were always reasonably well defined. Politics were different. He'd never been comfortable with greasy-mouthed politicos, and he'd spent a great deal of his time in office keeping people like Sakanami Hideoshi and Pericles Waldeck *out* of office.

He sighed, feeling the full weight of his age. He supposed those two—and especially Waldeck—bothered him so because he was at least partly responsible for their existence, but they represented a new and dangerous power in the Assembly, and what Anderson didn't know about their plans worried him far more than what he did.

He'd always been unhappy over the chartered companies, yet the Federation of a century ago could never have built the Navy *and* financed colonization without ruinous taxation. The Khanate had simply been too big to match credit-for-credit, even with humanity's greater productivity, so something had to give, and that something had been BuCol.

It had made good financial sense to license chartered companies to finance colonization as a profit-making proposition. It had freed current revenues and expanded the tax base at an incredible rate, and Anderson knew he'd been at least as strident about the need to fund the Fleet as anyone. But the companies had been too successful. The Assembly had been unable to resist turning them into money machines, offering ever greater incentives. Before the practice finally ended in 2275, some of the chartered companies had acquired virtual ownership of entire worlds.

Yet Anderson was less concerned by the planetary oligarchies the chartered companies had birthed on what were coming to be known as the "Corporate Worlds" than by the way those oligarchies were extending themselves into an interstellar political machine of immense potential power.

The chartered companies had concentrated on choice real estate in strategic star systems, which had suited the Federation's military needs by providing populations to support Fleet bases and fortifications in choke point systems. But the Corporate World oligarchs were more concerned with the economic implications of their positions. Their warp lines carried the life blood of the Federation's trade, and they used that advantage ruthlessly to exploit less fortunately placed worlds.

Anderson found their tactics reprehensible, and he was deeply concerned by the hostility they provoked among the Out Worlds, but he would be safely dead before *that* problem came home to roost. He'd done his best to sound a warning, yet no one seemed to be listening, so he'd concentrated on more immediate worries, particularly military policy.

Now that the oligarchs had it made, they were far from eager to create potential rivals, so they'd cheerfully repealed the chartered company statutes and resurrected BuCol. They'd been less interested in paying for it, however, and they'd beaten off every effort to raise taxes. Instead, their Liberal-Progressive Party had found the money by slashing military appropriations.

The Fleet was badly understrength, and the state of the Reserve was scandalous. Officially, BuShips' mothballed Reserve should have at least seventy-five percent of Battle Fleet's active strength in each class, yet it boasted barely thirty-six percent of its authorized numerical strength ... and less than ten percent of its authorized tonnage. And the ships it *did* have hadn't been modernized in thirty years! It was bitterly ironic, but the worlds settled under a military-economic policy of expedience were now killing the very military which had spawned them.

The LibProgs might point to the Treaty of Valkha and fifty years of peace, but Howard Anderson knew better than most that when something went wrong it usually did so with dispatch, and Battle Fleet was twenty percent understrength for its peacetime obligations. In the event of a shooting war, any substantial losses would be catastrophic.

Which, he reminded himself, straightening in his chair, was why Sakanami's current policy was the next best thing to certifiable lunacy.

"Chien-lu," he said softly, "they *can't* send that much of the Fleet into Lorelei. Not until we know exactly what we're *really* up against."

"Then you'd better convince them of it," Admiral Li sighed. "For your personal—and private—information, Admiral Brandenburg and I said the same thing. Loudly. We have, however, been overruled by the defense minister and President Sakanami. And that, as you must realize as well as I, is that."

Anderson began a hot retort, then stopped and nodded unhappily.

"You're right," he said. "I'll just have to take the bastards on again and hope. In the meantime, how's the family?"

"Well, thank you." Admiral Li's smile thanked him for the change of subject. "Hsu-ling has emigrated, you know."

"No, I didn't know, but I approve. The Heart Worlds are getting too damned bureaucratic for my taste. If I were a half-century younger, I'd go out-world myself. Where is he?"

"He and my charming daughter-in-law signed up for the Hangchow Colony, and you should see the holos they've sent back! Their planetary charter is a bit traditional for my taste, but I'm seriously considering retiring there myself."

"You do that, Chien-lu, and I'll load this ancient carcass on a ship for a visit."

"It's a deal," Admiral Li said, and grinned toothily.

". . . and so," Defense Minister Hamid O'Rourke said, "in accordance with the President's directives, the required units have been ordered to rendezvous in the Redwing System to proceed to Lorelei in company with Special Envoy Aurelli. That concludes my brief, Madam Speaker."

"Thank you, Mister O'Rourke." Speaker of the Legislative Assembly Chantal Duval's cool, clear voice carried well. Now her image replaced O'Rourke's on the huge screen about her podium. "Is there any discussion?"

Howard Anderson pressed his call key and watched Duval's eyes drop to her panel.

"The Chair recognizes President Emeritus Howard Anderson," she said, and the mutter of side conversations ended as Anderson replaced her image on the huge screen behind her podium. Even after all these years, his ego found the attention flattering, and he propped himself a shade more aggressively on his cane as an antidote.

"Thank you, Madam Speaker. I will be brief, but I would be derelict in my duty if I did not voice my concern—my very *grave* concern—over the Administration's plans." The silence became a bit more profound, and he saw a few uneasy faces. His caustic attacks on the Sakanami-Waldeck military policies had a nasty habit of singling out delegates who'd received their kilo of flesh to support them.

"Ladies and Gentlemen, we have agreed to assume the role of *khimhok* in this confrontation between the individuals who call themselves 'Thebans' and the Khanate. As one who knows Khan Liharnow personally, I may, perhaps, have a better grasp than many of his tremendous concession in allowing us to do so, and, as President Sakanami, I see no alternative but to accept it. Yet we must be cautious. While circumstantial evidence certainly appears to confirm that the Thebans are descendants of the Lorelei Massacre's survivors, all the evidence to date is just that—circumstantial. And even if they have been correctly identified, aspects of their conduct both before and since their attack on the Tenth Destroyer Squadron cause me to have grave reservations.

"First, they have, as yet, failed to explain to my satisfaction why they refused even to consider that Lieutenant Johansen's messages outlined the true state of affairs. It is evident from the courier drones the Khanate has made available to us that they never had the least intention of making rendezvous to confirm or disprove her statements; their sole purpose was to close to decisive range and annihilate Lord Talphon's command.

"Second, they have permitted only unarmed courier vessels to enter Lorelei since our first attempts to communicate with them, and they continue to refuse all physical contact. Their visual links to our courier ships have also been most unsatisfactory, and I find these 'technical difficulties' of theirs suspiciously persistent.

"Third, they continue to refuse to explain how colony ships survived transit into the Theban System when no survey ships have done so.

"Fourth, they have *now* refused all further negotiations until we demonstrate our ability to protect them from Orion reprisals by dispatching to Lorelei sufficient forces to mount a creditable defense of the system. Coming after their steadfast refusal to permit even a single destroyer into the system, this seems a trifle peculiar, to say the very least."

He paused to gauge the effect of his remarks. One or two faces looked thoughtful, but most were bored. None of what he'd said, after all, was new.

"I can readily understand that a colony which has been isolated for almost a century would be cautious. I can even understand a certain degree of paranoid intransigence, given the traumatic circumstances which carried their ancestors to Thebes in the first place. What I do *not* understand is why that cautious culture should now obligingly invite us to send no less than thirty percent of Battle Fleet to their very doorstep. It is all very well to call it a major step forward, but it is a step which appears to make very little sense. If they are truly beginning to feel more confident, why do they not invite one of our harmless, unarmed courier craft to make the first contact? Surely that would be the rational approach. *This* sounds entirely too much like their offer to Lord Talphon."

This time, he saw some concern in his audience when he paused.

"Certainly it would be insane of any single planet to challenge both the Orions and us, but we may err seriously if we assume they are rational by normal standards. Were the Fleet up to strength, I might feel less concern, but the Fleet is *not* up to strength, and we can neither be certain what a potentially irrational culture may do nor risk substantial Fleet losses."

He paused once more, wondering if he should state his case even more strongly, then decided against it. The LibProgs already called him a senile crackpot in private.

"Madam Speaker, while military and diplomatic policy fall within the purview of the Executive, the Constitution grants the Assembly an oversight role, specifically confirmed by the Executive Powers Act of 2283. I therefore move that this Assembly instruct the Administration to hold its 'Peace Fleet' at readiness in Redwing pending a fresh approach to the Thebans, and that the Thebans be informed that the Federation requires direct, face-to-face contact before any Federation warship enters the Lorelei System. If these people are sincerely eager to rejoin the rest of humanity, they will accept. If they are not sincere, it would be the height of foolhardiness for us to expose so substantial a portion of our Navy to risk without overwhelming support.

"Thank you."

He sat in silence, and Speaker Duval's image reappeared.

"It has been moved that the Administration be instructed to hold the 'Peace Fleet' in Redwing until such time as the Thebans agree to direct contact with Federation negotiators," she said clearly. "Is there a second?"

"Madam Speaker, I second the motion." It was Andrew Spruance of Nova Terra, one of Anderson's Conservative Party allies.

"Ladies and Gentlemen of the Assembly, the motion has been seconded. Is there any debate?" An attention chime sounded almost instantly, and Duval looked up. "The Chair recognizes the Honorable Assemblyman for Christophon."

"Thank you, Madam Speaker." Pericles Waldeck, the LibProg Assembly leader and Anderson's personal *bête-noire*, smiled from the screen. "As the distinguished President Emeritus, I will be brief.

"No one in this Chamber can match President Anderson's lifetime of experience. As both war hero and statesman, he deserves our most serious attention. In this instance, however, I am unable to agree with him. Prudence, certainly, is much to be admired, but President Sakanami has been prudent. Three months have passed since the regrettable attack on the Orion squadron—three months in which no Theban vessel has attempted to depart the Lorelei System or fired upon any of our courier craft within it. They have been cautious, true, and perhaps less than courteous and forthcoming by our standards, but let us remember their history. Is it reasonable to expect any culture which began in massacre and desperate flight from the Orions, which must have spent virtually an entire century in preparation to return and, if necessary, confront those same Orions, to react in any other way?

"I am not well versed in technical matters, but many experts have agreed that the communications problems cited by the Thebans are, indeed, possible, particularly when technologies attempt to interface once more after a ninety-one-year separation. And their sudden about-face in requesting a powerful Fleet presence does not strike me as inconsistent. After all their people have endured, an element of 'show me' must be inevitable where their very survival is concerned.

"Finally, let us consider the strength President Sakanami proposes to commit to his Peace Fleet. We will be dispatching twenty-one capital ships, fifteen fleet and light carriers, and a strong escort of lighter units. The Thebans have shown no reluctance to allow our couriers to approach Charon's Ferry, and their fleet strength in Lorelei has never exceeded seventy vessels, only twelve of them capital ships. While this is an impressive strength for any isolated system—indeed, a strength which, following the Thebans' reunification with the rest of humanity, will do much to repair the weakness which President Anderson has often decried in our own Navy—it cannot be considered a serious threat to the Peace Fleet.

"With all of this in mind, and conceding every argument which urges caution, I cannot support President Anderson's contention that still more caution is required. Let us not jeopardize the chance to achieve a quick and peaceful resolution by an appearance of irresolution. Ladies and Gentlemen of the Assembly, I ask that President Emeritus Anderson's motion be denied.

"Thank you."

He sat, and Anderson leaned back, his own face expressionless, as the LibProg steamroller went smoothly to work. A dozen delegates rose to endorse Waldeck's words. They couldn't have been more respectful and deferential towards the Federation's "Grand Old Man," yet their very deference emphasized that he was an *old* man—one, perhaps, whom age had rendered alarmist.

And, he was forced to admit, many of their arguments made sense. A dangerously complacent sense, perhaps, but one against which he could offer little more than instinct. It might be an instinct honed by over a century of military and political service, but it couldn't be quantified as ship strengths could, and it wasn't enough to convince the Liberal Democrats or the handful of Independents to join his Conservatives in bucking a powerful president and his party under the terms of an act whose constitutionality had always been suspect. . . .

The final vote rejected his motion by more than three to one.

CHAPTER FOUR

A Slaughter of Innocents

Fleet Admiral Li Chien-lu frowned as Special Envoy Victor Aurelli entered his private briefing room and sat. Aurelli's patrician face wore a faintly supercilious smile, and Li was hard pressed to keep his frown from becoming a glare as he placed a memo chip on the conference table.

"Thank you for coming so promptly, Mister Aurelli," he said.

"You sounded rather emphatic," Aurelli replied with a slight shrug.

"I suppose I did. And if I did, Mister Aurelli, *this*"— Li tapped the chip sharply, eyes suddenly dagger-sharp— "is to blame."

"I take it those are my modest amendments to your . . . battle plans?"

"No, Mister Aurelli, they're your unwarranted intrusion into my standard operational directives."

Two pairs of eyes locked across the conference table, and there was no affability in either.

"Admiral," the envoy finally broke the silence, "this is a diplomatic mission, not an assault on a Rigelian PDC, and I do not propose to permit you or anyone else to jeopardize its success. This crisis is too grave to justify offering gratuitous insult to Theban sensibilities."

"Considering those same Thebans' record to date," Li returned coldly, "I fail to see how any prudent deployment of my forces could be deemed a 'gratuitous insult' to their gentler natures. And, sir, while you may command the mission, *I* command this task force."

"Which is a subordinate component of the over-all mission, Admiral. I direct your attention to paragraph three of your orders."

Aurelli's gentle smile made Li wish briefly that they were on one of the Out Worlds which had resurrected the code duello.

"I am aware of my instructions to cooperate with you, sir, but Fleet orders are for a flag officer's guidance. If in his judgment the situation on the spot requires prudent and timely precautions not visualized when those orders were written, he is expected to take them. And, Mister Aurelli, this latest Theban 'request' requires the precautions laid down in my ops order."

Aurelli sighed. The admiral was a typical Academy product: dedicated, professional, and utterly unable to see any further than his gunnery console. Of course the Thebans were acting irrationally! What else could anyone expect from a colony with their history? How would Admiral Li have felt if a "negotiator" allied with the Rigelians had told *him* the Third Interstellar War was all a misunderstanding?

That was why this was too important to botch by letting the military fumble around in charge of it.

"Admiral Li," he said, "you may not believe this, but I sympathize with your concerns. As a military commander, it's your duty to project possible threats and counter them. I accept that. But in this instance, I must insist that you follow the instructions I've given you."

"No." Aurelli's eyebrows rose at Li's flat refusal. "The

Thebans have 'requested' that we rendezvous with them on their warp point with our entire strength. That will place my carriers and battle-cruisers twenty hours from the nearest friendly warp point. My battle-line units will be over a full day from it. I will not place my ships and my people in a position from which they cannot withdraw in the event of hostile action."

It was Li's turn to lean back and glare. Victor Aurelli was an ass. The sort of idiot who chopped away at every military budget on the theory that if the Fleet could do its job—somehow—last year, it could do it with a bit less this year. And now he wanted a third of Battle Fleet to advance beyond withdrawal range into a star system occupied by a fleet which had already demonstrated that it would shoot a man out from under a flag of truce?

"Admiral, have you detected any additional Theban units?"

"No, but a star system is a very large haystack. Against a ship with powered-down systems, our scanners have a maximum detection range of under five light-minutes under ideal conditions. The entire Orion Navy could be out there, and without a proper network of scan sats we'd never know it."

"But you have *not* detected any additional units?" Aurelli pressed, and Li shook his head curtly. "And if there were any such units, could they enter attack range without being detected?"

"Not without better cloaking technology than we know of," Li admitted.

"Excellent. Then whether there are additional Theban warships or not, we need concern ourselves immediately only with those we can detect. Given that, would you say you were confident of your ability to engage and defeat, if necessary, the forces you've so far identified?"

"Given that they have no radical technical or tactical surprises for me, and that there are no additional hostile forces hidden away, yes."

Aurelli hid a sigh. Why did the military always insist on qualifiers? They used the same worn-out tactic every time they demanded a bigger budget. If the Orions do this, if a new Rigelian Protectorate turns up, if the Ophiuchi do that, if, if, if, *if!*

"Admiral, if you were defending the Centauris System and the sole warp point to Sol, would *you* allow a hostile force into Centauris instead of trying to stop it at the warp points?"

"Under some circumstances, yes," Li said surprisingly. "If my forces were strong enough to defeat the enemy in a head-on engagement but too weak to block all potential entry warp points, I would concede the warp points rather than risk being defeated in detail. And"—his dark eyes stabbed the envoy like a force beam—"if I could, I'd suck the hostiles too deep in-system to run before I let them know I had the strength to smash them."

"I'm not going to argue anymore, Admiral." Aurelli's voice was cold. "You will muster the entire task force— not just a screen of cruisers and battle-cruisers—and advance to Charon's Ferry. You will rendezvous with the Thebans, and you will refrain from potentially provocative actions."

"Sir, I must respectfully refuse to do so," Li said equally coldly.

"You have no choice." Aurelli's thin smile was dangerous as he reached inside his jacket. "President Sakanami anticipated that there might be . . . differences of opinion between the military and civilian components of this mission, Admiral Li, and he took steps to resolve them."

Li unfolded the single sheet of paper, and his face tightened. The orders were crisp, cold, and to the point, and he refolded them very carefully before he returned them to the envelope.

"Do you really think they'll do it?"

First Admiral Lantu glanced at Fleet Chaplain Manak as he spoke, and the churchman shrugged. His yellow eyes were thoughtful as he stroked his cranial carapace, and his ring of office glinted on his three-fingered hand.

"Yes," he said finally. "I had my doubts when the

Prophet decreed it, but Holy Terra works in mysterious ways. It would seem the infidels have been blinded by our words."

"I hope you're right," Lantu grunted, turning back to his large-scale nav display. The light dots of the infidel task force moved steadily towards him, led by the single destroyer squadron he'd sent out as guides and spies. It was hard for Lantu to believe anyone could be this stupid.

"I believe I am," Manak replied with the serenity of his faith. "The cursed Orions fell into your snare, my son. If the Satan-Khan's own children can be taken so easily, should not the apostate fall still more easily?"

Lantu didn't reply. Satan's children or no, those Orions had shown courage. It had been obvious from the initial reports that the boarding attack had been a total surprise. There'd been no hope of organized resistance, yet somehow *Znamae*'s bridge officers had held long enough to blow their fusion plants . . . and take *Kepler* with them.

He glanced at the huge portrait of the Angel Saint-Just on the flag bridge bulkhead and closed his inner eyelids in sympathy. How must the Holy Messenger feel to see his own people brought so low?

Admiral Li sat on the superdreadnought *Everest*'s flag bridge and ignored Victor Aurelli. Neither training nor personality would let him show his contempt before his officers, but he was damned if he'd pretend he liked the man.

"Coming into scan range of the Ferry now, sir," his chief of staff reported. "The drive source count looks consistent."

"Thank you, Christine. Any new messages from the Thebans?"

"None, sir."

Li nodded and watched his display. The "Peace Fleet" continued its stately advance at four percent of light-speed, and he tried not to think of how far from home they were.

* * *

"Hmmmm . . ." Admiral Lantu studied the images relayed from his flanking destroyers, then gestured to his flag captain. "Look there. See how carefully they're protecting those units?"

"Yes, sir." Captain Kurnash rubbed the ridge of his snout, staring at the ships at the center of the infidel formation. "Those are the ones that carry the small attack craft, sir."

"I know." Lantu drummed on the arm of his command chair and thought. Their contact vessels had watched the infidels closely since they'd entered Lorelei, and he'd viewed the reports on those small craft with interest. Their routine operations had shown they were fast and highly maneuverable, though he had no idea what their maximum operating range might be or what weapons they carried. Missiles, most probably, but what sort of missiles? The People had nothing like them, and the lack of any sort of comparative meterstick bothered him.

"I think we'd better deal with them first, Kurnash," he said at last. "Can we get salvos in there?"

"Certainly, sir. We won't be able to get to beam range immediately, but if they really wanted to protect them, they should have left them out of missile range."

"Thank Terra for Her favors, Captain, and get your revised fire plan set up. Oh, and send a drone to the reserve with the same instructions."

"Approaching rendezvous," Commander Christine Gianelli reported. "Range to Theban flagship fifteen light-seconds. ETA to contact six minutes."

"And the Thebans' status?" Li asked sharply.

"Shields down, as our own. We're picking up a lot of primary and secondary sensor emissions—mostly point defense tracking stations, though CIC thinks some may be targeting systems—but no Erlicher emissions, so at least they aren't warming up any force beams or primaries."

"Thank you." Li turned his chair to face Aurelli at last.

"Mister Envoy, we are coming onto station," he said with cold formality. "I suggest you hail the Theban representatives."

"Thank you, Admiral, I think that would be an excellent idea," Aurelli said smugly, and Li nodded curtly to his com officer.

"The infidels are hailing us, Holiness."

Fleet Chaplain Manak glanced at his assistant and nodded.

"Are the computers ready?"

"They are, Holiness."

"Then we shall respond." Manak glanced at Admiral Lantu. "Are you ready, my son?"

"We are, Holiness." Manak noted the tension in Lantu's eyes and smiled. He'd watched the admiral grow to adulthood and knew how strong he was, but even the strongest could be excused a bit of strain at such a moment.

"Be at ease, my son," he said gently, "and prepare your courier drone. We shall give the infidels one last chance to prove they remain worthy of Holy Terra. If they are not, She will deliver them into your hand. Stand by."

"Standing by, Holiness."

"Greetings, Mister Aurelli. My name is Mannock."

The voice was clear, despite the poor visual image, and Victor Aurelli wondered what mix of colonist dialects had survived to produce its accent. The Standard English was crisp, but there was a hard edge to the vowels and a peculiar lisp to the sibilants. Not an unpleasant sound, but definitely a bit odd. And this Mannock was a handsome enough fellow—or might have been, if not for the flickering fuzz of those persistent technical problems.

"I'm pleased to meet you, sir," he replied, "and I look forward to meeting you in person."

"As I look forward to meeting you." The poor signal quality prevented Aurelli from noticing that the comput-

er-generated image's lips weren't quite perfectly synchronized with the words.

"Then let us begin, Mister Mannock."

"Of course. We are already preparing to initiate docking with your flagship. In the meantime, however, I have
a question I would like to ask."

"Of course, Mister Mannock. Ask away."

"Do you"—the voice was suddenly more intent—"accept the truth of the Prophet's teaching, Mister Aurelli?"

Aurelli blinked, then frowned at the com screen.

"The teaching of *which* prophet, Mister Mannock?"
he asked . . . and the universe exploded in his face.

"Incoming fire!" someone screamed, and Captain Na-
dine Wu, CO of TFNS *Deerhound*, stared at her display.
Missiles were coming at her carrier—not one, or two, or
a dozen, but scores of them!

"Impact in eighteen seconds—mark!" her gunnery officer snapped. "Weapons free. Stand by point defense."

"Launch the ready fighters!" Captain Wu ordered,
never looking away from her plot. The stand-by squadron
might get off before those missiles struck. No one else
would.

"Oh, dear God!"

The anguished whisper came from Victor Aurelli, but
Admiral Li had no time to spare the envoy.

"Execute Plan Charley!" he barked, and his answering
missiles whipped away. But he needed time to power up
the shields and energy weapons Aurelli had forbidden
him to activate on the way in, and *Everest* trembled in
agony as the first warheads erupted against her naked
drive field.

"Captain Bowman reports we're streaming air, sir," Gianelli reported. "Datalink gone—we're out of the net."

"Acknowledged. Get those beams up, Christine! We
need them badl—"

"Energy fire on *Cottonmouth*!" Li turned to his ops
officer in surprise. Energy fire? How? They hadn't picked

up any Erlicher emissions, so it couldn't be force beams, and the battleship was too far out for effective laser fire.

"Specify!"

"Unknown, sir. It appears to be some sort of x-ray laser."

"*X-ray laser?*" Li stole a second to glance at his own read-outs and winced as the impossible throughput readings registered.

"*Cottonmouth* is Code Omega, sir," Gianelli reported flatly. "And the carrier group's taking a pounding. *Deerhound* and *Corgy* are gone. So is *Bogue*, but she got about half her group off before they nailed her."

"Many hits on enemy flagship," Gunnery announced, and Li watched *Saint-Just*'s dot flash and blink. His missiles were getting through despite her readied point defense, but her armor must be incredible. Her shields were still down and fireballs spalled her drive field like hellish strobes, but she wasn't even streaming atmosphere yet!

"Admiral Li!" He looked up at his Plotting officer's summons. "We're picking up additional drive fields, sir—they're coming out of the Ferry!"

Dispassionate computers updated the display silently, and Li looked at the destruction of his task force. They must have had a courier drone on the trips, ready to go the instant Aurelli fumbled their question. Now the rest of their fleet—the fleet no Terran had ever seen—was coming through, and six more superdreadnoughts headed the parade.

He swore silently and ran his eyes back over his own battered force. The carriers had taken the worst pounding. Half were gone and most of the rest were cruelly mauled—the bastards must have gunned for them on purpose. His surviving units were getting their shields up at last, but most of the capital ships were already streaming air. At least half of them must have lost their datalink, which meant they'd be forced to fight as individuals against trios of enemy ships whose fire would be synchronized to the second. Worse, it was already obvious the

"Peace Fleet's" supposed numerical advantage was, in fact, a *dis*advantage.

They'd timed it well. If he'd been only a little closer to the Ferry, he might have been able to bull through and sit on it, smashing their reserves as they made transit. As it was, he couldn't quite get there in time, and trying to would only put him closer to those damned lasers. They were almost as long-ranged as his force beams and, unlike force beams, they could stab straight through his shields. If he got even closer to them—

"Pull us back, Christine." He was amazed he sounded so calm.

"Aye, aye, sir," his chief of staff said levelly, though she knew as well as he that backing off the warp point was tantamount to admitting defeat.

If only more of his fighters had gotten into space! The ones which had launched were doing their best, but once their missiles were expended they would have only their single onboard laser mounts, because there would no longer be any hangar decks to rearm them. Only *Elkhound* and *Constellation* had gotten their full groups off, and even now heavy missile salvos were bearing down on both frantically evading carriers.

"*Sir!*" The utter disbelief in Gianelli's voice wrenched his head around. She sat bolt-upright at her console, her face white. "*Greyhound* reports she's being *boarded*, sir!"

"Ramming Fleet in position, Admiral. First *samurai* salvos away."

"Thank you, Plot. Captain Kurnash, where are my shields? I—Ahhhh!"

Saint-Just's shields snapped up, and Admiral Lantu grinned fiercely. These infidels clearly had no lasers to match his own. He didn't know what those long-ranged energy weapons of theirs were, but they couldn't reach through a shield as his could, and the massive armor his ships mounted as an anti-laser defense had served them well. The damage in the first exchange had gone in the People's favor by a wider margin than he had dared hope.

"They're pulling back, sir."

"I see it, Plot. Maneuvering, the fleet will advance."

"Aye, aye, sir."

Li Chien-lu shut it all out for a moment, forcing himself to think.

That first deadly salvo had gutted his carriers and blown too many of his capital ships out of their datanets, and the enemy's ability to board ships under way made an already desperate situation hopeless. Captain Bowman had *Everest*'s Marines racing for the armories, but they would be pathetically out-numbered when those "capital missile" vehicles got around to her. In a stand-up fight with the strength bearing down on them, his task force would be annihilated in thirty minutes of close action.

"Commander Gianelli."

"Yes, sir?"

"Order all escorts, battle-cruisers, and carriers to withdraw. The battle-line will advance and attack the enemy."

"Aye, aye, sir."

Admiral Li turned back to his plot as his battered formation unraveled. One or two battle-cruisers ignored the order, their drives already too damaged to run, and he doubted very many of those fleeing units would escape, but—

"What are you *doing*?!" A hand pounded his shoulder, and he turned almost calmly to meet Victor Aurelli's stunned eyes.

"I'm ordering my lighter units to run for it, Mister Aurelli."

"But . . . but . . ."

"They may have the speed for it," Li explained as if to a child. "We don't. But if we can make these bastards concentrate on us while the others run, we can at least give them a chance."

"But we'll all be *killed*!"

"Yes, Mister Aurelli, we will." Li watched his words hit the envoy like fists. It was very quiet on the bridge, despite the battle thundering about *Everest*'s hull, and the admiral's entire staff heard him as he continued coldly, "That's why I'm so glad you're aboard this ship."

He turned away from the terrified civilian to Commander Gianelli.

"Let's go get them, Christine."

CHAPTER FIVE

"A *khimhok* stands alone, Mister President."

Howard Anderson switched off his terminal and rose, rubbing his eyes, then folded his hands behind him and paced slowly about his small study.

During his own naval career, courier drones had been the only way to send messages between the stars, but the slow extension of the interstellar communications relays was changing that. No com signal could punch through a warp point, but drones could, and deep-space relays could beam their contents across the normal space between warp points at light-speed. Their cost tended to restrict them to wealthier, populous systems, but the Federation had taken pains to complete links all along its frontier with the Khanate.

Which meant Old Terra had learned of the disaster in Lorelei ten times as quickly as it might once have . . . for what it was worth.

He looked around his study unseeingly. Eighty percent

of the "Peace Fleet" had died, but *Everest's* Omega Drones had gotten off just before she blew her fusion plants. The data base download had included Chien-lu's log, and Anderson's fury had burned cold as he read the thoroughly illegal bootleg copy an old friend had passed him.

He picked up the message chip in age-gnarled fingers and wondered what the summons meant. Perhaps Sakanami had discovered he knew and meant to shut him up? If so, he was about to discover the limits of the presidency's power.

The aide rapped on the ornate doors, then opened them and stood aside, and Anderson stepped wordlessly into a magnificent office. Its splendor was an expression of the power of the man in the president's chair, but he was unimpressed. He'd sat in that chair himself.

He stumped across the sea of crimson carpet, leaning on his cane. It was less of an affectation than it once had been. He'd been in his fifties before the antigerone treatments became available, and his body was finally beginning to fail. But his eyes remained as sharp as his brain, and they flitted busily about as he advanced upon his waiting hosts.

Sakanami Hideoshi sat behind the big desk, expressionless as a *kabuki* mask. Vice President Ramon Montoya and Hamid O'Rourke sat in armchairs by the coffee table, Pericles Waldeck stood gazing out the windows with ostentatious unconcern, and Erika Van Smitt, leader of the Liberal Democrats, sat across the coffee table from Montoya.

Quite a gathering, Anderson mused, choosing a chair beside Van Smitt. Add himself, and the people in this room represented the Administration and over ninety percent of the Assembly.

"Thank you for coming, Howard," Sakanami said, and Waldeck turned from the window with a smile. Anderson met it stonily, and it faded. The silence stretched out endlessly until Sakanami finally cleared his throat.

"I've asked you here because I need your advice, Howard."

"That's a novel admission," Anderson said, and the president winced.

"Please, Howard. I realize how you must feel, but—"

"I doubt very much," Anderson's voice was cold and precise, "that you have the least idea how I feel, Mister President." *If you did, you'd've had me searched for weapons, you son-of-a-bitch.*

"I—" Sakanami paused. "I suppose I deserved that, but I truly do need your help."

"In what way?"

"I need your experience. You've led the Federation through three wars, both as an admiral and as president. You understand what the Fleet needs to fight with and what it takes to produce it. I'd like to create a special cabinet post—Minister for War Production—and ask you to assume it."

"And what would the duties of this post be?"

"You'd be my direct representative, charged with rationalizing demand and output. If you took the post, I'd ask you to go out to Galloway's World. Admiral Antonov will be taking command in the Lorelei Sector, and I want you to help him coordinate the operations of the Fleet yard with its civilian counterparts before he ships out. Are you interested?"

"Would I retain the right to speak my mind, publicly as well as privately?" Anderson was surprised and—he admitted it—excited by the offer.

Sakanami glanced at Waldeck, then nodded firmly. "I couldn't expect the full benefit of your experience if you didn't."

"Then I accept, Mister President," Anderson said. His voice was still cold, but he was beginning to wonder if he'd misjudged Sakanami.

"Good. Good! And there's another thing I need from you, Howard. You're the only man on Old Terra who's ever personally met Khan Liharnow, and a message from you will carry more weight than one from me."

"A message to Liharnow?" Anderson's eyes narrowed once more. They'd shown him the carrot, now they were about to tell him how high he had to jump to get it. "What message?"

"We haven't released the report, but ONI has finished its analysis of Admiral Li's drones," O'Rourke answered for Sakanami. The defense minister faltered as Anderson turned his basilisk gaze on him, then continued.

"You must have heard rumors the Thebans aren't human after all. Well, we have positive confirmation they aren't. The battle-cruiser *Scimitar* got away, but not before she was boarded. The Thebans have some sort of personnel capsule—something like a short-ranged capital missile—that lets them literally shoot small boarding parties at a ship. They have to knock the shields down first, but they carry drive field penetrators like fighters and small craft. ONI puts their maximum range at about eight light-seconds.

"Anyway, *Scimitar's* Marines took out her boarders, and the bodies are definitely non-human." He paused, as if that explained everything, and Anderson frowned. Obviously they didn't realize he'd already seen the original reports, but what were they driving at?

"I fail to see," he said into the expectant silence, "what that has to do with my acquaintance with Liharnow."

"Surely it's obvious that this changes everything, Howard." Pericles Waldeck's patronizing manner was one of several reasons Anderson detested him.

"How?" he asked coldly.

"Mister Anderson"—O'Rourke seemed stunned by his obtuseness—"we lost eighty percent of Admiral Li's force—over ninety percent of its tonnage, since none of the battle-line got away. That's more than a quarter of Battle Fleet!"

"I'm familiar with the figures, Mister O'Rourke."

"Well, don't you see, we agreed to intervene and handle the situation alone because we thought we were dealing with *humans*! We're not—and we don't have the least idea how powerful these Thebans really are. They *said* they had only one system, but they could have dozens. We need to invoke the Alliance and get the Orions in here to help!"

Anderson stared at him.

"We can't," he said sharply. "It's absolutely out of the question."

"Howard," Sakanami stepped into the breach, "I don't think we have any choice. It'll take us months to redeploy the Fleet, and if we do it'll leave the frontiers almost naked. We need the Orions."

"Don't you understand the Orion honor code?" Anderson demanded. "A *khimhok* stands alone, Mister President. If you ask Liharnow for help now, you're rejecting the role you *asked* him to let you assume! The best we can hope for is that he won't hold *us* responsible if the Thebans hit him again."

"But we accepted the role because we thought the Thebans were humans, and they aren't," Waldeck explained with elaborate patience.

"Which doesn't matter a good goddamn!" Anderson shot back. "Jesus, haven't you even *talked* to your xenologists?! To an Orion, an obligation is an obligation. If he makes a mistake, takes on a responsibility because of a misunderstanding, that's his problem; he'll handle it anyway or die trying."

"I think you're overreacting," Sakanami said.

"Like hell I am! Damn it, Liharnow put his own honor on the line to let you handle the Thebans! You go to him with an idea like this, and you'll have the fucking Orion Navy on your back, too."

"I find your language offensive, Howard," Waldeck said coldly.

"Well, fuck you and the horse you rode in on!" Anderson retorted. "I'll help clean up your goddamn mess, Wonder Boy, but I'll be damned if I help you make it any worse!"

"Howard—" Erika Van Smitt started pacifically.

"You stay out of this, Erika! All you did was support

the Administration—don't screw up now and get roped into *this* insanity!"

"I've had just about enough of you, Anderson," Waldeck grated. "You *and* your holier than thou criticism! It's always the civilians, right? Always *our* fault! Well, Mister Anderson, this time your precious Fleet's in it up to its gold-braided ass!"

Anderson met the younger man's eyes contemptuously. Their enmity cut far deeper than mere politics—it was personal and implacably bitter. Waldeck would never forget that CNO Anderson had personally seen to it that Admiral Solon Waldeck was court-martialed and shot after ISW-1 for allowing the Orions to capture a copy of the Federation's entire astrogation data base . . . and attempting to conceal the fact. Other branches of the Waldeck clan had provided many a flag officer as distinguished as any family could wish, but Solon had been Pericles Waldeck's grandfather.

Now Waldeck's florid face darkened as the famous Waldeck temper roused. Sakanami looked alarmed and reached out a hand, but Waldeck ignored it.

"You're riding pretty high right now, aren't you, Mister Minister for War Production? All fired up to 'help' us after you warned us and we went right ahead and put our foot in it, right?"

"Something like that," Anderson said coldly.

"Well, just remember this—it was your precious Navy admiral who decided to take his task force right onto Charon's Ferry and got his command shot to hell! You remember *that* when you tell us what we can and can't do to get out of the mess *he* made!"

Anderson's lined face went white, and Waldeck's eyes glowed. But he'd misread the old man.

"You goddamned lying son-of-a-bitch!" The ex-president was on his feet, age forgotten in his rage, and the taller, younger man retreated a half-step in shock.

"*Howard!*" Sakanami's face was distressed as he stood behind his desk.

"You get this shit-faced fucker out of my face or I'll

ram this cane up his goddamned ass!" Anderson roared, and started for Waldeck.

"Mister Anderson!" O'Rourke had more guts than Anderson had guessed, for it was he who seized his arm to hold him back. "*Please*, Mister Anderson!"

Anderson stopped, quivering in every muscle, shocked by his own loss of control. He dragged in deep, shuddering breaths, and Waldeck recovered some of his lost composure.

"I'll overlook your outburst," he said coldly, "because I know you and Admiral Li were close. But he was in command, and he took his entire force into a position it couldn't possibly escape from. If he hadn't, we wouldn't *need* the Orions. So whether you approve or not, we're going to ask for them."

"I see." Anderson's voice was ice, and President Sakanami shifted uneasily as he turned his cold blue eyes upon him. "I'd wondered who really pulled the strings in this administration. But this time he's wrong."

"I—" Sakanami began, but a savage wave cut him short.

"Understand me. You will *not* ask the Orions for help. If you try it, I'll move for your impeachment."

A moment of shocked silence hovered in the office, then Waldeck spoke.

"On what possible grounds?" he asked tightly.

"The truth, Piss Ant," Anderson said contemptuously. "And I'll *enjoy* nailing you to the cross where you goddamned well belong."

"How?" Waldeck sneered.

"By producing the secret orders this administration handed Victor Aurelli after assuring the Assembly there *were* no such orders," Anderson said very softly.

He saw the shot go home, but Waldeck recovered quickly and managed a bark of laughter.

"Preposterous!"

"Mister President," Anderson turned to Sakanami, "I apologize for my intemperate language, but not for the anger which spawned it. I am in possession of a copy of

Admiral Li's log. In it, he recorded the orders he received over your signature, placing Aurelli in command
of the military as well as the diplomatic aspects of his
mission, and also the orders he was given *by* Aurelli . .
and obeyed under protest. I leave it to you to estimate
the effect of that log entry in the Assembly and press."

"You wouldn't dare!" Waldeck spluttered. "We'd—"

"Pericles, shut up." Sakanami's voice was cold, and
Waldeck's mouth snapped shut in astonishment. Anderson was almost equally astonished as the president sat
back down and turned his chair to face all of them.

"He's right," Sakanami continued in the same hard
voice. "I should never have issued those orders to Li.
whatever you and Aurelli thought."

"But, Hideo—"

"Be quiet," Sakanami said icily. "You may be the majority leader in the Assembly, but I'm not letting you
cut this administration's throat by pushing Howard into
making good on his threat."

"But we *need* the Orions!" Waldeck said desperately.

"Perhaps. But what if Howard's right about the Khan's
reaction? The last thing we need is to bring the Orions
in on the wrong side of a three-cornered war!"

"But, Mister President—" O'Rourke began.

"Please, Hamid." Sakanami raised a hand. There was
no affection in the gaze he turned on Anderson, but
there was a cold respect. "I'll make you an offer, Howard.
I will consult ONI's xenologists before I proceed with
any message to the Khan. If they concur with you, no
such message will be sent, nor will I assign public blame
for what happened at Lorelei to Admiral Li. In return,
you will promise not to publish his log entries until after
we're out of this mess. Is that acceptable?"

"Yes," Anderson said shortly. He felt like a traitor, but
he knew the people at ONI. They would never support
the idea of calling in the Orions, and that had to be
headed off at any cost. Even Chien-lu's name.

"Then I think that concludes our business. Thank
you."

Anderson nodded curtly and turned for the door, but Sakanami's voice stopped him.

"By the way, Howard, how soon can you ship out for Galloway's World?"

He turned back quickly, his face showing his surprise, and the president laughed sharply—a laugh that took on an edge of true humor at the matching surprise on Waldeck's face.

"You've always taken your politics too personally, Howard. I don't like you, and you don't like me, but I really do need your experience."

"I don't—" Anderson began, but Sakanami stopped him.

"Don't say it. Instead, reflect on your little victory here. You may not win the next round, but you called the tune today. Maybe you were even right. But whether you were or not, and whether or not I give in next time, I need you. So take the goddamned job. Please?"

Anderson stood irresolute for one more moment, watching the hatred on Pericles Waldeck's face and visualizing the inevitable battles if he took the post. But Sakanami was right—damn him. The situation was too grave to withhold any service he could give, and he nodded slowly.

CHAPTER SIX
The Path of the Storm

First Admiral Lantu stood on the bridge of the super-dreadnought *Hildebrandt Jackson*, double-jointed arms crossed behind him, and contemplated his visual display. The Alfred System was a distant G0/K2 binary, and each component had a habitable planet, yet only one was inhabited. Alfred-A IV, known to its inhabitants as New Boston, was on the dry side, but it lay within forty hours of a warp point. Alfred-B I, though suitably damp, was over a hundred hours from the nearest warp point—almost two hundred from the next closest. Lantu tended to agree with the infidels; there was little point wasting time going to Hel when Boston was so much closer to hand.

He rocked on his wide feet, watching another wave of shuttles slice into the planetary atmosphere. The space about New Boston was crowded with the ships of First Fleet of the Sword of Holy Terra, but he was beginning to think his concentration of firepower might be a bit excessive. Most of the survivors of the infidels' massacred fleet had escaped through the closest warp point, to the starless nexus JF-12 and the Blackfoot System. First Fleet's battle-line, headed by six superdreadnoughts and nine battleships, had encountered exactly five small frigates in Alfred, and those had fled at high speed. Lantu didn't blame them; there'd been no point in those ships sacrificing themselves to defend an unfortified world.

He shook his head at the blue and green planetary jewel on his display. There were over a million infidels on that gem, and not even a single missile platform to protect them. Incredible.

He settled into his command chair. Most of the infidels had blown their fusion plants when his *samurai* infantry sleds swamped them with boarders, but they'd fought well first. Captain Kurnash's beloved *Saint-Just* would be in yard hands for months, and her sister *Helen Borkman* would never fight again. The ferocity with which the infidel battle-line had turned on him, forcing him to let many of their light ships escape despite his initial success, had dismayed him. The Synod was pleased, but it saw only the destruction *he'd* wreaked without grasping what it had taken for the infidels to strike back so fiercely after their surprise, and the Church's obvious contempt for its enemies worried him.

Yet even he found the total lack of defenses in Alfred ... odd. Most of their Lorelei prizes had managed to dump their data bases before they were taken, but Thebes had learned much. Among other things, they'd learned of the "Treaty of Tycho," and Lantu was inclined to concede that only demonic influence could account for its irrationality. The original assumption that the accursed Khanate had conquered humanity might have been an error, but the infidels had certainly been seduced into apostasy somehow. How else could a victorious Federation not only have concluded peace with the Satan-Khan but *suggested* a prohibition against fortifying "transit" systems along their mutual frontier? It was insane enough not to destroy their enemies when they lay prostrate, but this—!

Lantu shook his head again, baffled. Of course, there were those none-too-clear references to "The Line." The Redwing System, five transits beyond Alfred, was its closest outpost, and he gathered from the scanty data that the infidels regarded it as a formidable obstacle, even though its fortifications were eighty and ninety Terran years old. But he and First Fleet would cross that bridge when they came to it. In the meantime, the shipyards could take the prizes apart and analyze away to their heart's content while Lantu tidied up by occupying all the systems the infidels had so obligingly left totally undefended.

Sergeant Angus MacRory of the New New Hebrides Peaceforce ran a hand through his wet, dark hair. His brown uniform was streaked with sweat, and his callused palms stung. His world was digging in, but they were almost as sadly deficient in construction equipment as they were in weapons.

He laid aside his pick and climbed out of the weapon pit to survey his handiwork while tools clinked all about him. New Hebrides' (natives routinely dropped the official first "New" of their planet's official name) pseudo-coral islands made digging hard, but his painfully hacked-out hole was well placed to cover New Lerwick's single airfield—for all the good it might do. Angus had been a Terran Marine Raider for seven years before the home-hunger drew him back, and though he didn't intend to admit it to his fellows, he knew their efforts were an exercise in organized futility. Not that they needed telling. Peaceforcers were policemen, ill-equipped for serious warfare.

Corporal Caitrin MacDougall leaned on her shovel beside him. She was tall—rivaling his own hundred and ninety centimeters—and broad-shouldered for a woman. Short, red-gold hair dripped sweat under her uniform tam-o-shanter, her snub nose was smeared with dirt, and she was as weary as Angus, but she grinned tiredly as their eyes met.

"Deep enough?" she asked.

"Aye," Angus replied. "Or if no, it's no gang deeper."

"You've got that right." Caitrin held a doctorate in marine biology, and six years of study on New Athens had muted her New Hebridan burr.

"Weel, let's be gettin' the sandbags filled." Angus sighed, reaching for his own shovel. "And if we're dead lucky, Defense Command may even find us a wee little gun tae put in it when we've done."

Captain Hannah Avram, TFN, stepped into the destroyer *Jaguar*'s briefing room. Commodore Grissom was bent over the holo tank, watching its tiny dots run through yet another battle problem, and she had to clear her throat loudly before he noticed her.

"Oh, hi, Hannah." He waved at a chair and put the tank on hold as he swung his own chair to face her.

"You sent for me, sir?"

"Yep. What's the status of your repairs?"

"We've got all launchers back on line, and one force beam. Shields are at eighty-six percent. Her armor's a sieve, but the drive's in good shape and datalink's back in . . . sort of."

" 'Bout what I expected," Grissom murmured, tugging at his square chin.

How the heavy-set commodore managed to sound so calm baffled Avram. His pathetic "New New Hebrides Defense Fleet" was a joke. Her own *Dunkerque* and her sister *Kirov*, all that remained of the Ninth Battle-Cruiser Squadron, were his heaviest ships. Admiral Branco, the Ninth's CO, hadn't made it out of Lorelei, and *Dunkerque* and *Kirov* were here only because they'd been cut off from the JF-12 warp point. Grissom had three cruisers—a heavy and two lights—and two destroyers to support them. That and a hodgepodge of twelve Customs Patrol frigates and corvettes.

"As I see it, I don't have a hope in hell of holding this system, Hannah," Grissom said, finally admitting what she'd known all along, "but we have to make the gesture."

He leaned well back, folding his hands on his ample belly and frowning up at the deckhead.

"There are six and a half million people on New New Hebrides, and we can't just abandon them. On the other hand, the Thebans have a lot of warp points to choose from in Lorelei, and I figure it's unlikely they'll just race off in all directions when they can't be certain how quickly we can regroup.

"If they were coming straight through, they'd already be here. They aren't, which may mean they're being cautious and methodical, and *that* means they may probe with light forces before they come whooping through the Alfred warp point. If they do, we might just manage to smack 'em back through it and convince them to go pick on someone else until Fleet can get its act back together and rescue us. That's a best chance scenario, but it looks to me like we've got to play for it and hope, right?"

He straightened quickly, eyeing her intently, and Avram nodded.

"Right," he grunted, and flopped back. "Okay, I'm giving you a brevet promotion to commodore and putting *Kirov, Bouvet, Achilles,* and *Atago* under your command." Avram sat a bit straighter. That was his entire battle-cruiser and cruiser strength. "I'll hold the tin cans and small fry right on the warp point to pound 'em as they make transit, and I want the cruisers close enough to use their force beams, but keep *Dunkerque* and *Kirov* back."

He paused, and Avram nodded again. Her battle-cruisers were *Kongo*-class ships with heavy capital missile batteries and weak energy armaments. They were snipers, not sluggers, and keeping them well back would also keep her wounded armor away from those godawful lasers.

"It's my duty to defend this system, Captain," Grissom said more somberly, his black face serious, "but I can't justify throwing away battle-cruisers when I figure they're worth more than superdreadnoughts were a month ago. So if I tell you to, your entire force will shag ass out of here."

"Yes, sir," Avram said quietly.

"In that case, you'll be on your own, but I recommend you make for Danzig." Avram nodded yet again. Danzig was in a cul-de-sac, a single-warp point system not covered by the Treaty of Tycho's prohibition against fortifying "transit" systems. It was fairly heavily industrialized, too, and Fortress Command had erected respectable warp point defenses.

"If you can help the locals hold, you'll suck off enemy forces to seal your warp point. More important, there are fifteen million people on Danzig. It'll be your job to protect them, Captain."

"Understood, sir. If it happens, I'll do my best."

"Never doubted it, Hannah. And now"—Grissom propelled himself explosively from his chair—"let's go find a tall, cold drink, shall we?"

Admiral Lantu rechecked his formation as Chaplain Manak's sonorous blessing ended. The tricky thing about warp point assaults was sequencing your transits so no two units emerged too close together and overlapped in normal space. That resulted in large explosions and gave the enemy free kills, which meant an alert defender always had an important edge. You had to come through carefully, and if he had the firepower he could annihilate each assault wave as it made transit.

Lantu doubted there was that much firepower on the other side of this warp point, but there could be enough to make things painful.

"All right, Captain Yurah," he told *Jackson*'s captain. "Execute."

"They're coming through, Skipper."

Acting-Commodore Avram acknowledged her exec's report as her tactical display lit with the first red dots. Grissom's light craft were a loose necklace around the warp point cursor, already launching while she waited impatiently for her own scanners to sort out the targets.

Aha! The symbols changed, shifting to the red-ringed white dots of hostile destroyers, and Grissom's ships were concentrating on the leaders.

"Gunnery, take the trailers!" she snapped, and *Dunkerque* bucked as the first salvo of capital missiles spat from her launchers and external ordnance racks.

Angus MacRory looked up from his hole. Night hung heavy over New Lerwick, lit only by the wan glow of Brigit, the smallest of New Hebrides' three moons, and the sudden glare tore at the eye. Searing pinpricks flashed and died against the cold, distant stars, and his lips tightened. Caitrin slid into the hole beside him, one hand gripping his shoulder bruisingly, as they watched their threadbare defenders meet the foe.

"Execute Plan Beta," Lantu said quietly to Captain Yurah. The first destroyer should already have returned if there was no resistance.

"Aye, sir," Yurah replied, and the battleship *Mohammed* moved forward.

"That's no destroyer, Skipper!" Commander Dan Maquire said, and Hannah Avram's heart sank as the crimson-on-crimson of a hostile capital ship burned in her plot. Another appeared behind it, and another.

The commodore's scratch team had done well against the first wave. Six destroyers had been blasted apart in return for a frigate and heavy damage to a corvette and one precious Terran destroyer, but this was no probe.

Her display flickered and danced with the violence of warheads, force beams, and the deadly Theban lasers, and Terran units vanished with dreadful, methodical precision. Capital missiles from her battle-cruisers blanketed the lead battleship, pounding down her shields and savaging her armor, but it wasn't going to be enough.

"Personal signal from Flag, sir."

Avram punched a stud, and Grissom's broad, dark face appeared on her com screen.

"All right, Hannah," he said. "Shag on out of h—"

His signal chopped off, and Hannah Avram's contralto was harsh.

"Execute Dunkirk, Maneuvering." Her lips thinned. "Gunnery, maintain fire on Target One until we lose the range."

"Jaysus!" someone murmured beside Angus's hole. The explosions had died away briefly, only to erupt with fresh violence minutes later. Waves of nuclear flame billowed, far hotter than before, and the Navy couldn't possibly throw that many missiles with what Angus knew they had out there.

The silent, white-hot flashes continued for perhaps two minutes, then began to scatter and die. A cluster of them sped off across the system as some of the defenders retreated under fire in a desperate effort to reach the Sandhurst warp point. Smaller clusters flashed and faded, and he clenched his fists. The enemy was picking off the cripples, but one glaring spark was bigger and brighter than any of the others. Someone was kicking hell out of something big up there, he thought fiercely, pounding it again and again and—

The spark suddenly flared still bigger, expanding in an eye-aching boil of light.

"They got one o' the bastards," he said softly.

Admiral Lantu read the message flimsy, then looked up at Yurah.

"Break off the pursuit, Captain."

"But, sir, we've got eight cruisers and six battle-cruisers after them. They can't—"

"You may overhaul the cruisers, Yurah, but not the battle-cruisers, and you'll lose more than you'll gain in the chase. Break off."

"Aye, sir." Yurah sounded a bit rebellious, but Lantu let it pass, unable to blame him for wanting the kills.

He'd gotten one of the lights, but infidel cruisers mounted more launchers; they were giving almost as good as they got. Lantu could still have them in the end—his ships had to score a crippling drive hit eventually—but meanwhile the infidel battle-cruisers were pounding their pursuers with those damnable long-ranged missiles.

The yards back home were putting matching weapons into production, helped by the fact that they, too, used standard Terran units of measure and tech notations, but he didn't have any yet. And, as he'd told Yurah, he'd lose more than he gained without them. Just as he'd already lost *Mohammed*.

He folded his arms behind him once more, rubbing his thumbs against his shoulder carapace. A single battle-ship, one heavy cruiser, and six destroyers wasn't an exorbitant price for an entire star system, but he was bothered by how well the infidels had done. Most of their minuscule ships hadn't even had datalink, yet he'd lost eight ships, and the damage reports from *Karl Marx* and *Savanarola* sounded bad. If the infidels ever managed to assemble a real task force, things might get nasty.

He shook himself out of his gloomy thoughts and glanced at Yurah.

"Shape your course for New New Hebrides, Captain."

Dawn bled crimson over New Lerwick Island, and Sergeant MacRory sat in his hole with his com link. There was no sign of the invaders here—which was just as well, since Major Carmichael had never gotten his promised heavy weapons—but there was heavy fighting elsewhere. New Hebrides was a world of archipelagoes and small continents, and her people were scattered too thinly to prevent the enemy from landing unopposed in far too many places. But the enemy wasn't interested in unopposed landings; he was dropping his troops right on top of the population centers.

The civilian com channels were a madhouse of civil defense signals, frantic, confused queries, and Theban broadcasts in perfect Standard English. Angus couldn't make much sense of the latter; they seemed to consist mainly of weird commands for all "infidels" to lay down their weapons in the name of "Holy Terra," and wasn't that a fine thing for aliens to be telling humans?

But the Peaceforce channels were clear . . . and filled with horror. The main landing had apparently been over the capital of New Selkirk on the continent of Aberdeen. The first few shuttles had fared poorly against the capital's hastily cobbled-up defenses, but the Thebans had put a stop to that. Two-thirds of New Selkirk had been obliterated by a kilotonne-range nuke, and there were reports of other nuclear attacks, apparently called in from orbit anywhere the defenders denied the Thebans a foothold.

MacRory leaned back in his hole, tam-o-shanter covering his eyes, and hatred and helplessness coursed through him. How the hell were they supposed to fight that sort of firepower in the hands of someone ruthless enough to use it so casually? He was thankful they hadn't come to New Lerwick yet, for he had no more desire to die than the next man, but he knew. The planetary president had died in New Selkirk, but as soon as the surviving government could reach a com, they would have no choice but to order a surrender.

He ground his teeth and tried not to weep.

CHAPTER SEVEN
The Faith of Holy Mother Terra

Archbishop Tanuk smothered his impatience as his shuttle entered the atmosphere of his new archbishopric, but try as he might, he could not suppress his pride.

A century before, the Angel Saint-Just had set forth to claim this very world for Holy Terra. Now the Holy Messenger's true People would complete his mission, even if they must wrest it from his own apostate race, and the Synod had elevated the son of a lowly mining engineer to the primacy of New New Hebrides to oversee that completion.

He folded his hands, watching his amethyst ring catch the cabin lights, and the incised sigil of Holy Terra glittered like a portent.

Angus MacRory tried to hold his head erect as he marched with the survivors of the New Lerwick detachment, coughing on the dust of their passage. The day was hot for Aberdeen—almost twenty degrees celsius—and they were far from the first to make this march.

Thousands of feet had churned the surface to ankle-deep powder, and their guards' odd, three-wheeled motorcycles trailed thick plumes as they rode up and down the column. Those bikes might look silly, but they made sense; the Thebans' short, stumpy legs would be hard-pressed to match even their prisoners' weary shuffle.

One of them puttered closer. He—at least Angus assumed it was a male—was dark skinned, his face covered with a fine, almost decorative spray of scales. His dark green uniform and body armor couldn't hide the strange angularity of the bony carapace covering his shoulders, and the smaller carapace over the top and back of his head gleamed under the sun. His amber eyes reminded Angus of a German Shepherd, but his blunt, vaguely wolf-like muzzle ended in flared, primate-like nostrils, and his large, powerful teeth were an omnivore's, not a carnivore's.

Angus had examined his captors carefully, and the first thing he'd thought of was an Old Terran baboon. The aliens' torsos were human-size but looked grotesque and ungainly perched on legs half as long as they should have been—an impression sharpened by their over-long arms. Yet they weren't baboons or anything else Old Terra had ever seen. Their limbs appeared to be double-jointed; their ankles sprang from the centers of broad, platform-like feet; they had three fingers, not four; and their thumbs were on the outsides of their hands, not the insides.

They were ugly little boggits. But though they might look like clumsy, waddling clowns and their planetary combat gear might be obsolescent by the Corps' standards—indeed, from what he'd seen, he suspected it wasn't quite as good as that issued to the paramilitary Peaceforcers—they were backed by starships and nukes. That was all the edge they'd needed to smash New Hebrides' pathetic defenses in less than eighteen hours, and their quick, ruthless organization of their prisoners soon finished off his amusement.

The officers and both chaplains had been singled out

and marched away even before they'd been shipped over
to the mainland, and Sergeant-Major MacIntosh had
been shot two days ago for jumping a guard. They'd
passed a line of civilian prisoners separated into three
groups—men in one, women in another, children in a
third—and the weeping bairns had pushed the big sergeant-major over the edge. MacIntosh's death had also
made Angus the senior surviving noncom, and he tried to
keep himself alive by reminding himself others depended
upon him.

Unlike the civilians, the military POWs hadn't been
segregated by sex. He didn't know if that was a good
sign or a bad, but as he'd told the others, if they'd meant
to shoot them all, they could've done it on New Lerwick
instead of shipping them clear across the Sea of Forth.

He lowered his eyes to Caitrin MacDougall's shoulders
as she trudged along in front of him and tried to believe
it himself.

"Welcome, Your Grace." Father Waman bent to kiss
Tanuk's ring.

"Thank you, Father, but let us waste no time on ceremony. We have much to do in Holy Terra's service."

"I've made a start, Your Grace, if you'd care to read
my report . . . ?"

"A brief verbal summary will do for now." Tanuk
waved the priest to a chair and settled back behind his
own desk.

"Certainly, Your Grace. The leaders of the heresy have
already been executed." Waman gestured distastefully.
He'd been astounded by how stunned the infidel priests
and government leaders had looked as they were lined
up to be shot. The military officers had seemed less
surprised.

"Of course," Tanuk said a bit impatiently. "And the
others?"

"That will take time, Your Grace. The infidels aren't
gathered in large cities but spread out in towns and villages. Almost half live on one and two-family farms and

aquaculture homesteads, but we've made a start, and the children are being segregated as you instructed."

"Excellent. If we can reach them young enough, perhaps we can wean them from their parents' apostasy."

"As you say, Your Grace. The ministers of Inquisition have completed their first re-education camps. With your permission, I've instructed Father Shamar to begin with the captured military personnel."

"Indeed?" Tanuk rubbed his muzzle. "Why?"

"I believe they will be the ones most steeped in fallacy, Your Grace. I fear few will recant, but we may learn much from them to guide us when we turn to the civilians. And if some sheep must be lost, best it should be such as they."

"I see." Tanuk frowned, then nodded. "So be it. You've done well, Father, and I shall report it to the Synod with approval. Continue as planned and inform Father Shamar I look forward to his first reports."

At least there were beds. For the first time in over a week, Angus wasn't sleeping on the ground, and he was clean, for the POWs had been herded into communal showers on arrival at the camp. Their captors still made no distinction between male and female, and he'd been forced to deploy his small washcloth with care as he and Caitrin bumped under the spray. He was eight years older than she, and he'd known her all her life, but he'd been away for four years before she left for New Athens, and she'd only returned last spring. The beanpole adolescent he remembered had vanished, and his body had been intent upon betraying his awareness of the change.

Yet it was hard to remember that pleasant tide of embarrassment as he lay on his hard, narrow cot. All the surviving noncoms shared one hut, and Caitrin lay two cots down, but his mind was full of what he'd seen of the camp.

It was near ruined New Selkirk, at the foot of the New Grampians, the rugged mountain spine of Aberdeen. New Hebrides' islands had been formed by eons of pseudo-coral deposits, but the continents were granite. The mountains had been air-mapped yet remained mostly unexplored, for the New Hebridans were a coastal folk. If he could slip his people away into the Grampians . . .

He snorted bitterly in the dark. Certainly. Just slip away—past three electrified fences and guards with automatic weapons. True, they seemed a bit casual, without a single proper weapon emplacement in the place, yet that gave him no hope. There were some good lads and lasses caged up with him—not Marines, but good people—and if he could have gotten his hands on a weapon it might have been different, but that was wishing for the moon.

No, he could only wait. Wait and hope . . . and maybe pray a bit.

"I am Yashuk," the alien announced, "and I am your teacher."

Angus and Caitrin exchanged speaking glances. Yashuk stood on a dais that brought his head to human height, and the two manacled humans sat in low chairs. Angus found the effort to place them at a disadvantage fairly crude, yet there'd been something peculiarly demeaning in submitting to the armed guards who'd split the noncoms into handcuffed pairs and marched Caitrin and him away to this small room.

He looked back at Yashuk. The alien wore a violet-colored, hooded robe, like a monk's, but there was nothing monkish about the businesslike machine-pistol at his side. A purple-stoned ring flashed on his narrow hand as he gestured with a thick metal rod, and the rheostats on that rod's grip made Angus uneasy.

He realized Yashuk had fallen silent, his head cocked, and wondered if he was showing impatience.

"To teach us what?" Caitrin asked. It seemed to be the right question, for Yashuk nodded almost approvingly. "It is well you ask." Angus hid a grin. Yashuk's Standard English was better than his own, despite his elongated palate, and his pomposity came through perfectly.

"You have been seduced into apostasy," the Theban continued. "Your race has fallen into sin, abandoning the way of Holy Terra to commune with the Satan-Khan. As the Angel Saint-Just brought enlightenment to my world, so now I return the Holy Messenger's gift to his own race."

Angus blinked. Yashuk seemed to feel his gibberish meant something, but what was an "Angel Saint-Just"?

"Excuse me, Yashuk"—it was Caitrin again, and Angus was content to let her speak; he'd never been very verbal even with other humans, and she was the one with the fancy education—"but we don't understand you."

"I know this," Yashuk said smugly. "The Truth has been concealed from you, but I shall open your eyes. Listen, and heed the word of Holy Terra."

He drew a small book from his robe and cleared his throat with a very human sound, then began to read.

"For ages, the People dwelt in darkness, worshiping false gods, and nations warred each upon the other for empire and the wealth of their world.

"Yet they were not suffered to remain in darkness, for in the Year of Annunciation, the Holy Messenger came upon them. Saint-Just was his name, and he was sent by Holy Terra as Her Angel to lead the People into light.

"But the Satan-Khan, who hates Holy Terra and all Her children, harried the Angel's fleet, destroying its ships, so that only three of the Messenger's vessels ever touched the soil of the world the Holy One named Thebes. On the Island Arawk they landed, and they were *Starwalker*, *Speedwell*, and *John Ericsson*. Scarcely ten score Messengers survived the Satan-Khan's attack, and they were sorely wearied and afraid when they came to the People.

"Yet great was their mission, and the Angel Saint-Just went forth among the People, sharing with them the science of Holy Terra. As children they were before Her knowledge, but freely he gave of it to them.

"Now other nations were afraid and sought to smite down the Messenger and the People of Arawk, but the Messenger and his Companions aided those who had received them. The guns and tanks of Arawk's enemies withered before the weapons Holy Terra placed in the hands of those who had succored Her Messengers, and their foes were brought low.

"But even in that moment of triumph, the Satan-Khan struck, sending a terrible pestilence upon the Holy Ones. Not one of all the People died, but only the Holy Ones, and the pestilence slew and slew until only the Angel Saint-Just and less than a score of his fellows lived, and they sorrowed for all the Satan-Khan's despite had slain.

"Yet they lived, and they gathered to them disciples, among them Sumash, Prince of Arawk, and taught them the Faith of Holy Terra. And the Angel Saint-Just said unto Sumash, 'Learn of Holy Terra's arts and gather your people, that they may gird themselves, for the day shall come when they will be called by Holy Terra to return the gifts She has given. The Satan-Khan presses Her sore, and it may be She shall fall even into his hand, but your people shall become the People of Holy Terra even as my own. They will go to Her as sons, mighty in Her Faith, and smite the Satan-Khan. They will raise Her up once more, and woe be unto the unbelievers in that day, for they shall be gathered up and cast into the Fire forever.'

"Thus the Holy Messenger taught Sumash, and he learned all the Angel Saint-Just set before him. He mastered *Starwalker*'s Holy Records and grew mighty in the knowledge of Holy Terra, yet always he remembered he was but Her humble servant, and greatly did he please the Messenger.

"Yet in the Eighth Year of the Holy One, the Satan-Khan's pestilence returned, more terrible than before, and slew even the Angel Saint-Just and all his Companions.

"Great was the despair of the People when the Messengers were taken from them, and some among the disciples proved false and turned from the Holy One's teaching of jihad, but a vision came upon Sumash. Holy Terra Herself appeared unto him, anointing him as Her Prophet and the Messenger's Sword, and he cast down the faint of heart and drove them from *Starwalker*. And when they went among the People, preaching sedition against him, the Prophet came upon them in terrible wrath, and he slew them for their apostasy."

Yashuk drew a deep breath, almost a sigh, and closed his book.

"Thus did the Angel Saint-Just come to Thebes and charge the People with their holy task," he said reverently, and Angus gaped at him.

"But, Yashuk," Caitrin said softly and carefully, "we've never heard of the Angel Saint-Just, nor of the Faith of Holy Terra."

"We know this," Yashuk said sorrowfully. "We have scanned your records, and the Faith has been extirpated root and branch. Even as the Holy One foretold, the Satan-Khan has brought Holy Terra to the dust and seduced Her own children into sin."

"Like hell," Angus grunted. "We kicked the Tabbies' arse!"

"You will not use such language to me," Yashuk said sternly.

"Get knotted!" Angus snarled. "An' as fer that load o' crap yer peddlin', I—"

Yashuk's yellow eyes flamed. His rod hummed, and Angus screamed and arched up out of his chair. Molten lead ran down his nerves, and torment hurled him to the floor, twisting and jerking, teeth locked against another scream.

Agony tore at him forever before it ended with the quiet snap of a released switch. He grunted in anguished relief, consciousness wavering, and Yashuk's voice was colder than the gulfs between the stars.

"Be warned, infidel. For the Messenger's love, we will teach you Truth once more, but if you cling to apostasy, then even as he foretold, you will be cast into the Fire, and all other unbelievers with you. Return to your Faith and embrace Holy Terra, or you will surely die."

Angus wasn't particularly religious, and he knew it was stupid to defy Yashuk, but there was too much Highlander in his heritage. The agony of the rod's direct neural stimulation punished every defiant word, and his brawny body grew gaunt, yet the grim denial in his hollow, hating eyes never wavered.

It seemed Yashuk's stubbornness matched his own. Half the noncoms vanished within a week, "cast into the Fire" by less patient "teachers," but he refused to admit Angus might defeat him, though Angus had no doubt the alien would already have sent him after the others if not for Caitrin.

She sought desperately to divert Yashuk, tying him up in conversation, seeking "enlightenment," and her keenly probing questions seemed to delight the alien. On a good day she could divert him into an hours-long explanation of some abstruse theological distinction while Angus sat quietly, gathering his strength as she watched him from the corner of one anxious eye. He knew she regarded Yashuk's drivel exactly as he did, despite her exasperation with his own stubborn, open rejection, but they were different people. She had the gift of words, the ability to dance and spar. Angus didn't, and even though enough defiance must exhaust even Yashuk's patience, he couldn't pretend.

It was the way he was.

"I weary of you, infidel," Yashuk said coldly, tapping his rod as he glared at Angus. "Caitrin seeks knowledge, yet you hold her back. You cling to your darkness like the Satan-Khan's own get! Will you die for it? Will you see your soul cast into everlasting damnation before you return to your Holy Mother?"

"Aye? Weel, I've had aboot enow o' *yer* drivel, tae," Angus said wearily, matching glare for glare. He was weary unto death, and a darkness had begun to grow in his brain. Not the darkness Yashuk yammered about, but despair. He knew Caitrin had not yet professed her "conversion" only because she was protecting him. But she'd felt the rod twice in the last two days for defending him too openly, and enough of that would get *her* killed.

"I've had you *and* yer maunderin'," he said now, coldly. "'Holy Terra' my left nut!"

"*Blasphemy!*" Yashuk screamed, and the dreadful rod whined.

Angus shrieked. He couldn't help it, couldn't stop the screams, yet within his agony was a core of gratitude. This was the end. This would kill him and set Caitrin free to—

His torment died in a high-pitched squeal; not his, but another's. Reaction's heavy hand crushed him to the floor, but he rolled his head and opened his eyes, then gaped in horror.

Somehow Caitrin had reached Yashuk while the alien concentrated on him. Now her wrists were crossed behind his neck, and the chain between them vanished into his throat.

Yashuk writhed, one hand raking bleeding furrows in his throat as it scrabbled at the chain. The other reached back, and his incredibly long arm clubbed her with his rod. Angus heard her grunt in anguish as the blows crunching into her ribs lifted her from the floor, but she held on grimly, and her forearms tightened mercilessly.

Angus groaned and dragged his hands under him, but he had no strength. He could only watch their lethal struggle while the alien's face darkened and his squeal became a strange hoarse whine. He smashed his cranial carapace into Caitrin's face again and again. Blood ran from her mouth and nose, and her knees buckled, but Yashuk was weakening. He stumbled to his knees and dropped the rod to paw at the chain two-handed in a weak, pathetic gesture. His limp hands flopped to the floor, and she braced a knee in his spine, her face a mask of blood and hate, and wrenched the chain still tighter.

She held it until the last light faded from the bulging

yellow eyes, and then she collapsed over the body of her foe.

Caitrin MacDougall opened swollen eyes, blinking as Angus's face swam above her, and stifled a whimper as simply breathing grated broken ribs.

"Bloody fool," Angus said softly. His brogue was more pronounced than ever as he dabbed at her face with a damp cloth from somewhere.

"Me?" she whispered through split, puffy lips. "He'd have killed you this time, Angus."

" 'Twas what I wanted, ye great twit. Ye took tae many chances fer me, lassie."

"Well, we've both blown it now," she sighed. She tried to sit up and collapsed with a moan. "What're you still doing here?"

"I cannae leave ye," he said reasonably.

"You're going to have to. If you move fast, you might even make it as far as the wire, but with me to slow you down—"

"Hisht, now! Ye'll no have tae run. We'll see tae that."

"We?" She rolled her head and gaped at the crowd of brown-uniformed men and women. Each of them seemed to be holding a Theban machine pistol or assault rifle. "What—?"

"Yon Yashuk had our handcuff keys and a knife, Katie," Angus said with an ugly smile, "and no a one of 'em expectin' an 'infidel' tae be runnin' aboot loose. I slipped around ahind the spalpeens and picked off a dozen o' our wee 'teachers.' They've had nowt tae worry at fer tae lang, and when I threw a dozen pistols in the hut door, weel. . . ."

He shrugged as if that explained everything, and Caitrin gawked at him.

"Do you mean you lunatics—?"

"Aye, lassie, we've taken the whole damned camp, and we started wi' the com shack. Sae just lie easy, Katie girl. We've a stretcher here, and ye're comin' wi' us!"

CHAPTER EIGHT
A Question of Authority

Senior Chief Petty Officer Hussein watched Captain—no, he reminded himself, *Commodore*—Avram stalk into *Dunkerque*'s boat bay and felt sorry for whoever the Old Lady was going to meet.

He sprang to attention with alacrity. The sideboys did the same, but Commodore Avram hardly seemed to notice. She saluted the Federation banner on the forward bulkhead with meticulous precision as the bosun's pipe shrilled, then stepped silently into her cutter, and the atmospheric pressure in the boat bay dropped by at least a kilo to the square centimeter as its hatch closed. It departed, sliding through the mono-permeable force field at the end of the bay, and Chief Hussein shook his head sadly.

Some poor bastard dirtside was about to grow a new asshole.

Hannah Avram sat on her fury and made herself lean back as the cutter headed for Gdansk, the capital city of

New Danzig. Despite her preparations, her position was unbelievably fragile, and venting her volcanic anger would do more harm than good, but still—!

She smoothed the cap in her lap and smiled unwillingly as she stroked the braid on its visor. That was the single card she had to play, and she'd built her entire strategy on it. And it helped enormously that Commodore Hazelwood was such a gutless wonder.

She shook her head, still unable to believe either the situation or how much she'd already gotten away with. Richard Hazelwood came from a distinguished Navy family, but now that she'd met him she understood how he'd gotten shunted off to Fortress Command in a system no one had ever dreamed might actually be attacked. She doubted Hazelwood would blow his own nose without authorization—in triplicate!—from higher authority.

Her arrival in Danzig with what was left of the New New Hebrides defenders—her own ship, *Kirov*, the heavy cruiser *Bouvet*, and the light cruiser *Atago*—had been bad enough. They hadn't even been challenged until they'd been in-system over two minutes! God only knew what *Thebans* might have done with that much time, and Hannah Avram had no intention of finding out. That was one reason *Kirov*, *Bouvet*, and *Atago*, along with the six destroyers which constituted Danzig's entire mobile local defense force, were sitting on the warp point under Captain Yan, *Kirov*'s skipper.

The only good thing about the entire bitched-up situation was that Hazelwood was such a wimp he hadn't even questioned her brazen usurpation of his authority. He'd been overjoyed to let her shoulder the responsibility by exercising a Battle Fleet commodore's traditional right to supersede a Fortress Command officer of the same rank. Of course, that assumed the Battle Fleet commodore in question was a *real* commodore and not simply a captain who'd been "frocked" by a desperate superior. Hannah had a legal right to the insignia she now wore, but her rank certainly hadn't been confirmed by Fleet HQ. It hadn't occurred to Hazelwood to ask about that, even though his personnel files had to list her as a captain, and she wasn't about to mention it to him.

Only her staff knew her promotion had been signed by Commodore Grissom rather than some higher authority, and she'd used the week since her arrival well, getting personally acquainted with all of Danzig's senior officers. For the most part, they were a far cry from their erstwhile CO, and they were delighted by her assumption of command.

But now that Hazelwood had gotten over his immediate panic he was proving a real pain in the ass. The man commanded a dozen Type Three OWPs, for God's sake! Admittedly, his forts were a lot smaller than The Line's, but they were still more powerful than most battleships and covered by a minefield whose strength had surprised even Hannah. He was also responsible—or had been, until she took the burden off his shoulders—for the protection of fifteen million Federation citizens. Yet he wanted to send out a courier ship to discuss "terms" with the Thebans!

She gritted her teeth against a fresh flare of anger. Bad enough to have an idiot as her second in command, but Hazelwood also had close ties to the local government. Well, that was to be expected after he'd spent six years commanding their defenses, but it also meant they were prepared to back him. Indeed, she suspected President Wyszynski had actually put Hazelwood up to it. Or it might have been Victor Tokarov. In fact, it sounded more like Tokarov than Wyszynski.

The president might, on a good day, have the independence to decide what color to paint his office without running it by the manager of the Cracow Mining Company. Danzig had been settled by Polish neo-ethnicists fifty years ago, but the planet's incredible mineral wealth had brought New Detroit's Tokarov Mining Consortium in almost from the beginning, which had contributed immensely to the speed of Danzig's industrialization. It had also moved the planet firmly into the Corporate World camp.

Backed by Tokarov money, Wyszynski could be re-elected planetary president three months after he died. Conversely, of course, if he irritated the Tokarov interests, he couldn't be elected dog-catcher. Assuming, that was, that there were enough dogs on Danzig to *need* a dog-catcher.

The more she thought about it, the more convinced she'd become that Tokarov had originated the suggestion. It was just the sort of brilliant idea to appeal to a business-as-usual financier. But neither Tokarov, Wyszynski, nor Hazelwood—damn him!—had been at Lorelei or New New Hebrides. They'd make out better negotiating with a saber-toothed tiger . . . or a *zeget*.

The cutter's drive changed note as it settled towards the pad, and she looked out the armorplast view port at the spaceport's orderly bustle. A dozen local shuttles full of additional mines were about ready to lift off, and there were another dozen Fleet personnel shuttles spotted around the pads. Most had their ramps down, and she could just see a platoon of Marines marching briskly off towards their waiting ground transport.

Her lips quirked wryly as she turned away from the view port. Her newest idea had horrified most of her fledgling staff, but they'd come through like champs. Danny had worked like a Trojan with Commander Bandaranaike, her legal officer, as well as finding time to handle the logistical side. And, she supposed, she might as well be hanged for a sheep. Besides—her smile vanished—Commodore Grissom had charged her with the defense of Danzig. If he could go down fighting knowing it was futile in defense of less than half as many people, then she could damned well do the same for Danzig's.

Even if she had to do it in spite of their government.

Victor Tokarov watched Commodore Avram walk in. She laid her briefcase neatly on the conference table, then sat and set her cap equally neatly beside it. She was smiling, but Tokarov had attended too many outwardly affable business meetings, and the good commodore's over-controlled body language spoke volumes. He could teach her a thing or two about stage-managing meetings. Not that he had any intention of doing so. Or perhaps, in a way, he did, he thought with a hidden smile.

President Josef Wyszynski nodded pleasantly to her. Commodore Hazelwood did not, but he'd made it clear he intended to distance himself from the entire discussion. It was a pity, Tokarov thought, that it was Avram who was the newcomer. She had so much more to recommend her as an ally, aside from her foolish insistence on "defending" Danzig. No single system could stand off the juggernaut which had smashed Battle Fleet at Lorelei and driven this deep into the Federation so quickly. Far wiser to make bearable terms locally, preserving Danzig's industrial infrastructure—and people, of course—from pointless destruction. The Navy would get around to rescuing them sooner or later, after all.

"Thank you for coming, Commodore," Wyszynski said. "I appreciate your taking the time from your busy schedule."

"Not at all," Hannah said with a tight smile. "I'd planned on paying a call as soon as convenient. I do rather regret pulling *Dunkerque* off the warp point at this particular moment, but I'd have had to turn her over to the local yard for permanent repairs sometime soon, anyway."

"Uh, yes, I see." Wyszynski cleared his throat. "Turning to the point which, I believe, Commodore Hazelwood has raised with you, it seemed a good idea for the planetary government's viewpoint to be—"

"Excuse me, Mister President," Hannah said calmly. "I presume you're referring to Commodore Hazelwood's suggestion that we seek a negotiated local *modus vivendi* with the Thebans?"

Wyszynski seemed a bit taken aback by her interruption, but he nodded. "Well, I'd hardly put it in quite those words, but, yes. I understand you oppose the idea, and of course, as the senior officer in Danzig you have every right to make your own tactical dispositions, but we feel—"

"Excuse me again, sir," Hannah interrupted, and Tokarov gave her high marks for tactics as she crowded the president, throwing him off stride and asserting her own authority. "Such negotiations—which, I feel I must point out, have *not* been authorized by President Sakanami or the Legislative Assembly—represent rather more than a simple tactical decision."

"Well, we know *that*," Wyszynski replied a bit tartly. "But President Sakanami is on Old Terra, not here."

"True. On the other hand, sir, any negotiations with a hostile power lie strictly within the purview of the Federal government, not of member planets. I direct your attention to Article Seven of the Constitution."

Wyszynski's mouth opened, and his eyes darted to Tokarov. The mining director swallowed a frown, but it was clear more direct action was in order.

"You're quite correct, Commodore. But while I realize I'm present solely as an economic and industrial advisor, I think President Wyszynski's point is that the Constitution makes no provision for a planet which finds itself cut off from the rest of the Federation *by* a hostile power. And Danzig, as a Federated World, has no Federal governor and hence no official representative of the Federal executive."

"I see." Hannah cocked her head thoughtfully. "Your point is that with no such official the planetary government must—strictly as an emergency measure—create its own foreign policy until contact with Old Terra is regained?"

"Exactly," Wyszynski said quickly.

"I see," Hannah repeated. She shrugged slightly and opened her briefcase. "Actually, gentlemen, I didn't come specifically to discuss this point. I'd intended to give you this"—she handed over a document chip folio—"which details my planned repair and construction policy. Given Danzig's industrial capacity, I believe we can easily triple the density of the present warp point minefields within two months. After that, I'd like to get started on the construction of destroyers and light carriers. I doubt we'll have time for anything much heavier, and the local population would be strapped to provide crews if we did. In respect to that point, it occurs to me that we may have to introduce conscription—on a hostilities-only basis, of course—and I'd intended to discuss that with you, as well."

Her listeners stared at her in shock. Even Tokarov's jaw had dropped just a bit, and she smiled at them.

"Still, if you feel we must resolve this negotiations question first, I am, of course, at your service."

Wyszynski blinked. Avram's fast, unpredictable footwork was hardly what one expected from a bluff, apolitical TFN officer. For his part, Tokarov eyed the commodore with new respect. She might not be very good at hiding emotions, but he made a mental note against equating that with lack of guile. Poor Josef was obviously uncertain how to proceed, so it looked as if it was going to be up to him.

"Speaking for Danzig's industrial interests, we'll certainly be glad to take the fabrication side of your requests under advisement. But I really think we have to determine whether or not such a program would accord with the government's intention to seek a cease-fire with the Thebans."

"Not really, Mister Tokarov. You see, there will *be* no negotiations."

"I beg your pardon?" Wyszynski demanded, swelling with outrage. "With all due respect, Commodore, this is a political question—and a legal one, of course—but certainly not a military one."

"On the contrary, sir." The steel glinting in Hannah's brown eyes gave Tokarov a sudden feeling of dread. "It most certainly is a military question. On the other hand, I wasn't speaking to its purely military aspects. I was, in fact, addressing those same legal and political points you just referred to."

"In what way, Commodore?" Tokarov asked.

"In this way, Mister Tokarov." She extracted another document from her briefcase, this time a printed hard copy, and handed it across the table to him. He looked down at it in some surprise.

"This seems to be a copy of the Articles of War," he said, playing for time and trying to deduce her intent.

"It is. If you'd take a look at Article Fifty-Three, please?" He thumbed pages, and those steely brown eyes shifted to Wyszynski like *Dunkerque's* main battery. "Since we have only one copy, I'll save a bit of time by citing the relevant passage for you, Mister President. Article Fifty-Three says, and I quote, 'The senior Naval officer present shall, in the absence of guidance from the relevant civil authorities, exercise his discretion in the formulation of local military and supporting policies, acting within the understood intent of previously received instructions.' "

Tokarov stopped turning pages. He didn't doubt she'd cited correctly, but he still didn't see where she was headed. Which didn't prevent a sudden sinking sensation. Commodore Avram looked entirely too sure of herself. She had something nasty up that silver-braided sleeve of hers.

"I fail to see," President Wyszynski said, "the relevance of that article, Commodore. We're not discussing military policy, except, perhaps, in the most indirect fashion. We're talking about a political decision made by the duly constituted local authorities. In fact, I believe we *are* the 'relevant civil authorities' in this case!"

"With all due respect, Mister President, I must disagree," Hannah said coolly, and Wyszynski gaped at her. "The document I've just cited from is the legal basis of the Federation Navy. It is not merely a military document; it is also a *legal* document, drafted by the Admiralty but approved and enacted by the Legislative Assembly and, as such, constitutes a portion of the legal *corpus* of the Federation, not of any single member planet. Under Article Two of the Constitution, Federal law, where existent, supersedes locally enacted law. As

such, I am not bound by your wishes, or those of Mister
Tokarov, in the formulation of my own 'military and supporting' policy. In fact, I am a direct representative of
the Federal government. Wouldn't you agree?"

"Well, I . . . I suppose that *sounds* like it makes sense,
in a way. Not," Wyszynski added hastily, "that I've ever
seen any documentation on the point. And constitutional
law is hardly my strong suit. I'd hesitate to make any
rash pronouncements or commitments."

"I realize that, sir, and I am, of course, equally desir-
ous of maintaining a scrupulous adherence to the law of
the Federation. Accordingly, I discussed this very point
at some length with my legal officer before I left to attend this meeting. At her suggestion, I refer you to *Har-
good-vs.-Federation* and *Lutwell's World-vs.-Federation*.
In both cases, the Supreme Court determined that the
senior Navy officer present was, in fact, directly representative of the Federal government. I'm certain your own
Attorney General could provide you with copies of those
decisions."

"All right, then," Wyszynski said. "But I still fail to see
how your authority to determine military policy applies
to a purely political question like negotiations with the
Thebans!"

"I invite your attention once more to the relevant portion of Article Fifty-Three, sir." Hannah smiled. Why,
she was actually beginning to enjoy herself! Odd. She'd
never *thought* she had a sadistic streak.

"*What* 'relevant portion'?" Wyszynski snapped.

"I refer," she said softly, "to the specific phrase 'military and *supporting* policies.' I submit to you, sir, that
my intention to defend Danzig and prevent any Theban
incursion therein, which is clearly a military policy and
hence within *my* jurisdiction, precludes any negotiation
with the enemy. And, as the proper authority to determine policies in support of my military intentions, I
must ask you to abandon any idea of those negotiations
and, instead, turn your attention to my industrial
requirements."

"Now just a moment, Commodore!" Tokarov said sharply. "You can't seriously suggest that we allow a military officer to dictate to a duly elected planetary government!"

"That, I'm afraid, is precisely what I'm suggesting, Mister Tokarov," Hannah said flatly, "though 'suggest' is, perhaps, not the proper word. I am *informing* you of my decision."

"This—this is preposterous!" Wyszynski blurted. "Why, you haven't got any more legal right to issue . . . issue *dictats* to civilian authorities than . . . than . . ." He slid to a halt, and Tokarov looked at Hannah with narrow eyes, all humor vanished.

"I believe President Wyszynski means to point out that while you may represent the Federal military, you have no *civilian* authority, Commodore," he said coldly.

"On the contrary." Hannah pulled out another thick book. It thudded onto the table, and Tokarov's eyes dropped to the cover. *Admiralty Case Law of the Terran Federation, Vol. XLVIII*, it said.

"And what, if I may ask, does *this* have to say to the matter?"

"Under Admiralty law, Mister Tokarov, the senior Federation Navy officer present becomes the Federation's senior *civil* officer in the absence of proper civilian authority. I refer you to *Anderson-vs.-Medlock, Travis, Suchien, Chernov, et. al.*, otherwise known as 'The *Starquest* Case.' Since we have all just agreed there is no local Federal authority in Danzig, I have no option but to consider myself acting in that capacity. This"—she extracted yet another document from the deadly magazine of her briefcase—"is a proclamation drawn up by my legal officer and myself. It announces my assumption of civil authority as Governor of the Danzig System in the name of the Federal government."

"You're insane!" Hazelwood blurted, speaking for the first time. "That's patently illegal! I refuse to listen to this driv—"

"Commodore Hazelwood," Hannah said very, very

softly, "you are in violation of Articles Seven, Eight, and Fourteen of the Articles of War. I am your superior officer, and you will bear that in mind and address me as such or I'll have your commission. Do you read me, Commodore Hazelwood?"

Hazelwood wilted into a confused welter of dying half-sentences, and Hannah turned back to Tokarov, dropping all pretense that anyone else in this room mattered.

"Commodore Hazelwood has just been relieved—on my authority—of his duties as Sky Watch commander." She glanced at her watch. "One hour ago, Captain Isaac Tinker turned command of *Bouvet* over to his exec and assumed Commodore Hazelwood's duties to free the commodore to act as my personal liaison with Danzig's industrial complex. I'm certain he'll carry out his new duties in the exemplary manner in which he carried out his previous responsibility for Fortress Command."

"You won't get away with this, Commodore," Tokarov said quietly.

"Governor, please," Hannah replied calmly. "I am, after all, speaking in my civilian persona. And I've already 'gotten away' with it, sir. With the exception of one or two defeatists, the officers and enlisted men and women of the Navy have no interest in negotiating with the Thebans. Nor, I might add, do the officers and enlisted people of the Marine detachments."

Tokarov swallowed, eyes suddenly very wide, as she reached into that deadly briefcase yet again. She extracted a small handcom and activated it.

"You may come in now, Major," she said into it, and the conference room doors opened. Ten Marines in unpowered body armor stepped through them, bayoneted assault rifles ostentatiously unthreatening in their hands. They took up properly deferential positions against the wall, paying absolutely no attention to the people sitting around the table.

"Now, gentlemen," Hannah's voice drew their pop-eyed stares from the silent Marines as she closed her briefcase with a snap, "I believe that completes our business."

"This—this is mutiny! *Treason!*" Wyszynski blurted.

"On the contrary, Mister President. This is a constitutional transfer of authority, in exact accordance with the legal precedents and documents to which I have drawn your attention."

"That's nonsense!" Tokarov's voice was more controlled, but his eyes were just as hot. "This is a brazen use of force to circumvent the legitimate local authorities!"

"That, Mister Tokarov, is a matter of opinion, and I suggest you consult legal counsel. If I've acted beyond the scope of my authority, I feel certain the Admiralty and Assembly will censure me once contact with those bodies is regained. In the meantime, we have a war to fight, and the organs of the Federal authority in this system—the Fleet and Marine units stationed herein—are prepared to do their duty, under my orders, as per their oaths to protect and defend the Constitution of the Terran Federation. Which, I'm very much afraid, makes your objections irrelevant."

"You'll never get away with this. My people won't stand for it, and without us, there's no industrial base to support your insane policy!"

"On the contrary, sir. Your managerial personnel may, indeed, refuse to obey me. Your labor force, however, *won't* refuse, and you know it. In the meantime, Marine units are on their way to your offices and major industrial sites even as we speak, and any act of sabotage or active resistance will be severely dealt with. You may, of course, at your discretion, elect to employ passive resistance and noncooperation. I should point out, however, that such a decision on your part will have the most serious postwar repercussions if, as I confidently expect, my actions are retroactively approved by the Assembly."

She held his eyes unblinkingly, and something inside him shied away from her slight, armor-plated smile. She waited a moment, inviting him to continue, and his gaze dropped.

"I believe that's everything then, gentlemen," she said calmly, standing and tucking her cap under her arm. "Good day."

She walked out amid a dead, stunned silence.

CHAPTER NINE
Ivan the Terrible

The VIP shuttle completed its approach run and settled on the landing platform with a sort of abrupt grace that would have looked inexplicably *wrong* to anyone who'd lived before the advent of reactionless, inertia-canceling drives. Its hatch slid open and a solitary passenger emerged into the light of Galloway's sun.

Fleet Admiral Ivan Nikolayevich Antonov was of slightly more than average height but seemed shorter because of his breadth, thickness, and—the impression was unavoidable—density. His size, and the way he moved, suggested an unstoppable force of nature, which was precisely what his reputation said he was. But he stopped at the foot of the landing ramp and saluted, with great formality, the frail-looking old man in civilian clothes who headed the welcoming committee. One didn't ordinarily do that for a cabinet minister ... but Howard Anderson was no ordinary cabinet minister.

"Well," Anderson growled, "you took your sweet time getting here, EYE-van."

"My orders specified 'Extreme Urgency,' sir," the burly admiral replied in a rumbling, faintly accented basso. "I had certain administrative duties to attend to before departure . . . but Captain Quirino is speculating about a new record for our route."

"So what are you doing standing around here now with your thumb up your ass?" was the peevish reply. The other dignitaries stiffened, and the painfully young ensign beside Anderson blanched. "Let's go below and make all the introductions at once. You already know Port Admiral Stevenson . . . he'll want to welcome you to The Yard." Ever since the First Interstellar War, the sprawling complex of Fleet shipyards and installations in the Jamieson Archipelago of Galloway's World had been called simply that.

"Certainly, sir," Antonov replied stonily.

Anderson led Antonov in mutual silence towards the luxuriously appointed office that had been set aside for his private use. The ensign who'd hovered at the old man's shoulder throughout the formalities scurried ahead to the door, but Anderson reached out with his cane and poked him—far more gently than it looked—in the back.

"I'm not yet so goddamned feeble I can't open a door, Ensign Mallory!" His aide stopped dead, face flustered, and Anderson shook his head in exasperation. "All right, all right! I know you meant well, Andy."

"Yes, sir. I—"

"Admiral Antonov and I can settle our differences without a referee," Anderson said less brusquely. "Go annoy Yeoman Gonzales or something."

"Yes, sir." Mallory's confusion altered into a broad smile, and he hurried away . . . after punching the door button. Anderson growled something under his breath as the panel hissed open, waved Antonov through, and used his cane to lower himself into a deeply-padded chair.

"*Puppy!*" he snorted, then glanced at Antonov as he settled back. "Well, so much for your introductions—and thank *God* they're over!"

"Yes," Antonov agreed as he loosened his collar and shaped a course for the wet bar. "Upholding your image as an obnoxious old bastard must be almost as great a strain as serving as the public object of your disagreeableness. Don't they keep any vodka here? Ah!" He held up a bottle. "Stolychnaya, this far from Russia!" He looked around. "No pepper, though."

Anderson shuddered. "Make mine bourbon," he called from the depths of his chair, "if there is any. Do you know," he went on, "what the problem's been with the TFN from its very inception?"

"No, but I have a feeling you're going to tell me."

"Too many goddamned Russkies in the command structure!" Anderson thumped the floor with his cane for emphasis. "I say you people are still Commies at heart!"

Anderson was one of the few people left alive who would even have understood the reference. But Antonov knew his history. His eyes, seemingly squeezed upward into slits by his high cheekbones in the characteristic Russian manner, narrowed still further as he performed a feat most of his colleagues would have flatly declared impossible: he grinned.

"Also too many capitalistic, warmongering Yankee imperialists," he intoned as he brought the drinks (and the vodka bottle). "Of which you are a walking—or, at least, tottering—museum exhibit! These last few years, you've actually begun to *look* a bit like . . . oh, what was the name of that mythological figure? Grandfather Sam?"

"Close enough," Anderson allowed with a grin of his own.

It was an old joke, and one with a grain of truth. The Federated Government of Earth, the Terran Federation's immediate ancestor, had created its own military organization after displacing the old United Nations at the end of the Great Eastern War. Twenty years later, China accelerated the process with her abortive effort to break free of the FGE. Not only did the China War have the distinction of being the last organized bloodletting on Old Terra, but it had encouraged the FGE to scale the old national armed forces back to merely symbolic formations . . . quickly.

Since the Chinese military had no longer existed, the Soviet Union and the United States had possessed the largest military establishments, and hence the largest number of abruptly unemployed professional officers. Inevitably, the paramilitary services that were later to become the TFN had come to include disproportionate numbers of Russians and the "American" ethnic melange in their upper echelons. Even now, after two and a half centuries of cultural blending had reduced the old national identities largely to a subject for affectation (on the Inner Worlds, at least), the descendants of the two groups were over-represented among the families in which Federation service was a tradition.

"I'm starting to feel about as old as a mythological figure," Anderson went on. "You're looking well, though."

It was true. Like other naval personnel who had declared their intention of emigrating to the Out Worlds later, Antonov had had access to the full course of antigerone treatments from an early age. At seventy-two standard years, he was physiologically a man in his early forties. He shrugged expressively and settled into the chair opposite Anderson's.

"I keep in condition. Or try to. For an admiral, it's about as hard as for this damned peacetime Fleet." He scowled momentarily, then gave Anderson a reproachful look. "But we're wasting perfectly good drinking time! Come on, Howard! *Ty chto mumu yebyosh?*" He raised his glass. "*Za vashe zdorovye!*"

They drank, Antonov tossing back his vodka and Anderson sipping his bourbon more cautiously, muttering something inaudible about doctors.

"That's another thing about you Russians . . . if you want to tell a man to drink up, why not just say so? 'Why are you fucking a cow?' indeed! Well, I'll say this much for you: your language is rich in truly colorful idioms!"

"Rich in every way!" Antonov enthused, refilling his

glass. "Ah, Howard, if only you knew the glories of our great, our incomparable literature—"

"I read a Russian novel once," Anderson cut in bleakly. "People with unpronounceable names did nothing for seven hundred and eighty-three pages, after which somebody's aunt died."

Antonov shook his head sorrowfully. "You are hopelessly *nekulturny*, Howard!"

"I'll *kulturny* you, you young upstart!" Anderson shot back with a twinkle. For an instant, the decades rolled away and it was the time of the Second Interstellar War, when Commander Nikolai Borisovich Antonov, his Operations officer, had learned of the birth of a son on the eve of the Second Battle of Ophiuchi Junction. They'd all had a little more to drink that night than they should have, but Nikolai had survived both the vodka and the battle. And toward the end of the Third Interstellar War, President Anderson had met Vice Admiral Antonov's newly commissioned son . . . who now sat across from Minister of War Production Anderson, tossing back his vodka so much like Nikolasha that for an instant it seemed . . .

Too many memories. We are not meant to live so long. Anderson shook himself. *That's enough, you old fart! Next you'll be getting religious!*

Antonov, watching more closely than he showed, sensed his change of mood, if not its cause. "How bad is it, really, Howard?" he asked quietly. "Even these days, the news is always out of date. I don't know much beyond what happened to Admiral Li."

"Then you know we've lost a third of the Fleet," Anderson responded grimly. "What you may *not* know yet, is that ONI's latest estimate, based on scanner reports from the Lorelei survivors, is that the Thebans actually deployed a fleet stronger than Chien-lu's was."

Antonov's eyes became very still, and Anderson nodded.

"Right. So far, we've actually observed twelve superdreadnoughts, eighteen battleships, and twenty-odd battle-cruisers, and I'm willing to bet there's more we *haven't* seen. They seem a bit weak in escort types, but that still gives them effective parity with our entire surviving battle-line, though we haven't seen any sign of carriers yet. On the other hand, we lost an even larger proportion of our carriers than we did of our battle-line, and, of course, they're concentrated with the interior position and the initiative. You can infer the strategic situation *that* leaves us with."

He pushed himself erect with his cane, reaching across the desk for a remote-control unit, and touched a button. A wall vanished, giving way to a holographic display of warp lines.

"It's at least as bad as you think, Ivan." (Preoccupied, he forgot to mispronounce the name.) "At the rate the Thebans—whoever or whatever they are—have pushed on from Lorelei; they're two or three transits out in all directions by now. All *our* directions, that is; they've stopped well short of the Orion border fortifications for the moment . . . another mystery, but one complication we don't have to worry about. Yet." He fiddled with the control, producing a pair of cursors which indicated two systems: Griffin and Redwing. "Some of Chien-lu's survivors are still picketing the approaches, and the way they're spreading out is attenuating some of their numerical advantage, but we don't have anything with a prayer of stopping them short of The Line.

"Now for the good news, such as it is. Our Ophiuchi allies have agreed to help. They're not going to commit forces to actual combat against the Thebans—they're a *long* way off, and the proper role of a *khimhok's* allies is a pretty fuzzy area—but they're arranging to take over some of our border obligations. That'll let us shift a lot of what's left of the Fleet to this sector, but it'll take time to concentrate our forces, and new construction is going to take even longer. For now, your 'Second Fleet' will have to depend largely on the mothballed units here at Galloway's World . . . such as they are. The big question concerns priorities in reactivating them." He raised an eyebrow, inviting comment.

"The *Pegasus*-class light carriers first," Antonov responded without hesitation. "And, of course, the reserve fighter squadrons."

"That decision didn't take long," Anderson remarked with a smile. "Are you certain? Those ships are as obsolete as dodoes, and they weren't anything much even in their day. Just very basic fighter platforms built early in ISW-3 . . ."

". . . for an emergency not unlike this one," Antonov finished for him. "As you've so rightly—and publicly—pointed out, my trip here took a while, so I've had time to think. Two points: first, we have more *Pegasus* class than anything else in the Reserve and they're relatively small. Coupled with their austerity, that means they can be reactivated more quickly than fleet carriers or battle-line units . . . and time is of the essence. We have to use what we have and what can be made ready in the next few weeks.

"The second point," he continued with a frown, "is a little more speculative. But from the courier drones Khardanish and Admiral Li were able to send off, it seems clear the Thebans don't have strikefighters and that Admiral Li, due to the circumstances in which he found himself, was unable to employ his fighters effectively. Taken together, these two facts suggest to me that the Thebans may not take fighters seriously. This attitude—while it lasts—could give us an advantage. But if we're to seize it, we have to deploy all the fighter assets we can in as short a time as possible."

"Very cogently put," Anderson approved. "As a matter of fact, I just wanted to hear your reasoning . . . which, it turns out, parallels mine. You must have noticed all the work going on in the orbital yards. The first three *Pegasuses* will recommission in a few days, with more on the way."

Antonov looked like a man who'd had one of several heavy weights lifted from his shoulders. "Actually, you forgot a couple of lines of good news." He smiled at Anderson's quizzical look. "Not even Russians are *always* gloomy, Howard. I'm referring to a few new developments which fortunately were already in the R&D pipeline. Captain Tsuchevsky's last post before joining my staff was assistant project officer on the strategic bombardment program to increase capital missile range, and he's given me a glowing report on the possibilities. Add that to this new missile with warp transit capability—whatever they've decided to call it—and the new warheads . . ."

"Right, right," Anderson interrupted, "but you're going to have to fight your first battle without any of the new hardware."

"Understood. But you know the old saying about light at the end of the tunnel." He paused. "There's something else that could mean even more to us . . . *if* it exists. In which case it's still classified 'Rumor' even for a fleet admiral. But one does hear things about a new breakthrough in ECM." He left the statement hanging.

"So one does. I'll look into it and see if there's anything to the rumor." Anderson was all blandness, and Antonov merely nodded. They understood each other.

"And now," Anderson said briskly, "there's someone I want you to meet." He touched another button. "Ask Lord Talphon to come in," he said.

Antonov's mouth didn't quite fall open, but his expression constituted the equivalent. Before he could formulate a question, a side door slid open to admit a tall Orion whose fur was the jet-black of the oldest noble bloodlines rather than the more usual tawny or russet shades. Antonov recognized his jeweled harness as being of the most expensive quality and noted the empty spots from which insignia of military rank had been removed.

"Admiral Antonov," Anderson said formally, "permit me to introduce Twenty-Third Small Claw of the Khan Kthaara'zarthan, Lord Talphon."

The massive admiral rose and performed the small bow one gave an Orion in lieu of a handshake.

"I am honored to greet you, Admiral Antaanaaav," Kthaara said, returning his bow just as gravely.

His voice was deep for an Orion, giving an unusual, almost velvety rumble to the gutturals of his language. Antonov was widely recognized as one of the TFN's "Tabby experts"—which, he knew, was one reason he'd been tapped to command Second Fleet—and now he savored Kthaara's patrician enunciation. Others might refer to the Orion language as "cat fights set to bagpipes" and bemoan the facts of evolution which made it impossible for the two species to reproduce the sounds of one another's languages, but not Antonov. He would have preferred to be able to speak Orion himself, but he differed from most of his fellows in the fact that he actually liked the sound of Orion voices. Which, Anderson had always maintained, was a perversion only to be expected from anyone who thought *Russian* was Old Terra's greatest language.

"Mister Aandersaahn is not altogether accurate concerning my status, however," Kthaara continued, "for I have resigned my commission, though it is true that I have been Lord Talphon and *Khanhaku'a'zarthan* since my cousin Khardanish died without issue."

Understanding dawned. "Please accept my condolences on the death of your cousin. He was a victim of treachery"—Antonov knew what that meant to an Orion—"but he died well."

"Thank you, Admiral," Kthaara reciprocated. "The circumstances of his death are the reason for my presence here. The *Khan'a'khanaaeee's* agreement to accept the Federation as *khimhok* satisfies the honor of our *race*, but I, as an individual and as Lord Talphon and—especially—as *khanhaku* of my clan, carry a special burden. Thus the *Khan'a'khanaaeee* has allowed me to set aside my military duties until this burden is lifted. I come to you as a private individual, to volunteer my services in the war against my cousin's killers!"

"Before you say anything, Ivan," Anderson put in, "Lord Talphon brings with him a certification from the Khan himself that he can act as an individual without compromising the Khanate's *khimhok* neutrality. And, I might also point out, he's regarded in the KON as one of their leading experts on strikefighter tactics."

Antonov scowled. The flower of the Federation's fighter jocks had perished with the "Peace Fleet," and now he was being offered the services of one of the top . . . he might as well say "people" . . . of a navy that specialized in fighters with a fervor that wasn't entirely based on cost/benefit rationality as humans understood it. For all of Orion history, their honor code had regarded personal combat as its only truly honorable expression. The Tabbies hadn't really been happy since the First Interstellar War, when small spacecraft had ceased to be effective combat units—a warrior with 150,000 tonnes of superdreadnought wrapped around him was hardly a warrior at all. The invention of the deep-space fighter had allowed them to be themselves again, and even the most prejudiced TFN officers admired their mastery of fighter tactics.

Yes, Antonov thought, *I can use him.* And, of course, to refuse his offer could hardly help Federation-Khanate relations, which needed all the help they could get, at the moment. But . . .

"Lord Kthaara," he began awkwardly, "I fully appreciate the significance of your offer, and I am grateful for it. But there are difficulties. As I don't need to tell you, any military organization has its professional jealousies . . . which can only be inflamed by bringing in an outsider to fill a billet as high as your rank and experience warrant. . . ."

"Rest assured, Admiral," Kthaara interrupted, "I will serve in any capacity you can find for me. If you want me to pilot a fighter, or operate a weapons console, I will do it."

And that, Antonov reflected, said a great deal about how serious Kthaara was. His clan had a high reputation, even among Orions, for the warriors it produced. Most Orion clan names and titles of nobility were identical, commemorating the heroism in battle which had earned their first Clan Father his lordship; the *khanhaku* of

Clan Zarthan bore a secondary title, which was a proud honor indeed. For Kthaara to accept such a subordinate position was an almost unheard of concession, but even so . . .

"Unfortunately, that isn't the only problem." Antonov took a deep breath. "Our races have been allies for fifty Terran years, but it is an alliance that many in the Navy are still uncomfortable with. You see, fighting you was the TFN's reason for coming into existence in the first place. Before we met you, our Federation had no real military forces at all. The humans of that era believed that war was something that would never happen again . . . that any advanced civilization, anywhere, *must* be nonviolent."

"Why did they think that?" Kthaara asked, genuinely curious.

"Er . . . never mind. The point is, and I must be blunt, that dislike of your race is something of a tradition in the TFN. I regret that this is the case; but it is my duty to consider the effect the prejudices of others may have on the morale and effectiveness of my forces."

"Admiral, I fully understand. There are those among my race who still think of Humans as *chofaki*, in spite of the history of the Third Interstellar War . . . and in spite of Humans like my cousin's liaison officer, whom I believe you knew."

"Lieutenant Johansen?" Antonov was surprised anew. "Yes, I knew her; she served with my staff before her posting to Lord Khardanish's squadron. She was a fine officer. But—"

"A fine officer whom you encouraged to perfect her understanding of the Tongue of Tongues," Kthaara agreed with the Orion ear flick of acknowledgment. "Which is why I think you will be interested to know that her name has been entered among the Mothers in Honor of Clan Zarthan. My cousin, in his last courier drone, requested this . . . and made clear that she was fully deserving of it, that none of the *Zheeerlikou'valk-hannaieee* could have better satisfied the demands of honor than she." He drew himself up. "I myself may do no less!"

For a moment, two pairs of eyes produced by two altogether separate evolutions met. Then Antonov spoke gruffly.

"Commissioning a foreign citizen is a little irregular, but with the good offices of such a dignitary as the Minister of War Production . . ."

Anderson smiled beatifically.

Admiral Antonov's staff contained an unusually high proportion of "Tabby experts." Despite that, and even though they'd known about it in advance, they couldn't quite hide their reaction when he entered the briefing room with a Whisker-Twister wearing a harness of TFN black-and-silver with the insignia of a commander in tow.

"As you were," Antonov rumbled, then continued matter-of-factly. "I would like to introduce Commander Kthaara'zarthan, who will be serving as Special Deputy Operations Officer of Strikefighter Operations." The title had been hammered out hours before, and the rank was a diplomatic courtesy. (The legal officer had been brought to the edge of a nervous breakdown by Kthaara's polite but relentless insistence that he was in no sense a diplomatic representative.) But none of that mattered. If Ivan the Terrible said the Tabby was a commander, then the Tabby was a commander. Very simple.

"Now," Antonov continued, with the air of a man who has made the most routine of announcements, "Lieutenant Commander Trevayne has prepared an intelligence update." He gestured to the intelligence officer, who activated a warp line display.

Winnifred Trevayne's face was dark, but her features were sharply chiseled and her speech held not a trace of the lilt an ancestor had brought from Jamaica in the late twentieth century; it was all clipped, upper-middle-class British.

"Thank you, Admiral. The Thebans have, at last report, secured the Laramie System." There was no reaction from the others; the news wasn't unexpected, and they were inured to shock by now. Trevayne summarized the fragmentary reports of fleeing survivors, adding: "This, combined with their known presence at QR-107, puts them in a position to attack Redwing along either—or both—of two axes. We do not know if they are in the same position vis-a-vis Griffin; the Manticore System has fallen, but at last report the Basil System had not."

"Thank you, Commander," Antonov said impassively. Then he addressed the room at large. "We now face the decision we knew must come. The Thebans have reached The Line at two points. They must know from captured data that they are finally about to run into something hard. Since there has been nothing stupid about their conduct of the war so far, we must assume they will concentrate their forces accordingly. The question is: will they attack Griffin or Redwing?" His voice seemed to drop an octave. "We must assume that their captured navigational data is complete. If so, they know Redwing is on the direct line to Sol. On this basis, I believe that Redwing is where they will attack. But, since we cannot be certain, I have no option but to divide our forces."

No one spoke. Antonov had invited neither comment nor advice. He'd taken the entire terrifying responsibility on his own massive shoulders.

"I will," he resumed, "take personal command of the Redwing task force. Captain Tsuchevsky," he said, turning to his chief of staff, "signal Vice Admiral Chebab. He will be taking the other task force to Griffin." Everyone present knew that dividing Antonov's new "Second Fleet" would result in two contingents whose size could scarcely justify the term "task force."

"And now, ladies and gentlemen," Antonov continued, "I believe we have a long night ahead of us."

CHAPTER TEN

"To Smite the Infidel. . . ."

First Admiral Lantu watched the display as the destroyer slipped into orbit about Thebes, and frowned. He was too dutiful a son of the Church to begrudge the Synod's orders to return and confer, yet he found himself resenting the priceless time it took.

So far, the infidels had failed to mass a proper force against either First or Second Fleet, but he'd spent too many hours poring over captured data to expect that to continue. He'd smashed far more of their fleet in Lorelei than he'd dared hope, but they had reserves. And the Federation had grown far vaster than the Synod had believed possible. The infidels had found some way to make colonies spring up like weeds since the Year of the Annunciation, and Holy Terra's Sword must strike deep, and soon, or be overwhelmed.

He sighed heavily, and Fleet Chaplain Manak chuckled beside him.

"Patience, my son," he murmured.

"Is it so obvious?" Lantu asked with a grin.

"To one who has watched you grow from childhood? Yes. To the Synod? Perhaps not, if you keep your wits about you."

"I'll bear it in mind," Lantu said softly.

The chairs in TFS *Starwalker*'s briefing auditorium were uncomfortable for Theban legs, but no one had ever even considered replacing them. The Synod of Holy Terra sat in state in its hallowed meeting place, eyes bright as Lantu entered with a measured tread and genuflected to the Prophet. He basked in their approval, yet he felt tension hovering like smoke.

"The blessing of Holy Terra upon you, my son," the Prophet said sonorously. "You return on the wings of victory, and we are well pleased."

"I thank you, Your Holiness," Lantu murmured, and the Prophet smiled.

"No doubt you begrudge time away from your fleet, First Admiral." Lantu glanced up in surprise, and the Prophet's smile grew. "That is only to be expected of a warrior, my son. We are not all"—the Prophet's glance rose to brush the grizzled bishops and archbishops—"too old and weary to understand that." There was a mutter of laughter, for the Prophet was even younger than Lantu.

"Yet it was necessary to recall you briefly. You are our warlord, the anointed champion of Holy Terra, and we require your advice."

"I am at your disposal, Your Holiness."

"Thank you." The Prophet gestured at a chair beside him. "Please, be seated, and I will explain our quandary."

Lantu obeyed, though he would have preferred to remain standing. It seemed impious to sit in the Prophet's presence.

"Now," the Prophet said briskly, "there has been some lively debate in this chamber, First Admiral. Your victories in Lorelei began our jihad with great success, yet success sometimes breeds dissension."

Lantu swallowed unobtrusively and looked out from the stage to find Manak. As First Fleet Chaplain, the old man was second only to the Prophet in rank, and his smile was comforting.

"The Messenger himself warned that Holy Terra might fall into the Satan-Khan's power, yet none of us ever truly anticipated the horror you discovered, my son," the Prophet continued, "and the truth has thrown us into turmoil. Our goal was to launch our jihad against the Satan-Khan, but the discovery of the Federation's apostasy divides us over how best to proceed. One portion of the Synod believes we should return to our original plan; another believes we must first crush the apostate. Both are infidel, so there is merit on both sides, and since we have not reached consensus, we ask you to speak your mind. Tell us how *you* think best to smite the infidel."

Lantu had suspected what they would ask, but the Prophet gave no sign of his own opinion, and the admiral gathered his thoughts with care.

"Your question is difficult, Your Holiness, and Holy Terra did not call me to the priesthood, so I can speak only to its military aspects. Is that satisfactory?"

"It is."

"Thank you, Your Holiness. In that case, I would begin by setting forth the military position as I now understand it.

"So far, we have occupied ten of the apostates' star systems and four of their starless warp junctions. We've also taken three unpopulated star systems from the Satan-Khan, which brings us almost into contact with the permanent fortifications of both of our enemies. Only one apostate system—Danzig—has withstood us. We could take Danzig, but the system's warp point is heavily fortified; our initial probe was thrown back with heavy losses, and I have decided against further attacks until we can deal decisively with the infidels' remaining fleet strength. The cost of Danzig's final conquest, though not unbearable for the capture of an entire star system, will be high. Indeed, no matter which direction we next strike, we will confront permanent defenses and, I fear, pay a high price to break through them. It is for that reason that I wish to defer attacks against nonessential objectives in the immediate future.

"Our losses to date are not severe in light of our achievements: a superdreadnought, four battleships, seven battle-cruisers, five heavy and light cruisers, and a dozen or so destroyers. Several more ships are under repair, but most of our losses will be made good by the repair of our prizes."

He paused and folded his hands before him.

"Before I continue, Your Holiness, may I ask Archbishop Ganhad to explore the question of weapons production for us?"

"Of course." The Prophet gestured for the stumpy old archbishop, the Synod's Minister of Production, to rise.

"Thank you, Your Holiness." Lantu turned to Ganhad. "Your Grace is more knowledgeable than I. Could you explain briefly to the Synod how what we've learned of the infidels' weapons affects our own production plans?"

"I can." Ganhad turned to face his fellows. "The infidels have attained a generally higher level of technology than the People," he said bluntly. "The gap is not tremendous, and some of our weapons surpass theirs, yet it exists.

"They have no equivalent of our *samurai* sleds, nor have we seen any equivalent of our Ramming Fleet, and their lasers, while somewhat more sophisticated in manufacture, are much less powerful and shorter ranged than our own.

"It would appear that they possess only four major weapon systems which we do not, and one is merely a highly refined development of another.

"First of these is the so-called 'capital missile,' which marries a long-ranged drive and powerful seeking systems with a heavy warhead. Such weapons can engage us from beyond our own range, and they carry ECM systems which make them difficult for point defense to stop. Accordingly, we've made their development our first priority, and our own capital missiles will begin reaching the fleet shortly.

"Second are the attack craft they call 'fighters.' These are one- and two-man craft, armed with short-ranged missiles and light lasers, capable of operating up to several light-minutes from their carriers. Their data base and tactical manuals indicate that they think highly of this weapon, but it has not proven effective in any of our engagements. Further, the infidels have developed the 'AFHAWK'—a small, high-speed missile with a light warhead but very sensitive homing systems—for anti-fighter defense. This weapon is ingenious but straightforward and is already in production. In light of the inefficacy of their fighters to date and our possession of the AF-HAWK, we've given development of our own fighters a low priority.

"Third is the device they call a 'force beam.' While somewhat longer-ranged than our lasers, with a better power-to-mass ratio, it is simply a powerful Erlicher generator—or tractor beam—of alternating polarity. In essence, it wrenches its target apart by switching from tractor to presser mode in microsecond bursts. Although it cannot penetrate intact shields as lasers can, it remains a most formidable weapon. Since, however, it is no more than an application of technology we already possess, we can put it into production rapidly if we so desire.

"Fourth, but perhaps most important, is their 'primary' beam. In simplest terms, this is merely a vastly refined force beam so powerful and focused as to overload and penetrate shields locally. In addition, its power is sufficient to punch through the thickest armor or, indeed, anything in its path. It is slow-firing and its focus is extremely narrow—no more than four or five centimeters—but that is quite sufficient to disable any system. Since, however, it is basically only a powerful force beam, development of the one should lead naturally to development of the other, and we expect to have both in production shortly, although we will assign a higher manufacturing priority to the primary in light of our laser weapons' superiority."

He turned to Lantu with a courteous bob of his head.

"I trust that covers your question, First Admiral?"

"It does, indeed, Your Grace." Lantu chose not to mention that his own reports had suggested giving rather more priority to the fighter. The infidels hadn't yet had a chance to employ them as their tactical doctrine decreed, and the prospect of facing swarms of small, fast attackers operating from ships he couldn't reach was an unpleasant one. But development and production facilities had to be prioritized somehow, and a warrior—as he'd been rather pointedly told—fought with the weapons he had, not the ones he wished for.

He turned back to the task at hand.

"As I see it, Your Holiness, we have two strategic options and, within them, two operational problems.

"First, we may attack the Satan-Khan. This must, of course, be our ultimate goal. Until he's defeated, Holy Terra can never be safe, yet he has so far been content to let us smite the apostate unhindered. No doubt he finds this entertaining, but it may well prove his downfall.

"Second, we may continue to attack the apostate, and this, I think, is the wiser choice. We've occupied three of their inhabited worlds, and all we've seen suggests that it shouldn't be difficult to convert their industrial plants to our own use. If, in addition to this, the Holy Inquisition can bring substantial numbers of infidels to recant and embrace the True Faith, we will acquire large additions to our labor force. Finally—forgive me, I realize this is a spiritual consideration, yet it must be mentioned—we may liberate Holy Terra Herself much more rapidly if we continue to advance towards Her.

"If the Satan-Khan is prepared to allow us to defeat the Federation and add its industry to our own, then his own conceit will be his undoing."

He paused and saw Manak's approving nod. More importantly, he saw several other prelates nodding slowly.

"That is well-argued, my son," the Prophet said softly. "But what of these operational problems you mentioned?"

"Your Holiness, we've driven as far into infidel space

as we can without confronting their fortifications. I lack sufficient data on what they call 'The Line' to evaluate its strength, but while the forts are quite old, the infidels seem to consider them powerful, which suggests they've been refitted and updated heavily. Certainly the only fortifications we've actually encountered—those of the Danzig System—are, indeed, formidable.

"Further, we know their reserves have not yet been committed. I would feel happier if they had been, preferably in bits and pieces we might defeat in detail. Instead, the infidels seem intent on gathering strength for a heavy blow.

"Our problems thus are, first, whether or not to continue to advance and, related but separate, *how* we shall advance.

"At the moment, we have near parity with the infidels, and no other sectors to guard. We are concentrated, if you will, to an extent they cannot match. But if we suffer heavy losses, we may forfeit that advantage.

"On the other hand, we occupy systems they must eventually seek to regain. I suggest, therefore, that we stand temporarily on the defense and let them come to us in order to eliminate as much as possible of their reserves before we assay 'The Line.' "

"Stand on the defense?!" An elderly bishop jerked upright in shock. "When you've defeated them so easily at every attempt?"

Lantu glanced at the Prophet, who nodded for him to reply.

"Forgive me, Your Grace, but to date we've had the advantage of surprise and overwhelming numbers against naked warp points. Contested warp point assaults will be costly, particularly if we attack fleet units supported by fixed defenses. If, on the other hand, we revert to a defensive stance, we invite their attack and *we* hold the defender's advantage."

"So your defensive stance is actually an offensive one?" Manak asked.

"Exactly, Holiness," Lantu said gratefully.

"Yet you yourself point to their greater resources!" the bishop protested. "If we yield the initiative, may they not assemble such force as to overwhelm us, defensive advantage or no?"

"That is, of course, possible, but the infidels are not wizards. It takes time to build ships, and if much time passes without an attack, we may rethink our own deployments. But it seems wiser to me to tempt them into a mistake than to make one ourselves."

"Hmph!" the bishop snorted. "These are not the words I expected of a warrior! You say our losses are scarcely a score of ships, while they have lost many times that many—is this not a sign their apostasy has sapped their ability to fight? With Holy Terra at your side, do you fear to confront so contemptible a foe?"

Lantu bit off a hot retort as he recalled the stubborn, hopeless fight of the infidel battle-line at Lorelei. Whatever else it was, the Federation was *not* a "contemptible foe," but he must be wary of charges of cowardice.

"Your Grace," he said carefully, "with Holy Terra at my side, I fear neither to confront any foe nor to die. I only advocate caution. We have won great victories against a powerful enemy; I would not see them thrown away through overconfidence."

He dared say nothing stronger, but he saw disagreement on the bishop's face—and others—and his heart sank. The Synod hadn't personally faced the infidels. They had only his reports, and the bishop hadn't seen—or had ignored—the warnings he'd tried to give.

"Thank you, my son," the Prophet said expressionlessly. "You have spoken well. Now we ask you to retire while the Synod debates."

"Of course, Your Holiness." Lantu effaced himself and left, trying not to let his apprehension show.

More than an hour passed before Manak rejoined Lantu in the small antechamber. The old churchman's expression was heavy as he beckoned to Lantu, and the admiral fell in beside him as he headed for *Starwalker*'s ramp. The chaplain rested one hand on his shoulder and shook his head.

"They've heeded you, in part. We will let the Satan-Khan wait. It makes good sense to gain the Federation's resources, and it is our duty to reclaim the apostate for the Faith, so you left little to argue on that point. But they reject your proposal to stand on the defensive."

"But, Holiness—"

"Hush, my son." Manak looked about quickly, then spoke in a softer voice. "I expected that to come from old Bishop Wayum, but the Prophet himself agreed. The matter is closed. We will continue the attack."

"As the Synod decrees," Lantu murmured, but he closed his inner eyelids in disquiet as he descended *Starwalker's* sacred ramp.

CHAPTER ELEVEN

"The Line will hold!"

"Attention on deck."

The assembled officers rose silently as Admiral Antonov entered the briefing room, accompanied by Kthaara and Captain Tsuchevsky.

"As you were." The admiral's bass voice was quiet—ominously so, Tsuchevsky thought. He'd known Antonov for years, and he knew the signs. In particular, he noted that the boss's faint accent was just a trifle less faint than usual.

"Commodore Chandra," Antonov addressed the CO of Redwing Fortress Command, "I have reviewed your proposals for defensive dispositions. I believe the essence of these is that all orbital fortresses be tractored to within tactical range of the Laramie and QR-107 warp points, there to fight a delaying action while Second Fleet covers the evacuation of essential personnel to Cimmaron."

"Correct, sir," Chandra acknowledged. He and the others were actually showing relief at Antonov's calm and measured tone, Tsuchevsky noted with a kind of horrified

114

fascination. "Of course," Chandra babbled on, "I've given a high priority to detaching part of Second Fleet's assets to cover the Novaya Rodina warp point during the withdrawal. I was certain this would be a matter of special concern to you and—" an unctuous nod "—Captain Tsuchevsky."

"I took note of this, Commodore. I also took note," Antonov continued just as emotionlessly, "that the 'essential personnel' to be evacuated included the upper management levels of the Galloway's World industrial interests with branches here . . . as well as everyone in this room." The increase in volume was so gradual only the most sensitive souls perceived it. Chandra was not among them.

"Er, well, Admiral, there are, after all, a hundred and fifty million people on Redwing. Since we can't possibly evacuate all of them, we have to consider who among those we *can* evacuate will be most useful to the war effort, so certain hard choices . . . yes, Hard Choices . . . must be made. And, obviously, special consideration must be given to—"

"You are relieved, Commodore." Antonov's voice cut Chandra's off as if the latter hadn't existed. "There is a courier ship leaving for Terra at 22:00; you will be on it . . . along with my report to Admiral Brandenburg."

Chandra blinked stupidly. "But, but, Admiral, sir, I only . . ."

"Do you wish to add insubordination to charges of incompetence and cowardice, Commodore Chandra?" Antonov wasn't—exactly—shouting, but his voice had become a sustained roar from which everyone physically flinched. "*Yob' tvoyu mat'!*" Realizing he'd lapsed into Russian, he obligingly provided a translation. "Fuck your mother! Get out of here and confine yourself to quarters until departure, you worthless *chernozhopi!*"

Chandra's staff sat paralyzed as he stood clumsily, face pale, and then stumbled from the room. Tsuchevsky sighed softly in relief that Antonov hadn't continued his translation—the fine old Russian term of disapprobation "black ass" might have been even more offensive than the admiral intended. Every other face was blank . . . except Kthaara'zarthan's. The Orion watched Chandra with a grin that bared his ivory fangs.

"Now," Antonov continued, not quite as loudly (one could merely feel the vibrations through the soles of one's feet), "the rest of you will continue in your present duties . . . on a probationary basis, contingent upon acceptable performance of those duties. And I trust I have made clear my feelings on the subject of defeatism." His voice lost a little volume but became, if possible, even deeper. "There will be no more talk of retreats or evacuations! The Line will hold! As of now all leaves are canceled. Captain Lopez!" That worthy jumped in his chair. "You are now a commodore. You should regard this not as a promotion but as an administrative necessity for you to assume Commodore Chandra's duties. You will coordinate with Captain Tsuchevsky to schedule operational readiness exercises around the redeployment of this system's defenses." He activated the room's holographic unit and indicated the orbital works surrounding the Laramie and QR-107 warp points. "All of these fortresses are to be tractored *here*." The cursor flashed across the planetary system to the Cimmaron warp point.

The Fortress Command staff's shock was now complete. Lopez found his tongue. "But, sir, what will we use to defend the Thebans' entry warp points? And what about the Novaya Rodina warp point?"

"Nothing is to defend the ingress warp points, Commodore," Antonov rumbled. "If we try to defend them, not knowing which the Thebans will choose, we must divide our forces. And even if we stop them, they will simply bring in reinforcements and try again. And *they* have reserves available now." He glared around the table. "I will attempt—*one more time*—to make myself clear: this is not a delaying action. Our objective is to *smash* the Thebans! If any one of you fails to understand this, or to carry out my orders, I'll break him.

"As for the Novaya Rodina warp point," Antonov continued after a pause of a few heartbeats, "its defenses are not to be reinforced. Novaya Rodina is a major warp nexus—but mostly of warp lines leading to uninhabited systems. The Thebans must know this. And, so far, they've consistently advanced toward the Inner Worlds. I believe they will continue to do so."

The briefing room was silent again, but this time not entirely from fear. Everyone present knew Antonov had relatives on Novaya Rodina . . . and that Pavel Sergeyevich Tsuchevsky was one of the first native-born citizens of that fledgling colony.

"And now," Antonov resumed, "we have much planning to do. In particular, it is necessary that Fortress Command and Second Fleet coordinate fighter operations. Commander Kthaara'zarthan will be in charge of this project." He paused, then continued in the calm, low voice no one in the room was ever likely to misinterpret again. "Is this a problem for anyone?"

The disorientation of warp transit faded as *Hildebrandt Jackson* followed her escorts into Redwing, and First Admiral Lantu watched the superdreadnought's displays confirm his advance elements' incredible report. The warp point was undefended.

It was anticlimactic . . . and disquieting. Holy Terra's warriors had prepared themselves for Her sternest test yet: an assault on a warp point of the infidels' long-established, much-vaunted "Line." But already his scouts were proceeding unmolested across the system as his capital ships emerged into an eerie calm which shouldn't exist.

"I don't like this, Holiness," he said, but quietly. His subordinates must not see his uncertainty. "All our data speaks of massive fortifications at *all* of Redwing's warp points, and simple sanity says the infidels *must* commit their available mobile forces to its defense. So where are they?"

"Ah, my son, who can fathom the minds of the apostate?" Manak said too calmly. *He* knew better than to fall into the Synod's complacency, and Lantu started to say so, then paused before the unspoken worry in the prelate's eyes. The Fleet Chaplain wasn't getting any younger, he thought with a sudden pang.

"Holiness. First Admiral." Lantu looked up at Captain Yurah's voice. "The scouts have reached sensor range of the other warp points. They're downloading their findings now, and—"

The flag captain paused as fresh lights awoke in the master plot's three-dimensional sphere. Most of them were concentrated at one point.

"So," Lantu murmured. "*That's* where they went, Holiness! The infidels have tractored everything but the planetary defenses to our projected *exit* warp point. It would seem they've anticipated our objectives ... but why not contest our entry transit?" The first admiral rubbed the bridge of his muzzle unhappily. "Even their energy weapons could have hurt us badly at a range that low. It makes no sense. No *military* sense," he added. "Surely even heretics ..."

"Remember, my son, that these fortifications are old. Indeed, they date almost from the days of the Messenger! Perhaps they're feebler than we thought." Lantu carefully took no note of Manak's self-convincing tone, but the fleet chaplain frowned. "Still, perhaps it would be wise to wait until after they've been reduced before detaching units against the planet."

"I agree, Holiness. Captain Yurah, inform Commodore Gahad that the Fleet will execute deployment Plan Gamma. He is not to detach his task group without my specific instructions."

"Aye, sir," Yurah confirmed, and Lantu watched his display as First Fleet of the Sword of Holy Terra advanced steadily towards the clustered fortresses. He didn't like it, but the Synod's instructions left him no choice.

"Enemy fleet is proceeding towards the Cimmaron warp point, Admiral."

Antonov grunted. They'd had some bad moments as the Theban scouts approached within scanner range of this stretch of the asteroid belt between the system's gas-giant fourth and fifth planets. But the scouts had been mesmerized by the mammoth orbital forts. They hadn't been looking for ships with their power plants stepped down to minimal levels, lurking amid the rubble of an unborn planet.

He looked around the improvised flag bridge of TFNS *Indomitable*. A *Kongo*-class battle-cruiser wasn't intended to serve as a fleet flagship, and accommodations for his staff were cramped. But there'd been no question of flying his lights on one of the capital ships holding station in the Cimmaron System, thirty-two light-years distant in Einsteinian space but an effectively-instantaneous warp transit away, awaiting the courier drone that would summon them when the moment was right. No, he would live or die with the ships that would be trapped in Redwing if his plan failed and the Thebans secured its warp points.

Kthaara approached. "Admiral, they are nearing Point Staahlingraad." He gestured at the scarlet point in the navigational display.

Antonov nodded, watching from the corner of one eye as Kthaara's ears flattened and his claws slid from their sheaths. Labels like "Felinoid" were usually misleading, he thought; an Orion, product of an entirely separate evolution, was less closely related to a Terran cat than was a Terran lizard, or fish, or tree. The resemblance was mere coincidence, bound to happen occasionally in a galaxy of four hundred billion suns. But Kthaara was nonetheless descended from millions of years of predators . . . and Antonov was just as glad humans weren't this day's prey.

"Commodore Tsuchevsky," he said unnecessarily, "when Thebans reach Point Stalingrad, you will bring fleet to full readiness and await my word."

"Understood, Admiral." Tsuchevsky knew how much strain the boss was under when he started voicing redundant orders . . . and when his Standard English started losing its definite articles.

"Commander Kthaara," Antonov continued, "you will order our fighter launch at your discretion, within parameters of operations plan." Once that would have been unthinkable, but not after the past few weeks' exercises. There might still be officers who didn't accept the Whisker-Twister; none of the fighter jocks were among them.

He settled back in his command chair and waited.

Aboard the command fortress, other eyes watched the Thebans approach Point Stalingrad. They reached it.

"Launch all fighters!"

Commodore Lopez committed Fortress Command's full fighter strength, and, for the first time, the TFN's fighters hurled themselves at the Thebans in a well-organized, well-rehearsed strike from secure bases.

Lantu hunkered deeper into his command chair as his tactical sphere blossomed with new threat sources. He'd been afraid of this. Those well-ordered formations were a far cry from the scrambling confusion he'd faced at Lorelei, and they might explain why the infidels had conceded the entry warp points. It was clear their fighters had even more operational range than he'd feared—enough, perhaps, to fall back and rearm to launch a second or even a third strike before First Fleet could range on their launch bays.

But First Fleet wasn't entirely helpless, he reminded himself grimly.

Lieutenant Allison DuPre of Strikefighter Squadron 117 led Fortress Command's fighters towards the enemy, hoping Admiral Antonov and the Tabby were right about Theban underestimation of their capabilities. They'd better be. She was one of the very few veteran pilots Fortress Command had, and they'd need every break—

Her wingman exploded in a glare of fire.

"AFHAWKs!" she snapped over the command net. "Evasive action—*now!*"

Only then did she permit herself to curse.

Lantu watched the first infidel fighters die and thanked Holy Terra Archbishop Ganhad had agreed to make AF-HAWK production a priority, but he didn't share his staff's satisfaction. The kill ratio was far lower than predicted; clearly the infidels had devised not only an offensive doctrine to *employ* the weapon but defensive tactics to *evade* it, as well. No wonder their tactical manuals stressed that the best anti-fighter weapon was another fighter!

The survivors streamed forward past the wreckage of their fellows. They would be into their own range all too soon.

Lieutenant DuPre's surviving squadron spread out behind her, settling into attack formation, and she felt a glow of pride. They might be newbies, but they'd learned their stuff. And the Tabby had known a few wrinkles even DuPre had never heard of. She watched her display as the cursor marking their initial point flared. Any moment now—

There!

"Follow me in!" she snapped, and massed squadrons of fleet little vessels screamed through a turn possible only to inertia-canceling drives. They howled in, streaking in through the last-ditch fire of lasers and point defense missiles, breaking into the sternward "blind spots" of ionization and distorted space created by the Theban capital ships' drives.

One-Seventeen lost two more fighters on the way in . . . including Lieutenant DuPre's. But the three survivors broke through into the blind spots where no weapons could be brought to bear. And then, at what passed for point-blank range in space combat, their weapons spoke, coordinated by their dead skipper's training and energized by vengeance.

*   *   *

Lantu kept his face impassive, but he heard the fleet chaplain's soft groan as the infidels broke through everything First Fleet could throw. Their weapons were short-ranged and individually weak, but they struck with dreadful, beautiful precision. Entire squadrons fired as one, wracking his ships' shields with nuclear fire, then closing to rake their flanks with lasers as they streaked forward past the slow, lumbering vessels. None of them had targeted *Jackson*, but the superdreadnought *Allen Takagi* was less fortunate. Her shields went down, and even her massive armor yielded to the insistent pounding of her attackers. She faltered as a drive pod exploded, but she lumbered on, bleeding atmosphere like blood.

"They're breaking off, sir," Yurah reported, but the admiral shook his head. They weren't "breaking off." They'd executed their attack; now they were withdrawing to rearm for another.

"Sir, *John Calvin* and *Takagi* can no longer maintain flank speed. Shall I reduce Fleet speed to match?"

"Negative. Detail extra escorts to cover them and continue the advance at flank. We've got to hit those forts as soon as possible."

"Aye, sir."

"Admiral," Tsuchevsky reported, "the Fortress Command fighters are fully engaged. The enemy has sustained heavy damage and seems to be detaching some destroyer formations for fighter suppression—a task for which"—he added with satisfaction—"they clearly lack the proper doctrine and armament. But their heavy units are proceeding on course for the warp point. They'll be within capital missile range of the fortresses shortly."

Antonov nodded as he stared fixedly at the system-wide holo display. To communicate with the fortresses would be to risk revealing himself. He could only trust that Lopez would play his part.

"Commodore Tsuchevsky," he spoke distinctly and formally, "Second Fleet will advance."

The deck vibrated as *Indomitable*'s drive awoke. On the view screens, the drifting mountain that had concealed her slid to one side, revealing the starry firmament, and reflected starlight gleamed dimly as other ships formed up on the battle-cruiser while the last fighter warheads flashed like new, brief stars amid the Theban fleet.

Antonov sat back and heaved a sigh. Then he leaned over and spoke in Tsuchevsky's ear. "Well, Pasha, we're committed. Let's hope Lopez doesn't have his head too far up his ass."

"*Da*, Nikolayevich," Tsuchevsky replied just as quietly.

Fortress Command's fighters fled back to their bases to rearm, pursued by a badly shaken Theban fleet. Few ships had been destroyed—the orbital forts had too few fighters for a decisive strike, as Kthaara had observed with exasperation—but many were damaged. Some were injured even more seriously than *Calvin* and *Takagi*, and keeping formation was becoming a problem, but Lantu pressed on at his best speed. He wanted very badly to get within missile range and smash those looming fortresses before they relaunched their infernal little craft for a second strike . . . if he could.

His fleet entered capital missile range, and he braced himself again as the big missiles began to speed toward First Fleet.

The Thebans had encountered those missiles before; what they hadn't encountered were the warheads Howard Anderson had somehow managed to get to Redwing ahead of all realistic schedules. Not many of them, but a few. And as one of them came within a certain distance of its target, a non-material containment field collapsed, matter met antimatter, and the target ship experienced something new in the history of destruction. The field-generator was so massive that little antimatter could be contained—but even a little produced a blast three times as devastating as a warhead of comparable mass that relied on the energies of fusing deuterium atoms.

Some Thebans panicked as the hell-weapons crushed shields with horrible ease and mere metal vaporized . . . but not on Lantu's flag bridge. Face set, the first admiral ordered still more speed, even at the expense of what remained of his formation. There was no doubt now. He *had* to close the range and stop the terrible fighters and missiles at their source. And the new technology *must* be captured and turned to the use of Holy Terra. But even as he passed the word for the boarding parties to prepare themselves, infidel superdreadnoughts began to emerge ponderously from the Cimmaron warp point and the first rearmed fighters spat from the fortresses.

All of which meant that neither organic nor cybernetic attention was directed sternward in the direction of the barren asteroid belt they'd passed earlier. So the small fleet of carriers and their escorts that proceeded in First Fleet's wake went unnoticed.

Indomitable's flag bridge was silent. Antonov intended to take full advantage of Kthaara's instinct for fighter operations, so the Orion must be given the free hand he'd been promised. As was so often the case, once battle was joined the commanding officer's role was largely reduced to projecting an air of confidence.

Suddenly, Kthaara spoke a string of snarling, hissing noises to his assigned Orion-cognizant talker. The talker passed the orders on in the name of Fleet Command, and two fleet carriers and nine *Pegasus*-class light carriers launched their broods as one.

The thermonuclear detonations surrounding the battling Theban ships and Terran fortresses were dwarfed less and less often by the greater fires of negative matter, Lantu noted as he ordered the *samurai* sleds launched. Holy Terra was merciful; the infidels' supply of their new weapon was clearly limited. But his relief was short-lived.

"First Admiral! Formations of attack craft are approaching from astern!" Fresh lights blinked in the display sphere to confirm the incredible report, and Lantu blanched. The fortresses' fighters looming second strike would, at these ranges, arrive and be completed just before these mysterious newcomers struck, and understanding filled him. There *were* mobile infidel units; somewhere behind him was a fleet of unknown strength, in position to pin him against The Line like an insect pressed against glass.

He did what he could, cursing himself fervently for not having paid still more attention to the infidels' tactical manuals. A few minutes' desperate improvisation with his maneuvering officer rearranged his ships—some of them, at least—to cover one another's blind zones, producing a ragged approximation of the classic echelon type of anti-fighter formation. There were too many uncovered units, too many weak spots, but at least his ships could offer each other *some* mutual support. And, he reminded himself, his boarding parties should reach their objectives any time now. . . .

Gunnery Sergeant Jason Mendenhall, Terran Federation Marine Raiders, led his squad through the outermost spaces of the command fortress. Though normally the realm of service 'bots, these passages were designed for human accessibility if the need arose, so the Marines moved under artificial gravity through passageways that were large enough to accommodate them . . . barely.

There was no way they could have made it through inboard spaces in the old powered armor, the sergeant reflected. It had served well enough in the Third Interstellar War, but it could never squeeze into these close quarters. Which, after all, was exactly why this handier new version had been designed—and thank God for it! The designers had never expected to repel boarders in deep space (*Eat your hearts out, pirates of the Spanish Main!*), but now that they knew. . . .

Some R&D smartass with an historical bent had resurrected the name "zoot suit" early in the development program, and the official term "Combat Suits, Mark V" had somehow been altered to "combat zoots." Mendenhall didn't care what anyone called them. He didn't even care how badly he stank inside one. He'd seen the demonstration of assault rifle bullets bouncing off a zoot ... and he knew the capabilities of the weapon he carried.

The dull *whump!* of an explosion came around a corner, and air screamed down the passageway, confirming Tactical's projection of where the Thebans would breach the hull. Sergeant Mendenhall waved his troopers flat against the bulkhead. They didn't have long to wait before their helmet sensors picked up the sounds of the advancing boarders through the rapidly thinning air. Mendenhall grunted in satisfaction and motioned the squad forward, then swung his combat-suited body around the corner with his weapon leveled.

He was prepared for the appearance of the Theban he confronted, but the Theban was not prepared for a two-and-a-half-meter-tall armored titan out of myth. He was even less prepared for the looming troll's weapon. The center of its single-shot chamber contained a hydrogen pellet suspended in a super-conducting grid, and now converging micro-lasers heated the pellet to near-fusion temperatures. The resulting bolt of plasma was electromagnetically ejected down a laser guide beam, leaving a wash of superheated air that would have fried a man protected by anything less than a combat zoot. Mendenhall wore such a zoot; the Thebans did not.

The gout of plasma engulfed the lead boarder, and his brief, terrible scream ended in a roar of secondary explosions as the heat ignited the ammunition he was carrying.

Most of his fellows died almost as quickly as he, their vac suits' refrigeration systems overwhelmed by a thermal pulse that seared the bulkheads down to bare alloy, and the survivors were stunned, frozen for just an instant as the rest of Mendenhall's squad deployed and opened fire. Not with plasma guns but with cut-down heavy anti-personnel launchers that fired a rapid stream of hyper-velocity rockets—powered flechettes, really. Theban vac-suits had some protective armor, but against the weapons the Marines' exoskeletal "muscles" let them carry, they might as well have been in their skivvies.

It was a massacre, but the Thebans didn't quite go alone. One of them carried a shoulder-fired rocket launcher to deal with blast doors and internal bulkheads, and Gunny Mendenhall's combat zoot received, at point-blank range, a shaped-charge warhead designed to take out a heavy tank.

First Admiral Lantu fixed bitter eyes on the tactical display as he listened to Captain Yurah. Not a single boarding party had reported success, and the brief snatches of their frantic battle chatter were the last datum he needed. Another ambush, he thought coldly. First Fleet had stumbled into ambush after ambush, and the fact that he'd warned against the attack only made his bitterness complete.

The Line's fighters had struck hard . . . and the mystery fighters had struck harder. *Takagi* was gone. *Calvin* was practically immobile. Other ships were almost as badly damaged, and the fighters which had wreaked such havoc were already returning to the shadowy carriers hanging at the very edge of detectibility. They'd suffered less losses than those from the fortresses, too, for they'd *started* in First Fleet's blind spot. Nor did he dare turn to deprive them of their tactical advantage while he engaged The Line; allowing those demonic fortresses to fire their far more powerful missiles into that same blind spot would be suicidal. Worse, the capital ships from Cimmaron, though few in number, were starting to make a difference in the energy-weapon slugging match which now raged with the fortresses.

And the supply of AFHAWKs wouldn't last forever.

"Holiness, we must disengage," he said quietly, and Manak stared at him with shocked eyes. "The infidels have trapped us between the fortresses and their carriers; if we don't break off, our entire fleet may be destroyed."

"We can't, my son! Our losses are heavy, but if we

reduce the fortresses—secure the warp point—the *apostate* will be trapped, not us!"

"I wish it might be so, Holiness," Lantu said heavily, "but Cimmaron is also fortified. Even if we crush The Line, its forts will be waiting when we make transit. And if we *don't* make transit, the infidel carriers will pick our bones while we squat amid the wreckage. But even if we held the warp point, we could never trap their ships, Holiness; their carriers are as fast as our fastest units, their fighters out-range our best weapons, and they can always withdraw on Novaya Rodina."

"But the Synod, Lantu! The Prophet himself decreed this attack—how will we explain to the *Synod*?"

Lantu's head lifted. "*I* will explain to the Synod, Holiness. This fleet is my command; Holy Terra has trusted me not to waste Her People's lives, and persisting blindly will do just that. The decision is mine alone; if it is faulty, the fault will be my own, as well." Yet even as he said it, Lantu knew, guiltily, that he didn't believe it. The fault lay with those who had ignored his counsel and commanded him to execute a plan in which he did not believe. With those who'd fatuously assumed generations-old orbital forts hadn't been upgraded and modernized. Those for whom his fleet had sacrificed so much . . . and would now be required to make still one more sacrifice—

"No." Manak touched his arm. "You are our First Admiral, but I am Fleet Chaplain. The decision is mine, as well, and—" he met Lantu's eyes levelly "—it is the right one. *We* will explain to the Synod, my son. Do what you must."

"Thank you, Holiness," Lantu said softly, then drew a deep breath and turned to his communications officer. "Connect me with Admiral Trona," he said in a voice of cold iron. "It will be necessary for the Ramming Fleet to cover our withdrawal."

Commodore Lopez looked about the command center, watching people as weary as he try to coordinate damage control in the blood-red glow of the emergency lights. Surely, he thought, this battle could not go on.

It couldn't. A tired cheer went up as the Theban fleet began to swing away. Lopez started to join it, but an anomaly on the battle plot caught his eye. Why were those battle-cruisers and heavy cruisers detaching from the withdrawing enemy and moving toward his forts at flank speed?

It is practically impossible for one starship to physically ram another, given the maneuverability conferred by reactionless drives. Even if one captain is suicidal enough to attempt it, the other can usually avoid it with ease. And, in the rare instances in which it can be contrived, the damage to both ships is almost invariably total, unless one vessel's drive field is extraordinarily more massive than the other's. It is not a cost-effective tactic, for a warship heavy enough to endure a defender's fire while closing *and* to smash a capital ship is too valuable a combat unit to expend on a single attack, however deadly.

But the Thebans had found a way. It cost them something in speed and power efficiency, but in return they could manipulate the drive field itself, producing a "bow wave" or spur which was, in effect, an electromagnetic ram. The TFN had never imagined such a thing, for even with the ram, damage aboard the attacking vessel was dreadful as abused engine rooms consumed themselves, and the attack was still fairly easy for a mobile unit to avoid.

But The Line's fortresses weren't mobile.

The cruisers of the Theban Ramming Fleet were crewed by the most fanatical members of the Church of Holy Terra. They carried little except the mammoth machinery required to deform a drive field ... and assault sleds set for automatic launch after ramming.

"Admiral," Tsuchevsky spoke urgently, "the fortresses have taken heavy damage from this new attack system and their Marine detachments are again engaged with

boarders. Our second strike is just entering attack range
. . . they could be diverted against the ramming ships that
haven't reached their targets. . . ."

Antonov cut him off with a chop of his hand. "No,"
he said, loudly enough to be heard by his entire staff.
"That's what the Thebans want. The fortresses will have
to defend themselves as best they can. Our first priority
must be their capital ships. Every one of those that es-
capes, we'll have to fight again one day." He'd been as
shaken as anyone else by the Thebans' latest manifesta-
tion of racial insanity, but he couldn't show it. "The
fighters will proceed with their mission."

Kthaara looked at him oddly, clearly thinking the admiral would have made a good Orion. Antonov knew his
human officers were thinking precisely the same thing.

It was over. The Theban survivors had completed their
skillfully directed withdrawal from the system, and Second Fleet had rendezvoused with the fortresses to lend
whatever aid it could. Antonov looked expressionlessly at
the scrolling lists of confirmed dead . . . the many dead.
Including Commodore Antonio Lopez y Sandoval, killed
at his station when a Theban battle-cruiser disembowled
his command fortress with a spear of pure force.

He heard a voice from the group of staffers behind
him and turned around. "What is it, Commander Trevayne?"

"I was just thinking, sir," the intelligence officer replied softly, "of something a countryman of mine said
centuries ago. 'Except for a battle lost, there is nothing
so terrible as a battle won.'"

Antonov grunted and turned back to the names on the
phosphor screen.

CHAPTER TWELVE
Like the Good Old Days

The ground car settled as pressure bled from the plenum chamber, and the passenger hatch unsealed itself. Howard Anderson climbed out unaided and stumped past Ensign Mallory on his cane, glad the earnest young man had finally learned not to offer assistance. Even an aide with a bad case of hero worship could learn not to coddle his boss if he was chewed out enough, and all ensigns should be pruned back occasionally. It served them in good stead later.

Mallory scurried ahead to punch the elevator button, and this time Anderson gave him a brief nod of thanks as he stepped into it. He regretted it almost instantly when the ensign beamed as if, Anderson thought sourly, he were wagging the tail he didn't have. Then his thoughts flicked away from Mallory and he stood silently, drumming gently on the head of his cane as floor lights winked. If ONI had found what he expected, he was going to tear someone a new asshole . . . and enjoy it.

The elevator stopped, and the old man and the young

stepped out. An unbiased witness might have reflected on how much the ensign looked like a vastly younger version of his boss, but if that had been suggested to Anderson he would have felt a bit bilious. He liked young Mallory, but it would have wounded his *amour-propre* to remember ever having been *that* green.

"Those reports ready, Andy?" he asked as they neared his office.

"Yes, sir."

"Good."

His office door opened, and he waved Yeoman Gonzales back down as she started to shoot upright. She settled back with rather more aplomb than Mallory would have shown, and he spared her a smile as he passed on his way to the inner office.

He shooed Mallory out of the room as he switched on his terminal. His gnarled fingers tapped at the keyboard with surprising agility, and his blue eyes hardened as a file header appeared.

"Why, hello, Mister Anderson. This is a pleasant surprise."

Lawrence Taliaferro stood as the Minister for War Production entered his sumptuous office. He was a chunky man, going rapidly to fat, with a broad face. At the moment his gray eyes were wary, and Anderson wondered idly how many different reasons Taliaferro had to worry. Probably quite a few, but the one which brought him here would do for starters.

"Thank you," he said graciously, sitting as Taliaferro personally drew a comfortable chair closer to his desk.

"Not at all. Not at all. May I offer refreshment?" Taliaferro's finger hovered over his call button, but Anderson shook his head. He found the Corporate World nobility's ostentatious employment of personal servants distasteful. Besides, he approved of the Orion habit of never accepting food or drink from *chofaki*.

"Well, then!" Taliaferro said brightly. "What brings

you here, Mister Anderson? Anything we can do for you would be an honor."

"Why, thank you again," Anderson said genially. This was the first time he'd actually met Lawrence Taliaferro. The Taliaferro Yard had done a good job reactivating Antonov's ships, but so they damned well should have. They owned half the Jamieson Archipelago in fee simple after forty years of gobbling up chunks of their competitors. Even for a world whose constitution enshrined monolithic capitalism, the Taliaferros were over-achievers.

He eyed his host thoughtfully. Lawrence was the grandson of Winston Taliaferro, founder of the family empire. Anderson remembered Winston well from ISW-1, and he considered it a great pity the old man had died before antigerone therapy became available. He'd been a hard, merciless old pirate, but he'd been a *man*. And for all his ambition, he'd never, to Anderson's knowledge, played fast and loose with the safety of the Terran Federation. Fortunately, the population of Galloway's World had grown enough that Lawrence would have to agree to emigrate if *he* wanted the antigerone treatments.

Taliaferro fidgeted under those thoughtful, silent old eyes, feeling betrayed after all the credits he'd contributed to Sakanami Hideoshi's campaign chest. He knew they were at war, but had it really been necessary to send this horrible old dinosaur to *his* world? And what brought the old bastard here now? Those bright blue eyes were like leveled missiles, summoning up a long mental list of the Taliaferro Yard's hidden infractions.

"Mister Taliaferro," Anderson said finally, "I've been reading some interesting technical reports in the past few days. Some very exciting ones."

"Oh?" Taliaferro relaxed just a bit.

"Yes, indeed. There've been a lot of changes since my day. If I'd had some of the new hardware at Aklumar or Ophiuchi Junction, well . . ." He shrugged, and Taliaferro beamed.

"Yes, we're rather proud of our achievements. Our

men and women in uniform deserve the very best, and—"

"I quite agree," Anderson interrupted smoothly, "and now that we've got the Reserve reactivated and cleared the decks, as it were, I've been considering the prioritization of new construction. It looks like a lot of credits will be flowing through The Yard and Galloway's World generally. A lot of credits."

"Oh?" Taliaferro repeated, sitting straighter, and avarice gleamed in his eyes. Anderson observed it with pleasure.

"Indeed. And I want to personally inform you of the disbursement plan which will cover the Taliaferro Yard's share of the preliminary work."

"Why, that's very kind, sir. I'm sure—"

"In particular," Anderson said affably, "of why the Taliaferro Yard will be performing the first one-point-five billion credits of work gratis."

"*What?!*" Taliaferro jerked up out of his chair, eyes bulging, and the old man smiled coldly. "You can't—I mean, we . . . *Preposterous!*"

"On the contrary, Mister Taliaferro," Anderson's suddenly icy tone cut like a flaying knife, "I'm being quite lenient."

"But . . . but . . ."

"Sit down, Mister Taliaferro." The industrialist collapsed back into his chair, and Anderson leaned forward on his cane. "I've been most impressed by your R&D on new ECM systems. Your people are to be commended. If I'm to believe the evaluation of BuShip's technical personnel, they've achieved a breakthrough into a whole new generation of electronic counter measures. A single installation which can not only provide both fire confusion and deception ECM but also substantially negate hostile fire confusion *and*, if the test results are to be believed, actually cloak a ship. Invisibility at ranges as low as eleven light-seconds, Mister Taliaferro. A priceless tactical advantage."

"Well, of course," Taliaferro said, "but there have been—"

"I'm aware of the 'difficulties' you've encountered," Anderson said softly. "What *you* may not be aware of is that under its war powers, the Office of Naval Intelligence plays a much broader oversight role and examines all sorts of things it's legally barred from exploring in peacetime. Including the records of military suppliers."

Taliaferro paled, and Anderson smiled thinly.

"Since November 2294," he continued precisely, "the TFN has disbursed to the Taliaferro Yard over a billion credits for R&D on next-generation ECM. I find that very interesting, since ONI has obtained in-house reports from your own technical staff indicating that on November 18, 2294, their equipment surpassed Fleet specs under field conditions."

"But we needed more tests, and—" Taliaferro said in a sick voice.

"You always do," Anderson said coldly. "In some ways, I suppose, it's just as well. The new systems would've done Admiral Li little good in the . . . tactical position he faced in Lorelei, and no doubt the enemy would have obtained specimens. Since then, however, your actions have undoubtedly cost hundreds if not thousands of lives by depriving the Fleet of a system it needs desperately. Moreover, according to your last funding request to BuShips, you require another thousand megacredits for 'crash development' to get the system operational. Rather greedy of you, Mister Taliaferro. First you steal a billion credits by suppressing test results, and then you propose to extort *another* billion as your kilo of flesh for turning an already operational system over to the Fleet after another six months of 'development.' "

"You can't prove that!"

"Oh, but I can. And if I have to, I will. Complete documentation is already in my files and those of ONI on Old Terra."

"But what you're saying—! It would ruin us!"

"No, it won't. You'll miss quite a few dividends, but if

we turn it over to the Procurator's Office, the fines will be at least twice as high. And, of course, you'll spend the next few decades in prison."

"But BuShips authorized every step of the program!"

"I know. Did I mention that Vice Admiral Wilson is en route to Old Terra to face a general court martial?" Taliaferro's pudgy body wilted. "I'm still awaiting the final ONI report on exactly how BuShips came to award you this development contract in the first place. I'm fairly certain we'll find Admiral Wilson at the bottom of that, too, and I have no more doubt of his trial's verdict than you do. But we don't have time to waste, and I imagine that if you comply with my modest arrangements now, the post-war government won't do much more than slap your wrist with a few megacredits of fines."

"I can't—" Taliaferro began, then stopped and slumped as arctic blue eyes bored into him. "All right," he said dully. "You win."

"Thank you, Mister Taliaferro. The first work orders will be in your hands by this afternoon."

Anderson stood, leaning on his cane, and Taliaferro made no effort to rise. He only stared at the old man with mesmerized eyes, and Anderson paused.

"Before I go, let me just add that I knew your grandfather and your father. They were both experts at squeezing the last centicredit out of a contract, and we had our run-ins in the good old days, but neither of them would have been stupid enough to try this. Perhaps you might consider that if neither of *them* ever won a round with me, it'll be a cold day in Hell before a miserable little piss ant like you does. Good day, Mister Taliaferro."

He felt more spry than he'd felt in decades as he left the office and headed for the next unfortunate industrial magnate on his list.

Commodore Angelique Timoshenko, acting head of the TFN's Bureau of Ships, pressed a button on the work table. A schematic glowed to life on its surface, and her slender finger tapped a blinking line.

"There it is, sir," she said crisply, and Howard Anderson nodded. She was, he reflected, a far cry from her late, unlamented boss. Though young for her rank, and even more so for her new position, she was as brilliant as she was attractive. And no shrinking violet, either. Antonov had addressed her as "Commodore Timoshenkova" when they met, and she hadn't turned a hair as she politely—but firmly—corrected him. Her family had left Russia and its naming conventions behind in the second decade of the twentieth century, but it still took nerve for a junior to correct Ivan the Terrible.

"So that's how they do it," he murmured.

"Yes, sir. Ingenious, isn't it?"

"And goddamned dangerous," he growled.

"No question about that," Timoshenko agreed.

Anderson straightened thoughtfully. He was no longer as up to date technically as he would have liked, but sixty years in naval command gave a man a fair grasp of basic principles. If he couldn't be on a flag bridge, watching BuShips tear into the first specimens of captured Theban equipment was the next best thing, and this showed an audacious—if risky—ingenuity that appealed to him, even if an enemy had thought of it first.

He pursed his lips, remembering his own reaction to the force beam. That had been an Orion development during ISW-1, but, fortunately, they'd committed it in driblets. By the time they'd had it ready for mass production and called in their fleet for refit, the TFN had known about it and been producing its own version—and had carried through and produced the primary *before* the Orions.

"They must have the occasional accident," he observed now.

"Yes, sir. This gives them a hellacious throughput, but their mag bottle technology's cruder than ours, and it takes an *extremely* dense field. If it hiccups—blooie!"

"Agreed." The commodore was probably understating, but it certainly explained how the Thebans could produce a bomb-pumped laser without a bomb. They didn't; they simply detonated the bomb *inside* their ship.

He frowned at the schematic, tracing the lines of light with a finger. Each laser-armed Theban ship contained at least one installation walled with truly awesome shielding, all wrapped around a mag bottle many times as dense as that of a standard fusion plant containment field. When they fired those godawful lasers, they detonated a nuclear warhead inside the mag bottle, which trapped its explosive power but not its radiation. Heavily armored and shielded conduits focused and channeled that dreadful radiation, delivering it to up to four laser projectors. But it all depended on the containment field, for, as Timoshenko said, if that field faltered, the firing ship would die far more spectacularly than its intended victim. And even with it, the detonation chamber—and everything within meters of it—must quickly become so contaminated that total replacement would be required on a fairly frequent basis.

"Do you have any projections on their failure rate?"

"They're rough, but it may be as high as three percent. The system's supposed to shut down when the fail-safes report field instability, but it may fail catastrophically in about ten percent of those cases. Call it point-three percent, maybe a little less, for a serious event."

"Um. I don't know if I want to incorporate anything that ... fractious into our own ships, Commodore."

"I don't think we have to." Timoshenko touched a button on the work table and the schematic changed to a modified TFN blueprint.

"I'd say they've adopted this expedient because lasers were the best energy weapon available as of the Lorelei Massacre. It looks to me like they simply never considered the potential of the force beam, so they concentrated all their efforts on improved lasers, whereas we were diverted from the whole laser field, in a way, by other developments. In a sense, we've neglected their chosen field just as they've ignored ours."

"Which means?"

"Which means, sir, much as I hate to admit it, that we've overlooked quite a few potentials of our own systems. Our technology's better, and I think we can substantially improve on their current approach, but we're going to need at least several years of R&D before I'd be prepared to recommend it. In the meantime, however, we can improve the performance of our standard shipboard lasers dramatically. We won't be able to match their maximum effective range, but I think we can actually improve on their effective throughput figures, at least on a power-to-mass ratio."

"And how will we do that?" Anderson's eyes glinted at Timoshenko's enthusiasm; he'd always enjoyed watching bright people solving difficult problems.

"Like this," Timoshenko said, tapping the schematic, "by using a pair of heterodyning lasers in exact wavelength de-synchronization. Originally, we thought we'd need two separate projectors, but now that we've looked into it a bit, we think we can mount a pair of emitters in a single projector about fifty percent larger than a standard laser mount—the same size as a capital force beam, in other words. At shorter ranges, we should get very nearly the same destructive effect they do, without the potential for disaster built into their system. And without the need for all their shielding or to replace expendable lasing cavities between shots, the mass required for each projector will be less than fifty percent of theirs. We won't have as much range, but effectively, we can squeeze twice as many weapons into the same hull."

"That many?" Anderson was impressed, but he'd been a field commander waiting on the backroom types in his time. "How long?"

"The big problem's going to be maintaining optimum frequency control as the lasers heat up under repeated firings, but Commander Hsin is working on it. I've studied his reports, and it looks like we can handle most of it with modified Tamaguchi governors. Most of the changes will be to software, not hardware, if he's on the right track, and I think he is. So, assuming he can get the modified governors up and running as estimated, and given that most of what we're talking about is simply a new application of existing technology, I think we could have the first unit ready for testing in about five months. From successful test date to production would take another three to four. Call it eight months—ten at the outside."

"And to put this bomb-pumped system into production unchanged?"

"We might save three months. I don't think we could cut much more than that off it."

"All right." Anderson took his cane from the work table and headed for the door, gesturing for her to accompany him. "I'm inclined to think you're onto something, Commodore, but money's no problem, and neither is manufacturing priority. Push both systems full bore."

"Yes, sir. And this 'ram' generator of theirs?"

"Let it lie for now. It won't help forts, and Admiral Antonov seems to feel his mobile units can handle it with evasive maneuvering and anti-drive missiles now that he knows about it."

"Yes, sir."

"I'm impressed, Commodore," he said, pausing at the door and offering his hand. "I wish I'd had you around ninety years ago."

"Thank you, sir. I take that as a compliment."

"You should," he snorted cheerfully.

CHAPTER THIRTEEN
The Blood of Patriots

This time Lantu had company as he awaited the Synod's pleasure. Fleet Chaplain Manak sat beside him ... and two cold-eyed, armed Church Wardens flanked them both.

Lantu sat very erect, pressing his cranial carapace against the bulkhead behind him, and tried to ignore the Synod's policemen. He'd always found Wardens vaguely distasteful—had some intuition warned him he might someday find himself under their inspection?

His eyes tried to stray to Manak again. The fleet chaplain worried him, for Manak was old, and he was taking this waiting, grinding tension poorly. He sat bent-headed, inner lids closed and arms crossed before him. They'd been separated for days, yet his old friend had said not a single word in the dragging hours since the Wardens had "escorted" them here.

He sighed internally, maintaining his external impassivity. They'd known their retreat might rouse the Church's ire, but he hadn't counted on the heat of the Synod's reaction. It wasn't as if his fleet had been destroyed, after all. True, a disturbing percentage of the battle-line was in yard hands, but his withdrawal had prevented far worse, and he'd managed it in the face of massed fighter attacks launched from ships so distant his own vessels could hardly even *see* them!

Yet the Quaestors' harsh questions had ignored his achievement in preserving Terra's Sword, and he knew their attitude reflected the Synod's. The churchmen saw only that he'd failed to drive the Sword home in The Line's vitals, and it seemed the fact that he'd warned them of the danger ahead of time only made them angrier. Certainly the Quaestors had harped on that point, asking again and again if he had not gone into battle *expecting* defeat and so fled prematurely.

Lantu had answered calmly, yet he labored under a keen sense of injustice. He'd been overruled and ordered to attack by the Synod and the Prophet himself, so why must he and Manak bear the stigma of failure?

Because, a small, still voice whispered, you're a single admiral and Manak a single prelate. You're expendable; the Synod isn't.

The hatch opened, and the soft, sudden sound startled even Manak into looking up. A Warden major stood in the opening.

"First Admiral. Fleet Chaplain. The Synod requires your presence."

The approval of Lantu's last appearance before the Synod was notably absent, and cold eyes burned his back as he followed Manak down the central aisle. The Prophet's white robes were a flame, but the violet stole of the Holy Inquisition was a dark, dangerous slash of color across them.

Lantu raised his head proudly but not arrogantly. The Prophet's regalia indicated his readiness to pronounce judgment *ex cathedra*, with the infallibility of Holy Terra Herself, and the admiral was prepared to submit to Her will. Yet he'd done his best. Any error resulted from his effort to serve Her to the very best of his merely mortal ability.

"First Admiral Lantu," the Prophet said sternly. "Fleet Chaplain Manak. You have been summoned to hear the judgment of Holy Terra on your actions at the Battle of Redwing. Are you prepared?"

"I am, Your Holiness." Lantu was pleased by how firmly his reply came, and shocked by the slight quaver in Manak's echoing response.

"It is the judgment of Holy Terra that you have failed Her holy cause. It is Her judgment that if you had pressed your attack, trusting—as you ought—in Her guidance and support, Her Sword would have smitten the infidels' defenses into dust and that, once those defenses were breached, you would have trapped the infidels' ships behind your own, to be crushed by Second Fleet. By your weakness and lack of faith, you have failed Her most holy Self, and imperiled Her jihad."

Lantu swallowed, but his eyes refused to waver. Beside him, Manak's shoulders hunched in misery.

"Your lives are forfeit," the Prophet continued inexorably, "yet your past actions stand to your credit, and Holy Terra is merciful. Thus you will be given an opportunity to atone in Her eyes.

"Our Holy Inquisition has not prospered on New New Hebrides. As this world was the original goal of the Messenger, we must strive mightily to return its apostate people to the Faith, yet they have not only rejected Holy Terra's message but raised armed, unholy resistance against Her. You, First Admiral, are a military man. You, Fleet Chaplain, are a shepherd of the Faith. It shall be your task to aid Archbishop Tanuk in bringing these infidels once more into Holy Terra's arms. Success will atone for your recent actions; failure will not be tolerated by Holy Terra.

"Holy Terra has spoken." The Prophet brought his crosier's heel sharply down upon the stage, then moved his eyes to the Warden major. "Escort the admiral and chaplain to their shuttle, Major," he said softly.

* * *

Angus MacRory finished field-stripping the Shellhead grenade launcher and reached for his cleaning kit. It was cool under the long, streamer-like leaves of the massive banner oaks, and he was grateful for his warm civilian jacket. It was hardly proper Peaceforce uniform, but it was immaculately clean, and the sergeant's chevrons pinned to its collar were polished.

Caitrin dropped down across the blanket from him and picked up the old toothbrush, working on the action as he swabbed the launcher's bore. Her long fingers had become as rough as his own, and her hands were equally deft.

He watched her, not exactly covertly but unobtrusively. Her red-gold hair was longer now, gleaming in a short, thick braid from under her sadly tattered tam-o-shanter. Its decorative pom-pom had been snatched away by a bullet, but, unlike Angus, she'd found an almost complete uniform when they raided the New Glasgow Peaceforce supply dump. They'd lost six men and two women on that one, but the guns they'd recaptured had been worth it.

"The com shack's picked up something," she said after a moment.

"Aye?" Angus raised the launcher's barrel and squinted down its gleaming bore. The guerrillas never used coms, and the Shellheads seemed not to have considered that they might have any. They certainly didn't have any decent sense of communications security, anyway.

"There's a security alert in the New Greenock sector. Someone important's making an inspection of the camps Monday."

"Are they, now?" Angus murmured. He laid the launcher barrel across his thighs, and she smiled as he met her eyes thoughtfully.

The guerrillas had done far better than he'd dared hope. A dozen bands now operated from the mountainous continental interiors. They couldn't reach the islands—they were too far away and too small to dodge patrols—but fishing boats still operated under the Shellheads' supervision, for people had to be fed, and they managed an occasional crossing between continents.

Angus had never expected to find himself the senior commander of his home world's defenders. It had just . . . happened. Was it his Marine training coming to the fore? More likely it was simply the fact that none of the Peaceforce's officers survived and that he'd managed to last this long. He'd never been to OCS, but his own tactical ability had surprised him, though he relied heavily on Caitrin as his exec.

His unalterable rule that no recruit with relatives in the Occupied Zones would be accepted for operations had served them well in decreased vulnerability to reprisals, yet it held their numbers down. His own band, built around the re-education camp escapees and civilians picked up since, numbered scarcely six hundred, with barely another thirty-five hundred spread among the other bands, and to pit four thousand people against an occupation force backed by orbiting warships was lunacy. He knew that, but just as he'd been unable to pretend with Yashuk, he was unable to consider not fighting back. The Shellheads couldn't do anything much worse than they already had, and he was damned if they were going to have it all their own way.

Caitrin understood that. In fact, she understood *him* better than anyone else ever had, and she had an uncanny ability to extract the kernel of his plans from his sparse descriptions and make others understand them, as well. Surprisingly, perhaps, he understood *her* just as well. Despite very different personalities and educations, they'd fused in some mysterious way into a whole greater than its parts, and the strength of her amazed him. It was she who had first confronted their feelings for one another—something he would never have dared to do— which explained how they'd become lovers.

"Ammo?" he asked now.

"We've got four units of fire for our own small arms," she replied without consulting her notebook. "About three-and-a-half for the captured Shellhead weapons. The mortar section lost a tube at Hynchcliffe's farm, but they've got two units of fire with them and about five times that back at Base One. The Scorpion teams are down to about a dozen rounds, but we could hit that dump at Maidstone for as many Shellhead SAMs as we can carry."

"Um." He wished he had more mortar ammo, but fetching it from Base One would take too long. The mountains slowed even the colonists' Old Terran mules to a crawl, but they were the guerrilla's friends, too, rugged and heavily forested for Shellhead GEVs and infantry bikes, and Shellheads on foot could never keep up with the longer-legged humans. Their choppers were another matter, but the Scorpion teams had taught them circumspection. Unfortunately, they were running out of Scorpions.

In fact, they were running out of *all* military ammunition. They'd hit all the Peaceforce armories they could, but the Shellheads had caught on to that one fairly quickly and simply destroyed their stockpiles of captured weapons. By now, half the guerrillas' human-made small arms were civilian needle rifles, ill-suited to military targets. Their tiny projectiles relied on incredible velocities for effect, and while a single hit could reduce a limb to jelly, they lacked the mass to punch through body armor.

Fortunately, captured Shellhead weapons were taking up the slack. The troop reminders stamped on them—in English—helped, but they weren't really necessary, since the weapons themselves were based on original (if venerable) Terran designs. Awkward dimensions posed a much greater problem, for the Shellheads' over-long arms put triggers and butt plates in odd places. A determined man with a hacksaw could do a lot about that, but safeties placed for thumbs on the wrong side of the hand were another matter.

"Aye," he said finally. " 'Tis a gae lang way, but we can do it. Send runners tae Bulloch and Ingram—there's nae time fer the others. Sean can hit Maidstone; after that, 'twill be a repeat o' the Seabridge raid."

"I'll get right on it." Caitrin rose and walked away, and Angus watched her with a smile, confident she understood exactly what he intended. She was a bonny lass, his Katie.

Archbishop Tanuk's tilt-engine vertol sliced cleanly through the air, five minutes from the Inquisition's New Greenock camps, as the prelate ignored Father Waman and his staff and peered moodily out a window.

These infidels were incredibly stubborn. Even the handful who'd professed the Faith were riddled by secret heretics, and the terrorist renegades in the mountains were true devils. Their raids had grown increasingly audacious—they were even infiltrating and attacking the People's housing areas! He'd come to them in love, prepared to be stern to restore their souls to Holy Terra, but they clung to their blindness. The infidels outside the Occupied Zones still hid their heretical priests, and it was almost as bad *inside* the OZ. Just last week he'd learned three "converts" who'd been allowed to help manage the New Selkirk camps were in contact with the terrorists. Unfortunately, they'd helped almost four hundred infidels escape before they were executed.

The most stringent counter-measures seemed useless. Colonel Fraymak's garrison was doing its best, but these mountains were impossible, and his helicopter and vertol strength had taken dreadful losses. The archbishop had hardened his heart and authorized Warden Colonel Huark to shoot hostages and even entire villages as reprisals, but it only seemed to make these infernal heretics more determined to cut his soldiers' throats in the dark!

He rubbed his ring of office and sighed. He was Holy Terra's servant, and somehow She would help him bring his charges back to Her, but it was hard. He feared even sterner measures would be required, and made a mental note to remind Father Shamar to provide his Inquisitors with infidel lie detectors. Perhaps they could at least sort

out the honest converts that way. And if they could do
that, then——

His aircraft lurched suddenly, and he looked up ques-
tioningly as his military aide hurried back from the
cockpit.

"Your Grace, New Greenock is under attack! The terrorists have cut their way through the perimeter and
taken out the main barracks with mortars. Now they're——"

The aide broke off, gaping out the window, and Tanuk
turned quickly. The last thing he ever saw was a Scorpion
missile streaking towards him.

CHAPTER FOURTEEN
Options of War

The wide armorplast view port was partly blocked by Ivan Antonov's bulk as he stared at the panorama before him. Redwing's orbital yards seethed with activity such as they had not known since their original erection for the sole purpose of building The Line as men and machines swarmed over the torn and blistered skins of wounded orbital fortresses, and the light of laser welders flickered as the work of repair went on in shifts around the clock.

In some cases, those repairs looked all too much like rebuilding . . . but in the Federation's present pass, none of them could be written off. And the fortresses that had gotten off lightly enough to be considered operational by the elastic definitions that obtained these days had already been tractored to the QR-107 warp point, for the trap he'd sprung on the Thebans could be sprung only once.

At least the more-or-less operational fortresses were being reinforced by more and more mobile units as the

Federation's unimaginable industrial potential was gradually mobilized. Antonov watched a newly-arrived *Thunderer*-class battleship slide into orbit, fresh from mothballs and bristling with old-fashioned but still lethal energy weaponry. He was glad to see her; there had been few ships of her weight in the Reserve, and she was one of the few heavy units that had yet reached Redwing. Most of his gradually increasing trickle of reinforcements were still of the lighter classes.

Even more welcome were the lowly freighters carrying more antimatter warheads . . . and also something new. The great problem of space warfare since the chance discovery of warp points—those ill-understood anomalies in space/time that allowed instantaneous transit at an insignificant energy cost—had been an assault against an alerted defense. Even when a fleeting edge of surprise could be seized, attacking ships emerging one by one from a warp point into concentrated defensive firepower were at such a disadvantage that military historians could only compare them to infantrymen advancing across an open field of Flemish mud against machine-gun emplacements. Indeed, they were in even worse case, for these defenders could not be "prepared" by bombardment; nothing as small as a missile could carry the necessary instrumentation for a warp transit *and* a controlled attack.

But now a way around the conundrum had been found, thanks to new developments in artificial intelligence. (Could the "sentient computers" of the early— and vastly over-enthusiastic—computer pioneers be far away? Antonov rather hoped they were.) An unmanned carrier pack, smaller than any starship but far larger than a missile, could make a one-time warp transit and release its trio of "SBMHAWK" missiles against preprogrammed classes of targets. The missiles' "homing all the way killer" guidance circuits did the rest. Commodore Timoshenko promised eventual production of reusable packs with better on-board systems and larger missile loads, but even this early version would be an immeasurable advantage, and they'd begun arriving at Redwing at last ... a few of them. Always too few.

Pavel Tsuchevsky approached from his right. "That fort there was one of the hardest hit to survive at all," he said grimly, pointing to a hulk whose original shape was barely discernible. "A second rammer got through after the impact of the first overloaded its shields and station-keeping drive. Most of its crew were killed by the concussion—we've never thought it was worthwhile to install first-line inertial compensators on forts. They're not exactly intended for high-gee maneuvering."

"But they held," Antonov growled.

Winnifred Trevayne stepped up to the left. "By the time the last waves of boarders arrived, many of the Marines had exhausted their zoot power cells," she said sadly. "They had to switch to ordinary battle dress. From what I've heard in the debriefings, the fighting was inde-scribable ... toward the end, it was actually hand-to-hand."

"But they held," Antonov rumbled from deep in his cask of a chest.

Kthaara'zarthan spoke from directly behind him. "Most of the Fortress Command fighters managed to launch before the rams hit. They did what they could to blunt the attack, but many had to launch before they had rearmed. At least one managed to physically ram a Theban ship; he could not destroy it outright, but he left it unable to complete its attack run. Our report recommends the pilot for the Golden Lion of Terra." The last four words were barely understandable, but the tale flowed out naturally in the Tongue of Tongues, which throughout history had been a medium for such tellings. "We believe at least two other pilots did the same, but their mother fortresses were destroyed. Without the fortress records, we cannot identify them to record their names in honor as they deserve."

A raised hand showed its claws and clenched, sinking those claws into its fisted palm. Bright drops of blood welled as it opened in ritual salute.

"They fought as *farshatok*," he said softly. "When it was over, there were fewer usable recovery bays than there were fighters. By the time our carriers returned, many had exhausted their life support."

"But they held!" Antonov's voice was a deep, subterranean sound, welling up like magma from beneath the crust of one of humankind's planets. He turned heavily to face the half-circle of his subordinates.

"We've given the Thebans their first check, and they seem to have reverted to a holding operation in QR-107. Now, we don't know anything about their philosophy, or whatever is driving them, but their behavior so far suggests fanaticism of some stripe or other." He glanced at Winnifred Trevayne, who nodded. "If they're like human fanatics, they deal well with success, but poorly with defeat. After all, they *expect* success; their ideology tells them they alone understand the will of God, or"—a wry expression, almost a wince—"the dynamics of history, and that this enables them to ride the wave of the future. Failure is inexplicable, and shakes their faith."

He drew himself up against the backdrop of the stars, the mammoth orbital constructs, and the lovely blue-white curve of Redwing II.

"It is therefore essential we maintain pressure on them, remind them that they have lost the initiative. We remain too weak in heavy units to risk a decisive fleet action; but we can, and will, conduct a series of nuisance raids into QR-107, using our light carriers. I imagine," he added with a wintry, closed-lipped smile for Kthaara, "their earlier contempt for fighters has now turned into a very healthy fear, and that they're still feeling their way toward effective anti-fighter tactics."

Tsuchevsky cleared his throat. "Also, Admiral, the new SBMHAWKs give us a unique opportunity to clear the warp point for the raiders. The carriers and their escorts can be loose in QR-107 space before the Thebans understand what's happened!"

Antonov shook his head. "No, Pavel Sergeyevich. I know, it's tempting to give the SBMHAWKs an operational test . . . and, of course, reduce our casualties. But then the Thebans would know about the weapon. The shock value would be gone, and they could start to develop counter-measures. No, the system cannot be used at all until circumstances are such that it can be used to decisive effect."

Tsuchevsky looked almost mutinous. "But, Admiral . . . we used the antimatter warheads as soon as we had them. . . ."

"With great respect, Captain Tssssuchevssky," Kthaara cut in, "the circumstances are different. Our ability to hold this system was very much in doubt. We had to take every possible advantage, and the new warheads may have made the difference. Now, we have won the luxury of . . . I believe the Human expression is 'Playing our cards close to our chest.' And the need to make decisive use of a new weapon is a lesson the *Zheeerlikou'valkhan-naieee* learned well from the Federation in the Wars of Shame. Yes," he raised a blood-dotted, unhuman hand, forestalling Tsuchevsky's protest, "we will lose more people this way. But . . . they are Warriors."

There was silence. There were no anti-Orion bigots in this group, but the fact remained that Kthaara was dispassionately discussing *human* deaths. And yet . . . everyone knew the bond that had formed between the big Tabby and Second Fleet's fighter pilots, many of whom would die if the SBMHAWKs weren't used. And everyone knew better than to think for a moment that he would ever play "yes-man" for the Admiral.

There was no further protest.

Second Admiral Jahanak entered *Hildebrandt Jackson*'s briefing room with Fleet Chaplain Hinam. His new staff, headed by Flag Captain Yurah, rose expressionlessly, but Jahanak felt their resentment.

He understood, and he knew how much worse it would have been had the Synod followed its first inclination to strip Lantu of his rank and name Jahanak First Admiral in his stead. His own jihad had been respectable, but scarcely as brilliant as Lantu's, and these officers had shared the first admiral's heady triumphs. And his defeat ... if defeat it was.

Jahanak had his own thoughts on that, but no intention of voicing them. Unjust as Lantu's disgrace might be, there was no point refusing to profit over a matter of principle which could help neither of them in the end.

He took his place at the head of the table, Hinam at his right hand, and looked down its length at Captain Yurah. The flag captain looked back with just a trace of ... defiance? No, not quite that, but something akin.

"Gentlemen," Jahanak's voice was brisk but precise, "we shall shortly be reinforced by a third of Second Fleet. Our own damaged units will be reassigned to Second Fleet as they're repaired, but until then Second Fleet will, of course, be understrength. First Fleet, on the other hand, will be restored to full strength, and large additional stores of AFHAWKs are being forwarded to us. So reinforced, my orders—*our* orders—are to resume the offensive and secure the Redwing System as soon as practicable."

He carefully did not note the flinch which ran around the assembled staff officers, but there was frank dismay on several faces. He felt Fleet Chaplain Hinam bristle and unobtrusively touched the churchman's arm under the table. Unlike the Synod, Jahanak didn't believe Lantu's staff had been "infected" by his "defeatism." He knew too many of these officers, just as he did Lantu; if they were dismayed—even frightened—they had their reasons.

He laid his hands on the table and studied them, weighing the staff's reaction against his own evaluations. And, he admitted, against its bearing on his own position.

"I've read your reports ... and First Admiral Lantu's," he said finally, and Captain Yurah seemed to relax slightly as he spoke Lantu's name with no trace of condemnation. Lantu always had inspired intense personal loyalty, Jahanak reflected without bitterness. His own strengths lay in more calculated maneuvers. "I ask you now if you would change—or expand upon—anything you said in them. Captain Yurah?"

"I would expand only one point, Second Admiral," the flag captain said flatly, "and that is to emphasize even more strongly the danger represented by the infidels' fighters. Our tonnage advantage over their mobile units was on the order of five-to-one, but even with due allowance for the destruction inflicted upon their fortresses, our damage was at least three times theirs. Had the first admiral not withdrawn"—he met his new commander's eyes levelly—"the Sword would *have* no First Fleet."

"I see." Jahanak glanced around the other faces. "Would anyone disagree with the flag captain?" No one spoke, and he gave a wintry smile. "I assure you, gentlemen—neither Fleet Chaplain Hinam nor I will hold honesty against you. No one has more respect for the Synod than I, but *you* are the officers who confronted these fighters. If you agree with Captain Yurah, say so."

The silence lingered a moment longer, then died in a soft rumble of agreement, and Jahanak sat quietly, listening as much to how his officers spoke as to what they said. His face showed nothing, but his hands folded together on the table as he absorbed the staff's intensity.

"Very well." He brought their comments to a close at last and glanced at Fleet Chaplain Hinam from the corner of one eye, but Hinam was carefully expressionless, refusing to challenge him. Jahanak hid his wry amusement. There were advantages in claiming the First Prophet as an ancestor.

"In all honesty, gentlemen, what you say only confirms my own initial impression. Before accepting this command, I strongly endorsed First Admiral Lantu's request that development of our own fighters be given absolute priority." Captain Yurah's eyes lit, and Jahanak nodded slightly. "That request has been granted. Archbishop Ganhad informs me it will take time—I understand the major difficulty lies in duplicating the infidels' small fusion plants—but the process is under way.

"With that in mind," he said more briskly, "it is certainly our duty to advise the Synod of prudent strategic decisions enforced by our existing weapons mix. As it stands, the infidels are able to strike from ranges far beyond our own. If they possess sufficient fighters—and we must assume from Redwing that they do—they can afford to exchange them for capital ships in quite large numbers. Until our own fighters can interdict them short of the battle-line, we must assume the infidels will welcome battle in deep space, where they can make full use of their range and speed advantage over our stronger battle-line. Does this accurately reflect your joint view of the situation?"

There were relieved nods, and Jahanak smiled faintly.

"In that case, I shall recommend to the Synod that we assume a defensive stance until such time as our own fighters become available. QR-107 is a starless nexus— useless to us but an ideal battleground for the infidels— and, of course, we have no fortifications to support our mobile units in defending the QR-107-Redwing warp point. To hold against a determined attack would require the forward deployment of our battle-line, but this would place our slowest, most powerful, least expendable vessels far from retreat should the infidels muster sufficient firepower to break through in strength.

"In view of these facts, I intend to withdraw our battle-ships and superdreadnoughts to Parsifal and cover the warp point with lighter units—specifically with *Nile*-class light cruisers and *Ronin*-class battle-cruisers. With their heavy missile armaments, they can deliver massive AF-HAWK fire should the enemy enter QR-107."

He paused, feeling Hinam's unspoken opposition. His major concern was easing the hostility of his staff, but even so . . .

"Understand me, gentlemen," he said crisply. "We are *not* surrendering this nexus without a fight. I intend to bleed each infidel sortie from Redwing and, at the same time, gain experience against the fighter threat. We must evolve proper anti-fighter tactics before we once again expose capital ships to their attack, and this nexus will provide both our laboratory and a forward picket for our battle-line in Parsifal. I would prefer to implement the Synod's wishes and launch a new and immediate attack on Redwing. Given the situation, I do not believe this to be possible. We shall therefore convert our disadvantages into advantages while building the weapons we need for the new attack we most assuredly *will* launch against The Line."

The eyes which met his now were almost enthusiastic, and he smiled.

"Thank you, gentlemen. Please return to your duties. I want complete status reports on your departments in two hours. Dismissed."

He watched the hatch close behind the last of his staff before he turned to Hinam with a wry expression.

"I gather my battle plan fills you with less than total enthusiasm, Holiness?"

"It does not fulfill the Synod's bidding, Second Admiral," Hinam said frostily. "The Prophet will not be pleased."

"And do you think *I* am pleased?" Jahanak asked more acidly. "Holiness, I am but mortal, as is my staff. Indeed, even the Synod and the Prophet are mortal . . . and fallible." Hinam swelled with indignation, and Jahanak smiled thinly. "Recall, Holiness," he said softly, "that even my holy grandsire met occasional failure in Holy Terra's service."

Hinam's mouth closed with a snap, and Jahanak hid a grin. His kinship to the First Prophet wasn't a card he dared play often, but when he did, it was with effect.

"As mere mortals, Holiness Hinam," he went on calmly, "we can but offer Holy Terra our best. You saw my staff's initial reactions. They served First Admiral Lantu—as I, myself, have—and they've learned to expect victory in Holy Terra's cause. They don't understand what happened, but they can't believe—or won't, perhaps—that it was Lantu's fault, nor do I know that I blame them. *I* wouldn't have believed he would retreat from the Satan-Khan himself, yet he withdrew. And, Holiness, anything we may do for the jihad begins from that point . . . and depends upon those officers. I *must* enjoy their support, and I won't win it by casting aspersions upon the officer they believe saved their Fleet for Holy Terra's further service."

"I . . . can see that," Hinam said unwillingly. "Yet to take it upon yourself to alter the Synod's strategy is—"

"Is one of the functions of a flag officer, Holiness," Jahanak interrupted as he sensed victory. "I don't challenge the Synod's essential strategy, but they cannot be as well aware of the severity of the situation as we who directly confront it. Had Lantu done his duty and secured Redwing, thus breaking The Line decisively," Jahanak felt a brief twinge at his own words but continued smoothly, "then I could do *mine* by continuing the advance. As it is, I dare not expose our battle-line to the infidels' fighters. Too many of our ships are out of action to confront fighters *and* fortresses until we have carriers of our own. I'm sorry, Holiness, but my sorrow can't change facts. I must gain my officers' trust, renew their courage and faith in Holy Terra, and build my own strength before I once more challenge The Line. The Synod," he finished gently, "will thank neither of us if we compound Lantu's failure by a more serious one of our own."

The fleet chaplain sat silent, staring down as he turned his ring of office on his finger. Jahanak leaned back, waiting patiently. Given his birth, he'd seen more of senior churchmen than most officers, and he felt confident of Hinam's final reaction.

"Very well," the chaplain sighed at last. "I don't like it, and the Synod will be displeased, but perhaps you're right. I will support you in this, Second Admiral." He raised his head and tried to put a glint of steel into his gaze. "For now."

"Thank you, Fleet Chaplain," Jahanak said gratefully . . . and carefully kept the laughing triumph from his own yellow eyes.

*   *   *

Ivan Antonov tried again.

"You see," he began as he poured another round for himself and Kthaara, "your race's unity came after a series of wars that almost destroyed it. Whole nations and cultures vanished, and those that were left were smashed down to bedrock. So when one group finally established control over what was left of your home planet, it was able to remake the entire race in its image. Culturally, the slate had been wiped clean." He paused, saw that Kthaara understood the expression, then resumed.

"So all Orions today share a common language and culture. We got off lightly by comparison. Our Great Eastern War was destructive enough, but not on the scale of your Unification Wars—there was no wholesale use of strategic nuclear weapons, and we avoided biological warfare entirely. So our cultural diversity survived our political unification, and today we still cling to what's left of it. Some of us," he added, raising his glass, "more than others. *Za vashe zdorovye!*"

"*T'chaaigarna*," Kthaara responded, and tossed off his vodka. Alcohol affected the two species in the same way, and both had surrounded its use with traditions, including the according of special prestige to imports. Since the Alliance, the Orion upper classes had acquired a fondness for bourbon. At least, Antonov thought, he'd managed to cure Kthaara of *that*.

"I think, perhaps, you overstate the consequences of the Unification Wars somewhat," the Orion said, claws combing his whiskers thoughtfully. "Unlike Old Terra, we had enjoyed a single world-state within our own recorded history, long before we ever discovered the scientific method. Yet it is true our cultures were far more diverse before their differences were overwhelmed by the survival imperatives which followed the Wars."

"Precisely," Antonov replied, leaning over the table. "But that *didn't* happen to humans."

"Yes," Kthaara said slowly, "and it explains much we find incomprehensible about you—and not just the idea that an advanced, united race can have so many different kinds of personal names! My people have always looked at your pluralism and seen chaos, but now much becomes understandable—including your notorious inventiveness." His tooth-hidden smile reminded Antonov anew that the Orion face (like humanity's, and unlike Terran cats') had evolved as a tool of self-expression.

"That has always been hard for us to understand. Naturally, we could never accept the idea that you were simply more intelligent, nor was there any scientific evidence for such a notion. My sire, Kornazh'zarthan, had a theory, which I see now was correct—though he used to get into terrible arguments with my grandsire, the first Lord Talphon! He believed your secret was your unimaginable diversity. What a constant creative tension it must generate! And what an incredible range of options it must open to each individual: a banquet of novel perspectives and modes of thought!" He sighed, an almost startlingly human-like sound. "Thus it must have been on Old Valkha once, before the Unification Wars. We have lost much."

They were both silent for a space, gazing out the transparent view port in Antonov's quarters, one of the privileges of rank the admiral most treasured. Kthaara had become a frequent visitor here during his and the admiral's off-duty hours. Socially, his position was ambiguous: still officially a mere commander in an ill-defined staff position, but with the "permanent rank" of small claw of the khan (approximately a commodore) and more and more Antonov's *de facto* fighter commander. Anyway, Antonov liked him.

The communicator chimed, and Captain Tsuchevsky's face appeared in the screen as Antonov keyed acceptance.

"Admiral, the debriefs from our latest QR-107 raid are complete. They seem to confirm what we've seen the last few weeks. The Thebans aren't seriously opposing entry by small groups of raiders, now that we've demonstrated we have enough battleships to clear the warp point of any defense they seem inclined to mount just now. At the same time, we've encountered enough opposition deeper in to make it appear the enemy could fight a major fleet action if we force one by entering the system in strength. I'll download the full report later."

Kthaara leaned forward into a near-crouch, mobile ears twitching in a way Antonov had come to recognize. "So, Admiral, they are willing to continue this war of raids and counter-raids, gaining experience in anti-fighter operations and thinking we lack the strength to seek a full-scale fleet engagement." The ears flattened. "So perhaps now is the time to force such an engagement! We could brush aside the light forces on their side of the warp point and transit our new fleet carriers before they realized what was happening!" Beneath all of Kthaara's sophistication lay an elemental Orion, Antonov reflected. When a large-scale decisive battle beckoned, the philosophical detachment which had recognized the need to defer use of the SBMHAWKs went by the boards, a feeble thing to set against the instincts of all Orion history and prehistory.

"No," the admiral said slowly. "The new Theban commander—and I'm convinced they have a new one—is trying to gauge our strength. We'll let him think we don't have enough of the big carriers to risk a pitched battle yet. For now, we'll continue our probes and raids as planned." He smiled at the disappointment which confronted him. "Remember what you've told me of the lessons of the Wars of Shame, Kthaara'zarthan!"

Kthaara relaxed, seeming to deflate a bit.

"You are correct, of course, Ivaaan'aantaahnaav," he said with the same surprisingly expressive smile as before, and reached for his vodka glass once more.

CHAPTER FIFTEEN
The Stewards of Holy Terra

"Your presence honors us, First Admiral."

Colonel Fraymak's respect actually seemed genuine, Lantu thought. Perhaps it was. Despite his disgrace, the Ministry of Truth had labeled his last campaign a resounding triumph, though it hadn't occurred to him the Church might lie to its own warriors. He toyed with the notion of telling Fraymak the truth, then pushed the thought aside. It would only undercut his own authority, and he disliked his own strange, base temptation to shake the colonel's faith.

"Thank you, Colonel," he said, "but our work is cut out for us. Have you caught up with the terrorists who killed Archbishop Tanuk?"

"Ah, no, First Admiral." Fraymak looked out the window of Lantu's new and luxurious—*very* luxurious—office, and frowned. "In fact," he continued unhappily, "I don't expect to, sir."

"No?" Lantu rocked back in his chair and stroked his cranial carapace. It took a certain courage to make that sort of admission to a superior who'd been on-planet barely three hours. "Why not, Colonel?"

"Sir," the colonel focused his eyes above Lantu's head like a first-year cadet, "I have one reinforced infantry brigade, supported by one light armored regiment and two vertol battalions. That's not enough to garrison the re-education camps *and* organize reaction teams on a planetary scale."

"Why should you have to garrison the camps?" Lantu asked in some surprise. "They're the responsibility of the Inquisition and Wardens."

"The archbishop ... requested"—Lantu noted Fraymak's careful phrasing—"that I assist the Wardens, sir." His suddenly lowered eyes met Lantu's. "That was right after the New Selkirk inmates massacred the Warden guard force and escaped *en masse.*"

"I see." Lantu stroked his carapace even more thoughtfully. No one had reported *that* little fiasco to Thebes. "So basically we're just chasing around behind the infidels after they hit us?"

"Unfortunately, that's a fair way to put it, sir."

"How many terrorist groups are we talking about, Colonel?"

"We're not certain. None of the New Hebridans still awaiting re-education ever see anything, of course, but our best estimate is between seven and fifteen major groups. There are at least three here on Aberdeen, two on Scotia, and one each on Hibernia and New Gael. So far, there are none on the islands, but even with confiscated transport, I can't move troops around quickly enough to cover all four continents."

Lantu ran the tip of a letter-opener over the map on his desk, hiding a wince at the contour lines of the continental interiors. No wonder the colonel had problems. "And they hit targets near the mountains, then pop back into them and laugh at you, right?"

"Yes, sir." Fraymak made no effort to hide his relief at Lantu's understanding tone, but he shifted uncomfortably for a moment before he continued. "And, sir, with all due respect to the archbishop and Father Shamar, I don't really believe we should consider them 'terrorists.' "

"No?"

"No, sir. They hit mainly military targets, sir, and they've got excellent tactics. They're short on heavy weapons, but that actually lets them move faster and through rougher terrain. By now, about half their weapons are captured equipment. Every time I stick a squad or a platoon out on its own to cover the Wardens, I might as well be handing that many weapons over to them," he ended bitterly.

"I understand, Colonel, but we're here to support the Church, not vice-versa." The colonel nodded, and Lantu dropped his letter-opener. "Have we considered moving our installations out of reach from the mountains?"

"We can't, sir. The continental coastal strips are barely two hundred kilometers wide and heavily forested, and these trees are incredible; a mature 'banner oak' stands over ninety meters, with foliage too dense for thermal scan penetration. The guerrillas don't *have* any heavy equipment, so there aren't any electronic emissions and magnetic detectors are virtually useless. Small parties just filter through the trees, link-up, hit their targets, then disappear again. It's like trying to spot fish in muddy water, sir."

Lantu understood the colonel's frustrated professionalism perfectly. The late archbishop had scattered his troopers in penny-packets, and the terrorists—guerrillas, he corrected himself, mindful of the colonel's point—held the initiative. All Fraymak could do was react *after* he was hit.

"I assume they have bases. Can't we even locate them?"

"Warden Colonel Huark raised that same point, sir," Fraymak said tonelessly. "The answer is no. These mountains are riddled with caves and deep valleys. Without more scan sats, I can't even cover the valleys adequately, much less spot them through thirty or forty meters of rock."

"Colonel Huark raised the point?" Lantu was surprised. The Warden colonel hadn't impressed him when he greeted his shuttle.

"Yes, sir," Fraymak said even more tonelessly. "I believe he intended to call in nuclear strikes on them."

Now that I can believe. It's just the sort of idiocy a Warden would come up with. I'm surprised he hasn't suggested a saturation bombardment of the entire continental interior! Lantu started to say as much, then stopped. It would only be another attempt to shake Fraymak's faith. Besides, the colonel's expression made him half-afraid Huark had suggested just that.

"I think," he said instead, "that we have the resources—properly used—to kill this fly with a slightly smaller sledgehammer, Colonel."

"Yes, sir!" The colonel's profound relief made Lantu smile.

"All right. I think we'll begin by informing Colonel Huark that camp security is *his* responsibility. Pull in your men and organize battalion-sized reaction forces, then work out a deployment grid that gives us optimum response time to all our own installations."

"Yes, sir." The colonel paused, manifestly struggling with himself, then took the plunge. "Uh, sir, while I agree whole-heartedly with your orders, I think I should point out that we're going to get hit hard, at least initially."

"Why?"

"The Wardens aren't—well, they aren't very good at security, sir, and the guerrillas *really* hate them. Especially the extermination squads."

"The what squads?" Lantu asked very quietly, and Fraymak swallowed.

"The extermination squads, sir. They're special units."

"So I gather. But what, exactly, do they do, Colonel?"

"They're in charge of reprisals, sir," Fraymak said uncomfortably.

"Reprisals." The single word came out with glacial coldness.

"Yes, sir. Counter-reprisals, really." Lantu crooked his fingers, inviting the colonel to continue. "The guerrillas make a point of hitting installations near the camps with the highest execution totals. They . . . don't leave much behind when they do. So Warden Colonel Huark and Father Shamar organized the extermination squads. Whenever we get hit, they pick out hostages or a village that hasn't been brought in for re-education yet and they, well, they *exterminate* them, sir."

Lantu closed his eyes, and his own words about supporting the Church were bitter on his tongue. How could something like *that* serve Holy Terra? He sat very still for a moment before he opened his eyes. "Well, Colonel Fraymak, you're under my orders, not Colonel Huark's, and we'll do this my way. Adjust your deployment to cover dependent and civilian housing, but the *extermination* squads are just going to have to look after themselves."

"Yes, sir." The colonel's gaze met his with grim satisfaction before he executed a snappy salute and withdrew.

Lantu watched the door close and shook his head. Extermination squads. Sweet Terra, no wonder this planet was a shambles!

Not until much later did he realize Fraymak hadn't used the word "infidel" once.

"First Admiral?"

Lantu looked up at his secretary's soft, sweet voice and smiled. Hanat was tall for a Theban woman, her head reaching almost chest-high on him, and he'd instantly recognized who really kept things moving around here. She was a curious blend of the efficient and the traditional, managing somehow to handle everything that crossed her desk without ever overstepping the bounds which would set an old-fashioned male's teeth on edge.

"Yes, Hanat?"

"You were due in the fleet chaplain's office ten minutes ago."

"What?" Lantu looked at his chronometer and grimaced. "Damn. Excuse me," he apologized automatically, and she laughed softly. "Fortunately, I've known him a long time—I doubt he'll have me shot just yet." He stood and took down his pistol belt, buckling it distastefully. He shouldn't have to walk around armed inside the HQ compound.

"Don't forget your meeting with Colonel Huark at fourteen-thirty, either," Hanat admonished.

"As if I could." Lantu didn't bother to conceal his opinion of the Warden. "Did you get those figures to the fleet chaplain?"

"Yes, sir," she said with revulsion. That was why he didn't hide his contempt for Huark from her. "You were right. They're twelve percent over Archbishop Tanuk's execution ceiling."

"Terra!" Lantu muttered. "Well, I'll read them when I get back. Copy the data to my computer while I'm out."

"Of course." She reached out to adjust his pistol belt's buckle. "There. Can't have my boss looking sloppy."

Lantu grinned at her and walked out of the office, humming.

"Sit down," Manak invited, and the admiral dropped into a chair. His pistol caught on its arm, and he muttered a curse as he wrestled with it.

"Language, my son. Language!" Manak's gentle mockery made Lantu feel better. The old chaplain had been monosyllabic and despondent for days after their conviction by the Synod. Even now there was little of the old sparkle in his eyes, and Lantu sometimes thought he sensed a disquieting brittleness about his inner strength. Lantu had been a baby when his parents died, and the fleet chaplain had raised him as his own son. Seeing him so cavalierly reduced was one more coal in the admiral's smoldering resentment.

"Sorry," he said, then sighed in relief as the pistol came unsnagged. "Holy Terra, I *hate* having to wear this thing."

"As do I." Manak frowned and looked around what had been Archbishop Tanuk's office. Its splendid luxury had yielded to the fleet chaplain's spartan hand, and Lantu found its present austerity far more comfortable.

"I've received word from the Synod," Manak continued. "They've decided—for the present, at least—to confirm me as acting archbishop." He snorted. "I imagine none of the regular bishops wanted the job."

"Wise of them." Lantu was careful to limit the bite in his tone.

"Unhappily true. But that means *I* set policy now, and that's what I wanted to see you about. Colonel Huark and Father Shamar have both protested your new deployment orders."

"I'm not surprised, Holiness, but if they want to stop these attacks instead of just responding to them, then—"

"Peace, my son. I know you too well to question your judgment . . . unlike some others." The fleet chaplain's face was momentarily bitter, but he shook the expression aside. "I've told them you have my full support. In return, I'm going to need yours, I think."

"Oh? In what way, Holiness?"

"I've read the report your charming secretary put together." Manak smiled slyly, and Lantu grinned—Manak had badgered him for years about his duty to take a wife as Holy Terra expected—but the churchman sobered quickly.

"You're right. The execution totals are far too high, even excluding reprisals. If your figures are as accurate as I expect, we've killed almost thirteen percent of the population. That is *not* the way to win converts."

Lantu nodded feelingly.

"What you may not realize," Manak went on, "is that our conversion rate—our *claimed* conversion rate, I should say—is under five percent. I find that truly appalling. Surely infidels should be willing to at least *pretend* conversion to escape death."

"They're stubborn people, Holiness," Lantu said mildly.

"Indeed they are, but this is still highly disturbing."

"I suspect, Holiness," Lantu said cautiously, "that the Inquisition has been . . . over zealous, let us say, in its use of punishment."

"Torture, you mean," Manak corrected bitterly, and Lantu relaxed. That sounded like the Manak he knew and respected. "One shouldn't speak ill of the dead, perhaps, especially not of martyrs in the cause of Holy Terra, but Tanuk never could tell right from left without an instruction book."

"I never knew the archbishop—"

"You missed very little, my son. His faith was strong, but he was ever intolerant. It's one thing to carry the jihad home against the infidels; it's quite another to slaughter them out of frustration, and that's precisely what the Inquisition is doing. If they prove impossible to reclaim, then we may have no option, but the Inquisition will win more converts with love than with hate. And whatever they may have become, they are still of the race of the Messenger. If only for the love we bear him, we must make a true effort to restore them to their Faith."

"I agree, Holiness. But I think our problem may be more difficult than simply *restoring* their Faith."

"Oh?"

"Holiness," Lantu considered his next words carefully, "I've been studying the planetary data base ever since we got here. There are many references to Holy Terra, but only as another world—the mother world, to be sure, but with no awareness of Her divinity. Could the infidels be telling the truth when they say they never heard of the Faith, much less rejected it?"

"Of course they are." Manak sounded a bit surprised. "I thought you understood that, my son. The Satan-Khan's influence is pervasive. All references to the Faith have been suppressed."

"But, Holiness," Lantu said cautiously, "I see no gaps, no evasions. Could something so profound be suppressed so tracelessly?"

"Lantu, this planet was settled nine years *after* their apostate Treaty of Tycho. Believe me, it wouldn't be difficult to delete all reference to the Faith from a colonial data base and keep it deleted. When we liberate Holy Terra, we'll find the evidence."

He sounded so positive Lantu merely nodded, but the admiral found his very assurance disturbing. The Church had always been zealous to protect its children from spiritual contamination, which was why access to the original Holy Writ in *Starwalker*'s computers was so restricted. But Manak's confidence suggested something else. Was it possible he knew how simple it would be to suppress data because it had already—?

He chopped off that dangerous thought in a hurry.

"Getting back to my original point, though," Manak continued, "I'm going to disband the extermination squads—which Huark will hate—and I'm going to cut Archbishop Tanuk's camp execution levels in half. Shamar will hate that, and he'll hate it even more when I send in chaplain inspectors to limit his use of torture and make sure he abides by *my* quotas. They've both got powerful sponsors in the Synod, too; that's why I need your support."

"You have it, of course. What do you need me to do?"

"Just stand around and look efficient," Manak said dryly. "I'm basing my case on military expediency by arguing that a reduction in 'punishment' and the death totals will undermine popular pressure to support the terrorists."

"I see." Lantu fingered his muzzle. "It should have that effect, to some extent, at least. But it won't end it, Holiness."

"I know, but if I can justify it militarily long enough to raise the conversion rate, I won't need to justify it on any other grounds."

"I see," Lantu repeated, nodding with renewed respect. "And if I should just happen to score a few successes in the field—?"

"Exactly, my son," Manak said, and smiled.

* * *

"Jaysus!" Angus MacRory threw himself flat as yet another vertol swept overhead. A cluster of armored GEVs snorted through the underbrush like a herd of near-hippos barely a klick down-slope, and he heard the putter of infantry bikes following the paths the GEVs had flattened.

"My sentiments exactly," Caitrin muttered, and raised herself cautiously, peering uphill. "I think the rally point's still clear."

"Aye, and let's hope it *stays* clear." Angus drew the AP clip from his grenade launcher and replaced it with one of shaped-charge HEAT grenades. They had enough punch to deal with a lightly-armored GEV . . . assuming they got past the reactive armor's explosive strips first.

The thick smoke billowing through the canopy of distant treetops on the lower slopes had been a Shellhead extermination center, and Angus hoped the hostages they'd released had made a clean getaway. The guerrillas' civilian supporters were waiting to spirit them out to isolated farmsteads beyond the OZ, and they should be safe there. If they ever *got* there.

The speed of the Shellhead reaction had been almost as astounding as its strength. There must be at least two companies out there, and they'd dropped out of the sky before he and his people had gotten more than fifteen kilometers from the site of the raid. Fortunately, the Grampians thrust a stony tentacle close to the coast here, but—

He looked up as a rocket motor snarled and a captured Shellhead SAM raced for a lumbering personnel vertol. Its proximity fuse exploded close to the port engine, and the aircraft lurched away, trailing smoke. Angus smiled grimly. They weren't going to find any handy clearings to set that beastie down in.

His smile vanished as a heavily-armored attack helicopter darted at the SAM team's position. A ripple salvo leapt from its rocket pods, followed by a hurricane of tracers. Then the chopper flashed over the spot, and the orange glare of napalm belched through the shattered trees.

Unless that team had been very, very lucky, it was dead. These new, powerful response teams were going to make things ugly.

"Weel, let's gae," he sighed, waving for Caitrin to proceed him while he lay still to cover her. She darted to their next chosen bit of cover, and he rose, jogging quietly past her.

It had to be the new Shellhead military type. The one called Lantu. The Shellhead com techs had finally begun to develop an awareness of basic security—probably another gift from this Lantu—but the resistance was still picking up enough to identify its new foe.

It might, Angus mused as he flopped down behind the fallen tree and waited for Caitrin to lope past him, be worthwhile to see if they couldn't find a way to send him to join Archbishop Tanuk.

CHAPTER SIXTEEN
The Blood of Warriors

The surge of the electromagnetic catapult, the queasiness of departure from the ship's artificial gravity, the indescribable *twisting* sensation of passage through the drive field, the instant of disorientation as "up" and "down" lost all meaning in the illimitable void of space (lacking even the reassuring reference point of a sun in this segment of nothingness men had labeled "QR-107"), the familiar grip of the fighter's drive as it assumed control of acceleration and inertia—all were behind him now. Kthaara'zarthan stretched out as far as the confines of the Human-designed fighter's cockpit allowed, then relaxed, muscle by muscle, and heaved a long sigh of contentment.

The Humans had modified the cockpit of this fighter to accommodate him and link with his Orion-designed life support suit months before. He had taken her on practice runs in Redwing until she responded like an extension of his own body, with a smoothness of control that could hardly have been bettered by that "direct neural interfacing" of which the Khan's researchers (and, he had been amused to discover, the Humans', as well) had blathered for centuries without ever quite overcoming those irritating little drawbacks which would kill a pilot outside the safe confines of a laboratory. Especially in the stress of battle.

He snorted into his helmet—a very Human sound of amused disgust that ended in a high-pitched sound no Human could have manufactured. He would believe in neural interfacing when one of those *droshokol mizoa-haarlesh* who preached its virtues were willing to risk their own pelts flying it in combat. Which, he reflected, nudging his controls with sensual pleasure, was not to say he would welcome it, for it was difficult to believe anything could equal the sheer delight of holding his fleet little vessel's very soul between his claws. Yet not even this pleasure could substitute for personal combat against his cousin's killers. Even the Humans—some of them, at least—could understand that.

Humans. Kthaara gave the clicking sound equivalent of a man's rueful headshake. Who could understand them? He had seen them in battle, and he would have words for the next cub of his clan who called them *cho-faki*. Yes, and more than words, if more was required. But the fact remained that there was no understanding them, with their wildly inconsistent ethics and their seemingly limitless capacity for self-deception. Howard Anderson had once quoted to him from a Human philosopher: "We have met the enemy, and he is us." A great philosopher indeed, Kthaara had acknowledged. Truly, Humans were a race forever at war with themselves—at once the source of their unique vitality and the price they paid for it. The *Zheeerlikou'valkhannaieee*, knowing precisely who and what they were, could see the universe precisely as it was; their follies resulted from inability to subordinate their innermost nature to some bloodless balancing of advantage and disadvantage, and not from the strange tendency of most Humans to painstakingly construct an unreal universe and base their actions thereon. Not all Humans—certainly not Ivan Antonov.

There was, of course, another barrier to empathy with Humans which no well-bred Orion would ever dream of revealing to them. Besides, Kthaara was a cosmopolite; he had long since learned to overcome the physical revulsion any normal mind must feel in the presence of such a species. But it was hard. It would have been better if they were completely hairless; their spotty, patchy growth made them look diseased. It was fortunate they had the decency to keep their bodies covered with fabric . . . most of the time.

He had learned that since their industrial revolution they had abandoned their nudity taboos. Well, most of them had, at any rate, he amended, marveling anew at the multiplicity of utterly incompatible value systems Humanity embraced. It was maddening. Each time he thought he had brought a definitive idea of what Humans believed within claws' reach, he discovered yet *another* level of disagreement within their complex melange of cultures. He still couldn't imagine how *they* kept track of it, much less how any rational species could be expected to do so. And those who had discarded the traditional religious view of the naked human body as an obscene sight were actually proud of themselves. Kthaara couldn't imagine why.

Yet the faces were the worst, flat, without the slightest trace of a muzzle, with eyes and mouth surrounded by bare and unmistakably wet-looking skin. The males, in obedience to the dictates of current fashion, made it even worse by shaving what facial hair they did possess in an odd and perverse throwback to primitive self-mutilation.

But give them their due: though they might not be aware of their own ugliness, they at least recognized the handsomeness of the Orions—which must, he reflected, be intrinsically obvious to any truly sensitive mind! He had, however, been taken aback to learn that the Human reaction to his own species was due in part to a pleasing and comforting resemblance to a Terran domestic animal!

He shook loose from the thoughts as he maneuvered his fighter into place in the strike formation. Excessive concern with appearances was an adolescent characteristic few Orions completely outgrew until old age. But it, too, could be overcome. He reflected on the insignificance of the physical body that housed an Ivan Antonov, and thought back to the staff conference that had led to his presence here. . . .

"No, Admiral Berenson," Antonov had said implacably. "This has been discussed before. Our probes have established that the ingress warp point is covered by light craft, supported by nothing heavier than battle-cruisers. The SBMHAWKs must not be used until we reach a warp point defended by heavy units."

"With great respect, Admiral," the commander of Second Fleet's light carriers replied, not sounding particularly respectful, "we have to fight our way through QR-107 before we can even reach such a warp point! And I cannot answer for the ability of my units to contribute much to that end after the losses they're bound to take in forcing the warp point under the present plan." He drew a deep breath. "Sir, I believe an unused weapon is a useless weapon. As you've so rightly pointed out, we know exactly what ship classes are waiting on the other side of the warp point. This makes the situation ideal for SBMHAWK deployment; they can be programmed with precision."

Antonov scowled. He could count on solid support from his own staff on this—Tsuchevsky had come around to Kthaara's way of thinking. But Berenson, a relatively recent arrival who possessed a solid reputation as a fighter pilot and commander of fighter pilots, remained unconvinced.

"Our battle plan has been formulated with an eye to minimizing losses to your light carriers, Admiral," Antonov replied in his very best effort at a conciliatory tone of voice. "Of course, the fighters can expect a certain percentage of casualties, but our assessment is that these should be within acceptable levels—"

" 'Acceptable levels,' Admiral?" Berenson cut in, shocking even his own supporters in the room. (*Nobody* interrupted Ivan the Terrible.) He glanced at Kthaara, who was known to have been one of the plan's principal authors, then back to Antonov. "Perhaps, sir, what we need here is a *human* definition of 'acceptability'! "

"*Yob' tvoyu mat'!*" Antonov exploded, with a volume that seemed to cause the entire orbital fortress to vibrate. Even Berenson flinched visibly. "Who the fuck ever told you this was safe occupation? It is objective that matters. We—all of us—are expendable. Your pilots understand that even if you don't, you motherless turd!" He paused, then continued in a mere roar. "I have broken bigger men for less cowardice than yours, Admiral! For cowardice in face of enemy, I swear I will have anyone—whatever his rank—shot! If you feel you cannot carry out plan as it stands, it is your duty to so inform me, so I can replace you with someone who can. Do I make myself clear?"

"Perfectly clear, Admiral." Berenson's face was paler by a couple of shades, but he hadn't gone into a state of shock like almost everyone else in the room. "Your orders will, of course, be carried out to the letter."

"Good." Antonov rose. "This meeting is adjourned. Captain Tsuchevsky and Commander Kthaara, please accompany me to my quarters."

Once the three of them were in the elevator, Antonov sighed deeply, knowing what was coming next.

"You're going to have a stroke one of these days, Ivan Nikolayevich," Tsuchevsky scolded sternly, and Antonov held up his hand wearily.

"I know, I know, Pasha. I promise I'll stop losing my temper." He glanced at Kthaara, who was looking ill at ease, and smiled faintly. "What, nothing about your request?!"

The Orion relaxed slightly. "This is hardly the time,

Admiral. I find I owe you an apology." Antonov raised an inquisitive eyebrow, and Kthaara explained bleakly. "I now understand what you meant at our first meeting when you spoke of the problems I would cause you."

"Oh, that!" Antonov gave a sound halfway between a laugh and a snort. "Don't give it another thought. You see, Berenson was talking about me as much as he was about you."

"I know there are those among your officers who feel you understand my race all too well—better than a Human has any right to," the Orion replied slowly. "They may have a point." A sudden carnivore's grin signaled the mercurial mood-shift the two humans had come to know so well. "So perhaps it *is* time to renew my request!"

A low moan escaped Antonov.

"Kthaara, you can't really be serious," Tsuchevsky put in. "You know better than most what a problem command-and-control poses in strikefighter operations, even under the best circumstances! And you know you can't take your talker along in a single-seat vehicle!"

"Command-and-control is not a factor, Paaavaaaal Saairgaaiaavychhh," replied Kthaara (who'd been around these two long enough to grasp the nuances of modes of address), "for I seek to command no one. It will be enough if I am assigned to a squadron whose commander understands the Tongue of Tongues, so that I will be able to report to him."

Antonov gazed narrowly at the being who stood before him like Nemesis, overhead lights gleaming on midnight fur. "Do I understand, then, that you're requesting to take part in the coming battle as a common fighter pilot? And do *you* understand how much more good you could do—how much more damage you could do the Thebans—on the flag bridge?" He drew a deep breath. "Kthaara, as much as I'd hate to see you do it, I must tell you you could go home to Valkha right now and know you'd avenged your cousin many times over by what you've already contributed. You don't need to do this!"

"Yes, I do, Admiral." Kthaara's reply was quiet, but the elemental predator looked out of his slit-pupilled eyes. "You know I do. I have only planned and organized the killing of Thebans by others. No amount of this can meet the demands of honor. Ever. This may be unreasonable . . . but honor itself is unreasonable."

A couple of heartbeats of brooding silence passed before Antonov spoke, with the kind of gruffness that told Kthaara he'd won. "Well, if you must play the fool, I believe Commander Takashima understands Orion well enough. . . ."

The emergence of the first wave of *Pegasus*-class light carriers from warp told the Theban defenders of QR-107 another raid was underway. The second group, and the third, made them wonder. They'd expected any major infidel incursion to be led by battleships. But Ivan Antonov was still hoarding his battleships.

At any rate, Admiral Tharana, CO of the light covering forces and fifteen *Ronin*-class battle-cruisers that supported them, knew his duty. He reported the attack to fleet command, five-and-a-quarter light-hours away near QR-107's other warp point. Then, while his messages winged across the endless light-minutes, his units converged on the invading carriers, which were their primary targets. Their new anti-fighter training told them fighters with their bases destroyed were only temporary threats, but Antonov also knew that. On his orders, the light carriers now performed an old trick—one that was an Orion favorite and, in particular, of Kthaara'zarthan.

The reactionless drive didn't really cancel inertia, and Berenson's carriers couldn't instantaneously reverse direction without loss of velocity like those "flying saucers" Terrans had been wont to observe during the decades of endemic mass hysteria preceding the Second Millennium. But they could (and did, immediately after launching their fighters) make a far tighter 180-degree turn than would have been imaginable in the days of reaction drives, and vanished back into the warp point, leaving the fighters to slash into badly bewildered Theban formations. Back in Redwing space, they swung about again, paired off with *Scimitar*-class battle-cruisers, and returned to the carnage of QR-107 in time to retrieve and rearm their fighters.

It was the kind of complex tactical plan which ordinarily invites disaster by requiring a degree of precision which cannot be counted upon in the field. It worked because it was conceived in the cross-fertilization of two winning—but very different—traditions, practiced to exhaustion under the lash of Ivan Antonov's will, and executed by David Berenson, whose abilities were such that Antonov had to tolerate him. The Thebans were thrown onto the defensive against an enemy whose strength grew steadily as more and more ships emerged. By the time Admiral Tharana finally exercised the discretion the communications lag had forced Second Admiral Jahanak to grant him, it was almost too late.

The battered Theban survivors withdrew from the vicinity of the warp point, and as they did, it became harder and harder to render accurate reports of the number and tonnages of the arriving infidel ships. But it wasn't until his rampaging fighter squadrons had driven them out of scanner range altogether that Antonov allowed certain ships to disappear.

Electronic countermeasures had always been a crucial element of space combat, in which the unaided human eye was largely useless. Early-generation ECM suites had operated purely in fire-confusion mode; their only function was to make the ships that carried them more difficult targets, for the massive energy signature of an active drive field was simply impossible to hide. Later systems could play more sophisticated games with enemy sensors and make a ship seem, within limits, to be significantly more or less massive, but no one had ever been able to devise a way of concealing from today's broad-spectrum active and passive sensor arrays the fact that *something* was out there. Until now.

The new system was hideously expensive, and too massive for small ships, but its capabilities were on a par with its cost and tonnage penalty. It could perform all the functions of the earlier-generation systems and more for any ship which mounted it. Sophisticated computers wrapped a force field bubble about the betraying energy signature of its drive field—a very unusual bubble which trapped the energy that turned a starship into a brilliant beacon and radiated it directly astern, away from hostile scanners. Other, equally sophisticated computers monitored the strengths and frequencies of active enemy sensors, playing a fantastically complex matching game with their frequency shifts and sending back cunningly augmented impulses to blind their probing eyes. For the first time since humanity had abandoned primitive radar, true "stealth" technology had become feasible once more.

It wasn't infallible, of course. Though passive sensors were useless against it, active sensors had been found to be able to penetrate the ruse between fifteen and twenty percent of the time. But active scanners were far, far shorter-ranged, and that success rate had been achieved in tests whose participants had known exactly what they were looking for. Against an enemy who didn't even suspect the device's existence . . .

Thus it was that Antonov's eight *Wolfhound*-class fleet carriers ceased masquerading as light cruisers. They vanished from the ken of detection instruments and split off from the emerging Terran formation, advancing deep into the void of QR-107 on a wide dog-leg, unaccompanied by their usual escorts and protected only by the invisibility conferred by a new and untried system.

Second Admiral Jahanak's thumb caressed the switch on his light pencil in an unconscious nervous gesture as he waited. Tharana had waited overlong to break off, he thought sourly. But sufficient light units remained to

maintain a scanner watch over the advancing infidel fleet
while Tharana's surviving battle-cruisers fell back on the
main body at maximum. Now Jahanak watched Captain
Yurah listening intently to the voices in his earphone and
possessed his soul as patiently as he could.

"Second Admiral. Holiness." The flag captain paused
to nod politely to both of his superiors and Jahanak managed not to snap at him. "Admiral Tharana's reports indicate this is a major attack. His units have been pushed
back to extreme scanner range, but he estimates the enemy's strength at approximately six superdreadnoughts,
twelve battleships, nine battle-cruisers, and twelve to
fourteen light and heavy cruisers. They appear to be accompanied by eighteen to twenty destroyers and eight to
ten of their cruiser-size carriers. They are advancing directly towards us at five percent of light-speed. ETA is
approximately ninety-three hours from now."

"Thank you, Captain." The switch on Jahanak's light
pencil clicked under his stroking thumb, and he switched
it quickly off again, then slipped it into his pocket. It
would never do, he thought sardonically, to admit he,
too, could feel anxiety.

"Well, Holiness," he turned his command chair to face
Hinam, "it seems the infidels are finally seeking a decisive battle. The question is whether or not we grant it
to them."

Hinam leaned forward, looking alarmed. "Surely, Second Admiral, there can be no question! The infidels are
so inferior in both numbers and tonnage that not even
the diabolical weapons their satanically-inspired cunning
has allowed them to develop can . . ."

Jahanak tuned it out, maintaining a careful pose of
grave attention, and thought hard. Yes, they were obviously counting on their fighters and those incredible new
warheads to make up the force differential. But how
many fighters could they have? The reports from the
fighter-development project back on Thebes gave him a
fair idea how much carrier tonnage it required to service
and launch each fighter. The approaching fleet included

only cruiser-size "light carriers" such as had been encountered at Redwing, and not many more of them than had been engaged there. Was the enemy's supply of fighters—or pilots—subject to some unsuspected limiting factor?

It seemed unlikely from captured infidel data, but there clearly couldn't be enough fighters aboard that handful of carriers to even the odds between the two fleets. Especially not here, where there could be no ambush and the infidel fighters would have to approach from ahead, through the entire range of his AFHAWKs. Of course, the enemy's antimatter warheads would be a problem, but the infidels couldn't know his *Prophet*-class battleships and the refitted *Ronin*-class battle-cruisers he'd held back from the warp point now carried copies of their own long-range missiles—as did the external racks of all his other capital ships, as well. If their previous tactics held good, they would close to just beyond standard missile range in order to maximize accuracy, allowing him to get in the first heavy blows, and once they closed to laser range—

Yet the infidel who'd commanded at Redwing was manifestly no fool. Still, one didn't have to be a fool to fall victim to overconfidence. . . .

He realized Hinam had stopped for breath, allowing Yurah to resume. "Only one thing bothers me," the flag captain frowned. "There seems to be a discrepancy between the ship counts reported during the earlier stages of the battle and the ones we're getting now. A few light cruisers seem to be missing from that formation."

"The earlier reports were confused and contradictory," Hinam declared dismissively. Which, Jahanak knew, was true. "And the infidels could now be using ECM in deception mode to confuse us." He turned to Jahanak, eyes bright. "This is your hour, Admiral! Don't spurn the chance Holy Terra has offered—seize it!" His gleaming eyes narrowed shrewdly. "The Synod will hardly complain about minor past deviations from policy on the part of the hero who smashes the main infidel fleet!"

Jahanak hid an incipient frown. Little as he liked Hinam, the fleet chaplain's last point had struck home. A decisive victory would vindicate his strategy, demonstrating that he'd been right and the Synod wrong. (Oh, of course he wouldn't put it that way. But everyone would know.) He lifted his head and spoke urbanely.

"As always, Holiness, I am guided by your wisdom in all things. Captain Yurah, the battle-line and all supporting elements will engage the enemy as per Operational Plan Delta-Two."

"At once, Second Admiral!" Yurah's eyes blazed, and Jahanak smiled, remembering the hostility of their first meeting. The flag captain's eagerness augured well.

The second admiral leaned back, watching his display as the fleet moved forward. Forward, but not too far forward. They'd had time to consider, to plan for all contingencies that might arise in QR-107, and now the Sword of Holy Terra unsheathed itself with practiced smoothness.

Eleven superdreadnoughts, fourteen battleships, and thirty battle-cruisers took up their positions, screened ahead and on the flanks by massed cruiser flotillas and destroyer squadrons. Even if those carriers had lost no fighters at all in breaking into QR-107 (and they *had* lost, Jahanak thought coldly), they wouldn't be enough to even *those* odds. Not against ships who knew, now, what fighters could do . . . and what to do about them, in turn.

Yet it wouldn't do to become overly confident himself. That was why he'd selected Delta-Two, which wouldn't take his battle-line overly far from the Parsifal warp point. If the infidels were foolish enough to come to him, he would oblige them by crushing them, but his fleet represented too much of Terra's Sword to risk lightly.

The two fleets swept closer and closer, and the phantom carriers swung wide around the ponderous Theban formation, circling until they entered its wake, cutting between it and the Parsifal warp point. They had plenty of time to position themselves before the two battle-lines drew into capital missile range. And just as the opening salvos were being exchanged, two hundred and forty fighters, piloted by two hundred and thirty-nine humans and Kthaara'zarthan, entered the Theban battle-line's blind zone from nowhere.

Kthaara felt an almost dreamy sense of fulfillment as his squadron charged up the stern of the Theban super-dreadnought. The massive vessel, warned by frantic reports from its screening units, began an emergency turn—slow and incredibly clumsy compared to a fighter . . . and too late. Far too late. His fighter shuddered, slicing through the curdled space of the huge ship's wake, closing to a shorter range than he'd ever thought possible. His entire being, focused on his targeting scope, willed his heavy, short-ranged close-attack missiles through the wavering distortion of this unreal-seeming space as the 509th Fighter Squadron fired.

Neither he nor his Human *farshatok* could miss at this range—electromagnetic shielding and drive field alike died in a searing cluster of nuclear flares, and the stern of the mammoth ship seemed to bulge outward, splitting open in fissures of hellfire, as a warhead Kthaara was certain was one of his made the direct physical hit no mobile structure could withstand. No human who heard it would ever forget his banshee howl of vengeance.

"Let's keep the noise down," Commander Takashima called as they pulled up with a maneuverability possible only to craft such as theirs. There was no reproach in his voice—his understanding of the Tongue of Tongues, and those who spoke it, had turned out to be far less superficial than Antonov had implied. "Good job, everyone. Let's get back to the barn and—"

Takashima's voice died in a burst of static as the glare of his exploding fighter almost overloaded their view ports' automatic polarization. It faded, revealing the Theban light cruiser that had, by who knew what fanatical efforts, managed to swing about and come within AFHAWK range on a converging course that would soon bring it close enough to use its point defense lasers, as well.

"Evasive action!" The voice in Kthaara's helmet phones was that of the squadron ops officer, a painfully young lieutenant. (But he also understood the Tongue of Tongues, Kthaara had a split second to reflect; yes, per- haps Antonov's choice of a squadron to attach him to hadn't been so casual after all.) "Back to the ship—fast!"

"A course for the ship will carry us directly through the Theban's optimum AFHAWK envelope, Lieutenant Paapaas," Kthaara said without having time to reflect. "We can turn about and outrun him, but such a course will take us further from the carrier than we can afford to get." Let's see . . . how to put this? "May I suggest that the squadron reform on me, as I seem to be in the best position to . . ."

"Certainly, Commander!" Pappas couldn't quite keep the gratitude out of his voice. Kthaara waited for him to give the other pilots the order, then wrenched his fighter around and accelerated directly towards the Theban, corkscrewing madly. He had time to see that Pappas and the others were glued to him, and to feel a kind of pride in them that couldn't be put precisely into any Human language.

The Theban crew were new arrivals; they'd trained intensely and listened to the stories of the veterans of Redwing. But they'd never actually faced fighters. And they were shaken to the core by what Holy Terra was allowing to happen to their fleet. Their point defense should have taken toll of these fighters that so unexpect- edly swept past them at an unthinkable relative velocity, clawing their ship's flanks with lasers. But in less than an eye-blink the little crafts were in their blind zone, reced- ing rapidly . . . and Kthaara saw that all four of his com- panions were still with him.

He was, he decided, really getting too old for this.

"But where *are* they?" Hinam's voice wavered on the edge of hysteria as he stared over the scanner crews' shoulders, searching as they for the carriers to which the mysterious fighters had returned. "Where—"

"Be silent," Jahanak said curtly. Shock had the desired effect—fleet chaplains simply weren't spoken to that way. But on this flag bridge at this time, no one noticed. Hinam subsided, and Jahanak continued to absorb reports that told of the light carriers' massed fighter launch—a launch whose delay was no longer quite so inexplicable. Those fighters would hit his badly shaken fleet while the first attackers were rearming aboard their phantom carriers, and dealing with this fresh strike would require a compact formation which couldn't spread out to search for the invisible ships which had launched the first one. Meanwhile, the infidel battle-line was keeping scrupulously out of laser range and continuing the long-range capital missile duel in which their antimatter warheads nearly canceled out his own more numerous launchers.

"Signal to all units, Captain Yurah. Withdraw immediately and transit to Parsifal." This contingency had also been planned for. Turning to meet Hinam's stricken gaze, he continued smoothly. "It would seem, Holiness, that we've achieved our minimal objective of learning more about the infidels' capabilities and lulling them into overconfidence before unleashing our own fighters upon them. We can thus withdraw to Parsifal . . . as we intended to do all along."

Hinam stared at him, then shifted his gaze to a repeater screen showing the fleet's damage reports, then stared back at Jahanak again, as at a lunatic. He tried to speak but failed, and Jahanak went on remorselessly.

"You will, of course, be able to help explain our true intention in seeking this battle—as you urged my staff and myself to do—to the Synod." His eyes held the fleet chaplain's for a cold, measured heartbeat before he continued thoughtfully. "It is, after all, essential that we present a consistent report to avoid any possible misunderstanding on the Synod's part. Wouldn't you agree, Holiness?"

He turned away from the now speechless fleet chaplain and gave his attention to the battle. Yes, Hinam would go along, if only out of self-preservation. That, and the occasional, judicious mention of his own lineage, should get them past this debacle, in spite of the hideous losses his fleet still must take. Thank Holy Terra they hadn't ventured too far from the Parsifal warp point. The fighters from the cloaked carriers would only have the opportunity for one more strike before his survivors were through the warp point to the safety of Parsifal.

The lighter, faster Terran units, including Berenson's command, were already closing in on the Parsifal warp point, surging ahead of the lumbering battle-line when the battle had turned into a pursuit, and the cloaked fleet carriers, having dodged the retreating Thebans with almost ludicrous ease, moved to join them. The only living Thebans in QR-107 were the scattered light units that hadn't made it through the warp point with the main body, and which were now being hunted down.

Kthaara—just arrived by cutter aboard Antonov's new flagship—entered TFNS *Gosainthan*'s flag bridge to see Rear Admiral Berenson's face, contorted with suppressed fury, filling the main com screen.

"Your orders have been carried out, Admiral," Berenson was saying through tightly compressed lips. "Three *Shark*-class destroyers have been detached, and have now transited the warp point. No courier drones have been received, as yet. Wait." He turned aside, listened to someone off-screen, and spoke briefly. Then he turned back, and the fury in his face had congealed into hate. "Correction, Admiral. A courier drone—*one*—has returned from Parsifal. I have ordered its data downloaded to the flagship." Even as he spoke, the information appeared on a screen. "You will note," Berenson went on in a tightly controlled voice, "that it concludes with a Code Omega signal for all three ships."

Antonov, face expressionless, studied the data. "Yes," he finally acknowledged in a quiet voice. "I also note that they were able to record for the drone their sensor read-outs on the Theban defenses." Kthaara saw it, too; the shocking total of orbital fortresses in whose teeth the three destroyers had emerged into Einsteinian space. Antonov continued just as quietly. "You said it yourself, Admiral Berenson, at the last staff conference: to employ the SBMHAWKs with maximum effectiveness, we need to know exactly what is waiting at the other end of the warp line. We now have that information. And, as *I* said on the same occasion, it is the objective that matters." As the message crossed the few light-seconds that still separated them, he cut the connection. Then he turned to face Kthaara.

"You look like shit," was his greeting. For once, the Orion hadn't taken time to groom himself.

"So do you." Nothing ever really wore Antonov down; he was like planetary bedrock. But he was showing a certain undeniable haggardness.

"I heard what you did out there." Was it possible the Human smiled, a trifle?

"I saw what you just did here." Kthaara spoke seriously, but he, too, showed the beginning of his own race's smile. "You are more like my people than even Baaara-aansaahn thinks. And that is why . . ." He seemed to reach a decision. "You know of the oath of *vilkshatha*, do you not?"

Antonov blinked at the seeming irrelevancy. "Of course. It's the 'blood binding' that makes two Orion comrades-in-arms members of each other's family."

"Correct: two *farshatok* of the *Zheeerlikou'valkhan-naieee*. To my knowledge, the ceremony has never involved a member of any other race. But as Humans say, there is a first time for everything . . . Ivaaan'zarthan!"

For a couple of heartbeats, Antonov was as motionless as he was silent. Then he threw back his head and bellowed with gargantuan laughter.

"Well," he managed when he had caught his breath, "I hope you know what you're doing . . . Kthaara Kornazhovich!"

CHAPTER SEVENTEEN

"I need those ships!"

The Marine honor guard clicked to attention in the echoing spaces of the superdreadnought *Gosainthan*'s boat bay, and Antonov stepped forward to the VIP shuttle's ramp. "Welcome to Redwing, Minister."

Howard Anderson didn't acknowledge the greeting. He merely stared, then pointed with his cane. "And just what the hell is *that*?"

"I believe it's my face." Antonov was all imperturbability. Anderson was not amused.

"You *know* what I mean!"

"Oh, that." Antonov rubbed his jaw. At least the stubble phase was past. It was getting almost fluffy. "Well, I've always wondered what I'd look like with a beard. Somehow, it just came up in conversation with Commander Kthaara'zarthan." He gestured in the direction of the big Orion, who was looking insufferably complacent. "He urged me to try it, just to see how it would turn out. I think it's coming along rather well, don't you?"

"You look," Anderson replied, eyeing the burgeoning facial hair with scant favor, "like something out of an early twentieth-century political cartoon about Bolsheviks!" Then he glanced at Kthaara again. There was, he decided, no other way to describe it: the Orion looked like he'd swallowed a canary built to scale.

"Well," Anderson sighed, setting down his empty glass with a click. "Congratulations, Ivan. I don't need to tell you what you've accomplished here." Antonov, silhouetted against his stateroom's view port, gave an expressive Slavic shrug.

"We've been lucky. And part of our luck has been the new hardware you've sent us—especially the new ECM. Trying to guess what Father Christmas will pull out of his bag next has become the Fleet's favorite pastime."

"Ho, ho, ho! Well, as it happens, I *do* have a little something to satisfy your curiosity. I'm sure you've read the preliminary reports on how the Thebans manage to produce those lasers of theirs?" Antonov nodded. "And may I assume you're not particularly wild about the thought of exploding nukes rolling around the insides of your own ships?"

"You may, indeed." There was very little levity in Antonov's rumbling voice. "But if there's no other way to match their beams—" He broke off with another expressive shrug.

"Ah, but there *is* another way!" Anderson looked briefly very like Kthaara'zarthan as he smiled. "What would you say to a laser with about seventy-five percent of the Thebans' range, no bombs, and damned near two-thirds again as many projectors per tonne?"

"*Bozhemoi!*" Antonov said very softly and sincerely. "There truly is such a weapon?" Anderson nodded smugly, and the admiral grinned. "Then Father Christmas has outdone himself, Howard!"

"No, this time it's *Mother* Christmas," Anderson corrected. "In the form of Rear Admiral Timoshenko. She calls them 'hetlasers,' and I saw a full-scale field test just before I personally rammed her promotion through the board. You should have heard old Gomulka howling about promoting her out of the zone!" His eyes gleamed with fond remembrance.

"They don't pack quite as much punch per projector, but the numbers more than make up for it across their range, and I've had BuShips modify the plans for the new superdreadnoughts and battleships. I'm afraid it'll put our building schedules back a couple of months, but I was pretty sure you'd think it was time well spent."

"Indeed," Antonov nodded. "The only real tactical advantage the Thebans have left is in energy-range combat. With that gone, and with an initial SBMHAWK bombardment, there's no way they'll be able to keep us out of Parsifal. And we haven't used the extended range capability of the standard SBMs yet, either; as far as they know, their missiles' range will match ours, now that they've developed capital missiles of their own."

He paused and frowned slightly. "But, Howard, under the schedule you've just outlined, we'll have enough SBMHAWKs long before we have enough new capital ships. And the longer we wait, the more time they'll have to strengthen their defenses. Why not refit my existing heavy ships with hetlasers now?"

"That's been thought of, of course. But withdrawing your battlewagons to Galloway's World for refitting—even in shifts—will mean going on the defensive for now in QR-107."

Antonov looked at him sharply. "Why, of course, Howard—by definition. The whole purpose is to enable us to break into Parsifal without crippling losses, so naturally we won't be attacking until the work is completed. Besides, we've already taken up a mobile defensive posture that doesn't involve capital ships. Rear Admiral Berenson is in command there now, with the cloaked *Wolfhounds* as well as his own light carriers, disposed to sting the Thebans to death if they try to counterattack from Parsifal. Surely," he went on, looking unwontedly concerned, "you understand—"

"Of course *I* understand, Ivan. Whatever you think, I'm not senile yet. I only mentioned the point because of political factors."

"*Political* factors?" Antonov started to take on a dangerous look. "What political factors? We're talking about a military decision!"

Humanity had left instantaneous communications (and the tendency to micro-manage military operations to death) on Old Terra, and the Federation had always granted its admirals broad authority to run wars on the frontier. If it hadn't, it would long ago have been replaced, as a simple matter of natural selection, by a polity that did.

"Remember, Ivan," Anderson said, "this isn't a normal situation. Having gotten us into this mess in the first place, the politicos are still shitting their pants. Once we unmistakably gain the military upper hand, I expect them to turn vindictive; at present, they're merely scared, and they won't respond well to any suggestion of 'irresolution' on the military's part! Trust me—I'm talking from seventy years of political experience."

"Experience I don't envy you in the slightest!" Antonov snapped. He visibly controlled himself. "Look, Howard, surely even politicians can understand an elementary matter of military necessity like this—at least after you explain it to them. Can't they?"

Anderson laughed shortly. "Not these fuck-ups. And don't count on my explanations doing much good—at least as far as Waldeck goes. You know he hates me about as much as I do him."

"*Sookin sin!* Son-of-a-bitch! So the military objective—and the lives of my people—are secondary to enabling gasbags like Sakanami and slime molds like Waldeck to evade the consequences of their own stupidity?"

Anderson gave a theatrical wince. "I *do* wish you wouldn't say things like that, Ivan! Where's your respect for properly constituted civilian authority?"

Antonov exploded into a spate of Russian, and the little Anderson understood made him just as glad he didn't understand the rest. Finally, the massive admiral calmed down sufficiently to communicate in Standard English.

"Why am I even surprised? Mass democracy! Ha! The

divine right of political careerists!" He glowered at Anderson. "Does such a regime even deserve to survive?"

"Hey," Anderson said, alarmed. "Don't go Russian-nihilistic on me, Ivan! Not now!"

Antonov let out a long breath. "Oh, don't worry, Howard. I'll follow orders. But," he continued grimly, "in order to do so, I need those ships. You'll just have to explain the facts of life to Sakanami and Waldeck and even that cunt Wycliffe." (This time Anderson's wince was sincere.) "If my battle-line has to go into Parsifal without hetlasers, or if I have to wait for the new construction, the losses will make them *really* shit in their pants." He leaned forward, and his voice dropped even deeper than was its wont. "I need those ships!"

"Well," Anderson said mildly after a heartbeat or two, "we'll just have to see what we can do about getting them for you, won't we?"

The cloud-banded blue dot swelled on TFNS *Warrior*'s visual display, and the light cruiser's captain turned to the old man at the assistant gunnery officer's station.

"You know, Admiral, it's eight years since I last saw Old Terra. She sure is pretty, isn't she?"

"Indeed she is, Captain. And thank you for letting me watch. It's been a lot more than eight years since *I* last saw her from a command deck."

"In that case, Admiral, would you care to take the con?"

Commander Helen Takaharu smiled, and Howard Anderson grinned back like a schoolboy. Then his grin faded.

"No, Captain. Thanks for the offer, but I'm afraid it's been too long. Besides, I'm not really an admiral anymore."

"You'll always be an admiral, sir," Takaharu said softly, "and I'd be honored if you accepted."

Color tinged Anderson's cheeks, but for once he felt no ire. There was no sycophancy in Takaharu's voice. He hesitated.

"Please, sir, I know I speak for *Warrior's* entire crew."

"Well, in that case, Captain Takaharu," he said gruffly, "the honor will be mine." He stood, and Takaharu rose from her command chair.

"I relieve you, sir," he said.

"I stand relieved," she replied crisply. He settled into her chair, and she moved to stand at his shoulder, her face creased in a huge smile.

"Maneuvering, stand by for orbital insertion."

"Standing by, aye, Admiral," the helmsman replied, and Howard Anderson stroked the command chair's armrests almost reverently.

"Out of the question," Irena Wycliffe said sharply. "Totally out of the question! I'm astonished Admiral Antonov could suggest such a thing."

Anderson leaned back and looked around the conference room. Hamid O'Rourke looked unhappy and avoided his eyes, and several other ministers fidgeted uncomfortably.

"Ms. Wycliffe," he said at last, "I fail to understand exactly which aspect of the Ministry of Public Welfare qualifies you to hold such a pronounced opinion?"

Wycliffe flushed and glanced angrily at the president. In point of fact, she wasn't expressing *her* opinion. She was one of Pericles Waldeck's closest supporters, his eyes and ears—and mouth—in the Sakanami Cabinet.

"I may not have your own long—and long *ago*—military experience, Mister Anderson," she shot back, "but I'm quite conversant with the course of *this* war! Admiral Antonov held Redwing by the skin of his teeth, and now, when he's finally pushed the Thebans back at last, he wants to *weaken* his forces? Even I know the thing for the Thebans to do is counterattack as quickly as possible!"

"Ladies and gentlemen, please!" Sakanami intervened mildly. "This is not a question to settle on the basis of personalities." He glanced at both disputants. "I trust I make myself clear?"

Anderson snorted in amusement and nodded. Wycliffe distributed her glare almost impartially between him and the president.

"Now, then," Sakanami continued. "Admiral Antonov is entitled to make his own tactical dispositions. No one disputes that. But I do feel we have a right to question the wisdom of such a fundamental strategic redistribution. Admiral Brandenburg?"

The chief of naval operations was a spare, white-haired man. Seventy years younger than Anderson, he actually looked older as he sat quietly erect in his space-black and silver uniform. Five years as CNO had taught him the tricks of the political jungle, but he'd commanded a task force himself in ISW-3, and he frowned thoughtfully.

"As a rule, Mister President, the commander on the spot usually has a clearer appreciation than GHQ, and Antonov's record to date certainly seems to suggest he knows what he's doing. I suppose there is a possibility of a counterattack, but as I understand it he's not talking about pulling the battle-line back *en masse*, is he, Howard?"

"No. He wanted to, but I convinced him it'd cause undue concern"— Anderson grinned wryly—"back home. Besides, Fritz, we're heavily committed to the new construction programs. We can only free up the space to handle about a third of his battle-line at a time without disrupting things, so we're talking about a temporary reduction, not a total rollback."

"Indeed?" Wycliffe put in. "But it's actually a *two*-thirds reduction, isn't it?"

"It is," Anderson agreed with unruffled calm. "One-third of his units will be put into yard hands immediately; the next third will start back to Galloway's World when they're finished. They'll pass one another *en route*, but for some weeks Second Fleet's battle-line will, indeed, be at one-third strength."

"Still," Brandenburg mused, "we're talking about a fleet defending a starless nexus, with no need to mount a warp-point defense."

"Which doesn't mean those ships won't be needed!" Wycliffe turned to Sakanami. "Mister President, such a policy would cause great disquiet in the Assembly. Important people will ask questions."

"Let them," Anderson said coldly.

"Oh, that's a wonderful idea! Wars, Mister Anderson, are not fought only on the front lines—and military people aren't the only ones with a stake in their outcome!"

"No, just the ones who do the dying," Anderson said even more coldly, and Wycliffe jerked back as if he'd slapped her. He pressed his advantage.

"Look, Fritz has already pointed out we've got plenty of depth and no population to defend. Any counterattack will be met with a mobile defense, not a point-blank battle on top of a warp point! Admiral Antonov is confident his fighters can stop any Theban attack cold, and I concur. Fritz?"

"On the basis of the reports I've seen," Brandenburg said mildly, "I'd certainly have to agree. In a mobile defense, the sluggers would only slow him down, anyway. He'd need carriers and fighters to pound them as they try to close, and carriers need escorts who can keep up with them."

"I see." Sakanami rubbed the conference table gently, then raised his fingers, as if inspecting them for dust. "Hamid?"

"I"—O'Rourke shot Wycliffe an unhappy glance—"have to agree with Admiral Brandenburg. If we're going to stand on the defensive in QR-107, the battle-line would definitely play a secondary role."

"But that raises another point." Anderson shook his head. Whatever else she was, Irena Wycliffe wasn't a quitter. "Should we even be talking about standing on the defensive? Why isn't Second Fleet pushing forward into Parsifal right now?"

"Because," Brandenburg's voice was unwontedly caustic, "a lot of people would die, Ms. Wycliffe. In a warp point assault, the enemy is right on top of you as you make transit. They'd be at their most effective range and working right through our shields from the outset; without matching weapons, *we'd* have to pound their shields flat before we could even get at them." He snorted. "That's why Antonov's insisting on this refit! Or would you prefer for him to wade right in and lose more ships and people than he has to?"

"Fritz is right, Mister President," Anderson said. "We could probably take Parsifal now, but the battle-line would take murderous punishment. They still will, even with the new lasers, but at least they'll be in position to reply effectively. You may face some political questions now, but what are your options? Push ahead too soon and get our people killed? Or wait till we have enough *new* ships for the attack—possibly as much as a year from now? At the moment the Thebans don't have any fighters, but give them that much time and they will. In which case"—he looked steadily at Wycliffe—"our losses will be even higher."

"I have to agree with Mister Anderson and Admiral Brandenburg." O'Rourke took the plunge at last.

"Why?" Wycliffe's cold tone warned of more than military consequences for Hamid O'Rourke if he crossed Pericles Waldeck.

"Because they're right," O'Rourke said sharply. "And if there are questions in the Assembly, I'll say so there. It's important to launch heavy, properly prepared attacks, and this is the quickest way to accomplish that. Mister President," he turned to Sakanami, "Admiral Antonov is right."

"Very well," the president said calmly. "If that's the opinion of the Chief of Naval Operations, the Minister for War Production, and the Defense Minister, the question is closed. Now, the next item on the agenda is—"

Anderson sat back. It had been easier than he'd expected after all. He'd known Brandenburg would support him, but he hadn't expected O'Rourke to overcome his fear of Waldeck's revenge. It seemed he owed the man an apology, and he made a mental note to deliver it in person.

CHAPTER EIGHTEEN
No Sae Bad . . . Fer a Shellhead

The vertol's cockpit was less impressive than a flag bridge, and he might become dead very quickly if he stumbled over a guerrilla SAM team, but it was worth it to get away from HQ. Or, Admiral Lantu amended wryly as the craft turned for another sweep, it had been *so* far. He knew it worried Fraymak, but he refused to be a mere paper-pusher. Besides, flying an occasional mission gave him at least the illusion of commanding his own fate.

Unlike many Fleet officers, Lantu was an experienced vertol pilot, and he habitually took the copilot's station. Now he leaned to the side, pressing his cranial carapace against the bulged canopy to peer back along the fuselage. A pair of auto-cannon thrust from the troop doors, and there were rocket pods under the wings, but the vertol's sensor array was their real weapon. It probed the dense forest below with thermal, electronic, and magnetic detectors, its laser designators ready to paint targets for their escorting attack aircraft, not that Lantu expected

199

to find any. The guerrillas knew what they were doing, and it was the Satan-Khan's own task to get any reading through these damnable trees, especially once they split back up into small groups. But at least his sensors *forced* them to break up and stay broken up . . . he hoped.

It was a frustrating problem. How did he know if he was winning? Body counts were one way, but the guerrillas seemed to have an inexhaustible supply of recruits, thanks to Colonel Huark and the late archbishop. The lower incidence of attacks might have been a good sign, if their larger assault parties weren't gaining in firepower what they lost in frequency and proving a nastier handful for any reaction teams that managed to catch them.

Lantu sighed. The jihad's initial force structure had badly underestimated the need for ground troops, and replacing the Fleet's climbing losses took precedence over increases in planetary forces. And it seemed New Hebrides, for all its spiritual importance, had been demoted in priority as the general situation worsened. Replacements slightly outpaced losses—Fraymak's command was essentially an understrength division now—but there were never enough troops, for the colonel's comments about fish in muddy water had been accurate in more than one sense.

Pattern analysis convinced Lantu the guerrillas' active cadres were small, and prisoner interrogations seemed to confirm that, but without more troops, he couldn't expand the occupation zones, and beyond the OZs they simply vanished into the sparse general population. Even within them, they were hard to spot, and Fraymak couldn't put checkpoints *everywhere*. Nor, despite Huark's suggestions, could he provide sufficient guards to confine all the locals in holding camps. Moreover, he had to feed these people—and his own—somehow, and the agricultural and aquacultural infrastructure was too spread out for centralized labor forces.

He knew he was hurting them, but how *much*? Certainly not enough to stop them; the destruction of the New Perth Warden post which had sparked this search and destroy mission proved that. But at least there'd been only two more raids on civilian housing, and that was sufficient improvement for Manak to continue his more lenient re-education policies.

Lantu sat back, eyes skimming the treetops, and chuckled mirthlessly. Here he was, hunting guerrillas in the hope of killing a few of them in order to justify *not* killing their fellows in the Inquisition's camps! Holy Terra—if, as he was coming to doubt, there *was* a Holy Terra—must have a warped sense of humor.

Angus MacRory sweated under the thermal canopy and held his field glasses on the vertol. The old-fashioned glasses had none of the electronic scan features which might have been detected, and he hoped none of his SAM teams got itchy fingers and gave *their* position away. Five or six men and women might not be an unreasonable trade for an aircraft loaded with sensors and heavy weapons . . . if you had the people to trade.

He lowered his glasses and gnawed his bushy mustache. These new Shellhead operational patterns were enough to worry a man. He'd lost fifty-one people in the past two months—not many for a Marine division, but an agonizing total for his light irregulars. He had another twenty seriously hurt and twice that many walking wounded, but at least Doctor MacBride's deep-cave hospital camp was virtually impossible to spot.

His teams were still exfiltrating, but by now most of them could have given lessons to Marine Raiders. Unless the Shellheads got dead lucky, they wouldn't spot any of them, so he judged the raid had been a success. Yet he knew he'd picked New Perth because it could be hit, not for its importance. Clearly Admiral Lantu had other priorities than protecting Wardens too clumsy to protect themselves, which—despite the satisfaction of killing those particular vermin—was worrisome. It was only a matter of time before Lantu began using Wardens for bait . . . if he hadn't already. This particular response team had arrived suspiciously quickly even for him.

Angus tipped his bonnet to his opponent. Before he'd turned up, the momentum had been with the Resistance, and though Angus had never expected to *win* the damned war, he'd thought he might keep the bloody Shellheads on the defensive until the Fleet returned. Now he was being forced to plan operations so carefully the bastards were free to do just about as they liked within the Zones, and that wouldn't do at all, at all.

He could replace personnel losses, but newbies required training and he was short on arms. Those the New Perth Wardens no longer required would help, yet he needed to hit a real arms dump, and Lantu was being difficult. Still, the Shellies had just rebuilt their Maidstone base, and the New Rye ran right down to it. If he could divert the Knightsbridge response force . . .

He frowned. Yes, it might be done. It wouldn't be as effective as, say, picking off Admiral Lantu, but it would help.

Lantu walked wearily into his office and hung up his body armor, smiling tiredly in answer to Hanat's greeting.

"Any luck?" she asked.

"There are times," Lantu said feelingly, "when I'm inclined to accept Father Shamar's theories of demonic intervention."

"No luck, then," she observed as she poured him a cup of hot *chadan*. He took it gratefully, pressing a chaste kiss to her cranial carapace, and slumped behind his desk.

"No, no luck. Whoever's running them knows what he's doing."

"Among these people"—like Fraymak, Hanat never said "infidel" anymore; then again, neither did Lantu— "it might just be a *she*."

"So it might. Jealous?"

"Maybe," she said, then laughed at his expression. "I'm not about to ask for a rifle, First Admiral. Their women have the size for it and ours don't. It's just that there are things I *could* do as well as a man."

"Yes," Lantu considered the heretical thought, "yes, I suppose so. But—"

"But Holy Terra expects Her daughters to produce children—preferably sons—for Her jihad," Hanat said in a dry, biting tone.

"Hanat," Lantu said very seriously, "you can say such things to me, here, because I have my office swept by my own people every day. Don't ever say them where Colonel Huark might hear of it."

"I won't." She bent over his desk and sorted data chips. "Here are those reports you asked for, First Admiral. And don't forget your meeting with the Fleet Chaplain at fifteen hundred."

He nodded, and she headed for the door, but his voice stopped her.

"There *are* things you could do as well as any man in the service, Hanat. Would you really like to do them?"

"Yes," she said, without turning. "Yes, I wish I could." She opened the door and left, and Lantu watched it close behind her.

"Do you know," he said softly, "I wish you could, too."

". . . so your people will hit the MacInnis Bay fuel depot." Caitrin MacDougall tapped the plastic laminate of a New Hebrides Fisheries map with a bayonet and met Tulloch MacAndrew's frowning eyes. "Mortar the dump and rocket the guard shacks, but the main thing is to raise enough hell to draw the Knightsbridge battalion after you. When you do, bury the tubes, hide your equipment, and move deeper into the Zone, not out. With luck, they'll sweep towards the Grampians looking for you. Got it?"

"Aye, but that's no tae sae I like it. If we're tae draw the buggers oot, let's hit 'em here." Tulloch tapped a spot on the map even further from Maidstone, but Angus shook his head.

"Nay, Tulloch. If yon Shellies are willin' tae break up their 'extermination squads,' I'm willin' tae stop hittin' their housing."

"Then ye're a fool." Tulloch was as blunt as Angus himself. "Aye, I ken they've stopped 'reprisals,' but it's done nowt tae stop the killin' in the camps."

"It may not have stopped it, but the execution levels have dropped by almost seventy percent."

"An' grateful I am, Katie," Tulloch agreed, "but sae lang as they gae on killin' us, I'm game t'gae on killin' *them*."

"I hear ye, Tulloch," Angus said quietly. "And sae we will, but not today. I've a thought aboot that, but I need time tae work it oot."

His eyes held Tulloch's until MacAndrew nodded slowly.

Lieutenant Darhan cringed in his hole as the infidel mortars ripped off another four-shot clip. Ninety-millimeter rounds walked across the vehicle pool with metronome precision and a distinctive, easily recognized "Crack!" They were hitting him with weapons shipped here from Thebes, and doing it as well as he could have done himself.

The infidels must have scouted the base carefully—they'd probably watched it going up, for Terra's sake!—and the first rockets had taken out both com huts and the alternate satellite link aboard the command GEV. Captain Kyhar had gone up with his vehicle—dropping command on him—and Darhan didn't know if he'd gotten off a message before he died. But he did know none of his short-range tactical coms could if Kyhar hadn't.

His perimeter was already too big for his two platoons, and rockets and mortars had chewed up his own heavy weapons with malignant precision. One machine-gun had gotten two infidel sapper teams that rushed the wire too soon, but its crew had died in a hurricane of fire when they did.

A crackling hiss lifted his head out of the hole with a curse as rockets smoked over the perimeter, towing assault charges. The flexible cables unfolded their wing-like charges over the wire, then detonated. The glare of

HE not only blew the wire but cleared the mines in the gaps, and the mortars shifted back, dropping visual and thermal smoke to hide the holes.

"They're coming through the wire in Alpha Sector!" Darhan barked into his hand com. "Reserve to Alpha Two *now*!"

His small reserve force scuttled through the carnage on short, strong legs, and he pounded the dirt as he urged them to greater speed. If the infidels broke through, they could swamp him by sheer weight of numbers, and—

The smoke screen lifted, and Darhan gaped at the breached wire. There wasn't an infidel in sight! But why—?

A fresh roar of assault charges shook the base, and he whirled in horror as Sergeant Targan came up on the com.

"Gamma Sector! Wire breached in Gam—"

Darhan was already running, screaming for the reserve to follow him, when the sergeant's voice cut off with sickening suddenness. He stumbled over mangled dead and wounded, eyes slitted against the smoke as dirt and flame erupted all over Gamma Sector, and a tall, long-legged shape loomed before him. His machine-pistol chattered viciously and the shape went down, but there was another behind it, and something smashed into Darhan's body armor with terrific force. The blow slammed him onto his back, stunned and breathless, and an infidel loomed out of the smoke. She was short for a human, black hair streaming in a wild mane, and the bayonet on her Theban rifle pricked the base of his throat.

"Be *still*, ye miserable boggit!" she snarled, and he went limp, not knowing which hurt worse—the terrible ache in his bruised body or failure.

Colonel Fraymak tugged on his muzzle in puzzlement. MacInnis Bay was further from the mountains than the guerrillas normally struck, and the attack pattern was . . . odd. Their short, vicious bombardment had scored heavily, killing or wounding a third of the guards and torching thousands of liters of fuel, but why hadn't they exploited that success? Had something gone wrong from their side and forced them to break off? But MacInnis Bay was in one of the rare timbered-off areas; his scouts should have found some sign of the raiders before they all got back under cover of the forests, for Terra's sake.

"Still nothing?"

"No, sir." Major Wantak shook his head. "I've sent in additional units from New Bern. This far into the Zone, we ought to be able to spot *something* before they get away."

Fraymak paused, arrested by how Wantak's comment echoed his own thoughts. Something about what his exec had said . . .

"Satan-Khan!" he hissed. Wantak recoiled from the venomous curse, and Fraymak shook himself. "It's a diversion! They *wanted* to draw our reaction!"

"But—" Wantak broke off, cranial carapace gleaming under the CP lights as he cocked his head. "It makes sense, sir, but what are they diverting us *from*? We haven't had any reports of other attacks."

"No." Fraymak was bent over the map table, scrolling quickly through the projected map sheets until he had the Knightsbridge sector. "But whatever they're after, they drew Lieutenant Colonel Shemak's force first." He slapped the table, yellow eyes narrow in thought. There were over a dozen likely targets in the sector, from re-education camps to the Maidstone depot.

"Get on the satellite net. I want a status report from every unit in the Knightsbridge sector right now!"

Lieutenant Darhan squatted in the dust on short, folded legs with the survivors of his command. Most of the infidels had already vanished into the heavily-timbered slot of the Rye River valley, leading sturdy Terran mules and New Hebridan staghorns laden with ammunition, small arms, and rocket and grenade launchers. He'd seen Theban camouflage sheets draped over the

weapon loads, and he wished to Holy Terra the quarter-
master had never shipped them in. Designed to foil the
thermal and magnetic detectors the infidels didn't have,
they worked quite well against those the People *did* have.

The last raiders ringed his survivors, and he wondered
why they hadn't already been shot. As far as he knew,
the infidels never left anyone alive. Of course, they usually hit Wardens, not regulars, but even so. . . .

A pair of infidels waded through the debris towards
him. The man was big, brawny, and dark, and Darhan
had seen enough infidels by now to know he was older
than the almost equally tall woman beside him. The lieutenant noted the polished chevrons on the man's collar
as they drew nearer.

"Ye're the senior officer?" the man demanded, and
Darhan nodded. "Good. We're gang now, but I've sum-
mat fer ye tae gi' Admiral Lantu."

Darhan blinked both sets of eyelids. Did that mean
they *didn't* mean to kill him?

"Here." Darhan took the envelope numbly, and the
man touched his tattered bonnet in a jauntily-sketched
infidel-style salute. The lieutenant responded automatically, and the man grinned, then waved his Theban grenade launcher at his followers, who faded into the trees
behind him.

Lieutenant Colonel Shemak's battalion came screaming in from the south forty-five minutes later.

"It might have been worse," Manak sighed. "At least
they didn't massacre their prisoners."

"True, Holiness." Lantu once more debated telling his
old mentor about the message the guerrillas had left with
Lieutenant Darhan. Once he would already have done
so, but Manak grew more brittle with every day, as if his
natural aversion to following in Tanuk's footsteps was
at war with an increasing desperation. His fulminating
diatribes against Admiral Jahanak, for example, were
most unlike him. He seemed to be retreating into a spiri-

tual bunker and venting his fury and despair on purely
military matters to avoid any hint of doctrinal weakness.

"Perhaps they truly are learning from our own restraint," the fleet chaplain mused.

"Perhaps," Lantu agreed. He folded his arms behind
him and wrinkled his lips in thought. "Holiness, I would
like to propose something which, I fear, Father Shamar
and Colonel Huark will hate."

"I wouldn't worry about that," Manak said with a ghost
of his old humor. "They're already about as upset as they
can get."

"In that case, Holiness, I'd like to put at least a temporary halt to any further executions for heresy."

"What?" Manak looked up quickly, his voice sharp.
"My son, we can take no chances with the Faith!"

"I'm not proposing that we should, Holiness," Lantu
said carefully. "We have a double problem here. Certainly we must win the infidels"—the word tasted strange
these days—"for the Faith, but to do so, we must hold
the planet without killing them all. The degree to which
we've already relaxed the Inquisition's severity seems to
have brought an easing in the ferocity of the guerrillas'
tactics, as witnessed by the lower incidence of attacks on
civilian housing and the fact that Lieutenant Darhan and
his troops weren't shot. I believe the Fleet's manpower
requirements will grow even greater in the immediate
future, so substantial reinforcements here seem unlikely.
If only as a temporary expedient to reduce the burden
on our own troops, a ruling—even a conditional one—
that infidels will be executed only for specific violations
of regulations might be most beneficial."

"Um." Lantu felt a chill as Manak looked down at his
hands. Just months ago, the old churchman would not
only have recognized his true goal but helped achieve it.
Now the thought of tying the camp firing squads' hands
actually upset him, but he nodded slowly at last.

"Very well, my son, I will inform Father Shamar that—
purely as a matter of military expedience—infidels are to
be executed only for active infractions. But—" he looked

up sharply "—*I* will decide what constitutes an infraction, and if the *terrorists*"—the gentle stress was unmistakable—"begin attacking non-military targets once more, I will rescind my decision."

"I think that's wise, Holiness."

"That is because you have a good heart, my son," Manak said softly. "Do not permit its very goodness to seduce you from your duty."

A sharper, colder chill ran down Lantu's spine, but he bent his head in mute acquiescence and left silently.

Hanat was waiting anxiously in his office. Unlike anyone else at HQ, she'd read the guerrillas' message. Now she watched him silently, her delicate golden eyes wide.

"He's agreed to suspend executions for simple apostasy," Lantu said quietly, but she didn't relax. Instead she seemed to tighten even further.

"Are you sure this is wise, Lantu?" She seemed unaware she'd used his name with no title for the first time, and he curled one long arm about her in a little hug.

"No," he said as lightly as he could. "I'm only sure I have to do it. And at least we know who their leader *is* now."

Hanat nodded unhappily, and he hugged her again, more briskly, before he sat and reached for pen and paper. This was one message he dared not trust to any electronic system.

"Weel, now," Angus murmured, as he refolded the letter Tulloch MacAndrew had delivered to him. His burly, beetle-browed subordinate still seemed amazed to be alive, much less back among his fellows. It was pure bad luck he'd been scooped up by the Shellhead checkpoint, but Angus recognized the additional, unspoken message of his release as Lantu's courier.

"He's agreed?" Caitrin asked.

"Aye. That's tae sae he's convinced his ain boss tae stop the killin's fer aught but actual resistance sae lang as we keep our word tae engage only military targets.

And—" Angus chuckled suddenly "—he'd nowt tae sae at all at all aboot the Wardens we might chance upon."

His gathered officers laughed. The sound was not pleasant.

"D'ye think he means it?" Sean Bulloch asked skeptically.

"Aye, I do," Angus said. "He's a braw fighter, this Lantu, but he seems a trusty wee boggit. He's no sae bad at all . . . fer a Shellhead."

CHAPTER NINETEEN

"We must all do our duty, Admiral Berenson."

"Before we begin," Ivan Antonov rumbled, eyes sweeping his assembled officers, "Commander Trevayne has prepared an intelligence update based on new findings. Commander."

"Thank you, Admiral." The newly promoted intelligence officer rose. In an era when defects of eyesight had not been biochemically corrected, Winnifred Trevayne would surely have had a pair of spectacles perched on the end of her nose, the better to peer over them at her class. "As you all know, the Thebans have always followed a policy of destroying their ships to avoid capture. On the few occasions when they've been prevented from doing this, they have nonetheless suicided as individuals after activating an automatic total erasure of their data bases. So we've been able to ascertain their physiology but little else, other than their seemingly inexplicable use of Standard English and of ship names from human history and languages.

211

"Now, however, we've finally had a spot of luck. One of the Theban destroyer squadrons trapped in QR-107 managed to avoid interception far longer than any of the others, largely by hiding where we never expected to find them: on the deep-space side of the Redwing warp point. They might be hiding still, if their commander hadn't elected to launch a virtual suicide attack on the fleet train and run straight into the convoy escorts. Most of them were destroyed, but one of them took a very lucky—from our viewpoint—hit which set up a freak series of breakdowns in its electronics, involuntarily shutting down its fusion plant and also crippling the crew's ability to lobotomize the computer. With no power, they couldn't evade, and our Marines got aboard." She turned to Antonov. "Incidentally, Admiral, our report specifically commends Captain M'boto, the Marine officer who led the boarding party. He not only secured their fusion plants before they could restore power but also dispatched a hand-picked force directly into their computer section, which prevented them from physically destroying their data. There were, as usual, no prisoners—but we're now in possession of priceless information. Far from complete information, of course . . . but I'm now in a position to tell you what this war is all about."

A low hubbub arose, stilled as much by everyone's eagerness to hear more as by Antonov's glare. They all knew about the captured Theban destroyer, but Trevayne had been playing its significance very close to her chest. This was due partly to a natural reticence that her profession had only reinforced, and partly to sheer inability to credit her own findings and conclusions. Only Antonov had heard what she was about to reveal.

She began—irrelevantly, it seemed—with a story most had heard many times: the colony fleet, bound for New New Hebrides in the darkest days of the First Interstellar War, all but wiped out in the Lorelei system, whose survivors had fled down Charon's Ferry from whence no ship had returned before or since. But the tale took a new twist as Trevayne neared its end.

"Now we know why the early survey ships hadn't returned," she stated flatly. With unconscious drama, she activated a holo display and gave them all their first glimpse of the Thebes System. "As you will note, the Theban end is a closed warp point inside an asteroid belt." She held up a hand to still her audience's incredulous sound. "Yes, I know it's a freakish situation—possibly unique. But, as you can see, that system is bloody *full* of asteroids, as is often the case with binaries; the secondary sun's gravitation prevents planetary coalescence throughout a far wider region than does a mere gas giant. At any rate, the point is that those colony ships—big brutes equipped with military-grade shields because of the war—survived the meteor impacts which pulverized small survey ships with prewar meteor shielding."

Most of the officers sat speechless, dealing as best they could with a surfeit of new facts. Berenson was the first to make, and accept, the logical conclusion.

"So, Commander," he grated, leaning forward as if to come physically to grips with the unknown. "You're telling us those colonists—or, rather, their descendants—are behind this war? That this is why the Thebans speak Standard English? I suppose it would account for the ship names from human history . . . but what about the ships with human names no one can identify?"

"As a matter of fact, Admiral, it was those names that put me onto the scent—those and repeated references to an 'Angel Saint-Just' in the Theban religious material of which the data base is full. I was afraid I was going to have to send back to Old Terra, but fortunately the archives at Redwing contain exhaustive personnel records of the old colonization expeditions in this region. A computer search of that fleet's complement turned up all those ship names—and one Alois Saint-Just."

Her eyes took on a faraway look. "Finding specific information on Saint-Just himself wasn't as hard as it might have been, as he seems to have made an impression on everyone who met him. A xenologist by profession, he was also a student of history, with a particular interest in ancient Egypt; hence the name 'Thebes.' He had many other interests as well." Her voice grew somber. "A brilliant man—and a very troubled one. He was obsessed with a foreboding that Terra was going to lose the war—a not unreasonable supposition at that time." She shot an apologetic glance at Kthaara, who sat listening impassively. "After he disappears from sight, we're thrown back on inference from the Theban religious references. But there are so *many* references we can form a pretty clear picture of what happened.

"The survivors, led by Saint-Just, found a Theban society on the threshold of the Second Industrial Revolution, but whose *ancien regime* was still in political control, and which had retained an unhealthy predilection for religious mania. They landed on a largish island-nation, to which—in direct contravention of the Non-Intercourse Edict of 2097—they gave modern technology so that it could forcibly unify the planet into a world-state, a potential ally for the Federation against the Khanate.

"The plan worked—up to a point. Then most of the humans died of what must have been a Terran microorganism that mutated in the new environment. Saint-Just and a few others lived, but they were so few they became more and more dependent on high-ranking Thebans, especially a noble named Sumash. He seems to have been of an unusually mystic bent even for a Theban, and he must have regarded himself as Saint-Just's chief disciple. I like to hope Saint-Just himself hadn't come to think in these terms, but we'll never know . . . for shortly, the same bug returned, in an even more virulent form, and killed all the remaining humans, leaving Sumash to his own devices.

"The colony ships' data bases must have held lots of Terran religious history. Using this for raw material, Sumash proceeded to manufacture a theology in which Saint-Just and the other humans had been messengers sent by God to bring the fruits of technology to Thebes, and the Orions who'd killed so many of these benefactors"—(another embarrassed glance at Kthaara)—"became the minions of the devil, led by the 'Satan-Khan.' Saint-Just had explained that the Orions were in control of Lorelei, at the other end of the warp line, so Sumash—the 'First Prophet,' as he's now remembered— proscribed all outside contact until Thebes was capable of mounting a full-scale jihad—"

"—which has now commenced," Berenson finished for her grimly. "But, Commander, if we humans are some kind of angels according to this crazy ersatz religion, why have the Thebans attacked *us*?"

"As often happens, Admiral, this religion took unintended turns after its founder's death. In particular, there was a shift of emphasis from *humans* to *Terra* as the fountainhead of enlightenment. It must have been a shock for them, finally emerging into Lorelei, to hear a *human* voice challenging them from an Orion warship. Clearly, the Angel Saint-Just's worst fears had been confirmed: his own race had been conquered or seduced by the Satan-Khan, leaving the Thebans standing alone as the true children of Holy Mother Terra."

This time it was Tsuchevsky who grasped it first. "Good God, Winnie! Are you telling us the Thebans' goal is to . . . to *liberate* Terra—from the *human race*?"

Trevayne nodded slowly. "I'm afraid that's exactly what I'm telling you—as insane as it may sound."

"But it's absurd!" Berenson's outburst shattered the stunned silence. "They must have learned by now, in the human systems they've occupied, that we *won* the First Interstellar War, and that we've never heard of any religion of 'Holy Mother Terra'!"

"I'm afraid, Admiral, that you underestimate the True Believer mentality's capacity for convoluted rationalization. The facts you've cited merely 'prove' the Satan-Khan and his human quislings have succeeded in reducing humanity to a state of hopeless apostasy by falsifying history and expunging all memory of the true faith!"

Antonov's basso sounded even deeper than usual in the flabbergasted stillness that followed. "Thank you, Commander . . . and congratulations on a brilliant piece of intelligence analysis." Everyone knew Antonov wasn't given to—nor, it was widely believed, capable of—fulsome praise. "However, the data on the Lorelei defenses are of more immediate military interest."

"Of course, Admiral." Trevayne manipulated controls and the holo projection changed to display Lorelei's five uninteresting planets, its six considerably more interesting warp points . . . and what appeared to be a rash of red dots infesting the regions of the four warp points connecting with Federation space.

"You realize, of course," Trevayne began earnestly, indicating the read-out of the warp point defenses, "that these data are somewhat out of date and therefore almost certainly on the conservative side, as the Thebans have had time to . . ." Her voice trailed off as she saw the needlessness of what she was saying. They were impressed quite enough by the raw data.

"This changes things," Antonov stated quietly. "The defenses of Lorelei are at least twice as powerful as we'd believed possible. But that was before we realized how heavily industrialized Thebes is, or what kind of fanaticism is driving them. And Lorelei is, after all, their final line of defense outside their home system. To break these defenses, we must hold one surprise in reserve." He gazed directly at Berenson. "I have therefore decided that we will forgo use of the SBMHAWKs at Parsifal and rely on our hetlaser-armed capital ships, as soon as sufficient of them become available, to break into that system."

The room was deathly silent. Antonov had invited neither discussion nor questions. But Berenson rose slowly to his feet. For several heartbeats, he and Antonov stared unblinkingly at each other. When he spoke, it was in an anticlimactically quiet tone—almost a *pleasant* tone, compared to the explosion they'd all anticipated.

"A point of information, Admiral. Are we to understand that the entire rationale for sending the crews of three destroyers on a suicide run into Parsifal has now become . . . inoperative? That those crews died for absolutely nothing?"

"Hardly, Admiral Berenson." Antonov's voice was equally quiet and controlled. This clash of wills had reached a level at which mere noise was superfluous. "Intelligence information has uses other than programming SBMHAWK carrier packs. Tactically, that information will be priceless to us when we attack. Those crews did their duty . . . as we must all do our duty, Admiral Berenson."

"Of course, Admiral. Our duty. I will assuredly do my duty. I will also send a personal message to Admiral Brandenburg stating for the record my feelings concerning your conduct of this campaign. That, too, is part of my duty, as I conceive it."

Again, the entire room braced for Apocalypse. Again, they were both disappointed and relieved. Antonov only looked somberly at Berenson for a long moment, then let his face relax into what looked very much like an expression of grudging respect. "You must do as you feel you must, Admiral Berenson," he said slowly. "As I must."

One month later, Antonov stood on *Gosainthan*'s flag bridge, gazing at a view screen that showed wreckage drifting among the unfamiliar constellations of Parsifal.

That wreckage was unusual. Space battles seldom left visible evidence, so vast were the volumes in which they were fought. But the floating, tumbling aftermath of what had just occurred about the QR-107-Parsifal warp point was so thick it hadn't yet had time to dissipate even in these trackless outer reaches of the system.

The Thebans had been positioned to face the kind of attack they'd experienced at QR-107, with laser-armed fortresses close to the warp point and mobile forces further away, at maximum effective AFHAWK range. The former were to smash the infidel carriers as they emerged, the latter to pick off their fighters as they launched. Instead, the assault had been led by refitted

Thunderer- and *Cobra*-class battleships, supported by equally refitted *McKinley*-class superdreadnoughts, and two fleets, equipped with the most destructive laser armaments in the history of Galactic warfare, had fought it out at close energy-weapon range. It had been submachine-guns at ten paces: an orgy of mutual destruction in which defense had been largely irrelevant. The missile-armed Theban ships and fortresses had done what they could, pouring fire into the already superheated furnace of battle, and the losses among the first Federation waves had been appalling. But as Antonov had continued to unflinchingly commit wave after wave, the superior numbers of the Federation's hetlasers had begun to tell. Only when the defense was clearly broken had the carriers begun to make transit. Faced with a combination of fighters and the rearmed capital ships, Jahanak had elected to cut his losses, withdrawing his mobile forces to the Lorelei warp point and leaving the surviving fortresses to cover his disengagement.

Now Berenson's carriers and their cruiser/destroyer screen were harrying the retreating Thebans across the Parsifal system as Antonov listened with half an ear to the reports of the reduction of the last of the fortresses.

"Preliminary reports indicate we may have secured some current data, Admiral," Winnifred Trevayne was saying. "This will enable us to update our estimates of Lorelei's defenses."

"Yes." Antonov spoke absently. He continued for a moment to gaze at the drifting wreckage. Then, abruptly, he swung around and activated a holo representation of Lorelei and motioned for Tsuchevsky and Kthaara to join them.

"Look here: the fortresses are heavily concentrated at the warp point connecting with this system, and I doubt if that's changed since these data were current. And that's bound to be where most of their mobile forces will concentrate after they're through running. After all"—he changed the display to a warp line schematic—"that's our most direct line of advance on Thebes itself. So they expect us to advance directly from here to Lorelei.

"But," he continued, maneuvering a floating cursor, "there is an alternate route to Lorelei: through this system's third warp point to Sandhurst, then to New New Hebrides—stupid name!—then to Alfred, and finally to Lorelei, through"—he reactivated the display of Lorelei—"*this* warp point, which is naturally the least heavily defended."

Kthaara looked skeptical. "But, Admiral, the delay . . ." he began. The direct approach was programmed into his genes.

"But," Tsuchevsky cut in, "think of the advantages. There are colonies in Alfred and New New Hebrides, and also in Danzig, whose only warp access is through Sandhurst. We'll be able to liberate those populations all the sooner."

"Eh?" Antonov looked up absently. "Oh, of course, Pasha. To be sure. But," he continued, his voice gaining in enthusiasm, "the point is that we'll force the Thebans to shift their defenses in Lorelei to meet a new threat, spreading their forces thinner. Remember, they won't be able to weaken the defenses of the Parsifal warp point too much; for all they'll know, the whole operation is a feint."

And so it was decided. Leaving a sufficient force in Parsifal to keep the Thebans guessing, the main strength of Second Fleet would advance through the Sandhurst warp point as soon as battle damage could be repaired and munitions replaced.

The human warships departed, moving onward to prepare for the next assault. In their wakes, the wreckage continued to drift, eventually dispersing by random motion into the infinite gulf between the stars, leaving nothing to show the battle had ever taken place.

CHAPTER TWENTY

Complications

The warp point at the Sandhurst end of the Parsifal-Sandhurst warp line lay nearly six light-hours from Sandhurst's orange-yellow G8 primary, which barely showed as a first-magnitude star at such a distance. It seemed even further to Ivan Antonov.

He'd been impatient enough after the numerous delays in repairing the ships damaged in the brutal Parsifal slugfest. Now, with the weak orbital fortresses that had guarded the warp point reduced to cosmic detritus and his fleet proceeding on a hyperbolic course toward the New New Hebrides warp point on the far side of the local sun, the less than 0.06 C his battle-line must maintain seemed excruciatingly slow.

Berenson was luckier, he brooded. The rear admiral led the faster screening force well in advance of the main body: battle-cruisers and heavy cruisers, sweeping ahead of the light carriers and their escorts. Fortunately, Sandhurst's third planet—a gas giant nearly massive enough to be a self-luminous "brown dwarf"—wasn't presently in such an orbital position as to complicate astrogational problems. And the asteroid belt it had created wasn't quite on the fleet's course and presented no hazards.

He tried to shake loose from his mood. *Stop being such an old woman, Ivan Nikolayevich!* There was no sign of mobile forces in the system; they must still be sitting in Lorelei, awaiting a direct attack from Parsifal. They'd shit in their pants—or whatever Thebans did— when the pickets at the Sandhurst-New New Hebrides warp point fled to Lorelei with the news. The absence of any opposition beyond the few fortresses was a clear indication he'd taken them completely by surprise, and if any mobile units were foolish enough to advance from Lorelei in the face of his fighters, his wide-ranging scout ships—already crossing the far edge of the asteroid belt ahead of Berenson's screen—would detect them and give him plenty of time to bring his fleet to general quarters.

Still, as he watched the lights on his display representing Berenson's ships approach the inner fringes of the asteroid belt in the scouts' wakes, he couldn't rid himself of a nagging worry—a feeling there was something he should have remembered.

Then it came to him.

Second Admiral Jahanak also watched a display, this one a holo sphere aboard the battle-cruiser *Arbela*, but his showed more than Antonov's. It showed the Theban ships concealed in this cluster of asteroids, not far from the New New Hebrides warp point.

He forced himself to relax. Things had been . . . difficult since his retreat from Parsifal. The Synod, merely restive before, was now in an ugly mood. His explanations that he'd never really wanted to fight so far forward were beginning to wear as thin with the panicky prelates as his references to his grandsire.

The situation had its compensations, though. He'd been able to argue that the forces sitting in the Manticore System watching the smaller infidel fleet in Griffin

were more needed to defend Lorelei, so at least there
were some reinforcements. Those, and the few captured
infidel carriers which were even now being converted to
bear Holy Terra's first operational fighter squadrons, let
him feel secure at last about holding Lorelei and gave
him enough freedom to search for an action to satisfy
the Synod's constant, hectoring demands that he Do
Something. But what?

The infidel's unexpected failure to stick their heads
into the trap of Lorelei's fortresses and fleet units from
Parsifal had suggested one possibility. Could it be they
meant to take the Sandhurst-New New Hebrides-Alfred
route instead? The notion contradicted their own tactical
manuals' insistence on following the shortest possible
route wherever possible, but whoever was commanding
the infidel forces seemed not to have read those manuals,
judging from his earlier tactics.

And if they *were* taking the longer route, it would be
as well to at least try to reduce their carrier strength
along the way. If they weren't, a strong force at Sandhurst would be well-placed to slice in behind any force
that might depart Parsifal for Lorelei.

Thus it was Jahanak had led his battle-cruisers and an
escorting force of lighter units to Sandhurst, where he'd
discovered this asteroid cluster. (Contrary to the mental
picture many have, asteroids are sparse in asteroid belts.
Yes, there are millions of them, but only where they
cluster do conditions even approach those depicted in
popular entertainment.) Fleet Chaplain Hinam had been
upset by his decision not to support the warp point fortifications, but the cluster had been decisive. It was big
enough to conceal his entire force in a volume of space
small enough for light-speed command and control to be
practical, and close enough to the New New Hebrides
warp point for him to strike and run. Besides, sacrificing
the fortresses might even convince the infidel commander that his strategy of misdirection had worked.

Now, looking into *Arbela's* holo sphere, he knew Holy
Terra was with him. The infidel carriers that were his

target had crossed the system to him, escorted by nothing heavier than destroyers, and were proceeding well behind the screen of cruisers. And the main infidel strength lumbered along too far in the rear to affect the outcome of the kind of battle he meant to fight.

"Second Admiral," Captain Yurah, who'd assumed command of *Arbela* (Jahanak had enough problems without having to break in a new flag captain) indicated the holo sphere, where the enemy cruisers were already receding from the asteroids, "the infidel carriers are nearing the closest approach to which their course will bring them."

Jahanak nodded. He wanted those carriers very badly. Of course, he had no way of knowing which of them carried the new cloaking device as they swept along at normal readiness. But if he could close with them before they could engage it, surely his sensor crews, working at short range and knowing the locations and vectors of what they were looking for, could penetrate it. The Satan-Khan-spawned thing wasn't magic, whatever they were saying on the lower decks!

He glanced sideways at Hinam as his thoughts reminded him of his fleet's morale problems. The fleet chaplain sat slumped in the listless posture which had become habitual for him since the battle of QR-107. He hadn't been giving much trouble lately—even his protests against leaving the fortresses unsupported had been halfhearted and *pro forma*—but he hadn't been much help, either. And the enlisted spacers had never needed spiritual reinforcement as much as they did now. Well, perhaps Hinam could be roused from his torpor.

"Holiness," he said briskly, "we'll be attacking momentarily. Do you wish to speak to the crews?" He glanced at Yurah to confirm that the fleet's com net was clear of any vital tactical data. The whisker lasers were virtually undetectable but could bottleneck communications badly. The flag captain checked his status board and nodded, and Jahanak indicated the fleet chaplain's communications console. Terra! Who would have believed he would ever have *wanted* Hinam to open his mouth?

The fleet chaplain stirred sluggishly, a faded memory of the old fire flickering in his eyes. He leaned forward, pressing the com button and hunching over the pickup, and spoke in the low, rasping voice which had replaced his one-time certitude.

"Warriors of Holy Terra," he began, "the infidels have been delivered into your hand at last. Their victories from Redwing to Parsifal and the Satan-Khan's unclean influence may fill them with false confidence, but they are empty as the wind before those filled by the Faith."

He paused as if for breath, and his eyes burned brighter. His voice was stronger, more resonant, when he resumed.

"Warriors of Holy Terra, we know—even as the ancient *samurai* who served Mother Terra in the days of the Angel Saint-Just—that death is lighter than a feather but duty to Her is as a mountain. Brace yourselves to bear that weight, knowing that She will give you of Her own holy strength in Her service! Even now Her foes approach the Furnace She has prepared for them, and you have been honored by Her trust, for it is to you She turns to thrust them into the purifying Fire! Gird your loins, Warriors of Holy Terra! Set your hands upon the hilt of Holy Terra's Sword, for the time is come to drive it home at last! The Jihad calls us! Advance, knowing that victory awaits!"

Hinam thundered his final words into the pickup with all the old fire, all the old faith, and his eyes blazed like yellow beacons as he released the button and leaned back in his chair.

"Thank you, Holiness," Jahanak murmured. "Your words have been an inspiration to us all." *At least I hope they'll do some good.* He frowned at the sphere as the infidel carriers reached the predetermined closest point on their course past *Arbela* and her consorts.

"Captain Yurah," he said more crisply, "begin the attack."

The order was passed, and he sat back with a sigh. Yes, it would be good to repay the infidels in their own coin, springing the same sort of trap they'd sprung on Lantu at . . .

. . . *Redwing!* It was like an explosion in Antonov's brain.

"Captain Chen!" he shouted at his flag captain. "Sound general quarters! And have communications raise Admiral Berenson. Tell him—"

It was too late. Even as he spoke, input was automatically downloaded to the silicon-based idiot savant that controlled his display, and the red lights of hostiles sprang into life, sweeping out of the asteroid belt and into energy-weapons range of the light carriers seventy-five light-seconds in the wake of Berenson's cruiser screen.

Berenson had already seen it—his scanners suffered from little time lag here as the Thebans erupted into his carriers at what passed for knife-range in space combat. Furiously, he ordered his command to general quarters and began to bring his ships about. But even with reactionless drives, a complete course reversal took time. Too much time, and he watched, nauseated, while the Thebans savaged the virtually unarmed carriers that frantically tried to launch as many of their fighters as possible.

"Admiral," Tsuchevsky's voice was harsh, "the Thebans seem to have their entire battle-cruiser strength here, with escorts. They're still concentrating on what's left of our light carriers, but they've managed to slip between them and the cruisers. They're forcing the carriers away from the screen. Admiral Berenson is cutting the angle and closing, but he still hasn't been able to bring his battle-cruisers into capital missile range. The fleet carriers have gone into cloaking mode, and are advancing at maximum speed, as per your orders."

Antonov nodded absently. Thank God he'd kept the

big carriers with the battle-line! It occurred to him that
the Thebans had never seen his fleet carriers; they probably thought the ships with the mysterious cloaking ability
were among the light carriers in the van, which would
help account for their single-minded pursuit of those vessels. And they'd cleverly positioned themselves close
enough to the New New Hebrides warp point to get
away before his battle-line—slower than their slowest
ship—could close to effective missile range. Or what they
thought was effective missile range. . . .

"Order the fleet carriers to come as close as they can
to the egress warp point. They can get fairly close to the
battle—the Thebans won't be scanning open space for
them. They're to launch all fighters as soon as the Thebans start to break off the engagement. And no, Kthaara,
there's no time to get you aboard one of them!" He
smiled grimly. "Our options appear to have narrowed.
We can no longer concern ourselves with concealing the
full capabilities of the SBMs. Signal Admiral Berenson
that he is authorized to use them at their maximum
range."

The order went out, and at effectively the same instant
as Berenson's acknowledgment was received, the scanners showed the strategic bombardment missiles speed-
ing from his battle-cruisers toward targets at their full
range of twenty light-seconds.

Jahanak cursed as his ships began to report hits by
missiles launched by the infidel battle-cruisers from beyond capital missile range. There weren't enough of
them, and the range was too extreme, for them to do
catastrophic physical damage. Their damage to his calcu-
lations was something else again. If mere battle-cruisers
had this new weapon (*another* new weapon!) he had to
assume the oncoming battle-line also had it, and in far
greater numbers. And that meant his estimate of how
soon that battle-line would become a factor had suddenly
become *very* suspect.

Even more unsettling was the failure of any of the

light carriers to fade out of his sensors' ken. Five of them had already been destroyed; surely the survivors would go into cloak when the alternative was destruction—*if they could*. Clearly, the ones with the cloaking capability were elsewhere. But where?

"Captain Yurah, the fleet will disengage and retire to New New Hebrides!"

The few fighters the light carriers had managed to launch had already shot their bolt; they wouldn't be able to mount an effective pursuit. And passing the infidel battle-cruisers at energy-weapons range held no terror. There was no indication from the intelligence analyses of the Battle of Parsifal that anything lighter than a battle-ship had been fitted with the new heterodyne-effect lasers, and if the infidel screen cared to exchange energy fire with his beam-heavy *Manzikert*-class battle-cruisers, it would be their last mistake. It was more than slightly infuriating to have sprung his trap so successfully and still fail to destroy the carriers he'd sought, but his ships *had* shattered the infidels' light carriers. Even as he watched his display, another carrier's light dot vanished, and most of those which survived would require lengthy repairs. Even if total success had eluded him, he'd still struck a weighty blow.

But then he glanced at Hinam. The fleet chaplain had sunk into his earlier lassitude, and suddenly, unbidden, there came to Jahanak the shades of a kindly cleric who'd taught him the grand old tales in his childhood, and another who'd been there when the first child of his young adulthood died in infancy. He reached out and laid a four-fingered hand on the fleet chaplain's arm.

"We haven't been defeated, Holiness," he said with unwonted gentleness. "We've inflicted crippling casualties on the infidel light carriers in return for trifling losses. Now we must retire, as we'd planned to do." And why, he wondered, should a simple statement of truth not *sound* like the truth? Were words tainted by use as rationalization, even as a whore was forever tainted despite a subsequent lifetime of virtue? Of course, came the unwanted thought, that analogy suggested it was people, not words, that became tainted, but . . .

The question became academic for Jahanak when hundreds of infidel fighters swept out of nowhere and streaked through space toward the blind zones of his retreating starships.

By the time Antonov's battle-line came within energy range, there was little for it to do besides help recover fighters whose light-carrier bases no longer existed. Of the eleven carriers Berenson had once commanded, only four remained, and all but one of the survivors were badly mauled. Nor, despite the SBM and its cloaked fleet carriers, had Second Fleet repaid the Thebans with proportionate damage. For the first time since Redwing, the enemy had scored a clear and punishing success, and it hurt all the more after the Federation's string of victories.

True, the fleet carriers' fighter squadrons had exacted a terrible revenge, but they'd had to break through the escorts before they could even reach the battle-cruisers, and there hadn't been time to rearm after their first strike and make it decisive. Berenson's screen had also wrought havoc, but his lack of hetlasers had forced him to remain at missile range. Again, his blows, though vicious, hadn't been decisive. The enemy heavy cruisers and escorts had paid dearly, but most of the battle-cruisers had escaped, though many trailed atmosphere as they vanished into the warp point, leaving a victorious but shaken Federation fleet in undisputed possession.

Kthaara, watching discreetly on *Gosainthan*'s flag bridge as Antonov and Berenson carried on a conversation that could now be conducted without annoying time lags, reflected anew on the impossibility of really grasping subtleties of expression in a race so very alien. It was as if *both* admirals were savoring the unaccustomed sensation of feeling crestfallen. Antonov, in particular, was as close to seeming awkward as the Orion had ever seen him.

"Well, Admiral Berenson," the bear-like Fleet Admiral

rumbled, "it would appear this route to Lorelei involves
. . . unanticipated complications." He looked like he'd
bitten into a bad pickle. "It would also seem that we are
not quite so free to decide when and where to commit
new weapon systems as we—as *I*—may have supposed."

"So it would seem, sir." For just an instant, Berenson's
face unmistakably wore the expression Kthaara had
learned to recognize as meaning "I told you so!" But only
for an instant. "I suspect we may all have been guilty of
cockiness—of underestimating the Thebans."

"Yes." Antonov nodded grimly. "But *never again*! To
begin, we mustn't assume there are no surprises waiting
in Danzig. We don't know what the Thebans may have
left behind there, so we can't leave it in our rear, unin-
vestigated. I'd hoped to seal it off and let its occupying
force wither on the vine, but much as I'd like to push on
immediately to New New Hebrides before the Theban
survivors can reorganize themselves there, we will first
proceed to the Danzig warp point and send a scouting
force through. After taking *all* precautions against a
counterattack!"

"Agreed, sir," Berenson said. "Shall I detail the
scouts?"

"If you would," Antonov replied. "I'll be attaching the
fleet carriers to support you. The battle-line will leave a
covering force for the New New Hebrides warp point
and follow your screen." He smiled grimly. "If anything
comes out of that warp point, Admiral, it won't be going
back into it again."

"Absolutely, sir," Berenson said. And, for the first time
in Kthaara's memory, the two admirals smiled at one
another.

CHAPTER TWENTY-ONE

Without Authorization

Hannah Avram sat on her flag bridge, scanning the latest shipyard report, and marveled yet again at the change the past dreadful months had wrought in Richard Hazelwood. The uncharitable might argue, she supposed, that his complete loss of support from the planetary government had left him no choice but to join her own team, but Hannah thought differently. He'd been sullen and uncooperative for a month or so after what President Wyszynski persisted in referring to as her *coup d'etat*, but he'd seemed to come alive after Danzig's defenders smashed the first Theban probe of the system without losing a single ship.

They'd done almost as well against the second, but they'd paid to stop the third. She glanced around her bridge with a familiar stab of anguish. She'd made too many mistakes the third time, starting with her hesitation in opening fire. The assault had been led by *Kongo*-class battle-cruisers, undoubtedly (in retrospect) captured at Lorelei, and the sudden appearance of Terran ships had

confused her just too long. They'd gotten off their initial
salvos while she was still convincing herself they weren't
a relief force.

Worse, she should have realized the Thebans would
develop their own capital missiles. She hadn't, and the
heavy external ordnance salvos of those leading ships had
blown her beloved *Dunkerque* apart. *Kirov* had survived,
though badly damaged, and *Dunkerque's* casualties had
been mercifully light—over two-thirds of her crew had
survived—but her ship's destruction had been agony . . .
and it had been Dick Hazelwood, of all people, who'd
helped her put it into its proper perspective.

She still remembered Maguire's astonished expression
when Hazelwood chewed her out—respectfully, but
without a ghost of his old wimpiness. She'd been hag-
ridden with guilt for having hesitated, and for having
decided against building additional capital missile-armed
units as a first priority. That decision had left *Dunkerque*
and *Kirov* to fight alone against the Thebans' initial long-
ranged salvos as their battle-cruisers squatted atop the
warp point, and her confident assumption of a monopoly
on capital missile technology meant she'd loaded her own
XO racks solely with offensive weapons.

She hadn't included any EDMs in her external loads,
and that had sealed *Dunkerque's* fate. The enhanced
drive missiles created extensions of a starship's drive
field, interposing those false drive fields to fool incoming
missiles' proximity fuses into premature detonation . . .
and there hadn't been any. She'd skimped on them,
"knowing" her battle-cruisers were beyond reach of any
Theban weapon and desperate to throw the heaviest initial salvos she could. And so her ships had been shattered
before their shorter-ranged consorts could close to effective range and the forts could come fully on-line, and
her own survival had seemed an utterly inadequate
compensation.

But Hazelwood had seen more clearly than she. He'd
accepted that she'd made mistakes, but it had also been
he who pointed out that her insistence on reinforcing the

minefields had been decisive. Danzig's minelayers had more than quadrupled the original density of the fields, and though no one could emplace mines directly atop an open warp point, where they would be sucked in and destroyed by the point's gravity stresses, their strength had prevented the Thebans from advancing in-system. Penned up on top of the warp point, they'd been unable to employ effective evasive maneuvering, and their concentration on her battle-cruisers had given the forts time to bring their own weapons—and defenses—to full readiness. The result had been the destruction of eight Theban battle-cruisers, four heavy cruisers, and six light cruisers in return for *Dunkerque*, *Atago*, three destroyers, and heavy damage to *Kirov* and two of the forts. And that, as Commodore Richard Hazelwood had finished acidly, was a victory by anyone's standards!

He'd been right, of course, and Hannah was grateful for his support. Just as she was grateful for the way he'd torn into his duties as her construction manager. He should, she thought, have been assigned to BuShips instead of Fortress Command from the beginning, for he certainly seemed to have found his niche, and he'd taken a far from hidden satisfaction in cracking the whip over Victor Tokarov and friends. His personal familiarity with the Danzig System's economic and industrial sectors told him where all the bodies were buried, and he'd exhumed the ones most useful to her with positive glee. Indeed, to her considerable surprise, she and Dick Hazelwood had become friends—a possibility she would flatly have denied when she first met him.

She turned her attention back to her screen, finishing his latest report. Her new flagship, the battle-cruiser *Haruna*, and her sisters *Hiei*, *Repulse*, and *Alaska*, were the largest units the Danzig yards had yet produced. When her fourth sister, *Von der Tann*, was commissioned next month, they and *Kirov* would give her a solid core of capital missile ships. She wished they had some true battle-line units with proper energy armaments—each Theban attack had been more powerful than the last, and she was acutely nervous over what they might come up with next—but there were limits to her resources. Committing so much of her limited yard space to the battle-cruisers was risky enough, and about as far as she could go.

At least she'd managed to build an impressive number of lighter units to support them. It could hardly be called a balanced fleet, but there was only one possible warp point to defend, and her "light forces" packed a hell of a defensive wallop. There were over thirty destroyers, uncompromisingly armed for close combat, with far lighter shields and far heavier armor than BuShips would have tolerated before meeting Theban lasers. And backing them were the real reason she'd come to think Hazelwood had missed his calling in Fortress Command: fourteen *Sand Fly*-class carriers built to his personal specifications.

They weren't the fleet or even light carriers of Battle Fleet, but tiny things, no larger than destroyers and thus suitable for rapid production. Their strikegroups were smaller than an *Essex*-class light carrier, but they were as big as the old *Pegasus* class, and they'd had time— thank God!—to bring their training up to standard. With the handful of local defense fighter pilots as a nucleus, they'd expanded their fighter strength at breakneck speed, and Danny Maguire had found a way to maximize their available flight decks by borrowing from the Rigelian Protectorate's ISW-3 tactics. Hannah had over three hundred fighters based on Danzig, the orbital forts, and a clutch of scarcely mobile barges. If battle was joined, she'd use the old Rigelian shuttle technique, staging them through her small carriers to strike the enemy. It was going to require some fancy coordination, but the exercises had been encouraging.

She sighed, closed the report file, and leaned back in her chair, running her fingers through her hair. With Dick to run the yards, Captain Tinker to run Sky Watch, and Bill Yan to deputize as her fleet commander, she'd been able to turn to the political side of her "Governor" role. She'd been lucky there, too. Commander Richenda Bandaranaike had proved a stellar legal gymnast, as devious as she was brilliant, and half of Hannah's civilian duties consisted of little more than confirming her recommendations. It had been a chastening experience for Wyszynski and Tokarov to confront Richenda's implacable ability to do whatever the governor wanted and then find some perfectly plausible legal justification for it.

The hardest part, as she'd feared from the beginning, was manpower. Danzig's population wasn't all that big, and manning and supporting her steadily growing naval force had strained it badly, but she'd been pleasantly surprised by the locals' response. Tokarov money or no, the old, defeatist planetary government was going to find the next election a painful experience, she thought gleefully. Wyszynski continued to cooperate as grudgingly as possible, beginning every discussion with a protest of her "patently illegal usurpation" of authority, but Danzig's citizens clearly disagreed. She hadn't even had to resort to conscription; volunteers had come forward in numbers too great for her limited training facilities to handle.

She stretched and checked the chronometer, then grinned tiredly and punched for another cup of coffee. It was late, and however capable her support team, there were never enough hours for everything. Assuming full responsibility for the political and military governance of an entire star system was even more wearing than she'd anticipated. Sometimes she almost hoped the Admiralty and Assembly *would* disapprove her actions. Once they cashiered her, she might actually get to sleep for six hours in a row!

Her steward appeared with the coffee as she turned to the next endless report, and she sipped gratefully. God, she was tired. And—

She jerked upright, cursing as coffee sloshed over her tunic. The shrill, teeth-grating atonality of the alarm blasted through her, and she shoved her reader display viciously aside, jerking her chair around to face Battle Plot.

The light codes of her own units flickered and changed as they rushed to general quarters with gratifying speed, but her attention was on the dots emerging from the Sandhurst warp point. Just as the last Theban attack had included those damned *Kongos*, the six lead ships of this attack were obviously more prizes. CIC identified them as *Shark*-class destroyers, and Hannah's lips twisted in a snarl. *Not this time, you bastards!*

"Dan! Switch the mines to manual over-ride!" If the Thebans had managed to put their prizes' IFF gear back into commission, the mines wouldn't attack without specific commands to do so.

"Aye aye, sir. Switching now."

"If they stay out of the mines, we'll take them with missiles. No point losing fighters or taking damage by closing into their shipboard range."

"Understood, sir." Maguire studied his own console for a moment. "We've got a good set-up, sir."

"Then open fire," Hannah said softly.

Captain Georgette Meuller, CO of Destroyer Squadron Nineteen, stared at her display in disbelief. Like every other member of DesRon 19, she'd entered the Danzig warp point expecting to die. Oh, there was always a chance of catching the defenders so totally off guard they could run before they were engaged . . . but not much of one. And unless they did, there was no way any of them were getting back to Sandhurst alive. Yet she'd understood why they had to go. But this—!

There were dozens of ships out there . . . and they were all *Terran*! Even the forts were still intact! It was impossible. Danzig had been cut off for twenty-five standard months, and there'd only been a half-dozen tin-cans to support the forts before the war. Where in God's name had they all *come* from?

"Sir!" Her senior scan rating's voice snatched her from her thoughts. "Those battle-cruisers have locked on their targeting systems!"

Georgette swung towards her com section.

"Raise their CO for me—quickly! Send in clear!"

Her communications officer didn't bother to reply—
she was already stabbing keys as the scan rating paled.

"They're *launching!*"

"First salvo away," Commander Maguire reported
tensely. "Impact in twenty-five seconds."

Hannah grunted, watching her display narrowly. *You
bastards are dead. You should've known better than to
send tin-cans through without support. Were you that
sure you could sucker me again?*

"Sir!" It was her communications officer. "I'm receiving an emergency hail!"

Hannah nodded. The Thebans had already demonstrated their ability to masquerade as humans over the
com, and if they could confuse the defenders, even if
only long enough to complete their scans and send
back courier drones with exact data on the defenses,
the advantage for their follow-on echelons would be
incalculable.

"What sort of hail?" she asked almost incuriously.

"They say they're Terrans, sir. It's from a Captain
Meuller."

"*What?!*" Hannah leapt from her command chair and
vaulted Maguire's console like a champion low-hurdler.
She landed beside the com officer, grabbing his small
screen and wrenching it around to stare at the face of
her best friend from the Academy.

Georgette Meuller watched the missiles tearing down
on her command. There wasn't time. Not to convince
whoever had fired them they were friendly units. She
and her people were going to die after all.

"Stand by point defense!" she said harshly, knowing it
was futile. Laser clusters trained onto the hurricane of
destruction streaking towards her, and she bit her lip. A
handful of capital missiles vanished in the fireball inter-
cepts of defensive missiles, but not enough to make any

difference at all, and she tightened internally as the lasers began to fire.

And then, with the lead missile less than ninety kilometers from impact, the visual displays polarized in a tremendous glare of eye-tearing light as more than eighty capital missiles self-destructed as one.

Haruna's cutter completed its docking maneuvers, the hatch slid open, and a tall, slender woman in the uniform of a commodore stepped through it. The bosun's pipe shrilled and the sideboys snapped to attention as Hannah Avram saluted the flag on the boat bay bulkhead, then turned to salute the stocky captain who awaited her. She'd never met Pavel Tsuchevsky, but they'd spoken over the com when he received her formal reports for his admiral. Now, as their hands fell from their salutes, her sinking sensation returned. The fact that Admiral Antonov hadn't come to greet her, coupled with his silence since receiving those same reports, was ominous.

"Commodore Avram." Tsuchevsky's voice was carefully neutral. "Admiral Antonov would appreciate your joining him in his staff briefing room. If you'll accompany me, please?"

Hannah nodded and fell in beside him, schooling her features into calmness and biting off her burning desire to ask questions. The answers would come soon enough— possibly *too* soon—but she was damned if she'd let anyone guess how anxious she was.

The intraship car deposited them outside the briefing room, and Tsuchevsky stood courteously aside to let her enter first. At least they were going to let her go on pretending to be a commodore until the axe fell. She'd never met Admiral Antonov, either, but from his reputation he was probably looking forward to chopping her off at the ankles in person.

Ivan Antonov looked up, face hard, as she stopped before the conference table, cap under her arm.

"Commodore Avram, reporting as ordered, sir," she said crisply, and he nodded. For the first time in two years, she was acutely aware of the insignia she wore as the admiral studied her coldly. He sat at the table, square-shouldered and unyielding, flanked by a dark-faced female commander and—Hannah just barely avoided a double-take—an *Orion*?

She wrenched her attention back from the Tabby and stood tautly at attention, wondering what Antonov had made of her reports. The complete lack of explanations which had accompanied his orders to rendezvous with *Gosainthan* in Sandhurst suggested one very unpleasant possibility. He was known for his own willingness to break the rules, but also for his ruthlessness, and as she faced him in silence she knew exactly why people called him "Ivan the Terrible."

" 'Commodore,' " his voice was a frigid, subterranean rumble, "do you realize how close you came to killing twelve hundred Fleet personnel?"

"Yes, sir." She locked her eyes on the bulkhead above his head.

"It might be wise," he continued coldly, "to double-check your target identification in future."

"Yes, sir," she said again when he paused. What else could she say? It was grossly unfair—especially after the Thebans had mousetrapped her once before in just that way—but perhaps it was understandable. And she still felt nauseated at how close she'd come to killing Georgette's entire squadron.

"I suppose, however," Antonov went on stonily, "that we might overlook that in this instance. I, after all, had not considered the possibility that there might not be Thebans on *your* side of the warp point, either. Had I done so, I might have sent through courier drones instead of destroyers, and this entire unfortunate affair might never have risen."

"Yes, sir," she said again.

"So," he said, "let us turn our attention instead to your other actions. It was, I trust you will admit, somewhat irregular of you to supplant another Fleet officer senior to you? But, then, you never bothered to inform him he *was* senior, did you?" Hannah said nothing, and the flint-faced admiral smiled thinly. "Then there were your fascinating, one might almost say precedent-shattering, interpretations of constitutional law. Your legal officer must be most ingenious."

"Sir, I take full responsibility. Commander Bandaranaike acted solely within the limits of my direct orders."

"I see. And is the same true of the Fleet and Marine personnel who assisted you in forcibly supplanting the planetary government? A planetary government, I might add, which has already requested your immediate court martial for mutiny, treason, insubordination, misappropriation of private property, and everything else short of littering?"

"Yes, sir," Hannah said yet again. "My personnel acted in accordance with my orders, sir, believing I had the authority to give those orders."

"Do you seriously expect me to believe, 'Commodore,' that none of your officers, none of your personnel, ever even suspected you were acting in clear excess of your legitimate authority? That *no one* under your command knew Commodore Hazelwood, in fact, outranked you?"

"Sir, they knew only that—" Hannah broke off and bit her lip, then spoke very, very carefully. "Admiral Antonov, at no time did I inform any of my personnel of the actual circumstances under which I was breveted to commodore. Under the circumstances, none of my officers had any reason to question my authority to act as I acted. I cannot speak to their inner thoughts, sir; I can only say they acted at all times in accordance with regulations and proper military discipline given the situation as it was known to them. And, sir, whatever your own or the Admiralty's final judgment as to my own behavior, I believe any fair evaluation of my subordinates' actions must find them to have been beyond reproach."

"I appreciate your attempt to protect them, 'Commodore,'" Antonov said coldly, "but it is inconceivable to me that not even the members of your staff were aware of the true facts and that you were, in fact, acting entirely on your own initiative without authorization from any higher authority." Hannah stiffened in dismay, and her eyes dropped to his bearded face once more. Dropped and widened as that stony visage creased in a wide, gleaming smile that squeezed his eyes almost into invisibility.

"Which means, *Rear Admiral* Avram," he rumbled, "that they are to be commended for recognizing the voice of sanity when they heard it. Well done, Admiral. Very well done, indeed!"

And his huge, hairy paw enveloped her slim hand in a bone-crushing grip of congratulation.

CHAPTER TWENTY-TWO
Knight Takes Queen

Angus MacRory's stomach rumbled resentfully as he waded through the cold mist, cursing softly and monotonously. The fog offered concealment from Shellhead recon systems, but its dripping moisture made the mud-slick trail doubly treacherous, and his next meal was ten hours overdue.

Caitrin skidded ahead of him, and he bit his lip anxiously as she caught herself and slogged wearily on. That was another worry, and he scrubbed sweat and mist irritably from his face.

New Hebrides had slipped into winter, and the Fleet had not returned. Prisoner interrogations said the Shellhead navy was in a bad way, but unless the Federation got back to New Hebrides soon, there would be no Resistance to greet it.

Angus cursed again, telling himself that was his empty belly talking. Yet he knew better. Admiral Lantu was finally winning, and the weather was helping him do it.

New Hebrides' F7 sun was hot but almost eighteen

light-minutes away, which gave the planet a year half again as long as Old Terra's neighbor Mars and cool average temperatures. Its slight axial tilt and vast oceans moderated its seasons considerably, but winter was a time of fogs and rainy gales. There was little snow or ice, yet the humid cold could be numbing, both physically and mentally. Worse, the titanic banner oaks were deciduous. Their foliage had all but vanished, and that, coupled with the colder temperatures, left the guerrillas far more vulnerable to thermal detection.

Yet Angus knew Lantu's success rested on more than the weather. The Shellhead admiral had already crushed the Resistance on Scotia, and now he was doing the same thing on Hibernia. He'd get to Aberdeen soon enough.

The first bad sign had been forced-labor logging parties assigned to clear fire zones around the Shellhead bases. Then they'd moved on, chopping away under their guards' weapons to cut wide lanes along the frontiers of the OZs. Angus hadn't worried at first; it was a tremendous task, and the Shellheads had little heavy equipment to spare for it. But then the shipments of defoliant arrived from Thebes, and the vertols swept back and forth along the frontiers, killing back the leaves.

The lanes could still be crossed, but at greater peril and a higher cost. About one in nine of his teams was being caught, and that was a casualty rate he could not long endure.

But that was only the first sign. The second was a redeployment of reaction forces to cover larger sectors—an arrangement the cleared lanes made workable. He'd wondered what Lantu meant to do with the troops he'd freed up, but only till the admiral transferred them all to Scotia, doubling his troop strength on that continent, and opened a general offensive. With the additional vertols and troops, extra scan sats, and defoliated kill zones, he'd pushed the Scotians hard, picking off their base camps one by one. Perhaps a quarter of them had escaped to Aberdeen; the rest were gone. Angus hoped some had managed to go to ground, but their casualties had been wicked.

And now, with the onset of winter, his own Base One had been spotted and destroyed. The SAM teams had cost the Shellheads some aircraft, and casualties had been mercifully light, but he'd lost a tremendous quantity of priceless equipment. Another strike had taken out Base Three, but his spotter network had spied that force on its way in. Most of his equipment and all his people had gotten away that time.

But he couldn't last forever. In the beginning, it had been the Shellheads who'd had to be lucky every time to stop him; now it was his turn. Lantu's relentless, precise attacks made the most of his material superiority, and Angus had learned the admiral was not inclined to do things by halves.

"Scratch one guerrilla camp, First Admiral," Colonel Fraymak crossed to the map and stuck a pin into the Hibernian mountains. "Strike recon says we got thirty percent of their on-site personnel and most of their equipment. Prisoner interrogation says we may have gotten Claiborne."

"Ah?" Lantu rubbed his cranial carapace. Duncan Claiborne was the Angus MacRory of Hibernia. If Fraymak's attack had, indeed, killed him, the Hibernian guerrillas would be in serious disarray.

"Yes, sir." Fraymak laid his helmet aside and frowned at the map, running a finger across the mountains. "Can we move the scan sats down this way? They didn't manage to burn all their records before we got to them, and there are indications of something fairly important down here."

"I suppose we could." Lantu moved to stand beside him. "Or there's a destroyer temporarily in orbit; I could swing her down to cover it."

"In that case, I think we can give you another camp this week, First Admiral. Maybe even wind up the Hibernian operation by the end of the month."

"Outstanding." Lantu tried to sound as if he really meant it, and the stubbornly professional side of him did. There was a grim satisfaction in the way his successes discredited Huark's bloody excuse for a strategy, but there was a deadness in his soul. As if none of it really mattered anymore.

He'd begun avoiding Manak. He knew it hurt the old man, but the fleet chaplain knew him too well. Manak's own faith might be hardening into a desperate conviction capable of ignoring the reality of impending defeat, yet he could hardly fail to spot the admiral's steady spiritual rot.

Not for the first time, Lantu cursed the stubborn streak in his own soul, for there was such a thing as too much integrity. If he could only have left well enough alone, he might not face these agonizing doubts. Might not have to worry that *he* might fall prey to the Inquisition.

Yet he was what he was, and he could no more have stopped himself than he could let his fleet die at Redwing. He'd been careful enough no one suspected—he hoped—but he'd delved deeply into the New Hebridan libraries and data base. He'd compared the Federation's version of history to that of the Church and found . . . divergences. Inconsistencies.

Lies.

And try as he might, he could not convince himself it was the humans who'd lied to him.

Caitrin's face was worn as she tossed another branch onto the fire. Then she leaned back against the cave wall, and Angus tightened his arm around her, trying to comfort without revealing his own anxiety. She would never admit exhaustion or fear, but he felt them sapping her inner strength like poison, and his hand brushed her ribs, then darted away from the slight swelling of her belly.

It was too much, he thought bitterly. A guerrilla war and pregnancy were just too much, and he cursed himself as the cause of it.

"Stop that." She caught his wrist and pressed his hand to the small bulge of their child. "I had a little something to do with it, too."

"Aye, but—"

"No 'buts'! It wouldn't have happened if I'd remembered my implant was running out—and if I weren't such a stubborn bitch, I'd have had it aborted."

Angus's arm tightened, and she pressed her face into his shoulder in silent apology. He would have understood an abortion—he'd spent seven years off-planet—but New Hebridans were colonials, not Innerworlders. Babies were precious to them in a way that went beyond logic, yet he knew Caitrin's decision went even deeper. She was determined to keep their child because it was part of *him*, and if the Shellheads caught up with him, she wanted that bit of him to remember and love.

He made himself loosen his embrace as Tulloch scooted into the cave.

"All under cover," he said tiredly, and Angus nodded. "We mun make better time tomorrow."

"Aye." Tulloch glanced at Caitrin from the corner of one eye, then shook himself. "Weel, I'm off tae set the sentries."

He vanished, and Angus frowned into the fire.

"I've been thinkin'," he said slowly. "'Tis but a matter o' time—and no sae much of it—afore the Shellies move back tae Aberdeen, Katie."

"I know," she said tiredly.

"Weel, then, 'twould be as well tae set up fall-backs now."

"Where?"

"Doon south. The weather's no sae cold, and we'd have better cover."

"That makes sense."

"Aye, sae I ken. But 'twill need one of us tae see tae it."

He felt her stiffen and stared steadfastly into the flames, refusing to meet her eyes. She started to speak, then stopped, and he knew she knew. If he sent her south, away from their current operational area, she'd have to cross an arm of the Zone, but the chance of interception was minute. And he might keep her safe . . . for a time, at least.

"How far south?" she finally asked tightly.

"A gae lang way—doon aboot New Gurock, I'm thinkin'."

"I see." He felt her inner struggle, her own stubborn strength rebelling against being sent to comparative safety. Had it been another woman and another child, she would have agreed instantly; that, too, was a factor in her thinking. And, he knew, she was thinking of him. Thinking of his need to see her as safe as he could make her.

"All right." Her voice was dull when she spoke at last. "I'll go."

Lantu flipped the last chip into his "Out" basket with a sigh of relief. Rain beat on the window, but the office's warmth enfolded him, and he stretched his arms hugely, rotating his double-jointed elbows.

"Lantu?"

He looked up quickly as Hanat closed the door behind her. Her face was anxious, and the use of his name warned him.

"Yes?"

"One of the flagged names has come up." She wrung her hands in an uncharacteristic gesture, and Lantu lowered his own hands to his desk and sat very still.

"Where?"

"Checkpoint Forty-One. Routine papers check and the Warden's stamp was wrong. At least—" she tried to look as if she felt it were a good thing "—it wasn't a Warden post."

"True." He studied his interlaced fingers. "Which name was it?"

"MacDougall," Hanat said softly. Lantu flinched, then gathered himself and met her eyes.

"Use my personal code to lock the report and have her brought here."

"Lantu—"

"Just do it, Hanat!" His voice was far harsher than he'd intended, and he smiled repentantly. "Just do it," he repeated more gently, and she nodded miserably and left.

"Nay, Angus!" Sean Bulloch shook him fiercely. "We cannae lose ye both, mon! Are ye gone clean daft?!"

"Stand out o' my way, Sean Bulloch," Angus said coldly.

"Sean's right, Angus." Tulloch MacAndrew was almost pleading. "And Katie'd no want ye tae do it, lad. Ye know that!"

"I'll no say it again. Stand out o' my way, the lot of ye!" Angus reached for his grenade launcher before he could make himself stop, and his dark eyes glared at his friends.

"Would ye do it fer anyone else, then, Angus MacRory?" Sean asked very softly, and Angus met his gaze squarely.

"Nay. But 'tis no anyone else, now is it?"

Sean held his eyes a moment, then his own gaze fell and he shook his head slowly and released Angus's shoulders.

"Then there's nowt more tae sae," Angus said quietly.

"But what d'ye think ye're gang tae do fer her?" Tulloch asked. "If the Shellies ken who she is, she's likely dead, mon!"

"I think ye're wrong. If they ken sae much, they ken I'll come fer her. Lantu's nae fool, Tulloch. He'll use her tae get at me."

"Which is nae less than he's done already!"

"As may be, I've nae choice."

"Then I'll no let ye gae alone." Angus glared, but his beetle-browed lieutenant glared right back. "D'ye think ye're the only one tae love her, ye bloody fool? If ye're mad enow tae gae, there's many o' us mad enow t' gae wi' ye."

"I'll no let any—"

"And how are ye tae stop us?" Tulloch asked scornfully. "If ye're daft enow tae try, we'll only follow. Better tae take a few lads willin', like."

Angus glowered wrathfully, but he saw the determination in Tulloch's eyes. When he looked to Sean the same stubbornness looked back, and his shoulders slumped.

"Weel enow," he sighed, "but nae more than ten men, Tulloch!"

CHAPTER TWENTY-THREE

An Admiral Heretical

Caitrin MacDougall sat on the low bed, braced against the wall, eyes closed, and fought despair. The Wardens had changed their travel permit stamps only two days ago, but she was Angus's chief intelligence officer. She should have *known*; she hadn't, and though she'd managed to wound three of the guards, she hadn't made them kill her, either.

That was what terrified her, for the way she'd been whisked away, the crisp commands for the guards to forget they'd ever seen her, the curiosity in her "escorts'" amber eyes, filled her with dread. The Shellheads had learned the value of intelligence since Lantu displaced Colonel Huark, and the way she'd been treated told her they knew who she was. *What* she was ... and what might be forced from her. Her death might have broken Angus's heart; her survival might kill him.

One hand pressed the swell of the new life within her, and a single tear crept down her swollen cheek.

* * *

Lantu had adjusted his uniform with care. It might be silly to worry over appearances, but he was about to meet an enemy he respected deeply. And, he reminded himself, one who might get him killed.

He walked down the hall slowly, arms crossed behind him, thankful he'd ordered the prisoner's injuries treated despite the risk of discovery. He was still uncertain whether professionalism or compassion had prompted him, but the doctor's report was the one hopeful thing he had.

He unfolded an arm to return the guards' salutes. The Fleet Marines, part of his personal security force, gave no sign of their thoughts as he knocked lightly, then opened the door and stepped through it.

The bedroom had been converted into a cell in haste, and the adhesive sealing the plastic bars across the window had dripped down over the sill in polymer icicles. There'd been no time to replace the Theban furniture, but if it was far too low for his prisoner's convenience, at least she was alive.

She'd gathered herself to confront him, warned by his knock, and dark green eyes met his steadily. Her face was calm, but he saw a tear's wet track on the cheek a rifle butt had split. She sat unmoving, hands folded, yet he wasn't fooled by her apparent docility. He out-massed her, despite her half-meter height advantage, but she'd wounded three trained soldiers—one mortally—with no more than her concealed combat knife.

"Good afternoon, Corporal MacDougall," he said finally. "I am Lantu, First Admiral of the Sword of Holy Terra." Her eyes glowed with a feral light at his name, and she'd already tried to make them kill her. Would the chance to take the People's military commander with her make her try again? Part of him almost wished she would.

"Since I know who you are, you must realize I also know you possess information I need. I do not, however, intend to force that information from you." He snorted softly, amused despite himself by the disbelief on her face, but she didn't even blink.

"The Wardens don't know I have you"—*I hope!*—"and I don't plan to tell them. Yours is one of several names I had flagged to be brought directly to me if captured, and you are *my* prisoner."

"Why?" She spoke for the first time, almost startling him.

"I'm not really certain," he admitted. "Curiosity, in part, but I have . . . other reasons. As you know, I've released other guerrillas"—her eyes narrowed as he avoided the word "terrorists"—"with messages to Sergeant MacRory. If I can keep certain others from learning of your capture or who you truly are, I hope to release you in the same way."

"Why?" she repeated.

"I—" Lantu stopped, unable to confess his doubts to a human. Instead, he only shrugged and returned her steady gaze. "In the meantime, is there anything else you need? Do you require additional medical attention?"

"No." He nodded and turned for the door, but her icy voice turned him back. "I expected better of you, First Admiral. Peaceforcers understand the 'good cop-bad cop' technique as well as you do."

He was briefly puzzled, but then he understood and laughed harshly. "You misunderstand, Corporal MacDougall. By the People's standards, I'm a *very* 'bad cop' just now. I won't bother you with why—you wouldn't believe me anyway—but one thing I will tell you. For the moment, you are completely safe, not simply from me, but from the Wardens and the Inquisition itself."

She glared at him in patent disbelief, and he shrugged.

"You're pregnant," he said gently. "Among the People, that's a very holy state, one not even the Inquisition would dare imperil."

"Why? I'm an 'infidel,' and I don't plan to change," she said coldly.

"Perhaps not, but your child has had no opportunity to choose, has it?" he asked quietly. "No. Even if your identity slips, you, personally, are safe for now. But—" he met her eyes "—that doesn't mean Colonel Huark wouldn't use you to lure Sergeant MacRory into a trap. So, please, Corporal MacDougall, pretend you believe I'm truly concerned for your safety and do nothing to draw attention to yourself."

The GEV whined down a security lane well inside the OZ, searchlights probing the dark. It was the fourth lane so far, but Angus didn't even curse. He merely lay in the chill mud, waiting, with every spark of human hope—or fear—frozen into stony purpose.

His hard eyes narrowed as a wheeled vehicle appeared, trailing the GEV with a quietly humming engine ... without lights. It grumbled softly past, its commander's bony head and bulky night optics protruding from the hatch, and he lay still for another ten minutes by his watch before he beckoned to Tulloch.

Eleven armed men slid deeper into the Zone like a grim band of ghosts.

"The fleet chaplain is coming to see you," Hanat said as Lantu returned from a late-night inspection. He paused, eyelids flickering, then nodded and continued towards his inner office, tossing his holstered machine-pistol onto the desk to unlatch his body armor and hang it up.

Hanat followed him, eyes wide.

"Don't you understand?" she said urgently. "He's coming *here.*"

"I understand."

"But— Does he *know*, Lantu?"

"Hush, Hanat." He cupped her head in his hands and stroked her cranial carapace gently. "If he knows, he knows."

"Oh, Lantu!" Tears gleamed, and he produced a hand-kerchief to dry them. "Why did you do it? *Why?*"

"I had to." Her wet eyes flashed angrily, and she began a sharp retort, but he silenced her with a caress. "Forgive me if you can, Hanat. I had no right to involve you."

"Idiot!" she said sharply. "As if I didn't—"

She broke off as an admittance chime rang softly. Her hands rose, gripping his caressing fingers tightly, then she straightened proudly—a small, slim figure with suddenly calm eyes—and went to answer it.

Angus glanced down at the inertial guidance unit's LED, checking its coordinates against the annotated City Engineer's map from the local civilian intelligence cell, and touched a ladder.

"We're here," he whispered to Tulloch, and MacAndrew nodded, his face shadowed in the sepulchral glow of his slitted torch beam. The rest of their team was a vague blur in the darkness of the service tunnel.

"Aye, but I'd feel better tae ken just where *she* is."

"The lad wi' the map said they'd fetched her here. And—" Angus grinned hungrily "—there's one Shellie bastard will tell me where tae find her, admiral or no . . . afore I kill him."

"Holiness." Lantu felt a flush of relief as the fleet chaplain closed the inner office door on his four-man bodyguard. If Manak had come for the reason Hanat feared . . . "What brings you here at this hour?"

"Forgive me." Manak sat heavily, his eyes dark. "I'm sorry to bother you so late, but I had to see you."

"I'm at your disposal, Holiness."

"Thank you, my son. But this—" Manak stopped and gestured vaguely.

"What's happened, Holiness?" Lantu asked gently.

"The infidels have driven the Sword from Sandhurst," Manak said wretchedly, and the admiral sat bolt upright. "They'll attack here within the week—possibly within days."

"Holy Terra!" Lantu whispered.

"You don't know the worst yet. Jahanak will defend neither New New Hebrides nor Alfred! The coward means to fall clear back to Lorelei before he stands! Can you believe it?"

Lantu stroked the gun belt on his desk. "Yes, I believe

it. Nor does it make him a coward. If he's been driven
from Sandhurst, his losses must have been heavy, and
there are no real fortifications here or in Alfred. He
needs the support of the Lorelei warp point forts." He
nodded. "Holiness, if I were in command, I would do
the same."

"I see." Manak fingered his ring, then sighed deeply.
"Well, if this is Holy Terra's will, we can but bend before
it. Yet it leaves us with grave decisions of our own, my
son."

Lantu nodded silently, his mind racing. He'd tried to
blunt the Inquisition's excesses, but when the humans
returned to New Hebrides and learned what had been
done to its people, their fury would be terrible. It was
unlikely they would recognize his efforts for what they'd
been, but his own fate bothered him less than what it
would mean for the People. If—

"We must insure the infidels do not defile this planet
yet again." The fleet chaplain's fervent words wrenched
Lantu's attention back to him.

"Holiness, Colonel Fraymak and I will do our best,
but against an entire fleet we can accomplish little."

"I know that, my son, but the infidels shall not have
this planet!" Manak's harsh voice glittered with a strange
fire. "This was the Messenger's destination. If no other
world is saved from apostasy, this one must be!"

"But—"

"I know how to do it, my son." Manak overrode Lantu
in a spate of words. "I want you to distribute our nuclear
demolition charges. Mine every city, every village, every
farmstead! Then let them land. Do you see? We'll *let*
them land, then trigger the mines! In one stroke, we will
return our souls to Holy Terra, save this world from
defilement, and smite Her foes!"

Shock stabbed the admiral, and he groped frantically
for an argument.

"Holiness, we don't *have* that many mines."

"Then use all we have! And Jahanak hasn't run yet,

Satan-Khan take him! I still have some authority—I'll make him send us more!"

Lantu stared at him, transfixed by the febrile glitter in his eyes, and horror tightened his throat. He'd sensed his old mentor's growing desperation, but *this*—! He searched those fiery eyes for some shadow of the fleet chaplain he knew and loved . . . and saw only madness.

"Holiness," he whispered, "think before you do this."

"I have, my son." Manak leaned forward eagerly. "Holy Terra has shown me the way. Even if we catch none of the infidel Marines in our trap, this world will be lifeless—useless to them!"

"That . . . isn't what I meant," Lantu said carefully. "Do you remember Redwing? When we fell back to save the Fleet?"

"Of course," Manak said impatiently.

"Then think why we did it, Holiness. We fell back to *save* the Fleet, to save our People—Holy Terra's People—from useless death. If you do this thing, what will the infidels do to Thebes in retaliation?"

"Do? To *Thebes*?" Manak laughed incredulously. "My son, the infidels will never reach Thebes! Holy Terra will prevent them."

Sweet Terra, the old man actually believed that. He'd *made* himself believe it, and in the making he'd become one more casualty of the jihad, wrapped in the death shroud of his Faith and ready to take this world—and his own—into death with him!

"Holiness, you can't do this. The cost to the People will—"

"Silence!" Manak's ringed hand slapped Lantu's desk like a pistol. "How *dare* you dispute with me?! Has Holy Terra shown *you* Her mind?!"

"But, Holiness, we—"

"Be silent, I say! I have heard the apostasy of others, the whispers of defeatism! I will not hear more!"

"You must, Holiness. Please, you *must* face the truth."

"Dear Terra!" Manak stared at the admiral. "*You*, Lantu? *You* would betray me? Betray the *Faith*?! Yes," he whispered, eyes suddenly huge. "You would. Terra forgive me, Father Shamar warned me, and I would not hear him! But deep in my heart, I knew. Perhaps I *always* knew."

"Listen to me." Lantu stood behind the desk, and Manak shrank from him in horror, signing the Circle of Terra as if against a demon. Lantu's heart spasmed, but he dared not retreat. "Whatever you think now, you *taught* me to serve the People, and because you did, I can't let you do this thing! Not to these people and never—*never*—to our own People and world."

"Stay back!" Manak jerked out of his chair and scuttled back. "Come no closer, heretic!"

"Holiness!" Lantu recoiled from the thick hate in Manak's voice.

"My eyes are clear now!" Manak cried wildly. "Get thee behind me, Satan-Khan! I cast thee out! I pronounce thee twice-damned, heretic and apostate, and condemn thy disbelief to the Fire of Hell!"

Lantu gasped, hands raised against the words of excommunication, and a dagger turned in his heart. Despite everything, he was a son of the Church, raised in the Faith—raised by the same loving hand which now cast him into the darkness.

But the darkness did not claim him, and he lowered his hands. He stared into the twisted hate of the only father he had ever known, and the stubborn duty and integrity that father had taught him filled him still.

"I can't let you do this, Holiness. I *won't* let you."

"*Heretic!*" Manak screamed, and tore at the pistol at his side.

Grief and terror filled Lantu—terrible grief that they could come to this and an equally terrible fear. Not for his life, for he would gladly have died before seeing such hate in Manak's eyes, but for something far worse. For the madness which filled his father and would destroy their People if it was not stopped.

Fists hammered at his office door as Manak's bodyguards reacted to the fleet chaplain's scream, but the stout door defied them, and the holster flap came free. The old prelate clawed at the pistol butt, and Lantu felt his own body move like a stranger's. His hand flashed out, darting to the gun belt on his desk, closing on the pistol grip.

"Die, heretic! *Die*—and I curse the day I called you *son!*"

Manak's pistol jerked free, its safety clicked off . . .

. . . and Lantu cut him down in a chattering blast of flame.

"Jaysus!"

Tulloch MacAndrew recoiled from the service hatch he'd been about to open as the thunder of gunfire crashed through it. The first, sudden burst was answered by another, and another and another!

"Mother o' God!" Davey MacIver whispered. "What i' thunder—?"

"I dinnae ken," Angus said, jacking a round into the chamber of his own weapon, "but 'tis now or naer, lads. Are ye wi' me still?"

"Aye," Tulloch rasped, and drove a bull-like shoulder into the hatch.

The access panel burst open, and Tulloch slammed through it, spinning to his right as he went. A single guard raced towards him down a dimly-lit hall, and his rifle chattered. The guard crashed to the floor, and Angus and MacIver led the others through the hatch and to their left, towards the thundering firefight, while Tulloch followed, moving backwards, swinging his muzzle to cover the hall behind them.

More bursts of fire ripped back and forth ahead of them, and then a Shellhead leapt out an open door. He wore the green of a regular with the episcopal-purple collar tabs of the Fleet Chaplain's Office, and he jerked up his machine-pistol as he saw the humans.

He never got off a shot. Angus's burst spun him like a marionette, and the guerrilla charged through the door, straight into Hell's own foyer.

The outer office was a smoky chaos, littered with spent cartridge cases. A Shellhead lay bleeding on the carpet, and two more sheltered behind overturned furniture, firing not towards the humans but towards the *inner* office! One of them looked up and shouted as Angus skidded through the door, but he and MacIver laced the room with fire. Fresh bullet holes spalled the walls, and the guards' uniforms rippled as the slugs hurled them down.

Angus's ears rang as the thunder stopped and he heard the distant wail of alarms, but confusion held him motionless. What in God's name—?!

A soft sound brought his rifle back up, and his finger tightened as a figure appeared in the inner doorway. He stopped himself just in time, for the Shellhead's smoking pistol pointed unthreateningly at the floor. He moved as if in a nightmare, but his amber eyes saw the chevrons on Angus's collar.

"MacRory," he said dully. "I should have guessed you'd come."

"Drap it, Shellie!" Angus grated, and the Shellhead looked down, as if surprised to see he still held a weapon. His hand opened, and it thumped the carpet. Another sound brought MacIver's rifle around, but he, too, held his fire as a Shellhead woman rose from the floor behind a desk. She raced to the Shellhead in the doorway—a tiny figure, slender as an elf—and embraced him.

"Easy, Hanat," he soothed. "I'm . . . all right."

"I hate tae mention it," Tulloch said tightly, "but there's a hull damned Shellie army aboot th' place, Angus!"

"Wait!" Angus advanced on the Thebans, and his rifle muzzle pressed the male's chest above the woman's head. "Ye know me, Shellie, but I dinnae know *you.*"

"First Admiral Lantu, at your service." It came out with a ghost of bitter humor.

"Ah!" Angus thought frantically. He'd planned a quiet intrusion, but all the gunfire had trashed that. They were in a deathtrap, yet the senior Shellhead military commander would make a useful hostage. Maybe even useful enough to get them out alive.

"Intae the office, Shellie!" he snapped, and waved his men after him.

"Back agin the wall!" he commanded, still covering the Thebans with his rifle, and the other guerrillas spread out for cover on either side of the door. Another body lay on the floor in the bloody robes of a fleet chaplain, and Lantu's face twisted as he glanced at it, but he drew himself erect.

"What do you hope to achieve?" he asked almost calmly.

"I think ye ken," Angus said softly, and the admiral nodded. "Sae where is she?"

"I can take you to her," Lantu replied.

"And nae doot clap us oop i' the same cell!" someone muttered.

"No—" Lantu began, but Tulloch cut him off with a savage gesture, and Angus's face tightened as he heard feet pounding down the corridor at last. He tried to think how best to play the single card he held, but before he could open his mouth, the Shellhead woman darted out the door with dazzling speed, short legs flashing. Rory MacSwain raised his weapon with a snarl, but Tulloch struck it down. It was as well, Angus thought. Lantu's eyes had glared with sudden madness when Rory moved, and Angus knew—somehow—that if Rory had fired the admiral would have attacked them all with his bare hands.

Which got them no closer to—

His thoughts broke off as he heard the woman's raised voice.

"Oh, thank Terra you're here!" she cried. *"Terrorists! They killed the fleet chaplain and kidnaped the admiral! They went that way—down the east corridor! Hurry! Hurry, please!"*

Startled shouts answered, and the feet raced off while the guerrillas gawked at one another. But their confusion grew even greater when the tiny Theban walked calmly back into the office.

"There. That was the ready guard force. You've got ten minutes before anyone else gets here from the barracks."

"What have you *done*, Hanat?" Lantu demanded fiercely. "What do you think will happen when they realize you lied to them?!"

"Nothing," Hanat said calmly. "I'm only a foolish woman. If you're gone when they return, they'll be ready enough to believe I simply confused my directions. And you've got to go. You know that now."

"I can't," Lantu argued. "My duty—"

"Oh, stop it!" She caught his arm in two small hands and shook him. It was like a terrier shaking a mastiff, but none of the guerrillas laughed. They didn't even move. They were still trying to grasp what was happening.

"It's *over*! Can't you see that? Even the fleet chaplain guessed—and what will Shamar and Huark do without him to protect you? You can't do your 'duty' if you're dead, so go, Lantu! Just go!"

"With *them*?" Lantu demanded, waving at the guerrillas.

"Yes! Even with them!" She whirled on Angus, and he stepped back in surprise as she glared up at his towering centimeters. "You must have some plan to get out. He'll take you to the one you want—he's kept her safe for you—if you only take him out of here. *Please!*"

Angus stared at the two Thebans, trying to comprehend. It was insane, but the wee Shellie actually seemed to make sense. And whatever else he'd done, Lantu had always kept his word to the Resistance.

"Aye," he said grudgingly. "We're gang oot th' way we came in, and if ye take us tae Katie—and if we're no kilt gettin' tae her—we'll take ye wi' us, Admiral. Ye'll be a prisoner, maybe, but alive. Ye've my word fer that."

"I—" Lantu broke off, staring back and forth between the tall human and Hanat's desperate face. Manak's body caught at his eyes, but he refused to look, and he was tired. So tired and so sick at heart. He bent his head at last, closing his inner lids in grief and pain.

"All right," he sighed. "I'll take you to her, Sergeant MacRory."

CHAPTER TWENTY-FOUR

"It's what I tried to *stop*!"

Second Admiral Jahanak sat on *Arbela*'s bridge once more, watching his repeater display confirm his worst fears. He'd hurt the infidels badly in Sandhurst, but not badly enough to stop them short of Lorelei. And they were being more circumspect this time; each carrier through the warp point was accompanied by a matching superdreadnought or battleship. If he'd cared to trade blows—which he emphatically did *not*—they had the firepower to deal with anything he could throw at them. But after the hammering his battle-cruisers and escorts had taken from those Terra-damned invisible carriers in Sandhurst, he was in no shape to contest their entry. With the newly revealed range of their heavy missiles to support their fighter strikes, any action beyond energy-weapons range would be both suicidal and pointless. It was going to require a full-scale, point-blank warp point ambush, with all the mines, fortresses, and capital ships he could muster, to stop them.

"Pass the order, Captain Yurah," he said quietly, ignoring the empty chair in which Fleet Chaplain Hinam should have sat. Hinam hadn't been able to contest his decision to retreat without a fight—he knew too much about what the second admiral would face in such an attempt—but neither had he been able to stomach the thought of further flight. With Fleet Chaplain Manak's death at terrorist hands, he'd found an out he could embrace in good conscience and departed for the planet with all the Marines Jahanak had been able to spare to join Warden Colonel Huark's hopeless defense.

And so Jahanak's surviving mobile units departed the system. Other than the necessary pickets, they wouldn't even slow down in Alfred. Of course, there wasn't much there now to slow down for. . . .

The thought worried Jahanak a bit, not that he intended to mention it to anyone. After all, Holy Terra would triumph in the end. No issues would ever arise concerning the People's sometimes harsh but always necessary acts on the occupied planets—planets they were endeavoring to bring back into the light against the will of the hopelessly-lost human souls that inhabited them.

Still . . . Jahanak also never mentioned to anyone his private hope that that dunderhead Huark would have the prudence to destroy his records.

"So that's the last of them, Admiral," Tsuchevsky reported. The Theban ships had moved beyond the scout's scanner range, and any pursuit was pointless. "They've left the planet's orbital defenses—and presumably their ground forces there—behind to surrender or die."

"And we know they will not surrender." Kthaara's statement held none of Tsuchevsky's distaste—it was entirely matter-of-fact. "Shall we prepare a fighter strike, Admiral?"

Antonov studied the display himself, watching Admiral Avram's small carriers—escort carriers, the Fleet was calling them—deploy with Berenson's surviving light carriers behind the protective shield of his cruisers and battle-cruisers. Thank God, he thought, that Avram had held

Danzig. It gave him an unexpected and invaluable secure forward base, and, after Sandhurst, those small carriers were worth their weight in any precious metal someone might care to name. Commodore Hazelwood's brilliantly improvised design made it abundantly clear his talents had been utterly wasted in Fortress Command, and the Danzig yards had made shorter work of repairs to Berenson's damaged units under his direction than Antonov would have believed possible. Certainly he'd put them back into service long before the fleet train's mobile repair ships could have.

He shook himself and glanced at Kthaara. "No. We lost enough pilots in Sandhurst. We'll stand off at extreme SBM range and bombard the fortresses into submission or into rubble." He had to smile at the Orion's expression. "Oh, yes, Kthaara, I know: they won't submit. But I'm hoping that afterwards, when we're orbiting unopposed in their sky, the ground forces will come to their senses." His tone hardened. "They must know by now that they're losing the war, and even religious maniacs may not be immune to despair when they're abandoned by, and utterly isolated from, their own people. At least," he finished, "it's worth a try."

"Why?" the Orion asked with disarmingly frank curiosity.

The guerrillas had been excited all day, though none of them had explained why. Now they were gathered in the cold mountain night, staring upward. The Theban who once had been a first admiral shambled almost incuriously out of the deep cave to join them, and a small pocket of silence moved about him with his guards.

As MacRory had promised, his life had been spared, though there'd been moments when he'd wondered if *any* of them would reach the mountains alive. He had no idea whether Fraymak had been searching for him to rescue or arrest him, yet it had been a novel experience to find himself on the receiving end of the relentless procedures he himself had set up.

But only intellectually so, for he hadn't felt a thing. After the terror of fighting for his life and the breathless tension of leading his captors to MacDougall's hidden cell, there'd been ... nothing. A dead, numb nothing like the endless night between the stars.

His memories of their escape were time-frozen snapshots against a strange, featureless backdrop. He remembered the ferocity with which MacRory had embraced MacDougall, and even in his state of shock, he'd been faintly amused by MacRory's laconic explanations. Yet it had seemed no more important than his own incurious surprise over the service tunnels under his HQ. It was odd that he'd never even considered them when he made his security arrangements, but no doubt just as well. And at least the close quarters had slowed his captors to a pace his shorter legs could match.

It was different once they reached open country. He'd done his best, but he'd heard the one named MacSwain arguing that they should either cut his throat or abandon him. He'd squatted against a tree, panting, unmoved by either possibility. Yet MacRory had refused sharply, and MacDougall had supported him. So had MacAndrew. It hadn't seemed important, and Lantu had felt vaguely surprised when they all started off once more. After all, MacSwain was right. He was slowing them, and he was the enemy.

There was another memory of lying in cold mud beside MacDougall while the others dealt with a patrol. He'd considered shouting a warning, but he hadn't. Not because MacDougall's knife pressed against his throat, but because he simply had no volition left. There'd been more Thebans than guerrillas, but MacRory's men had swarmed over them with knives, and he'd heard only one strangled scream.

There were other memories. Searching vertols black against the dawn. Whining GEV fans just short of the Zone's frontier. Cold rain and steep trails. At one point, MacAndrew had snatched him up without warning and half-thrown him across a clearing as another recon flight thundered overhead.

But like the three days since they'd reached the main camp, it was all a dream, a nightmare from which he longed to wake, with no reality.

Reality was an agony of emptiness. Reality was gnawing guilt, sick self-hate, and a dull, red fury against a Church which had lied. Five generations of the People had believed a monstrous lie that had launched them at the throats of an innocent race like ravening beasts. And he, too, had dedicated his life to it. It had stained their hands—stained *his* hands—with the blood of almost a million innocents on this single world, and dark, bottomless guilt possessed him. How many billions of the People would that lie kill as it had killed Manak? How many more millions of humans had it already killed on other worlds?

He was caught, trapped between guilt that longed to return to the security of the lie, fleeing the deadly truth, and rage that demanded he turn on those who'd told it, rending them for their deceit.

Now he bit off a groan as he watched brilliant pinpricks boil against the stars, like chinks in the gates of Hell. The human fleet had arrived to kill the scanty orbital forts . . . soon their Marines would land to learn the truth.

He sat and watched the silent savagery, despising himself for his cowardice. He should strike back against those who had lied, if only to atone for his own acts. But when the rest of humanity learned what had happened here, they would repay New Hebrides' deaths a thousandfold . . . and if Lantu couldn't blame them, he couldn't help them do it, either. Whatever he'd done, whatever his beliefs had been, he'd held them honestly, and so had the People. How could he help destroy them for that?

New New Hebrides had the cloud-swirling blue loveliness of almost all life-bearing worlds in the flag bridge view screens.

The light orbital weapons platforms had perished as expected, unable even to strike back at the infidels who smote them with the horrible mutual annihilation of positive and negative matter from beyond their own range. And now Second Fleet, TFN, deployed into the skies of the defenseless planet in search of someone from whom its surrender could be demanded.

Their search ended in an unexpected way.

"Admiral," Tsuchevsky reported from beside the com station, "we're receiving a tight-beam, voice-only laser transmission from the surface, in plain language—and it's not the Thebans. It's someone claiming to be a Sergeant MacRory of the planetary Peaceforce, representing some kind of guerrilla force down there. Winnie is running a check of the personnel records from data base to ... ah!" He nodded as Trevayne gave a thumbs-up from behind her own computer terminal. "So there *is* such a person. And he *is* using standard Peaceforce equipment. Shall we respond, sir?"

Antonov nodded decisively and stepped forward. "This is Fleet Admiral Antonov, Terran Federation Navy. Is this Sergeant MacRory of the New New Hebrides Peaceforce?"

"It is that," was the reply, in a burr that could saw boards. "An' 'tis a sight fer sore eyes ye are in our skies, Admiral! But I mun waste nae time, fer the Shellies— sorry, the Thebans—will be tryin' tae—"

"Excuse me, Sergeant," Antonov's basso cut in impatiently. "I had understood this transmission was in plain language."

"An' so it is!" MacRory sounded a bit miffed. "Och, mon, dinna fash yersel' ..."

Antonov turned to Tsuchevsky with a scowl. "What language do they speak on New New Hebrides, anyway? And why can't he use Standard English?"

Winnifred Trevayne smothered a laugh, then remembered herself and sniffed primly. "Actually, Admiral, I'm afraid that *is* English—of a sort. If you'll permit me...." She introduced herself to MacRory and then took over the com link, which resumed after a faint murmur from the receiver that sounded like "Rooskies an' Sassenach! Aye, weel. . . ."

The conversation continued for several minutes before she finally turned back to Antonov with a troubled expression. "The Theban commander on the planet is a Colonel Huark, sir. I've already keyed in the coordinates of his headquarters. But as for trying to persuade him to surrender . . . well, some of what Sergeant MacRory's been telling me about what the Thebans have been doing on this planet is, quite frankly, hard to believe. . . ."

Huark's was the first living Theban face any of them had seen, and the hot yellow eyes that glared from the view screen made it very different from the dead ones.

He'd accepted the transmission curtly in the name of Fleet Chaplain Hinam and listened stonily to the demand for unconditional surrender. His only visible reaction had been a hardening of his glare when Kthaara entered the pickup's field. Now Antonov finished, and a heartbeat of dead silence passed before Huark spoke.

"I have consented to hear you, infidel, only that I might see for myself the depths of apostasy to which your fallen and eternally-damned race has sunk. But I did not expect even you to be so lost to the very memory of righteousness as to come against the faithful in the company of the Satan-Khan's own unclean spawn!" A strong shudder went through him, and his curt, hard voice frayed, rising gradually to a shriek.

"This world, the destination of the Messenger himself in bygone days, will not be delivered to you to be profaned by you who consort with demons and worship false gods! You may bombard us from space, slaughtering your fellow infidels . . . but on the day the first of your Marines sets foot on this planet's surface, the mines we have planted in every city and town will purge it with cleansing nuclear fire! You may slay us, infidel, for we are but mortal, but Holy Terra's children will never be conquered! You will inherit only a worthless radioactive waste, and may you follow this Terra-forsaken world down into the torment and damnation of the eternal flame!"

Antonov leaned forward, massive shoulders hunched and beard bristling. "Colonel Huark, listen well. We humans have learned from our own history that threats to hostages cannot be allowed to prevent the taking of necessary actions—and that any actual harm to those hostages must be avenged! Not only you, personally, but your race as a whole will be held responsible for any acts of genocide against the populace of New New Hebrides. If you don't care about your own life, consider the life of your home world when we reach it!"

Huark started to speak, then laughed—a high, tremulous laugh, edged with the thin quaver of insanity, that had no humor in it—and cut the connection abruptly.

Antonov leaned back with a sigh. "Well," he rumbled softly, "they laugh. Odd coincidence. . . ." He shook himself. "Commodore Tsuchevsky, I think we'd better get back in contact with Sergeant MacRory. This time, try for a visual."

Angus MacRory nodded slowly. "Aye, Admiral. Nae doot aboot it. Yon Huark's nae mair sane than any Rigelian. If he's the means, he'll do it." The red-gold-haired woman beside him in the view screen also nodded.

Antonov was adjusting to the New Hebridan version of English, but he was devoutly (if unwontedly tactfully) grateful for Caitrin MacDougall's presence. Between her educated Standard English and Winnifred Trevayne's occasional, polite interpretation, communication flowed fairly smoothly. Now he rubbed his beard slowly and looked glum.

"I was afraid you'd say that, Sergeant, given what we've learned about the Thebans. But I don't suppose I need to tell you and Corporal MacDougall about *that*."

"No, Admiral, you don't," Caitrin agreed grimly. "The question is, what will you do now?"

"Do, Corporal MacDougall?" Antonov shrugged. "My

duty, of course. Which is to bring this war to a conclusion as quickly as possible. All other considerations must be secondary to this objective." The two New Hebridans noticed a slight thickening of his accent. Clearly he was troubled. Just as clearly, he would do whatever he felt to be necessary. The rising crescendo of terrorist outrages at the beginning of the twenty-first century had cured humanity of the twentieth's weird belief that terrorism's victims must be somehow to blame for it. Antonov wouldn't feel guilt over atrocities committed by his enemies. Which was not to say he looked forward to them; simply that he would never let the threat of them stop him.

"However," he continued, "while I cannot delegate responsibility, there is no reason I cannot ask advice. And I am asking yours now. Specifically, I'm asking you for an alternative to invasion. I'm prepared to listen to any suggestion that will enable me to prevent even greater mass murder on this planet."

"We understand, Admiral," Caitrin replied as they nodded in unison, "and thank you. We'll confer with our comrades . . . and with someone else."

"We mun talk," Angus said, and Lantu looked up from the fire with remote amber eyes.

"What about?" he asked from the drifting darkness of his mind.

"Aboot that bastard Huark's plans tae nuke the bloody planet!"

"*What?!*" Lantu jerked to his feet, his detachment shattered.

"He's gang tae nuke the cities and camps," Angus said coldly. "D'ye mean fer me tae think ye naer thought of it yer ainsel'?"

"It's what I tried to *stop!*"

"Is it, now?" Angus eyed him sharply, then sank down on another rock, waving Lantu back onto his own. "I almost believe ye, Shellie."

"I *do* believe him." Caitrin materialized out of the

cavern's dimness, and Lantu looked up at her, wondering if he should feel gratitude.

"It's the truth." His eyes hardened as horror banished apathy. "Tell me exactly what he said he'd do."

Angus sat silently, letting Caitrin describe their conversation with Admiral Antonov while he watched Lantu. For the first time since his capture (if that was the word) the Shellhead seemed alive, his questions sharp and incisive, and Angus realized he was finally seeing the admiral who'd almost broken the Resistance.

"Huark's a fool," Lantu said at last, folding his arms behind him and pacing agitatedly. "The sort of blind, bigoted fanatic who'd actually do it."

"Sae I ken. But what's tae be done? They've started killin' in the camps again, and he's no likely tae stop if the Corps *doesn't* land."

"They've resumed camp executions?" Lantu's spray of facial scales stood out darkly as he stared at Angus.

"Aye. They started the day after ye . . . disappeared. 'Tis that makes me think ye're tellin' the truth, Shel— Admiral."

Under other circumstances, Angus's sudden change in address might have amused Lantu. Now he scarcely noticed.

"I think you'll have to invade anyway, Sergeant MacRory."

"And have him nuke the planet? Are ye daft?!"

"No, and you and Corporal MacDougall should understand if anyone can. You escaped from the Inquisition." Lantu didn't even flinch as Angus's eyes narrowed dangerously. "I know what you must have endured, but it means you've heard first-hand what the Church teaches."

"Aye," Angus said shortly.

"It's a lie." Lantu's voice was flat. "I know that now, but Huark and Shamar don't, and you can't leave defeated people who *believe* in the jihad in control of this planet! They've killed almost a million people when they thought they were winning—do you think they're going to stop *now*?"

"Sae it's die slow or die fast, is it?" Angus asked wearily.

"No! It can't end that way! Not after——" Lantu shook his head. "I won't let them do that," he grated.

"And how d'ye mean tae stop 'em?"

"I may know a way—if you trust me enough."

Antonov cut the connection, blanking out the images of MacRory, MacDougall, and . . . the other. He swung about and faced the officers seated at the table. They all looked as nonplused as he felt. They'd all hoped for, and expected, a resistance movement to welcome them when they arrived as liberators—but a Theban defector hadn't been part of the picture.

Especially not the Theban who commanded their fleet until Redwing, he thought grimly. *The Theban who directed the massacre of the "Peace Fleet."* He'd been certain the Thebans had gotten a new commander after Redwing; the old commander was the last individual he'd ever expected to meet, much less to find himself allied with.

"Well, ladies and gentlemen," he growled, "we've heard the guerrillas'—or, rather, Admiral Lantu's—plan. Comments?"

"I don't like it, sir," Aram Shahinian said with the bluntness that was, as far as anyone knew, the only way the Marine general knew how to communicate. "We're being asked to send down a force of my Raiders, lightly equipped to minimize the risk of detection, and put them in this Shellhead's"—the New Hebridan term had caught on quickly—"hands." He almost visibly dug in his heels, and a hundred generations of stubborn Armenian mountaineers looked out through his dark-brown eyes. "I don't like it," he repeated.

"And I," Kthaara put in, through his translator for the benefit of those not conversant with the Tongue of Tongues, "most emphatically do not like being asked to trust a Theban."

"But what's the alternative?" Tsuchevsky asked. "The

guerrillas know Huark better than we do. They seem convinced he'll carry out his threat if we invade, and if we bombard, we'll merely be slaughtering the planet's population ourselves. We may as well let Huark do it for us! This plan involves risks—but does anyone have another idea that offers a chance of retaking the planet without civilian megadeaths?"

Winnifred Trevayne looked anguished. "We've already neutralized their space capability," she began with uncharacteristic hesitancy. "So Huark could pose no threat to our rear. We could simply proceed on to Alfred now. . . ."

"No." Antonov cut her off with a chopping motion. "I will not leave the problem for someone else to have to deal with later. And I will not leave this planet in the hands of a nihilist like Huark, to continue his butchery until someone with balls finally makes the decision I should have made!" He looked around the table, and at Kthaara in particular. "I don't trust this Lantu either—but Sergeant MacRory and Corporal MacDougall *do* seem to. And that they trust any Theban, after what they and their people have been through, must mean something!

"General Shahinian," he continued after a moment's pause, "your objections are noted. But we will proceed along the lines proposed by the New Hebridan Resistance. This decision is my responsibility alone. You will hold your full landing force in readiness to seize all cities and 're-education camps' as soon as the raiding party reports success—or to do what seems indicated if it does not."

"Aye, aye, sir." Shahinian knew Antonov well enough to know the discussion was closed. "I have an officer in mind to command the landing party—a very good man."

"Yes," Antonov nodded, "I think I know who you mean. See to it, General. And," he added with a slight smile, "we're going to have to do something about Sergeant MacRory, so have your personnel office prepare the paperwork. It won't do to have a sergeant in com-

mand of the liberation of an entire planet!" He looked
around. "Does anyone have anything further?"

"Yes, Admiral." Kthaara spoke very formally, looking
Antonov in the eye. The translator continued to translate,
but this was between the two of them. "I request to
be assigned to the landing party." He raised a clawed,
forestalling hand. "No fighter operations will be involved,
so I will be superfluous in my staff position. And since, as
General Shaahiiniaaaan has pointed out, powered combat
armor is contraindicated for this mission, my"— (dead-
pan)—"physical peculiarities will present no problem."

Antonov returned his *vilkshatha* brother's level stare.
He knew Kthaara would never trust any of
Khardanish'zarthan's killers, none of whom he'd yet had
the opportunity to avenge himself upon in the traditional
way of whetted steel.

And, Antonov knew, any act of betrayal by Lantu
would be the Theban's last act.

"Request granted, Commander," he said quietly.

Angus stood in the windy dark, praying the Raiders
had plotted their jump properly, for LZ markers were
out of the question. Their window would be brief, and
if any surviving scan sat detected anything . . .

Streaks of light blazed suddenly high above. The big
assault shuttles burned down on a steep approach, charging into the narrow drop window with dangerous speed,
and he held his breath. The plunging streaks leveled out,
dimmed, and swept overhead, then charged upwards
once more and vanished.

He waited, alone with the wind, then stiffened as a
star was blotted briefly away. Then another and another.
Patches of night fell silently, then thudded down with
muffled grunts and curses, and he grinned, recalling
night drops from his own time in the Corps, as he
switched on his light wand. It glowed like a dim beacon,
and a bulky shape padded noiselessly up to him.

"Sergeant MacRory?" a crisp Old Terran voice demanded, and he nodded. "Major M'boto, Twelfth Raider Battalion."

"Welcome tae New Hebrides," Angus said simply, and held out his hand.

The cavern was crowded by five hundred Terran Marines and two hundred guerrillas, their mismatched clothing more worn than ever beside the Marines' mottled battledress. The chameleon-like reactive camouflage was all but invisible, darkening and lightening as the firelight flickered, but weapons gleamed in the semi-dark as they were passed out, and soft sounds of approval echoed as the guerrillas examined the gifts their visitors had brought.

Major M'boto sat on an ammunition canister with Angus, facing Lantu, and the first admiral felt acutely vulnerable. The sudden influx of armed, purposeful humans had been chilling, even if he'd set it in motion himself, but not as chilling as the silent, cold-eyed Orion standing at the major's shoulder. His clawed hand gripped the dirk at his side, and even now Lantu had to fight a shiver of dread at facing one of the Satan-Khan's own.

"So," M'boto's black face was impassive, "you're First Admiral Lantu."

"I am," Lantu replied levelly. M'boto's black beret bore the Terran Marines' crossed starship and rifle, and Lantu wondered how many of the major's friends had been killed by ships under his command.

"All right, we're here. My orders are to place myself under Sergeant—excuse me, Brevet Colonel MacRory's orders. I understand *he* trusts you. For the moment, that's good enough for me."

"Thank you, Major." M'boto shrugged and turned to Angus.

"In that case, Colonel, suppose you brief me."

"Aye." Angus shook off a brief bemusement at learning of his sudden elevation and beckoned to Caitrin. "Fetch yer maps, Katie," he said.

*   *   *

Lantu crouched under a wet bush, no longer a sleepwalker stumbling in his captors' wake, and thanked whatever he might someday find to believe in that the guerrillas he'd faced had been so few and lightly-armed.

The seven hundred humans with him were all but invisible. The Marines had brought camouflage coveralls for everyone, but even without them, they would have been ghosts. The Raiders were better than he'd believed possible, yet the guerrillas were better still; they knew their world intimately and slipped through its leafless winter forests like shadows.

More than that, he'd learned the difference between the obsolescent weapons which had equipped the New Hebrides Peaceforce and first-line Terran equipment. Two Theban vertols had ventured too close during their night's march, but Major M'boto had whispered a command and both had died in glaring flashes under the Raiders' hyper-velocity missiles—five-kilo metal rods which were actually miniature deep-space missile drive coils. The HVMs had struck their targets at ten percent of light-speed.

He'd felt a brief, terrible guilt as those aircraft disintegrated, but he'd made himself shake it off. Far more of the People would pay with their lives for the Faith's lies before it ended.

Now Angus MacRory slithered quietly over to him with the major, and Lantu tried to ignore the silent presence of the Orion who came with them. Kthaara'zarthan had never been out of easy reach, and he was coldly certain of the reason.

"Huark's favorite HQ," he murmured. "We've made good time."

"I can see why he feels secure here." M'boto made certain his glasses' scan systems were inactive, then raised them and cursed softly.

A wide barricade of razor-wire fringed the inner edge of a cleared hundred-meter kill-zone, and heavily sandbagged weapon towers rose at regular intervals. The entire base was cofferdammed by thick earthen blast walls, and there were twelve hundred black-clad Wardens inside the wire and minefields, supported by two platoons of GEVs. Lantu eyed the vehicles bitterly, remembering his fruitless efforts to pry them loose from the Wardens.

"How deep did you say those bunkers are?"

"About forty meters for the command bunkers, Major."

"Um." M'boto lowered his glasses and glanced at Angus. "The outer works are no sweat, Colonel. The HVMs'll rip hell out of them, and the blast will take out most of the open emplacements and personnel, but forty meters is too deep for them." He sighed. "I'm afraid we'll have to do it Admiral Lantu's way."

"Aye," Angus agreed, and settled down to await the dark while M'boto and Lantu briefed their squad leaders.

Warden Colonel Huark sat in his bunker, staring at the small touchpad linked to the switchboard, and his fingers twitched as he thought of the mass death awaiting his touch. There had been no further word from the infidel admiral. Did that mean he would force the colonel's hand?

Huark stroked the touchpad gently and almost hoped it did.

" 'Tis time," Angus said softly, and Lantu nodded convulsively. The Orion beside him muttered something to M'boto in the yowling speech of his people, but the major only shrugged and extended a weapon to Lantu.

He took the proffered pistol. It was heavy, yet it didn't seem to weight his hand properly. Dull plastic gleamed as he opened his uniform tunic and shoved it inside.

"You'll know when it's time," he said, and Angus nodded and thrust out a hand.

"Take care," he admonished. "Yer no sae bad a boggit."

"Thank you." Lantu squeezed the guerrilla's callused, too-wide hand. Then he slipped away into the night.

* * *

Warden Private Katanak snatched at his rifle as something moved in the darkness. He started to squeeze the trigger, then made himself stop.

"Sergeant Gohal! Look!"

The sergeant reached for his pistol, then relaxed as a stocky, short-legged shape staggered from the forest into the glare of the perimeter floods.

"Call the lieutenant, Katanak. That's one of ours."

Lantu tried not to show his tension as he stumbled up to the gate. His hunched shoulders were eloquent with weariness, and the artful damage his human allies had wreaked on his uniform should help. But nothing would help if Huark had learned the truth about his "kidnapping."

"Who are—" The arrogant young lieutenant at the gate broke off and stared. "Holy Mother Terra!" he whispered. "*First Admiral Lantu?!*"

"Yes," Lantu gasped. "For Terra's sake, let me in!"

"B-b-but, First Admiral! We—I mean, how—?"

"Are you going to stand there and blither all night?" Lantu snarled. "Satan-Khan! I didn't escape from a bunch of murdering terrorists and sneak across a hundred kilometers of hostile territory for *that!*"

"Forgive me, sir!" The lieutenant's sharp salute was a tremendous relief. "We thought you were dead, sir! Open the gate, Sergeant!"

The gate swung, and Lantu stepped inside past the metal detector. The weapon inside his tunic seemed to scorch him, but there was no alloy in it.

"Thank you, Lieutenant." He injected relief into his thanks, but kept his voice tense and harried. "Now take me to the CP. Those Terra-cursed terrorists are planning— Never mind. Just get me to the colonel now!"

"Yes, sir!" The lieutenant snapped back to attention, then turned to lead the first admiral rapidly across the compound.

"He's in," M'boto murmured. "I hope he's been straight with us."

Angus only grunted, but Kthaara hissed something un-intelligible—and unprintable—in the darkness.

Lantu let his feet drag down the steep bunker steps, playing his role of exhausted escapee. The guards by the main blast door looked up boredly as the lieutenant hurried over, then whipped around to stare at Lantu under the subterranean lights. One of them—a captain—crossed to him quickly.

"First Admiral! We thought you were—"

"The lieutenant told me, Captain," Lantu said tiredly, feeling his heart race, "but I'm alive, thank Terra. And I must see the colonel at once."

"I don't—" The captain paused under Lantu's suddenly icy eyes. "I'll tell him, sir."

"Thank you, Captain," Lantu said frigidly. The officer disappeared, and seconds were dragging eternities until he returned.

"The colonel will admit you, First Admiral."

Lantu grunted, ignoring the insulting phrasing, and followed the captain into the bunker's heart. The smell of concrete and earth enveloped him as his guide led him swiftly to Huark's staff section.

"Sweet Terra, it *is* you." Huark sounded a bit surly—apparently he'd been less than crushed by his succession to command.

"First Admiral!" Another voice spoke, and he turned quickly, eyes widening as Colonel Fraymak held out his hand. Lines of weariness and worry smoothed on the colonel's face, and Lantu tried to smile as a spasm of bitter regret wracked him. Why in the name of whatever was truly holy had *Fraymak* had to be here?

"Colonel. Colonel Huark. Thank Terra I reached you! I have vital information about the terrorists' plans."

He made himself ignore Fraymak's flicker of surprise at his choice of words.

"Indeed?" Huark leaned forward eagerly. "What information?"

"I think it would be better if I shared it with you in

private," Lantu said, and Huark's eyes narrowed. Then he nodded.

"Everybody out," he said curtly, and his staff filed out. Lantu watched them go, willing Fraymak to accompany them yet unable to suggest it. Huark's eyes swiveled to his rival and he started to speak, but then he stopped, and Lantu's heart sank. Of course the Warden wouldn't risk his ire by ordering his most trusted subordinate to leave.

"All right, First Admiral," Huark said as the inner blast door closed behind his staff. "What is it?"

"The terrorists are planning a major attack," Lantu said, stepping back and casually engaging the blast door's security lock. "I stole one of their maps," he went on, reaching into his tunic, "and—"

His hand came out of his tunic with a bark of thunder.

"Now!" Major M'boto said harshly as a cluster of Wardens suddenly surged towards the HQ entrance. If Lantu had failed, three million human beings were about to die.

Colonel Huark lurched back, shocked eyes wide. Blood ran from his mouth as it opened. More frothed at his nostrils, and then he oozed down the wall in a smear of red.

Lantu ignored him. He was on auto-pilot, locked into the essential task he must accomplish, and his weapon barked again. The touchpad on Huark's desk shattered, and the main com switchboard spat sparks as he fired into it again and again, braced for the thunder of Fraymak's pistol. But when he whirled to face the colonel at last, his weapon was still holstered and he held his hand carefully away from it.

"F-First Admiral—?"

"I'm sorry, Fraymak. I couldn't let him do it."

Fists battered at the locked blast door as Fraymak stared at him.

"*Terra!*" he whispered. "You didn't *escape*, you—"

"That's right," Lantu said softly, and the world exploded overhead.

HVMs scored the night with fire, and gun towers vomited concussive flame. Blast and fragments scythed through exposed flesh like canister, sweeping the life from open gun pits as assault charge rockets snaked through the wire and mortar bombs thundered across the motor pool. Shocked Wardens roused in the perimeter bunkers and streams of tracer began to hose the night, but the HVM launchers had retargeted and fresh blasts of fury killed the guns. Flames roared from broken GEVs, and the mortars shifted aim, deluging the shredded perimeter wire in visual and thermal smoke.

"CIC confirms explosions on Target One, sir." Major Janet Toomepuu looked up from her com station aboard TFNS *Mangus Coloradas*, hovering above Huark's HQ in geosynchronous orbit, to meet General Shahinian's eyes. "No sign of nuclear explosions anywhere on the planet."

"Does Scanning report any signs of large-scale troop movements?"

Toomepuu relayed the question to the big assault transport's combat information center.

"No, sir," she said, and Shahinian nodded.

"Land the landing force," he said, and the assault shuttles of the First and Second Raider Divisions, Terran Federation Marine Corps, stooped like vengeful falcons upon re-education camps and Theban military bases scattered across the face of New New Hebrides.

Huark's stunned Wardens staggered from their bunkered barracks, rushing to man their positions, but the enemy was already upon them. Half-seen wraiths swept out of the smoke behind a hurricane of grenades and small arms fire, and the defenders died screaming as human assault teams charged through the bedlam towards assigned targets.

Angus hurdled a dead Warden, and his grenade launcher slammed on full auto as a Shellhead squad erupted from a personnel bunker. Fists of fire hurled them back, and he reloaded without breaking stride. Return fire spat out of the darkness, and he cursed as Davey MacIver went down at his side.

The HQ bunker entrance loomed before him, and a machine-gun swung its flaming muzzle towards him, but a Raider dropped a grenade into the gun pit. Another Raider seemed to trip in mid-air as his head blew apart, and the high-pitched scream of Clan Zarthan's war cry split the madness as Kthaara emptied a full magazine into the bunker slit from which the fire had come. A Warden popped up out of the HQ bunker, gaping at the carnage, and Angus pumped an AP grenade into his chest. The Shellhead flew apart, and Angus dodged aside as a Marine sergeant and his flamer squad inundated the steep passage in a torrent of fire. Screams of agony answered, and then he and Tulloch MacAndrew were racing down the shallow, smoldering steps, leaping over seared bodies and bits of bodies, with the Marines and Kthaara'zarthan on their heels.

A rifle chattered ahead of them, and Angus threw himself head-long down the stairs, grenade launcher barking. Three Marines went down before the bursting grenades silenced the enemy, and Angus tobogganed down the stairs on his belly, firing timed-rate as he went. The reek of explosives and burned flesh choked him, but he hit the bottom and rolled up onto his knees.

Tulloch charged through the open blast door. Dead Thebans littered the bloody floor, but interior partitions sheltered live ones. The lights went out, muzzle flashes shredded the darkness, and Tulloch upended a map table for cover as he fired back savagely. A thunderous explosion roared deep inside the bunker, and Angus cringed as he crawled to Tulloch's side under the whining ricochets, reloading and bouncing grenades off the roof and over the head-high partitions.

The defensive fire slackened, and Kthaara bounded

forward, the Marine sergeant cursing like a maniac as he tried to keep pace. Their weapons swept the bunker, and Angus followed them, slipping and sliding in a film of blood. There was a fresh bellow of automatic fire, and then, impossibly, only sobs and moans and one terrible, high-pitched, endless keen of agony that faded at last into merciful silence.

Angus straightened from his combat crouch, turning in a quick, wary circle to search out possible threats. There were none, and he stepped quickly into the short passage to Huark's offices.

"First Admiral?" he called, listening to the faint thunder still bouncing down the bunker steps from above, and a voice answered.

"Here, Colonel MacRory! Come ahead slowly, please."

Angus eased down the passage, flinching as the scattered, surviving emergency lights clicked on. A haze of gunsmoke hovered above at least a dozen Shellhead bodies, all faced away from the main bunker towards the sagging armored door a blastpack had blown half off its hinges.

But it hadn't gone down entirely, and he squirmed past it, then jerked his launcher up as he saw the Theban colonel, smoke still pluming from the muzzle of his machine-pistol. Lantu sat on the floor, holding one arm while blood flowed through his fingers, and his face was pale, but he shook his head quickly as Angus's launcher rose.

"Don't shoot, Colonel!" Angus and the Theban both looked at him sharply, and the admiral laughed a bit wildly, then hissed in pain. "I meant you, Colonel MacRory. It seems I had an ally after all. Colonel MacRory, meet Colonel Fraymak."

CHAPTER TWENTY-FIVE

A Gathering Fury

"I spoke to Admiral Al-Sana at BuPers about you, Andy," Howard Anderson said.

"You did, sir?" Ensign Mallory looked at him in some surprise.

"Yes. You'll be a full lieutenant next week, and he's promised you a transfer to BuShips or Second Fleet—your choice."

"Transfer?"

"Personally," Anderson said, peering out the ground car window, "I think you'd probably learn more with Admiral Timoshenko, but if you go to Second Fleet, you should arrive in time for the Theban invasion, and combat duty always looks good on a young officer's record, so—"

"Just a minute, sir." Young Ensign Mallory had matured considerably, and he broke in on his boss without the flustered bashfulness he once had shown. "If it's all the same to you, I'd prefer to finish the war with you."

"I'm sorry, Andy," Anderson turned to him with genuine regret, "but it just isn't possible."

"Why not? When you get back from Old Terra and—"

"I'm not coming back," Anderson said gently. "I'm resigning."

"You're resigning *now*? When everything's finally coming together?" Mallory looked and sounded shocked.

"As you say, everything *is* coming together. The production and building schedules are all in place, the new weapons are a complete success—" Anderson shrugged. "Admiral Timoshenko can manage just fine without me."

"But it's not fair, sir! You're the one who kicked ass to make it work, and some damned money-gouging industrialist'll grab the credit!"

"Andy, do you think I really *need* the credit?" Mallory blushed and shook his head. "Good." Anderson reached over and squeezed the young officer's knee. "In the meantime, there's something I have to do on Old Terra, and I can't do it as a member of the Cabinet."

Mallory glanced at him sharply as the car braked beside the shuttle pad. Then his brow smoothed and he nodded.

"I understand, sir. I should have guessed." He got out and held the door. Anderson climbed out and thrust out his hand, and Mallory took it in a firm clasp. "Good luck, sir."

"And to you, Lieutenant—if you'll forgive me for being a bit premature. I'll expect to hear good things about you."

"I'll try to make certain you do, sir."

Anderson nodded, gave his aide's hand a last squeeze, and climbed the shuttle steps without a backward glance.

Federation Hall had changed.

Anderson stood in an antechamber alcove, and the faces about him were grim. He wasn't surprised, for every newscast screamed the same story. The classified reports had leaked even before he reached Old Terra, and though he couldn't prove it, he recognized the hand behind the timing. It seemed unlikely the war could last much longer, the next elections were only eight months away, and the LibProgs were looking to the ballot box. Pericles Waldeck wanted to lead his party into them with a resounding flourish to head off any embarrassing discussion of just who had gotten the Federation into this mess, and the "bloody shirt" was always a sure vote getter.

Anderson snorted contemptuously and stepped out into the crowd, nodding absent replies to innumerable greetings as he headed for the Chamber. He was reasonably certain Sakanami hadn't been a party to the leaks. Not because he put cold-blooded political maneuvers past the president, but because Sakanami couldn't possibly want to further complicate the closing stages of the war, and one thing was certain—the news coverage was going to complicate things in a major way.

Anderson couldn't blame the public for its outrage. Of six and a half million people on New New Hebrides, nine hundred and eighty thousand had died during the Theban occupation. The same percentage of deaths would have cost Old Terra one and two-thirds billion lives, and the newsies had been quick to play up that statistic. It wasn't as if they'd died in combat, either; the vast majority had been systematically slaughtered by the Theban Inquisition.

Humanity's anger and hatred were a hurricane, and it would grow worse shortly. Second Fleet had not yet moved into Alfred . . . but Anderson had read the abstracts from the New New Hebrides occupation's records.

He shivered and settled into his seat, cursing the weariness which had become his constant companion. Age was catching up with him remorselessly, undercutting his strength and endurance when he knew he would need them badly. Ugly undercurrents floated through the Assembly, whispers about "proper punishment" for the "Theban butchers," and Anderson had heard such whispers before. Some of his darkest nightmares took him back to the close of ISW-3, when the Federation had agreed to the Khanate's proposals to reduce the central worlds of the Rigelian Protectorate to cinders. There had seemed to be no choice, for the Rigelians had not been sane by human or Orion standards. The Protectorate had never learned to surrender, and invasion would have cost billions of casualties. Almost worse, occupation garrisons would have been required for generations. Yet when the smoke finally cleared and the Federation realized it had been party not simply to the murder of a world, or even several worlds, but of an *entire race* . . .

He shook off the remembered chill and gripped his cane firmly as he waited for Chantal Duval to call the Chamber to order. Pericles Waldeck might be willing to condemn a race to extinction out of spleen and political ambition, but Howard Anderson was an old, old man.

He would not go to his Maker with the blood of yet another species on his hands.

The sight of New New Hebrides dwindling in the cabin's view port was lost on Ivan Antonov as he sat at his computer station, studying the final reports of the cleanup operation and stroking his beard thoughtfully.

A chime sounded, and he pressed the admittance stud. The hatch hissed open to admit Tsuchevsky and Kthaara.

"A final transmission from the planet, Admiral," Tsuchevsky reported. "The last of the high-ranking Wardens have been taken into custody and are awaiting trial with the surviving leaders of the Inquisition."

"Yes," Antonov acknowledged with a sour expression. "Trial for murder under the laws of New New Hebrides, I'm glad to say. I've never been comfortable with the idea of 'war crimes trials.'"

"So you mentioned." Kthaara's tone held vast disinterest in the legalisms with which humans saw fit to surround the shooting of Thebans. "Something from your history about the winners in one of your wars putting the losers on trial at . . ." He tried, but his vocal apparatus wasn't quite up to "Nürnburg."

Antonov grunted. "Those Fascists were such a bad lot it was hard for anyone to argue convincingly against putting them on trial. But when you start shooting soldiers for following orders to commit 'crimes against humanity,' the question arises: how does the soldier know what constitutes such a crime? How does he know which orders he's required to disobey? Answer: the victors will tell him after they've won the war!" He barked laughter. "So might makes right—which is what the Fascists had been saying all along!"

"I will never understand why Humans persist in trying to apply ethical principles to *chofaki*," Kthaara said with mild exasperation. "They can never be amenable to such notions. Honor, even as an unattainable ideal, is beyond their comprehension. Faced with a threat to your existence from such as they, you should simply kill them, not pass judgment on them! And if you insist on clouding the issue with irrelevant moralism, you find it growing even cloudier when dealing with an alien species. Especially," he continued complacently, "given your people's inexperience at direct dealings with aliens. Something else I will never understand is your 'Non-Intercourse Edict of 2097.'"

"The only nonhumans we'd discovered up to that time were primitives," Tsuchevsky explained. "Our own history had taught us that cultural assimilation across too great a technological gap doesn't work; the less advanced society is destroyed, and the more advanced one is left saddled with a dependent, self-pitying minority. Rather than repeat old mistakes, we decided to leave those races alone to work out their own destinies. Your race does have more experience in interacting with a variety of aliens—although," he couldn't resist adding, "historically, that interaction has been known to take the form of 'demonstration' nuclear strikes on low-tech planets."

"Well," Kthaara huffed with a defensiveness he wouldn't have felt a year earlier, "those bad old days are, of course, far behind us. And I will concede that this entire war would never have occurred if Saaan-Juusss had been more punctilious about observing the letter of the Edict. Still, there is something to be said for the insights our history gives us. Especially," he added pointedly, "now."

He referred, Antonov knew, to the two "guests" who occupied a nearby, heavily guarded stateroom. Lantu and Colonel Fraymak were in an ambiguous position; never having committed any of the crimes for which the Theban Wardens stood accused (even the Resistance admitted that they'd ordered no wanton murders or "reprisals" and had fought as clean a war as any guerrilla war can be), they hadn't been left to stand trial. So they, along with Sergeant—no, Colonel—MacRory, had departed with the Fleet. Kthaara had made no secret of his feelings about the two Thebans' presence, but everyone else seemed inclined to give some weight to Lantu's role in the relatively bloodless liberation of New New Hebrides.

But that, Antonov thought grimly, was all too likely to change.

An iron sense of duty had made him transmit to his superiors the findings culled from the records of New New Hebrides' Theban occupiers. But no one in the Second Fleet save himself, Winnifred Trevayne, and a few of her most trusted people knew what awaited them in the Alfred System. Not yet.

He really must, he decided, double the guard on the Thebans' quarters just before the warp transit.

It wouldn't have been as bad, Antonov reflected, gazing at the image of New Boston in the main view screen, if it hadn't come immediately after the euphoria of finding their entry into Alfred unopposed. Now, of course, they knew why that had been. The static from the communicators told them why, even before the images of radioactive pits that had been towns began to appear on the secondary view screens. There was nothing here to defend.

Kthaara was the first on the flag bridge to say it. "You knew," he stated, a flat declarative.

Antonov nodded. "New Boston has—*had*—only a little over a million people. The Thebans had no interest in trying to convert so small a population—not after the total failure of their 're-education' campaign on New New Hebrides. They just exterminated it as expeditiously as possible." His voice was at its deepest. "We will, of course, leave an occupation force to search for survivors; even a small human planetary population is hard to completely extirpate, short of rendering the planet uninhabitable." His voice trailed off. Then, suddenly, he sighed.

"A few very highly placed people on Old Terra already know. After this, it will be impossible to keep it from the public. The politicians and the media"—he made swear words of both—"will be like pigs in shit. It will be very hard, even for Howard Anderson, to argue successfully against reprisals in kind."

"*Minisharhuaak*, Ivaaan Nikolaaaaivychhh!" Kthaara exploded, causing heads to snap around. (The Orion oath was a frightful one, and he had never publicly addressed Antonov save as "Admiral.") "Anyone would think you actually feel *sympathy* for these treacherous fanatics!"

Antonov turned slowly and met the Orion's glare. And Kthaara, gazing across an abyss of biology and culture into the eyes of his *vilkshatha* brother, could for an instant glimpse something of what lay behind those eyes: a long, weary history of tyranny and suffering, culminating in a grandiose mistake that had yielded a century-long harvest of sorrow.

"I do," the admiral said quietly. Then he smiled, a smile that banished none of the sadness from his eyes. "And so should you, Kthaara Kornazhovich! Remember, you're a Russian now. We Russians know about gods that failed."

Like ripples from a pebble dropped into water, silence spread outward from the two of them to envelop the entire flag bridge.

"We will end this war," Antonov resumed in a louder, harsher voice. "We will end it in the right way—the only way. We will proceed to Lorelei and then to Thebes, and we will smash the Theban Church's ability to do to any other human planet what they've done to this one. We will do whatever we must to accomplish this objective.

But as long as I am in command, we will *not* act as fanatics ourselves! We owe the Thebans nothing—but we owe it to our own history to behave as though we've learned something from it!

"Commodore Tsuchevsky, have Communications ready a courier drone and summon the rest of the supply ships. We will have use for the SBMHAWKs."

"... completes my report, Second Admiral."

Second Admiral Jahanak leaned back in his chair in *Alois Saint-Just*'s briefing room, rubbing his cranial carapace.

"Thank you, Captain Yurah." Jahanak's thanks covered much more than the usual morning brief, for Yurah had come a long way from the distrustful days immediately after Lantu's "relief," and Jahanak had learned to rely upon him as heavily as Lantu himself must have. The flag captain wasn't brilliant, but he was a complete professional, and though he knew exactly how grave the situation was, he managed to avoid despair. Even better, he did it without the fatalistic insistence that Holy Terra would work a miracle to save Her children which had forced Jahanak to relieve more than one subordinate. Faith was all very well, but not when it divorced a naval officer from reality.

The second admiral studied the holo sphere and the glowing lights of his units clustered about the New Alfred warp point. He was confident the inevitable attack must come from there, for the infidels had moved too far from Parsifal to worry about that warp point, at least for now. It would take them weeks to redeploy that far, and they wouldn't care to uncover either New New Hebrides or Danzig once more. Especially, he thought, not now that they knew what had happened on New Boston.

But if—*when*—they attacked, his defenses would give them pause, he told himself grimly. Eleven superdreadnoughts hovered in laser range of the warp point, supported by fifteen battleships. He would have been happier with more superdreadnoughts, but then, any admiral always wanted more than he had, and if the infidels would only hold off another few weeks he'd be able to deploy another four of them fresh from the repair yards.

He would also feel happier with more battle-cruisers. His missile-armed *Ronins* had lost heavily in QR-107, Parsifal, and Sandhurst. Worse, a dozen of them—plus half that many beam-armed *Manzikerts*—remained in yard hands, with lower repair priority than battleships and superdreadnoughts. On the other hand, he had four infidel battle-cruisers, refitted for Holy Terra's service, and three of his eleven superdreadnoughts were infidel-built, as well. Losses in lighter units had been even worse proportionally, but the yards were turning out replacement cruisers and destroyers with production-line efficiency. It was the capital ships with their longer building times that truly worried him, which was why deploying his battle-line so far forward made him nervous.

Yet the infidels' advantage at extended ranges, despite the range limitations of their new lasers, ruled out any other deployment. Large-scale production of the long-ranged force beam had been assigned low priority because of faith in the Sword's initial laser advantage, and a belated acceptance of the absolute necessity of rushing Holy Terra's own fighters into service precluded any immediate changes. Jahanak couldn't argue with that—except, he amended sourly, for the fact that the fighter decision had been so long delayed—but it meant he had to get in close, under the infidels' missiles and force beams, and stay there. And that meant a forward defense in Lorelei.

Yet if he had to fight well forward, at least he had the massive fortresses and minefields to aid him. The individual OWPs might be less powerful than those of The Line, but there were dozens of them, surrounded by clouds of the lethal hunter-killer satellites, and his reports had inspired Archbishop Ganhad's Ministry of Production to provide some of them with lavish armaments of the new primary beams. If the infidel battle-line came through first to clear a path for the carriers, his own capital ships and laser-armed fortresses would be waiting to savage them at minimum range. If the infidel admiral was foolish enough to commit his carriers first, the primary-armed forts would riddle their fighter bays before they could launch . . . assuming they survived mines and laser fire long enough to *try* to launch.

Not that he expected them to survive that long, for First Fleet was poised at hair-trigger readiness. Indeed, a full quarter of his units were actually at general quarters at any given instant. It cost something in additional wear on the equipment, but it meant the infidels weren't going to catch him napping. No matter when they came through, at least twenty-five percent of his force would be prepared to concentrate instantly on their vastly outnumbered initial assault groups.

"Very well, Captain Yurah," he said finally, "I believe we're as well prepared as we can hope to be."

"Yes, sir," Yurah agreed, but he also continued in a carefully neutral voice. "Has there been any more discussion of the carriers, Second Admiral?"

Jahanak hid a smile. For a bluff, unimaginative spacer, Yurah had a way of coming to the heart of things.

"No, Captain, there has not," he said, and saw a wry glint in Yurah's eyes. Over the past months, the flag captain had developed an unexpected sensitivity to the reality beneath Jahanak's outward acceptance of the Synod's pronouncements. It wasn't something he would care for many people to develop, but it certainly made working with Yurah simpler.

"The Synod," he continued in that same, dry tone, "has determined that our careful and thorough preparations—plus, of course, the favor of Holy Terra—make our victory inevitable. As such, they see no need to commit the limited number of carriers we currently possess and every reason to prevent the infidels from guessing that we have them."

"In other words," Yurah said, "they're staying in Thebes."

"They're staying in Thebes. From whence, of course,

they will be available to surprise the infidels when we launch our counter-attack."

"Of course, sir," Captain Yurah said.

Antonov stared at the briefing room's tactical display a moment longer, then swung around to face the two whom he'd asked to remain after the final staff conference.

"Well, Admiral Berenson, Admiral Avram," he addressed the strikingly contrasted pair, "are you both clear on all aspects of the plan? I realize your duties elsewhere in this system prevented either of you from being present very much during its formulation."

There were other concerns, which he left unvoiced. Hannah Avram was a newcomer to his command team, and Berenson . . . well, it couldn't hurt to make sure of Berenson's full support. And, finally, they were both fighters who were being required not to fight until the coming battle's final stages. But they both nodded.

"We understand, Admiral," Berenson said. "The carriers will enter Lorelei in the last wave, to deal with any surviving Theban units." His eyes met Antonov's squarely, and Hannah sensed a rapport between them at odds with the stories she'd heard since linking with Second Fleet. There might be little liking there, but there was a growing—if grudging—mutual respect.

"Good." Antonov turned back to the display and the glowing dots representing his poised fleet: the serried ranks of superdreadnoughts in the first attack wave, the other battle-line units in the second, the carriers and their escorts in the third. But his somber gaze rested longest on the clouds of tiny, pinprick lights hovering nearest the warp point.

Screaming alarms harried the warriors of Holy Terra to their stations, and Second Admiral Jahanak dropped into his command chair, panting from his run to the bridge.

"Report, Captain Yurah?" he snapped.

"Coming in now, sir," Yurah said crisply. Then he

raised his head with a puzzled expression. "Look at Battle Three, Second Admiral."

Jahanak glanced at the auxiliary display, and his own eyes narrowed. *Something* was coming through the warp point, all right, but *what?* He'd never seen such a horde of simultaneous transits, and dozens of the tiny vessels were vanishing in the dreadful explosions of interpenetration.

Yet that was only a tithe of them, and his blood began to chill as more and more popped into existence. Had the infidels devised a warp-capable strikefighter? No, the things were far larger than fighters, but they were far too *small* for warships.

The first arrivals had gone to an insanely agile evasion pattern, eluding the fire of his ready duty units, and they were so fast even Lorelei's massive minefields were killing only a handful of them. But whatever they were, they were hardly big enough to be a serious threat . . . weren't they?

Specially shielded navigating computers recovered, and the Terran Navy's SBMHAWKs danced madly among the fireballs where less fortunate pods had destroyed one another, whipped into squirming evasion of hostile fire while their launchers stabilized.

Ivan Antonov's decision to withhold the SBMHAWK had yielded more than the advantage of surprise. It had also bought Admiral Timoshenko and BuShips time— time to refine their targeting systems, time to improve their original evasion programs, and, most importantly of all, time to put the new system into true mass production. Now dispassionate scanners aboard the lethal little robot spacecraft compared the plethora of energy signatures before them to targeting criteria stored in their electronic brains. Decisions were made, priorities were established, and targeting systems locked.

Jahanak gasped, half-rising in horror, as the dodging light dots suddenly spawned. *Missiles!* Those were *missile* carriers—and now their deadly cargo was free in Lorelei space!

He forced himself back into his chair, clutching its arms in iron fingers as a tornado of missile traces erupted across his display. He fought to keep his shock from showing, but nausea wracked him as Tracking began projecting the missiles' targets. This was no random attack. Scores of missiles—*hundreds* of them—sped unerringly for his fortresses, and more were launching behind them.

"Evasive action!" he snapped, and watched his surprised mobile units lurch into motion. It was a pitiable response to the scale of the disaster engulfing them, but it was all that they could do.

He met Yurah's eyes. The flag captain said nothing, for there was nothing to say . . . and no point in trying to.

The fortresses suffered first.

Trios of missiles slashed out from individual pods, joined by the fire of their brethren in a single salvo of inconceivable density. No point defense system yet constructed had ever contemplated such a tidal wave of fire. The tracking ability to handle it simply didn't exist, and the forts' active defenses collapsed in electronic hysteria. Some fire control computers, faced with too many threat sources to prioritize, lapsed into the cybernetic equivalent of a sulk and refused to engage *any* of them. Not that it made much difference; even if every system had functioned perfectly, they would have been hopelessly saturated.

Fireballs pounded shuddering shields with antimatter fists, and those shields went down. Armor puffed into vapor as more missiles screamed in, and more. *More!* Structural members snapped, weapon systems and their crews vanished as if they had never been, and Second Admiral Jahanak's hands were deathlocked on his command chair's arms as he watched his fortresses die.

The majority of Second Fleet's SBMHAWKs had been

targeted on the OWPs for a simple reason: Antonov's planners knew where to find them. They could be positive those targets would lie within acquisition range, but they'd been unable to make the same assumption about mobile units. Logic said the enemy must mount a crustal defense, but logic, as the TFN knew, was often no more than a way of going wrong with confidence, and so they had opted to assign sufficient of their weapons to guarantee the destruction of the forts.

They'd succeeded. Only a handful survived the thunder of the pod-launched SBMs, and that handful were shattered wrecks, broken and bleeding, without the power to affect the coming battle.

But that left the mobile units . . . and the SBMHAWKs which remained after the OWPs' deaths had been assured.

"There they go, Admiral," Tsuchevsky said unnecessarily.

Antonov grunted, eyes never leaving the flag bridge's master tactical display. The last SBMHAWK carrier pods of the initial bombardment moved into the warp point and vanished from the tidy universe of Einstein and Hawking, only to instantaneously re-emerge into it in the system of Lorelei, whose stellar ember of an M3 primary was invisible from Alfred, and where they would encounter . . . no one could say. There was every reason to assume the missiles had devastated the Theban fortresses as planned, but there was no way to be sure until living flesh committed itself to that warp transit.

And even as Antonov watched, the lead superdreadnoughts of the first wave moved up behind the departing SBMHAWKs. A half-dozen of those monster ships had been refitted with additional point defense armament for mine-sweeping purposes, which meant, of course, that something of their offensive armament had been given up in exchange. They could defend themselves well against missiles and mines, but their ability to fight back against whatever was left at the other end of the warp line was limited—especially at energy-weapons range, where the Thebans were always strongest. Behind the expressionless mask of his features, Antonov silently saluted those crews.

Angus MacRory stared down into the guarded briefing room's display as Second Fleet's first units disappeared into the warp point. He felt numb, wrapped around a taut, shuddery vacuum in his gut, and his own reaction surprised him. But only for a moment. It was knowing those ships' crews *knew* they were going to be pounded, and that they could only take it, that tied his insides in knots.

He raised his eyes to the two people seated across the table from him. Unlike Second Fleet's personnel, Angus had seen enough Shellheads to be able to read their alien expressions. Not perfectly, and not easily, but well enough to see the pain in Colonel Fraymak's eyes and sense the tormented clash of guilty loyalty with treason born of knowledge and integrity behind them. The colonel's face was the face of a being in torment, but the admiral's was the face of a being in Hell.

Angus shivered at the emptiness in Lantu's eyes, at the slack facial muscles and the four-fingered hands clasped tight about his agony. He shivered . . . and then he looked back at the display, for watching the light dots vanishing into the teeth of the Thebans' defenses was less heart-wrenching than watching Admiral Lantu's despair.

Jahanak clenched his teeth as still more missiles launched—not at the forts this time but at his warships. An involuntary groan went up from his staff as the superdreadnoughts *Eloise Abernathy*, *Carlotta Garcia*, and Yurah's old command, *Hildebrandt Jackson*, died, and the second admiral whipped around to glare at them.

"Silence!" The word cracked like a whip, wrenching their attention from the hideous displays to his blazing yellow eyes, and his voice was fierce. "We are the Sword of Holy Terra, not a pack of sniveling children! Attend to your duties!"

His officers jerked back to their instruments, and he returned his eyes to the display, grateful for the way his fury had cleared his own mind. He watched missiles shatter the battleships *Cotton Mather*, *Confucius*, *Freidrich Nietzsche*, and *Torquemada* while *Saint-Just* shuddered and lurched to hits of her own. None of his battle-line was unhurt—even his battle-cruisers were being targeted—and the missile storm was doing more than kill personnel and internal weapons. It was also irradiating his external ordnance, burning its on-board systems into uselessness before he had targets to fire it at. The infidel battle-line could not be far behind this hellish bombardment, and when it came through his shattered fleet could never stop it.

"Execute Plan Samson, Captain Yurah," he said flatly, and felt his words ripple across the bridge. No one had really believed Plan Samson would be required. Their defenses had been too strong, their tactical advantage too great—until they met the fury of the SBMHAWK.

The superdreadnoughts leading the first wave moved ponderously up to the warp point and began to vanish from Antonov's tactical display. The burly admiral watched them go with an odd calm—almost a sense of completion. His fleet was committed now, and he should soon get some definite word on what must be a maelstrom in Lorelei. Almost as soon, he would be entering that maelstrom himself. *Gosainthan* was among the capital ships of the second wave; she wouldn't transit in its lead group, but transit she would. Howard Anderson had ridden his flagship into the Battles of Aklumar and Ophiuchi Junction, and Ivan Antonov would do no less this day. TFN commanders accompanied those they commanded into battle. Always. This was no written regulation that could be evaded—it was a tradition that never could be.

The first Terran superdreadnoughts emerged into Lorelei on the SBMHAWKs' heels, and First Fleet of the

Sword of Holy Terra lunged to meet them. The avalanche of missiles had stunned the defenders, but these were foes they could recognize . . . and kill.

The superdreadnought *Saint Helens* led the Terran attack into a holocaust of x-ray lasers. She survived transit by approximately twenty-three seconds, then died in a boil of spectacular fury as a direct hit ripped her magazines open. Modern missiles and nuclear warheads were among the most inert, safest to handle weapons ever devised; antimatter warheads were not, and their prodigious power made magazine hits even more lethal than they had been in the days of chemical explosives. Now the Theban fire smashed the containment field on one—or two, or possibly three—of *Saint Helens'* warheads, and her own weapons became her executioners.

Her sister ship *Yerupaja* survived her by a few seconds—long enough to lock her main batteries and her full load of external ordnance on the wounded Theban superdreadnought *Commander Wu Hsin*. The two ships died almost in the same instant, and then the savagery became total.

"More Omega drones, Admiral," Tsuchevsky reported quickly. "Their targeting data is already being downloaded to the remaining SBMHAWKs."

Antonov nodded absently. The data transfer was totally automated: computers talking to each other at rates beyond the comprehension of their human masters while he watched the second wave's leading elements approach the warp point.

"You may commit the reserve pods when you are ready, Commodore Tsuchevsky," he said formally.

Second Admiral Jahanak bared his teeth as his ships charged forward through their own minefields. He'd planned on a close action, but not on one as close as this. Yet with his fortresses gone, he had no choice. Before it died, First Fleet must hurt the enemy as terribly as possible to buy time for the defenders of his home world, and all the careful calculation which had guided his career no longer mattered.

The remaining SBMHAWKs flashed through the warp point, emerging amid the fiery incandescence of dying starships. There weren't many of them, but the ships who led the assault had lived long enough to give them very precise targeting data indeed.

Jahanak cursed as two more superdreadnoughts exploded. The battleships *Jonathan Edwards* and *Ali* followed, but it seemed the infidels' supply of their newest hell weapon had its limits, and First Fleet was in amid the wreckage of the first wave of attackers when the second started through.

X-ray lasers snarled at ranges as low as fifty kilometers—ranges at which it was literally impossible to miss—and hetlasers and force beams smashed back with equal fury. Ships flared and died like sparks from some monster forge, and the superdreadnought *Pobeda*, command bridge demolished by a direct hit, stumbled from the clear zone about the warp point into the impossibly dense Theban minefields and a hundred explosions tore her apart.

Missile fire from the lighter Theban ships—those the SBMHAWKs hadn't targeted—ripped at the attackers' shields, smashing them flat, and scores of *samurai* infantry sleds sped through the carnage.

Hard on their heels came the ships of the Ramming Fleet.

The roar of explosions and the scream of rent metal filled the passageway as the hull-breaching charge ripped through *Dhaulagiri's* skin. The Marines flattened against the bulkhead in the combat zoots that kept them alive this close to the blast, flinching instinctively from the shock and flying debris, then swung back around even as the Theban boarders appeared, spectral in the smoke. In an instant, the passageway became a hell of explosions, plasma bolts, and hyper-velocity metal in which no unar-mored life could have survived even momentarily.

The Shellheads hadn't been able to develop powered armor, Lieutenant Amleto Escalante thought as he blasted one of them down. But they'd produced vac suits with as much armor as Theban muscles could carry, and these boarders were harder to kill than those he'd faced at Redwing. Still, the zoots gave the Marines an over-whelming advantage. Trouble was, an inner corner of his mind reflected dourly, there were so goddamned *many* infantry sleds this time. The improved tracking and com-puter projections that had placed his unit at the boarders' point of entry had also told them there would be other points of entry. And *Dhaulagiri*'s Marines couldn't be everywhere. Some of the boarding parties would meet unarmored, lightly-armed Navy personnel. Escalante couldn't let himself think about that.

He soon had to.

"Heads up, Third Platoon!" It was Major Oels, com-manding the superdreadnought's Marines from her sta-tion in Central Damage Control. It wasn't the sort of CP the Book had contemplated before the war, but damage control's holographic schematics gave her the best possi-ble information on a battle like this one.

"Intruders have broken through in Sector 7D." The voice rattled in his earphone. "They're moving around behind you. Watch your six!"

They must know the layout of our ships from the one's they've captured, Escalante had time to reflect before the first Thebans appeared in the passageway intersection behind his position, armed with the shoulder-fired rocket launchers they'd learned to use against zooted Marines. He barked an order, and his odd-numbered troopers turned to face the new threat as the even numbers fin-ished off the first boarders. It was too late for Corporal Kim ... a rocket took her from behind, and the front of her zoot blasted outward in a shower of wreckage and guts, spraying Escalante's visor with gore.

"*Escalante, if you puke, your rosy pink ass is mine,*

sweetheart!" The lieutenant blinked, head suddenly clear. Now what the hell was Sergeant Grogan, his OCS drill instructor, doing here? But, no, that hadn't been the battle circuit. . . . Half blind and wishing the zoot's gauntlets were any good for wiping, he sent a plasma discharge roaring down the passage towards the Thebans.

What a cluster-fuck, a part of him managed to mutter from some deep inner shelter in the midst of horror.

More and more capital ships emerged from the warp point, battleships fleshing out the superdreadnoughts, and their fire began to tell. Second Fleet paid a terrible price, but its fleet organization was intact, and the Theban squadrons had been harrowed and riven by the preliminary bombardment. Too many beam-armed ships had died; too many datalinks had been shattered. Their surviving ships fought as individuals against the finely meshed fire of Terran squadrons, and two of them died for every Terran they could kill.

Battle-cruisers and heavy cruisers of the Ramming Fleet charged headlong to meet the enemy, and shields and drive fields glared and died in deadly spasms of radiation, but the tide was turning.

The universe stabilized in the flag bridge's main view screen as *Gosainthan* emerged from warp transit into another kind of chaos. Reports poured in faster than living minds, or even cybernetic ones, could absorb them. Antonov sat in his command chair, an immovable boulder of calm amid the electrical storm of tense activity as highly-trained personnel fought to impose some semblance of order.

"Summarize, Commodore Tsuchevsky," he ordered quietly.

"We're mopping up their conventional ships, sir." Tsuchevsky gestured at the read-outs of confirmed kills and observed damage. His brow was beaded with sweat as tension and excitement warred with decorum. "Our losses have been heavy—the first wave is practically all gone, and their ramming ships have been pressing home attacks on the earlier groups of this wave. Many ships report multiple boardings."

"It would seem we need all the firepower at our disposal, Commodore," the admiral rumbled. He touched a stud on his armrest communicator. "Captain Chen, *Gosainthan* will advance and engage the enemy."

"Aye, aye, sir," the flag captain acknowledged. He paused. "Plotting reports that we've already been targeted by at least one enemy ramming ship."

"Fight your ship, Captain," Antonov replied, and leaned back, expressionless. The reactionless drive rose from a soft, subliminal thunder felt through feet and skin to something that snarled with fury, and TFNS *Gosainthan* accelerated into the hell of Lorelei.

Jahanak ran his eyes over the status boards one last time and felt almost calm. His fleet was done. More and more infidel ships emerged behind their dying sisters, joining their weaponry to the attack, slaughtering his lighter units. He watched a destroyer division lunge forward in a massed suicide run on an infidel superdreadnought, but they were too small to break through and defensive fire blew them into wreckage.

Only three of his mangled superdreadnoughts survived. At the moment, his light units' ramming attacks were forcing the infidels to ignore his capital ships while they defended themselves, but it was a matter of minutes—possibly only seconds—before that changed.

"Captain Yurah."

"Yes, Second Admiral?"

Jahanak looked into his flag captain's eyes and saw no fear in them. He nodded and drew his own machine-pistol, checking the magazine.

"Send the hands to boarding stations, Captain," he said calmly. "We will advance and ram the enemy."

"Aye, sir," Yurah said, and Second Admiral Jahanak of the Sword of Holy Terra closed his vac suit's visor as his dying flagship charged to meet her foes.

* * *

The damage control teams were finishing up and leaving, and the stench of burning was lessening on the bridge. Antonov didn't notice as he absorbed the tale told by the read-outs. Amazing, he reflected, how recently he'd thought of Parsifal as an appalling exercise in mass destruction. His standards in such matters had now changed. Would they change again when he entered the Thebes System?

Essentially, the entire Theban mobile fleet had been annihilated—but at what a cost! Of the twenty-four superdreadnoughts he'd taken into Lorelei, sixteen had been totally destroyed, and most of the survivors, including *Gosainthan*, were damaged in varying degrees. In fact, the flagship had gotten off very lightly compared to some. Only six of the fourteen battleships were total write-offs, but damage to some of the survivors was extensive. And personnel casualties were even heavier than might have been projected from the ship losses—Terran computer projections didn't have vicious boarding attacks by religious fanatics factored into them.

Winnie's precious Duke of Wellington should have been *here*, he thought grimly.

Thank God it had all been over by the time the carriers arrived in the third wave. They were unscathed, and even now Berenson and Avram were leading them in pursuit of the handful of Theban light units that had escaped. But unbloodied strikefighters or not, Second Fleet would need months to repair its damages, absorb all the new capital ship construction Galloway's World could send and, perhaps most importantly, replenish its stock of SBMHAWKs.

The armrest communicator chimed for attention and Antonov touched the stud, bringing his small com screen alive with a puzzled-looking Pavel Tsuchevsky.

"Admiral," the chief of staff began, "I've been talking to our guests. Admiral Lantu"—by common consent, the Theban still received the title—"has requested permission to speak to you on a matter of utmost urgency."

Antonov scowled. He wasn't really in any mood to talk to the Theban. But— "Put him on, Commodore."

Tsuchevsky stepped aside, and Lantu entered the pickup. Expressions were always difficult to read on alien faces, but Antonov had more practice than most. And he knew haunted eyes when he saw them.

"Admiral Antonov," the slightly odd intonation the Theban palate gave Standard English was more pronounced than usual, and Lantu's voice quivered about the edges, "as you know, I observed the battle with Colonel MacRory. I'm as appalled as you must be by this carnage, and—"

"Get to the point, Admiral," Antonov snapped. He wasn't particularly pleased with himself for his outburst, but he *really* wasn't in the mood for some sort of apology from the Theban. But Lantu surprised him. He drew himself up to his full height (it should have been comical in a Theban, but in Lantu's case it somehow wasn't) and spoke without his previous awkwardness.

"I shall, sir. This slaughter has removed my last doubts: my people must—and will—be defeated. But the kind of suicidal defiance we've all just witnessed is going to be repeated in Thebes. It has to be, only it will be worse— *far* worse—in defense of our home system. If your victory takes too long, or costs too much—well, Colonel MacRory's told me about the debate over reprisals among your political leaders. I can't say it surprises me, and I know the Church *deserves* to perish. But my race doesn't, Admiral Antonov ... and it will, unless this war can be brought to a quick end." He took a deep breath. "I therefore have no alternative but to place all my knowledge of our home defenses at your disposal."

For a long moment, Antonov and Lantu met each other's eyes squarely. Finally, the massive human spoke.

"I am ... very interested, Admiral Lantu. I will meet with you, Commodore Tsuchevsky, and my intelligence officer in my quarters in five minutes." He cut the connection, stood, and moved towards the intraship car.

He would be a priceless intelligence asset, he reflected.

But how far can I trust him? How liberated is he, really, from a lifetime's indoctrination?

There was no way to know—yet. But it was just as well Kthaara was off with the fighter squadrons, a good few astronomical units away!

CHAPTER TWENTY-SIX

"Buy me some time."

Ivan Antonov sat in his quarters, staring sightlessly through the armorplast view port at the glowing ember of Lorelei. His broad shoulders were squared, but the hands in his lap were very still and his mind worked with a strange, icy calm.

There had been few data bases to capture in Lorelei, but the fragments Winnie Trevayne's teams had so far recovered confirmed every word Lantu had said, and the thought of what that meant for his fleet was terrifying.

He stood and leaned against the bulkhead, searching the velvet blackness for a way to evade what he knew must be, but there was no answer. There would be none. The price Second Fleet had paid for Lorelei would pale into insignificance beside the price of Thebes.

He paced slowly, hands folded behind him, massive head bent forward. The far end of Charon's Ferry was a closed warp point. Unlike an open warp point, the gravity tides of a closed point were negligible. Even something as small as a deep-space mine could sit almost directly atop one, and the minefields the Thebans had erected to defend their system beggared anything Ivan Antonov had ever dreamed of facing.

And behind the mines were the fortresses. Not OWPs, but asteroid fortresses—gargantuan constructs, massively armed, impossibly shielded, and fitted with enough point defense to degrade even SBMHAWK bombardments. Dozens of them guarded that warp point. Enough SBMHAWKs could deal even with them, but he didn't have enough. He wouldn't have enough for months, and if Howard Anderson's letters from Old Terra were correct, he didn't have months.

A soft tone asked admittance, and he turned and opened the hatch, watching impassively as Kthaara'zarthan entered his cabin. The midnight-black Orion looked more like Death incarnate than ever, and Antonov studied his slit-pupilled eyes as Kthaara sat at a gesture.

"Well?" the human asked quietly.

"I have studied the intelligence analysis," Kthaara replied equally quietly. "I still do not share your concern for the Thebans, Ivaaan Nikolaaaaivychhh, for the *Zheeerlikou'valkhannaieee* do not think that way, but you and your warriors are Human. You cannot fight with honor if you act contrary to your honor. I accept that. But, clan brother, I do not see how such defenses may be broken in the time you say you have."

"Nor do I," Antonov rumbled, "but I have to find one. And there's only one person who may be able to find it for me."

"It goes against all I know and feel," Kthaara growled, and his ears flattened. "Thebans are *chofaki*, and you ask me to trust the very *chofak* who murdered my *khanhaku*."

"Kthaara Kornazhovich," Antonov said very softly, "the Orions are a warrior race. Has no Orion ever acted dishonorably believing he acted with honor?"

Kthaara was silent for a long, long moment, and then his ears twitched unwilling assent.

"I believe in Admiral Lantu's honor," Antonov said

simply. "He did his duty as he understood it—as he had been *taught* to understand it—just as I have and just as you have. And when he discovered the truth, he had the courage to act against the honor he had been taught." The admiral turned back to his view port, and his deep, rumbling voice was low. "I don't know if *I* could have done that, Kthaara. To turn my back on all I was ever taught, to reject the faith in which I was reared, simply because my own integrity told me it was wrong?" He shook his head. "Lantu is no *chofak*."

"You ask too much of me." Kthaara's claws kneaded the arms of his chair. "I cannot admit that while my *khanhaku* lies unavenged."

"Then I won't ask you to. But will you at least sit in on my conversations with him? Will you listen to what he says? I've never admitted helplessness, and I'm not quite prepared to do so now . . . but I feel very, very close to it. Help me find an answer. Even—" Antonov turned from the port and met Kthaara's eyes once more "—from Lantu."

Two very different pairs of eyes locked for a brief eternity, and then Kthaara's ears twitched assent once more.

"I just don't know, Admiral Antonov." Lantu ran a four-fingered hand over his cranial carapace, staring down into the holo tank at the defensive schematic he and Winnifred Trevayne had constructed. "I helped design those defenses to stop any threat I could envision—I never expected *I'd* be trying to break through them!"

"I understand, Admiral." Antonov raised his own eyes from the display. "We can break them, but it will take time, and our losses will be heavy. Commodore Tsuchevsky and I have studied the projections at length. Against these defenses, we anticipate virtually one hundred percent losses among our first four assault groups, losses of at least eighty percent in the next three, and perhaps forty percent for the remainder of the fleet. We simply do not have sufficient units to sustain such casualties and carry through to victory. We can build them ... but it will take over a year."

Lantu shivered at the unspoken warning in the human's tone. A year. A year for Thebes to build additional ships and strengthen its defenses still further. A year for humanity's entirely understandable thirst for vengeance to harden into a fixed policy. And when that policy collided with the casualties Second Fleet would suffer ...

"It's the mines," he muttered, wheeling abruptly from the tank. He folded his arms behind him, frowning at the deck. "The mines. You could deal with the fortresses with enough SBMHAWKs."

"True." Antonov watched the Theban pace. He could almost feel the intensity of Lantu's thoughts, and when he glanced at Kthaara he saw the glimmer of what might someday become sympathy in the Orion's eyes. "If it were an open warp point—if we had even the smallest space to deploy free of mine attack—" He stopped himself with a Slavic shrug.

"I know." Lantu paced faster on his stumpy legs, then stopped dead. His head came up, eyes unfocused, and then he whirled back to the display, and amber fire flickered in his stare.

"If you could break through the mines, Admiral Antonov," he asked slowly, "how long would it take you to prepare your assault?"

"Three months for repairs and to absorb and train new construction already *en route* from Galloway's World," Antonov rumbled, watching the Theban alertly. "But it will take at least a month longer for sufficient new SBMHAWKs to reach us. I would estimate four months. Commodore?"

He glanced at Tsuchevsky, and the chief of staff nodded. He was watching Lantu just as closely as his admiral.

"I see." Lantu rocked on his broad feet, nodding to himself. Then he looked up into Antonov's gaze. "In that case, Admiral Antonov, I think I've found a way to get you into the system."

*   *   *

Ivan Antonov sat before the pickup, recording his message, and his eyes were intent.

"I trust him, Howard," he rumbled. "I have to. No one who meant to betray us would have given us the data he has, and certainly he wouldn't have come up with an idea like this. It's not one we could afford to use often, but it's brilliant—and so simple I don't understand why *we* never thought of it.

"I know you're no longer Minister of War Production, but I need you to send me every tramp freighter you can find. Get them here as quickly as you can, even if you have to tow them on tractors between warp points. They don't have to be much—just big enough to be warp-capable. With them and enough SBMHAWKs, I am confident of our ability to break into Thebes.

"I recognize the stakes, and I will do my best, but even with the freighters and SBMHAWKs, Second Fleet will require at least four months to prepare the assault. It simply is not humanly possible to do it more quickly, and you must restrain the Assembly while we do. I don't know how—I'm no politician, thank God—but you have to."

He stared into the pickup, and his broad, powerful face was granite.

"Buy me some time, Howard. Do it any way you can, but buy me some time!"

Caitrin MacDougall walked slowly down the hall, wondering how her mother had survived five pregnancies. Her own was well advanced, and she hated what it was doing to her figure almost as much as she loved feeling the unborn infant stir. Knowing a new life was taking form within her was worth every backache, every swollen ankle, every moment of totally unanticipated yet seemingly inescapable morning sickness ... but that didn't mean she liked those other things.

"Hello, Caitrin," a wistful voice greeted her as the door at the end of the hall opened.

"Hi, Hanat."

Hanat held the old-fashioned door for her, and Caitrin sank gratefully into an over-stuffed chair. It was going to be hell to climb out of, but she chose to enjoy its comfort rather than think about that.

The slender Theban woman sat in a chair sized to her tiny stature, like a child sitting at Caitrin's feet, but Caitrin no longer felt like a kindergarten teacher. She'd come to know—and like—Hanat, and though Hanat tried to hide it, Caitrin knew how it hurt to spend her time under virtual house arrest. Yet there was no choice, for Hanat had been Lantu's personal secretary. Her fellow Thebans would have torn her limb from limb—literally—for his "treason," and she would have fared equally badly at the hands of any number of New Hebridans. Virtually every family had deaths to mourn, and the population as a whole had yet to learn how Lantu had fought to reduce the death toll. Even many of those who knew didn't really believe it. And so, in superb if bitter irony, Hanat's only true friend on New Hebrides was not merely a human but the Resistance's second in command!

"How are you, Caitrin?" Hanat asked, folding her hands in her lap with the calm dignity which was like a physical extension of her personality.

"Fine . . . I think. This little monster"—Caitrin rubbed her swollen abdomen gently—"has excellent potential as a soccer star, judging by last night's antics. But aside from that, I'm doing fine."

"Good." Hanat's inner lids lowered, and her voice was soft. "I envy you."

Caitrin nibbled on an index finger, studying the top of Hanat's cranial carapace as she bowed over her hands.

"I got a message chip from Angus last night," she said after a moment. "A long one, for him. I think there were at least ten complete sentences." Hanat laughed, and Caitrin grinned. She loved the sound of Hanat's laughter. It was very human and yet utterly alien, a silver sound totally in keeping with the Theban's elfin appearance.

"He says the admiral is fine. In fact"—Hanat looked

up quickly—"he and Colonel Fraymak are working with
Admiral Antonov's planning staff."

"Oh, dear," Hanat said softly, folded hands twisting
about one another in distress.

"Hanat." Caitrin leaned forward, capturing one of the
slender hands despite a half-hearted attempt to escape.
"You know he has to."

"Yes." Hanat looked down at the five-fingered hand
clasping hers. "But I know what it's costing him, too."

"Just tell me if it's none of my business," Caitrin said
gently, "but why don't you ever write him?"

"Because he hasn't written me. It's not seemly for a
Theban woman to write a man who hasn't written her."

"Somehow I don't see you as overly burdened by tradition, Hanat."

"I suppose not." Hanat laughed again, sadly, at Caitrin's wry tone. "But he hasn't written on purpose . . .
that's why I can't write him."

"Why not? If I'd waited for Angus to say something,
we'd've died of old age! Of course, he's not exactly the
verbal type, but the principle's the same."

"No, it isn't." Hanat's voice was so soft Caitrin had to
strain to hear her. "Lantu loves me—I know he does,
and he knows I know—but he won't admit it. Because—"
she looked up, and tears spilled slowly down her cheeks
"—he doesn't think he's coming back to me, Caitrin. He
thinks he's going to die. Perhaps he even *wants* to. That's
why I envy you and Angus so."

Caitrin bit her lip, staring into that tear-streaked alien
face. Then she opened her arms . . . and Hanat burrowed
into them and wept convulsively.

". . . outrage, Madam Speaker! This wanton blood-
shed—this *slaughter* wreaked against helpless civilians—
sets the Thebans beyond the pale! Fanaticism must not
be allowed to cloak butchery with any semblance of
excuse."

Yevgeny Owens paused, and a soft rumble of agreement
filled in the space. It was strongest from the LibProgs,

Anderson noted—not surprisingly, since Owens was Waldeck's handpicked hatchet man—but a disturbing amount of it came from Erika Van Smitt's Liberal Democrats. And, he admitted unhappily, from his own Conservatives. He made himself sit still, folded hands resting on the head of his cane, and waited.

"Madam Speaker," Owens resumed more quietly, "this isn't the first time humanity has met racial insanity, nor the first time we've paid a price for meeting it. I remind this Assembly that few political leaders of the time could believe the truth about the Rigelians, either. We are told the Thebans have committed these unspeakable atrocities—have resorted to torture, to the murder of parents in order to steal and 'convert' their children, to the cold-blooded execution of entire towns and villages as 'reprisals' against men and women fighting only to protect their world and people—in the name of religion. Of a *religion*, Madam Speaker, which deifies the very planet upon which we stand. And, we are told, that religion was concocted by humans in direct violation of the Edict of 2097.

"Perhaps it was, but what rational species could have accepted such a preposterous proposition? What rational species capable of interstellar travel, with all the knowledge of the universe that implies, could truly believe such arrant nonsense?"

Owens paused again, and this time there was only silence.

"I do not accept humanity's responsibility for this insanity," he finally continued, very softly. "We cannot hold ourselves accountable for the madness of another species, and only a species which *is* mad could wage 'holy war' against the race which first gave them the blessings of technology in the name of some half-baked agglomeration of pseudo-religious maunderings. But even if humanity is responsible for the unintentional creation of this menace, for providing a race of interstellar sociopaths with the weapons of modern warfare and mass destruction, that does not change the situation we now face. Indeed, if such is the case, are we not confronted by an added dimension of obligation? If our species has, in any way, however unintentionally, helped create the crisis we face, it becomes *our* responsibility to face and accept whatever its final resolution demands of us.

"Madam Speaker, Ladies and Gentlemen of the Assembly, this matter cannot be settled on the basis of what we would like to be true. It can be resolved only on the basis of what *is* true, and the Thebans have proven their irrationality. Events on New New Hebrides and New Boston have proven their murderousness. The most recent Battle of Lorelei has proven their fanaticism. And when a murderous fanatic actively seeks martyrdom, when he is not merely willing but *eager* to die for his cause, then the only defense is to help him find the death he seeks."

The silence was icy as Owens paused a final time, and his eyes swept the Assembly's members from the huge screen behind the Speaker's podium.

"And, Madam Speaker," he finished quietly, "what is true of an individual is a hundred times more true of an entire race of fanatics armed with starships and nuclear weapons. Not merely our own safety but that of the Galaxy itself requires that we override the Prohibition of 2249, and I now move that we so do."

He sat, and Anderson ground his teeth. Owens believed what he'd said; that was what made him so damnably convincing . . . and why Waldeck had chosen him to lead the LibProgs on this issue.

Anderson drew a deep breath and pressed his call key.

"The Chair recognizes President Emeritus Howard Anderson," Chantal Duval said, and he started to rise as his image replaced Owens', then changed his mind. His legs' aching unsteadiness was growing worse, and it made him look feeble at a time when he must show no sign of weakness, allow no suggestion that he spoke from senility rather than clear-minded logic.

"Madam Speaker, Ladies and Gentlemen of the Assembly." He was pleased his voice still sounded strong, at least. "Mister Owens argues that the Thebans are mad.

He argues, in effect, that humanity simply provided a vehicle through which that madness might express itself—that if it were not for 'the Faith of Holy Terra' they would have found some other madness to spur their actions. And he argues most cogently that we cannot make decisions on the basis of what we wish were true but only on the basis of what *is* true."

He paused for just a moment, then shook his head.

"He is, of course, correct." A shiver of surprise ran through the Assembly at his admission. "The worst mistake any governing body can possibly make is to allow hopes and expectations to twist its perception of reality. But, ladies and gentlemen, I must tell you that I have already seen *this* governing body do precisely that. Not simply once, but many times."

Feet shifted in a soft susurration of sound, and he smiled thinly.

"Oh, yes, ladies and gentlemen. I am an old man—a very old man, whom some of you call 'senile'—who has watched the Terran Federation grow and change for over a century. Over a *century*, ladies and gentlemen. I've served it as a naval officer, as president, and now as a member of this Assembly, and I have seen it prove the heights to which all the best in humanity may aspire. I have seen the Federation resist aggression. I've seen it suffer terrible losses and fight through to victory. I have seen it extend the values we hold dear to its member worlds and forge the community of Man across the stars.

"But I have also seen terrible, terrible mistakes. Mistakes made in this very chamber, with the highest of purposes and the most noble of intentions. Mistakes made by good and compassionate people as often as by those less good and more unscrupulous." Across the chamber from him, Pericles Waldeck stiffened angrily, but his face was expressionless.

"Ladies and gentlemen, in 2246 this Assembly made one of those terrible mistakes. It made it for the highest of moral reasons—and for the most base. It elected to endorse the decision embodied in Grand Fleet Headquarters Directive Eighteen, authorizing genocidal attacks on the civilian populations of the Rigelian Protectorate."

The silence was absolute as his wise old eyes swept the chamber.

"We had no choice," Anderson said softly. "That was what we told ourselves. The Rigelians were insane, we said. There were too many worlds of them, and they fought too fanatically. Every Rigelian regarded himself or herself as an expendable asset, and no more honorable end existed for him or her than to die attempting to destroy any being who challenged the supremacy of the Rigelian race. Conquest was virtually impossible; occupation forces would of necessity have been insupportably huge. The casualties we'd already suffered—casualties thousands of times greater than those we have suffered in *this* war—would have been multiplied a thousand-fold again had we sought to invade those worlds ... and in the end, we would have had to kill them all anyway.

"And so, ladies and gentlemen, the Terran Federation elected not to spend the lives of millions of humans and millions of our Orion and Ophiuchi and Gormish allies. The Federation elected instead to murder entire worlds with massive bombardments—bombardments very like that of New Boston—" spines stiffened at his quiet words "—because our only other option was to kill them one by one on the surfaces of those planets at the cost of too many of our own."

He paused once more, letting what he'd said sink in, then leaned closer to the pickup.

"All of those arguments were valid, but I was here—here in this very chamber, in the midst of the debate—and there was another argument, as well. One that was voiced only in whispers, only by implication, just as it is today. And that argument, ladies and gentlemen, was *vengeance*."

He hissed the last word, eyes locked on Owens' face across the floor, and saw the other man bite his lip.

"I do not say we could have avoided Directive Eighteen. I do not say that we *should* have avoided it. But I do say, as one who was there, that even if we could have avoided it we *would . . . not . . . have . . . done . . . so.*" The slow, spaced words were cut from crystal shards of ice, and the old, blue eyes on the master display screen were colder yet.

"We had too many dead. Half a million Terrans at Medial Station. Eight and a half million at Tannerman. One and a third billion on Lassa's World, a billion more in Codalus. A billion Orions on Tol, another ninety million on Gozal'hira, eight hundred fifty thousand in Chilliwalt. Our military deaths alone were over two million, the Orions' were far worse, and we weren't gods, ladies and gentlemen. We wanted more than an end to the fighting and dying. We wanted *vengeance* . . . and we got it.

"Perhaps it was also justice, or at least inevitable. I would like to believe that. I *try* to believe that. But it was more than justice. Our Ophiuchi allies knew that even before we did it. They refused to participate in the bombardments, and for that refusal some of us called them 'moral cowards' . . . until the smoke cleared, and we knew it too.

"And so the same Assembly which authorized Directive Eighteen drafted the Anti-Genocide Prohibition of 2249. Not because it knew it had murdered an entire species when it need not have, but because it was *afraid* it had. Because it had acted in haste and hatred, and it could never know whether or not it might have acted differently. The Prohibition doesn't forbid genocidal attacks, ladies and gentlemen. It simply stipulates that any such future act must be authorized by a two-thirds majority of this Assembly. In a very real sense, the blood debt for our own actions is that the Legislative Assembly must forever more assume—specifically, unequivocally, and inescapably—the responsibility for acting in the same way yet again.

"I had hoped," he said very quietly, "to be dead before a second such decision faced this Assembly. Most of my colleagues of that time are. A few of us remain, and when we look out over this floor and hear what is said, we hear ourselves and the ghosts of our dead fellows. We *know* what those who call for vengeance feel and think, for we have felt and thought those same things.

"But Thebans, ladies and gentlemen, are not Rigelians. They now hold but a single habitable system. We are not speaking of billions of casualties from assaults on planet after planet. And whether they are mad or not, whether their madness would have found a vehicle without the interference of Alois Saint-Just and his fellow survivors or not, the 'religion' which drives them *did* come from humanity. Perhaps they *are* mad, but have humans not shown sufficient religious 'madness' of their own? How many millions have *we* killed for 'God' in our time? Have we learned from our own bloody past? And if we have, may not the 'mad' Theban race also be capable of learning with time?

"I don't know. But remember this, ladies and gentlemen—on New New Hebrides their Inquisition did not, to the best of our knowledge, kill a single child. Certainly children died in the invasion bombardments, and certainly children died on New Boston, but even when entire New New Hebridan villages were exterminated, the children were first removed. We may call this 'stealing children' if we will. We may call preserving children who know their parents have been slaughtered cruelty, or argue that they did it only to 'brainwash' them. But they spared their lives . . . and Rigelians would not have."

He paused yet again, then shook his head slowly.

"Ladies and gentlemen, I can't tell you we can safely spare the Theban race. I can't tell you that, because until we reach Thebes, we simply cannot know. But that, ladies and gentlemen, is the purpose of the Prohibition of 2249—to *force* us to wait, to compel us to discover the truth before we act. And so, with all due respect to Mister Owens, I must ask you to withhold your decision. Wait, ladies and gentlemen. Wait until Admiral Antonov secures control of the Theban System. Wait until we know, beyond a shadow of a doubt, that we have no choice and that we are *not* acting out of vengeance and hatred.

"I am an old man," he repeated softly, "but most of you are not. I have paid my price in guilt and nightmares; you haven't ... yet. Perhaps, as I, you will have no choice, but don't, I beg you, rush to pay it. Wait. Wait just a little longer—if not for the Thebans, then for yourselves."

He cut the circuit and bowed his head over his folded hands, and utter silence hovered in the vast chamber. Then an attention bell chimed.

"The Chair," Chantal Duval said softly, "recognizes the Honorable Assemblyman for Fisk."

Yevgeny Owens stood. Anger still burned in his face and determination still stiffened his spine, but there were shadows of ghosts in his eyes, and his voice was very quiet when he spoke.

"Madam Chairman, I withdraw my motion pending the outcome of Admiral Antonov's attack on Thebes."

CHAPTER TWENTY-SEVEN
At All Costs

Ivan Antonov walked through the outer reaches of the Thebes System with light-second strides, and occasional asteroids whirled past him like insects. Not many—the Thebans had had generations to clear away a horizontal segment of the belt, as if it had been sliced across by a war-god's sword, and Antonov walked on a "floor" of artificially-arranged space rubble, while over his head there streamed a like "ceiling." Both held asteroids in a far higher density than anything in nature, but they were principally defined by the regularly spaced giant plane-toids that had been forged into fortresses of unthinkable strength. Considerations of weapons' ranges and fields of fire had created that pattern, and the precision of its geometry was almost beautiful, like a decorative tracery worked in the dull silver of dim, reflected sunlight that would have been lovely . . . save for the mass death it held.

He turned his two-hundred-thousand-kilometer body on its heel and started back toward the warp point, deep in thought. He reached it in a few steps, and the universe wavered, then dissolved, returning him to the human scale of things, facing the small group of people standing against the outer wall of *Gosainthan's* main holo tank.

Amazing how good these computer-enhanced simulations have gotten. Of course, this one was Winnie's pride and joy, painstakingly constructed with Lantu's help. He sometimes worried about the day when simulacra this good became commercially available—the sensation could become addictive. . . .

He shook off the thought and addressed his staff. "I have reviewed all aspects of our operational plan and can find no fault with it—except, of course, that it requires a force level that we don't have entirely in place as yet. Still, the build-up is on schedule, and that will soon change."

"True, Admiral." Lantu crossed his arms behind him as he studied the holo display Antonov had just left and gave the softly buzzing hum of a Theban sigh. "Yet I remain somewhat concerned over the one completely uncertain variable. I wish I knew what the Ministry of Production's done about strikefighter development in light of Redwing. I suspect recent events have lent the project rather more urgency than my own earlier recommendations."

He paused, and his yellow eyes met Antonov's with an almost-twinkle, half-apologetic and half-rueful. The human admiral looked back impassively, but there might have been the ghost of an answering twinkle, the commiseration of one professional with a fellow hamstrung by inept, short-sighted superiors. Lantu turned back to the holo with a tiny shrug.

"Of course," he continued wryly, "I haven't exactly been privy to the Synod's decisions *since* Redwing, so I can only offer the truism that knowing a thing can be done is often half the battle in matters of R and D."

Winnifred Trevayne gave the somewhat annoying sniff that, in her, accompanied absolute certitude about her own conclusions. "I don't entirely share First Admiral

Lantu's worries, sir. Permit me to reiterate my earlier line of reasoning.

"I don't think there can be any doubt that the Thebans have become well aware of the disadvantages imposed by their lack of fighters, but Lorelei's defenders obviously anticipated a desperate defensive action, as proved by their crustal defense and clearly pre-planned ramming attacks. This was natural, given Lorelei's crucial nature and the fact that the best they can possibly hope for against the Federation's mobilized industrial potential is a defensive war. Anyone prepared to expend *starships* in Kamikaze attacks would certainly have committed fighters to the defense of Lorelei *if they'd had them*." She glanced at Berenson, who nodded; the intelligence officer had stated simple military sanity.

"We can therefore conclude," she resumed, all didacticism, "that three months ago, when we took Lorelei, the Thebans did not possess fighters—not, at least, in useful numbers. Given this fact, they cannot possibly have built enough of them, or produced sufficient pilots and launch platforms, to make a difference when our attack goes in next month."

She stopped and looked around triumphantly, as if challenging anyone to find a flaw in her argument.

"Your logic is impeccable, Commander," Lantu admitted. "But permit me to remind you of the great limitation of logic: your conclusion can be no better than your premises. And one of your premises disturbs me: the assumption that the Church does, indeed, consider itself on the defensive ... or, at least, that it did at the time of the Battle of Lorelei."

They all stared at him, speechlessly wondering how the Synod could *not* so regard itself in the face of its disastrous strategic position. All but Antonov, who looked troubled.

Hannah Avram's feet rested inelegantly on the edge of the conference table as she watched the tactical simulation in the tank. It ended, and she grimaced. Dick had gotten her escort carriers up to sixteen units, and according to the tank, she'd just lost thirteen of them.

She rose to prowl *Haruna's* briefing room, fists jammed into her tunic pockets. The problem was, it all depended on the assumptions she fed the computer. *If* the Thebans followed their own tactical doctrine, and *if* they didn't know about her tiny carriers, then Antonov's devious ploy should get her into Thebes unscathed. And *if* she got in unscathed *and* got beyond shipboard weapon range, her fighters should sting the Shellheads to death, since nothing they had could reach her. If she ran the problem with those assumptions, the computer usually killed no more than three ships. If she changed any one of them, losses climbed steeply. If she changed any two of them, her command was virtually annihilated.

She came to a stop, frowning down into the tank. Her ships were so small, so fragile, without the shields and armor of fleet carriers. In a way, that ought to help protect them—they shouldn't look like worthwhile targets until they launched—but if anyone did shoot at them, they would certainly die.

Yet she'd gone over Antonov's ops plan again and again, and she couldn't argue with any of its underlying assumptions. Based on what they knew and had observed, it was brilliant. The only thing that could really screw it up was for the Shellheads to surprise them with fighters of their own, and she had to agree with the logic of Commander Trevayne's analysis.

But some deeply-hidden uncertainty nagged at her. Worse, she knew it nagged at Antonov, whether he chose to acknowledge it or not.

"Za vashe zdorovye!"

Kthaara responded with a phonetic approximation of the Russian toast of which he was extremely proud, but Tsuchevsky mumbled his response, clearly preoccupied.

"What is the matter, Paaavaaaal Saairgaaiaavychhh?" the Orion asked expansively. As always, his spirits had risen with the approach of decisive action. "Are you still worried by that Theban's misgivings?" He gave the choked-off snarl that answered to a human's snort of impatience, tossed off his drink, reached for a refill, then offered the bottle to Tsuchevsky. "Come, Paaaasha. Why are you fucking a *mairkazh?*"

It was the first time he'd essayed that particular transliteration, and Tsuchevsky sputtered into his vodka, spilling half of it to Kthaara's loud cry of anguish. But Antonov only allowed himself a brief smile. He hadn't shared the contents of Howard Anderson's latest message with the other two. There was no reason why they should have to share his own frustration at acting under politically-imposed time pressure. Besides, Kthaara wouldn't understand. To him, preparation for battle was an annoying necessity; he would never really be able to sympathize with a desire for more of it.

The admiral's slight smile vanished and he brooded down into his glass as he contemplated the machinations of that most loathsome of all human sub-species, the politico. There were, he conceded, occasional true statesmen in human history. Unfortunately, their rare appearances only made the lower orders of political life even more disgusting by contrast. Yevgeny Owens might have withdrawn his motion, but Pericles Waldeck had refused to accept defeat. He'd simply shifted to other, less-principled front men to keep the issue alive, and he was taking gradual toll of the anti-override mood (and, Antonov could tell, of Anderson's health). The attack could be postponed no longer. It would, as he'd just announced to his staff, commence in ninety-six hours.

Damn all politicians to hell! Antonov shook himself and tossed off his vodka. *Cheer up, Vanya! Things could be worse.*

The stupendous asteroid fortresses waited, three and a quarter light-hours from the binary star system's GO component. The distance-dimmed light of Thebes A woke spectral gleams from occasional surface domes and sensor arrays, but the fortresses' teeth were hidden at their iron hearts. It had been the work of decades to clear the cosmic rubble of the star's outermost asteroid belt away from the closed warp point, but the largest lumps of debris had been carefully saved when the rest went to the orbital smelters. The huge chunks of rock and metal, most as large or larger than Sol's Ceres or Epsilon Eridani's Mjolnir, had been bored and hollowed to receive their weapons and station-keeping drives, then towed by fleets of tugs to their new positions.

They floated within their own immense minefields, sullen with power, shielded and armored, fit to laugh at armadas. The Sword of Terra's final mobile units—destroyers and light cruisers, supported by a pitiful handful of superdreadnoughts and battle-cruisers, a scattering of captured infidel carriers, and the converted freighter "barges" the Ministry of Production had cobbled up—hovered behind them, beyond the projected range of the infidels' new weapons, but it was the fortresses which mattered. The smallest of those titans was seven times as powerful as the largest superdreadnought ever built; the biggest was beyond comprehension, its strength graspable only through abstract statistics. Once there'd been no doubt of their ability to smash any attack, but that was before the infidels revealed their warp-capable missiles.

Now construction ships labored furiously, modifying and refitting frantically in light of Lorelei. They couldn't possibly finish all they had to do, and too many of the new systems—the massed batteries of point defense stations and hastily constructed hangar bays—were surface installations, for there was no time to bury them deep, but the engineers and fortress crews had attacked their duties with desperate energy, for the People stood at bay.

The last bastion of the Faith lay behind those forts, and the Holy Messenger's own degenerate race hovered one bare transit away, poised to break through in this dark hour and crush the Faith it had abandoned. Beside such horror as that, clean death in Holy Terra's cause was to be embraced, not feared, for death meant less than nothing when the fate of God Herself rested in their merely mortal hands.

Ivan Antonov's eyes watched the first-wave SBM-HAWKs' cloud of tiny lights reach the warp point, waver slightly on the display, and vanish. Then they turned to the other precise clusters of matching lights, each indicating yet another wave that waited, quiescent.

It was different this time. Each of those waves had not a class of targets, but a single one.

He glanced across the flag bridge at Lantu, standing with Angus MacRory. It hadn't been easy to retrieve the data to permit such precise targeting. No conscious mind—least of all one whose primary concerns had lain in the realms of grand strategy—could hold such a mass of technical minutiae, and adapting the techniques of hypnotic retrieval to a hitherto-unknown race had been a heartbreaking labor. And, of course, however willing he might be, Lantu's subconscious couldn't yield up what it had never known—such as any last-minute refitting the forts might have undergone. But what they now knew should be enough. . . .

Lantu watched a smaller version of the same display through the cloudy veil of his inner eyelids. He forced his face to remain impassive, and he was glad so few humans had yet learned to read Theban body language.

The last of the first wave of lights vanished, and he closed his outer lids, as well, wishing he'd been able to stay away. Like Fraymak. The colonel had never questioned Lantu's decision, yet he hadn't been able to bring himself to watch the working out of its consequences. But Lantu couldn't *not* watch. He knew too much about what waited beyond that warp point, knew too many of the officers and men those missiles were about to kill. He had reached an agonizing point of balance, an acceptance of what he must do that had given him the strength to do it . . . but it was no armor against the nightmares. So now he watched the weapons he had forged for the

death of the People's defenders, for to do otherwise
would have been one betrayal more than he could make.

Angus MacRory never said much; now he said nothing
at all, but his hand squeezed Lantu's shoulder. He felt
it through his shoulder carapace, but he didn't open his
eyes. He only inhaled deeply and reached up to cover it
with one four-fingered hand.

A wave of almost eager horror greeted the first infidel
missile packs. Nerves tightened as the hell weapons
blinked into existence and the defenders realized the cli-
mactic battle of the People's life was upon them, but at
least it had come. At least there was no more waiting.

Captain Ithanad had the watch in Central Missile Defense aboard the command fortress *Saint Elmo* when the
alarms began to shriek. His teams were already plotting
the emerging weapons, and he swallowed sour fear as he
saw the blossoming threat sources.

"All units, engage!" he barked through the alarms'
howl.

Second Fleet's SBMHAWKs darted through the minefields virtually unscathed while the fortress crews rushed
to battle stations and the first defensive fire reached out.
Three squadrons of Theban fighters on standing combat
patrol swooped into the mines after them, firing desperately, and a few—a very few—of the wildly dodging packs
were killed. But not enough to make a difference. Targeting systems stabilized and locked, and hundreds of
missiles leapt from their launchers.

Captain Ithanad paled.

The missile pods weren't spreading their fire. The infidels must have captured detailed data on Thebes, for
every one of those missiles had selected the same target:
Saint Elmo, the very heart and brain of the defenses!

Hundreds of SBMs streaked towards his fortress in a
single, massive salvo, and Ithanad's lips moved in silent

prayer. Many of them were going to miss; more than four hundred of them weren't.

This time the SBMHAWK wasn't a total surprise, and *Saint Elmo* was no mere OWP. Her already powerful anti-missile defenses had been radically overhauled in the four-month delay Jahanak's stand had imposed upon Second Fleet, and not even that colossal salvo was enough to saturate her tracking ability. But it *was* enough to saturate her firepower.

Space burned with the glare of counter missiles. Laser clusters fired desperately. Multi-barreled auto-cannon spewed thousands upon thousands of shells, hurling solid clouds of metal into the paths of incoming weapons. Over two hundred SBMHAWKs died, enough to stop any previously conceivable missile attack cold . . . but almost two hundred got through.

Captain Ithanad clung to his command chair as the universe went mad. Safety straps—straps he'd never expected to need on a fortress *Saint Elmo*'s size—bruised his flesh savagely, and the thunder went on and on and on. . . .

Antimatter warheads wrapped *Saint Elmo* in a fiery shroud, and her surface boiled as her gargantuan shields went down. Fireballs crawled across her like demented suns, gouging, ripping, destroying. Her titanic mass resisted stubbornly, but nothing material could defy such fury.

The long, rolling concussion came for Captain Ithanad and his ratings and swept them into death.

The Sword of Holy Terra stared in horror at the sputtering, incandescent ruin. *Saint Elmo* wasn't—quite—dead. Perhaps five percent of her weapons remained. Which was a remarkable testimonial to the engineers who'd designed and built her, but not enough to make her an effective fighting unit.

And *Saint Elmo* had been their most powerful—and best protected—installation.

Tracking crews aboard the other fortresses bent over their displays, tight-faced and grim, waiting for the next hellish wave of pods.

"Second wave SBMHAWKs spotted for transit, Admiral," Tsuchevsky reported.

"Very well, Commodore." Antonov glanced at the chronometer. "You will launch in three hours fifty minutes."

"Aye, aye, sir." The chief of staff shivered as he turned back to his own displays, wondering what it must feel like to sit and wait for it on the far side of that warp point. He pictured the exquisite agony of tight-stretched nerves, the nausea and fear gnawing at the defenders' bellies, and decided he didn't really want to know.

He glanced at Admiral Lantu, hunched over the repeater display beside a tight-faced Angus MacRory, and turned quickly back to his instruments.

The alarms shrieked yet again, dragging Fifth Admiral Panhanal up out of his exhausted doze as the holo sphere filled with familiar horror. He didn't have to move to see it. He sat on the bridge of the superdreadnought *Charles P. Steadman*, just as he'd sat for almost a week now. He would have killed for a single night's undisturbed sleep or died for a bath, yet such luxuries had become dreams from another life. He stank, and his skin crawled under his vac suit, but he thrust the thought aside—again—and fought back curses as the fresh wave of missile pods spewed from the warp point.

He rubbed his eyes, trying to make himself think, for he was the Sword's senior officer since Fourth Admiral Wantar had died with Fleet Chaplain Urlad aboard *Masada*. That had been . . . yesterday? The day before?

It didn't matter. The devils in Lorelei had pounded his defenses for days, sending wave after wave of hell-spawned missiles through the warp point. They could have sent them all through at once, but they'd chosen to prolong their Terra-damned bombardment, staggering the waves, taunting the Sword with their technical superiority. Each attack was targeted upon a single, specific fortress, mocking the People with the totality of the data they must have captured. The shortest interval between waves had been less than fifteen minutes, the longest over nine hours, stretching the Sword's crews upon a rack of anticipation between the deadly precision of their blows.

He watched his units do their best to kill the pods . . . and fail. He'd brought his precious carriers to within forty light-seconds to maintain heavier fighter patrols, for the fortresses' exposed hangar decks had been ripped away by the crushing, endless bombardment. The fighters had gotten better at killing the pods . . . for a time. But their pilots were too green and fatigued to keep it up, and keeping them on standing patrol this way exhausted them further, yet even as their edge and reflexes eroded they remained his best defense.

The latest attack wave paused suddenly. He shut his eyes as the cloud of missiles slashed towards *Verdun*, the last of his fortresses, and behind his closed lids he saw the storm of defensive fire pouring forth to meet them. A soft sound—not really a moan, but dark with pain—rose from his bridge officers.

Panhanal opened his eyes and turned to the visual display as the terrible flashes died. Then he relaxed with a sigh. *Verdun* had been built into one of the smaller asteroids, and there was nothing left of her. Just nothing at all.

He leaned back, checking the status boards. Half a dozen of the once invincible forts remained, but all were broken and crippled, little more dangerous than as many superdreadnoughts. Indeed, *Vicksburg* and *Rorke's Drift* were less heavily armed than battle-cruisers. Forty years of labor had been wiped away in six hideous days, and Terra only knew how many thousands of his warriors had perished with them. Panhanal didn't know, and he never wanted to.

The infidels would come now that they'd killed the forts. But at least the minefields remained. He tried to cheer himself with that, for he knew what those mines would have done to any assault the People might have made. Yet the infidels had to know about the mines— the precision of their attacks proved they'd known exactly what they faced. And if they knew about them and still meant to attack, then they must think they knew a way to defeat them.

The thought ground at his battered morale, and he prayed his personnel felt less hopeless than he. Of course, the rest of the Sword didn't know Fleet Chaplain Sanak had excused himself briefly from *Steadman's* flag bridge last night. Not for long. Just long enough to go to his cabin, put the muzzle of his machine-pistol in his mouth, and squeeze the trigger. Panhanal made himself look away from the empty chair beside his own.

"Stand by all units," he rasped.

"Aye, sir. Standing by," his flag captain replied in a hoarse, weary voice.

The neat files of light dots moving slowly toward the warp point in Antonov's display belied the motley nature of the ships they represented.

Against all reasonable expectation, the tramp freighter had reappeared in the interstellar age. The reactionless drive represented a healthy initial investment, but its operating expenses were small, as it required no reaction mass. And the nature of the warp lines meant any vessel that could get into deep space could travel between the stars, so there was a vast number of hulls to be commandeered. The real problem—and the cause of much of the delay—had been the need to equip them with minimal deception-mode ECM so that they could fill the role Lantu had in mind for them. And if they did that, then they were worth every millicredit of the compensation that had been paid to their owners.

Tsuchevsky cleared his throat softly, and Antonov saw the time had arrived. The chief of staff—and, even more so, Kthaara—had been fidgeting for hours, but Antonov had been adamant. The Thebans must have time to feel their exhaustion and despair, just enough for their tense readiness in the wake of the final SBMHAWK salvo to ease a bit.

Now he nodded, and Tsuchevsky began transmitting orders.

Admiral Panhanal's crews had relaxed. Or, no, they hadn't "relaxed" so much as sagged in dull-minded weariness when no immediate attack followed *Verdun's* destruction. Panhanal knew they had, and even as he tried to goad and torment them into vigilance, his heart wept for them. Yet it was his job, and—

Two hundred superdreadnoughts erupted into the system of Thebes.

The admiral stared at his read-outs in stark, horrified disbelief as entire flotillas of capital ships warped into the teeth of his mines in a deadly, endless stream of insanely tight transits. Not possible! It wasn't *possible!* Not the Satan-Khan himself could have conjured such an armada!

"Launch all fighters!" he barked, and then the visual display exploded.

Despite himself Panhanal cringed away from its flaming fury. He peered at it through his inner eyelids, outer lids slitted against the incandescence, and a tiny part of his weary mind realized something was amiss. Wave after wave of ships appeared, dying in their dozens as the mines blew them apart, but they were dying too quickly. Too easily.

And then he understood. Those weren't superdreadnoughts—they were *drones!* They had to be. Fitted with ECM to suck the mines in if they were under manual control, perhaps, but not real superdreadnoughts, and his blood ran cold as he realized what he was seeing. The infidels weren't "sweeping" the mines; they were *absorbing* them!

He cursed aloud, pounding the padded arm of his chair. His mines were hurling themselves at worthless hulks, expending themselves, ripping the heart from his defenses, and there was nothing he could do about it!

The last freighter vanished into the nothingness of the warp point, and the lead group of the real assault's first wave—five superdreadnoughts converted for mine-sweeping—moved ponderously up. Antonov watched their lights advance, followed by those of the second group—three unconverted superdreadnoughts and three of Hannah Avram's escort carriers.

The lead group reached the warp point, and their lights wavered and went out.

The superdreadnought *Finsteraarhorn* blinked into reality, and the surviving Theban mines hurtled to meet her, but the tramp freighters' "assault" had done its job. Only a fraction of them remained, and *Finsteraarhorn's* heavy point defense handled the attacking satellites with ease. More ships appeared behind her, and their external ordnance lashed out at the air-bleeding wrecks of the surviving fortresses.

Return fire spat back, x-ray lasers and sprint missiles hammering at pointblank range. The last mines expended themselves uselessly, lasers lacerated armor and hulls, shields went down under the hammer blows of missiles that got through the mine-sweepers' point defense, yet they survived.

Rear Admiral Hannah Avram exhaled in relief as TFNS *Mosquito* made transit behind the superdreadnought *Pike's Peak*. *Mosquito* had survived—and that meant the anti-mine plan had worked.

Her eyes narrowed as her stabilizing plot flickered back to life. The lead group of mine-sweepers streamed atmosphere from their wounded flanks, yet they were all still there, and TFNS *Rainier* followed on *Mosquito*'s heels. The light codes of Theban capital ships blazed, but they were hanging back, obviously afraid Antonov had reserved a "mousetrap" wave of SBMHAWKs as he had in Lorelei. A half-dozen forts were still in action— no, only five, she corrected herself as the avalanche of *Pike's Peak*'s external missiles struck home—and the Shellheads were following their doctrine. They'd never seen her escort carriers, and they weren't wasting so much as a missile on lowly "destroyers" while superdreadnoughts floated on their targeting screens. Now to get the hell out of range before they changed their minds.

"All right, Danny. Course is one-one-seven by two-eight-three. Let's move it!"

"Aye, aye, sir!" MaGuire acknowledged, and she heard him snapping maneuvering orders as the next group of superdreadnoughts and escort carriers made transit behind them. It looked like the dreaded battle was going to be far less terrible than anyone had predicted, especially if—

Her heart almost stopped as the first fighter missile exploded against *Rainier*'s shields.

Admiral Panhanal bared his teeth, bloodshot eyes flaring. The ready squadrons had clearly taken the infidels unaware—there hadn't even been any defensive fire as they closed!—and now *all* of his fighters were launching.

TFNS *Rainier* shuddered as her shields went down and fighter missiles spalled her drive field, and her fighter/missile defense officer stared at his read-outs in shock. Fighters! The Shellheads had *fighters*!

His fingers stabbed his console, reprogramming his defenses to engage fighters instead of missiles, but there was no time. More and more missiles pounded his ship, and the fighters closed on their heels with lasers. He fought to readjust to the end, panic suppressed by professionalism, and then he and his ship died.

*   *   *

"Launch all—*No!*" Hannah chopped off her own instinctive order as Battle Plot's full message registered. Theban fighters speckled the plot, not in tremendous numbers, but scores more were appearing at the edge of detection, *and every one of them was the bright green of a friendly unit!*

She swallowed a vicious curse of understanding. The Thebans had duplicated their captured Terran fighters' IFF as well as their power plants and weapons—and that meant there was no way to tell *her* fighters from theirs!

"Communications! Courier drone to the Flag—Priority One! 'Enemy strikefighters detected. Enemy fighter emission and IFF signatures identical, repeat, identical, to our own. Am withholding launch pending location of enemy launch platforms. Message ends.'"

"Aye, aye, sir!"

"Follow it up with an all-ships transmission to the rest of the task group as they make transit. 'Do not, repeat, not, launch fighters. Form on me at designated coordinates.'"

"Aye, aye, sir. Drone away."

"Tracking, back-plot that big strike. Get me a vector and do it now!"

"We're on it, sir." Commander Braunschweig's voice was tight but confident, and Hannah nodded. More and more Theban fighters crept over the rim of her display, and she looked up at her fighter operations officer.

"You've got maybe ten minutes to figure out how our people are going to keep things straight, Commodore Mitchell."

The message from *Mosquito's* courier drone appeared simultaneously on Antonov's and Lantu's computer screens, and at effectively the same instant, their heads snapped up. Two pairs of eyes—molten yellow and arctic gray—met in shared horror. No words were necessary; it was their first moment of absolute mutual understanding.

"Commodore Tsuchevsky," Antonov's deep, rock-steady voice revealed how shaken he was only to those who knew him well. "Have communications pass a warning to assault groups that have not yet departed. And give me a priority link to Admiral Berenson."

TFNS *Mosquito* raced away from the besieged super-dreadnoughts, followed by her sisters. It took long, endless minutes for all of them to make transit, and Hannah's face was bloodless as she watched the first massed Theban strike smash home. Only a handful of fighters came after her "destroyers," and she forced herself to fight back only with her point defense. Her own pilots would have been an incomparably better defense . . . but not enough better.

Her conscious mind was still catching up with her instinctive response, yet it told her she'd done the right thing. If she'd launched immediately, her fighters might have made a difference in the fleet defense role, but their effectiveness would have been badly compromised by the identification problems. Worse, they would have further complicated the capital ships' fighter-defense problems; the superdreadnoughts would have been forced to fire at *any* fighter, for they could never have sorted out their true enemies. But worst of all, it would have identified her carriers for what they were, and there was no question what the Thebans would have done. Her tiny, fragile ships represented a full third of Second Fleet's fighter strength. Antonov couldn't afford to spend them for no return.

She winced as another Terran superdreadnought blew apart. And a third. She could feel her crews' fury—fury directed at *her* as she ran away from their dying fellows—and she understood it perfectly.

Fifth Admiral Panhanal tasted his bridge crew's excitement. The Wings of Death were proving more effective than they'd dared hope. The infidels had smashed his fortresses and won a space clear of mines in which to deploy, but it wouldn't save them. His strikefighters swarmed about them like enraged *hansal*, striking savagely with missiles and then closing with lasers. They were as exhausted as any of his warriors, and their inexperience showed—their percentage of hits was far lower than the infidel pilots usually managed—but there were many of them. Indeed, if they could continue as well as they'd begun, they might yet hold the warp point for Holy Terra!

He glanced at a corner of his plot, watching the fleeing infidel destroyers, and his nostrils flared with contempt. Only three of his fighter squadrons had even fired at the cowards! If the rest of their cursed fleet proved as gutless . . .

"Well, Commodore?" Hannah asked harshly.

The last of the superdreadnoughts had made transit and the first battleships were coming through. The warp point was a boil of bleeding capital ships and fishtailing strikefighters lit by the flash and glare of fighter missiles, and her own ship was sixteen light-seconds from it. Her rearmost units were less than twelve light-seconds out, but it was far enough. It had to be.

"Sir, I'm sorry, but we can't guarantee our IDs." Mitchell met her eyes squarely. "We're resetting our transponders, which should give us at least a few minutes' grace, but they've got exactly the same equipment. There's no way we can keep them from shifting to match us."

"Understood. But we *can* differentiate for at least a few minutes?"

"Yes, sir," Mitchell said confidently.

"All right. Bobbi, do you have those carriers for me?"

"I think so, sir," Roberta Braunschweig said. "We've got what looks like three or four *Wolfhound*-class carriers—prizes, no doubt—and something else. If I had to guess, they're converted freighters like our barges back in Danzig, but the range is too great for positive IDs."

Hannah turned back to Mitchell. "I know we don't have time to set this up the way you'd like, but I want you to hit those carriers. Retain four strikegroups for task group defense. All the rest go." Her gaze locked with his. "Those carriers are 'all costs' targets, Commodore," she said softly.

TFNS *Baden* reeled under repeated, deafening impacts, and only the bridge crew's crash couches saved them. Most of them. The deck canted wildly for a mad instant before the artificial gravity reassumed control, and the bridge was filled with the smoke and actinic glare of electrical fires.

"Damage control to the bridge!" Captain Lars Nielsen's voice sounded strange through the roaring in his head. His stomach churned as he felt his ship's pain, heard her crying out in agony in the scream of damage alarms, and his hand locked on his quivering command chair's arm as if to share it. She was too old for this. Too old. Taken from the Reserve and refitted to face this horror instead of ending her days in the peace she'd earned.

Another salvo of missiles smashed at her, and drive rooms exploded under their fury. *Baden's* speed dropped, and Nielsen knew she could never prevent the next squadron of fighters from maneuvering into her blind zone and administering the *coup de grace*.

He stared at his one still-functioning tactical display, eyes bitter as he recognized the amateurishness of the Theban pilots. They should have been easy meat for the fighters aboard the escort carriers—the carriers which had fled almost off the display's edge without even trying to launch.

God damn her. Nielsen was oddly calm as he looked around his ruined bridge and heard, as if from a great distance, the report of more incoming fighters. *God damn her to He—*

The universe turned to noise and flame and went out.

"Admiral Berenson is in position, sir," a haggard Pavel Tsuchevsky reported.

Antonov nodded. He felt like Tsuchevsky looked, but

order had finally been re-established. The plan for an operation of this scale was a document almost the size of the annual Federation budget, and changing it at the last moment was like trying to deflect a planet. But the fleet carriers Berenson now commanded had been pulled out of their position in the very last assault groups, moved to the head of the line, and paired off with battle-cruisers. Antonov didn't really want to send them in at all—they would be in combat before their cloaking ECM could be engaged, possibly before their launch catapults could stabilize. But he had no choice. His vanguard was dying without fighter support. Still he hesitated—and, as if to remind him, yet another Omega drone sounded TFNS *Baden's* death cry.

"Order Admiral Berenson to make transit as soon as possible," he told Tsuchevsky, all indecision gone.

"*Go!*"

Catapults roared with power aboard sixteen tiny ships, and one hundred and ninety-two strikefighters erupted from their hangars. Forty-eight of them formed quickly about their carriers, heavy with external gun packs to supplement their internal lasers. The others streaked away, charging for the Theban carriers just over a light-minute away.

Hannah Avram felt the whiplash recoil in *Mosquito's* bones and made herself relax. One way or the other, right or wrong, she was committed.

It took Panhanal precious seconds to realize what had happened. His exhausted thoughts were slow despite the adrenalin rushing through him, and the escort carriers were far away and his plotting teams were concentrating on the carnage before them.

Then it registered. Those fleeing "destroyers" weren't destroyers; they were carriers, and they'd just launched against *his* fighter platforms!

He barked orders, cursing himself for underestimating the infidels. There had to have been some reason they'd sent such tiny ships through in their earliest assault groups, but he'd been too blind, too weary and bleary-minded, to realize it.

His own fighters split. Two thirds curved away, racing to engage the anti-carrier strike, and his initial panic eased slightly. They were closer, able to cut inside the attackers and intercept well short of their bases.

Half his remaining pilots streaked towards the infidel carriers themselves. He could see they'd held back at least some of their own fighters for cover, but they didn't have many, and his strike would vastly outnumber them.

His remaining fighters continued to assail the infidel capital ships, yet they clearly lacked the strength to stop battle-line units by themselves. On the other hand, his starships had yet to engage. If he could get in close, bottle the attackers up long enough for his own fighters to deal with theirs and then return . . .

"Shellhead fighters breaking off attack, sir!"

The scanner rating was very young, and Captain Lauren Ethridge didn't feel like reprimanding him for his elated outburst—nor the rest of *Popocatépetl's* bridge crew for the brief cheer that followed it. They'd been engaged since the instant of their emergence, and the enemy fighters had made up in doggedness what they lacked in tactical polish. Then her scanners told her what Admiral Avram was up to.

Yes, she thought. *Let them have their elation. It won't last anyway.*

"Sir," the same scanner rating reported, this time in a quiet voice, "Theban battle-line units approaching at flank speed." He keyed in Plotting's analysis, and it appeared on the tactical screen. There was no doubt: every surviving unit of the Theban battle fleet was coming straight at them.

Shit. Captain Ethridge began giving orders.

"On your toes, people." Captain Angela Martens' voice was that of a rider gentling a nervous horse. She watched the untidy horde racing to intercept her strike, and despite the odds, she smiled wolfishly. They were about to get reamed, and she knew it, but that clumsy gaggle told her a lot about the quality of the opposition. Whatever was about to happen to her people, what was going to happen to the Shellies was even worse.

"Stand by your IFF," she murmured, eyes intent on her display. The lead Thebans were almost upon her, and she felt herself tightening internally. "Stand . . . by . . . *Now!*"

There was a moment of instant consternation in the Theban ranks as their enemies' transponder codes suddenly changed. It should have helped them just as much as the Terrans, but they hadn't known it was coming. And they weren't prepared for the fact that a full half of the Terran fighters were configured for anti-fighter work, not an anti-shipping strike.

The Terran escort squadrons whipped up and around, slicing into them, a rapier in Martens' hand against the clumsy broadsword of her foes.

Fifty Theban fighters died in the first thirty seconds.

The dimly perceptible wrongness in space that was a warp point loomed in TFNS *Bearhound*'s main view screen. David Berenson glowered at it as if at an enemy.

"Ready for transit, Admiral," *Bearhound*'s captain reported. Berenson acknowledged, then swung around to his ops officer.

"Well, Akira, will it be ready in time? And, if it is, will it work?"

Commander Akira Mendoza's face was beaded with sweat, but he looked satisfied. "Sir, I think the answers are 'Yes' and 'Maybe.' The fighters' transponders should be reset by the time we reach the warp point." There was no way for him to know he and Kthaara had, in a few minutes' desperate improvisation, independently duplicated Mitchell's idea. "And it ought to work . . . I hope." He outlined the same dangers Mitchell had set forth for Hannah Avram, but his professional caution fooled no one. He was a former fighter pilot, with his full share of the breed's irrepressible cockiness. So was Berenson, but he was a little older. He nodded thoughtfully as Mendoza finished, then sighed deeply.

"It'll have to do, Akira. We're committed." He leaned back towards his armrest communicator. "Proceed, Captain Kyllonen. And have communications inform Admiral Antonov we are making transit."

Hannah sat uselessly on *Mosquito*'s bridge. It was all in Mitchell's hands now—his and his handful of defending pilots. She watched the AFHAWKs going out as the lightly-armed escort carriers fired, and then her own fighters swept out and up to engage the enemy.

The Theban pilots were tired, inexperienced, and armed for shipping strikes. Fighter missiles were useless against other fighters, and the few without missiles were armed with external laser packs—longer ranged than the Terrans' gun armament and ideal for repeated runs on starships but less effective in knife-range fighter combat. The defensive squadrons closed through the laser envelope without losing a single unit, and their superior skill began to tell. Both sides' craft were identical, but the Terrans knew far more about their capabilities.

Theban squadrons shattered as fighter after fighter blew apart, but there were scores of Theban fighters. Terran pilots began to die, and Hannah bit her lip as the roiling maelstrom of combat reached out to engulf her carriers. *At least they haven't managed to shift their transponders yet.*

It was her last clear thought before the madness was upon her.

Admiral Panhanal fought to keep track of the far-flung holocaust. It was too much for a single flag officer to coordinate, yet he had no choice but to try.

Charles P. Steadman lurched as she flushed her external racks and blew a wounded infidel battleship apart. *Steadman* had only three surviving sisters, but they were

unhurt as they entered the fray, and Panhanal snarled as
their heavy initial blows went home. Yet infidel ships
were still emerging from the warp point, the forts were
gone, and his remaining warp point fighters had exhausted their missiles. They were paying with their lives
as they closed to strafe with their lasers, but they were
warriors of Holy Terra; the dwindling survivors bored in
again and again and again.

Panhanal stole a glance at the repeater display tied
into his carriers and blanched in disbelief. The escorting
infidel fighters had cut their way clear through his inter-
ceptors and looped back, and space was littered with
their victims. But his own squadrons had ignored their
killers to close on the missile-armed infidels, and fireballs
blazed in the enemy formation.

They were better than his pilots—more skilled, more
deadly—but there weren't enough of them. A handful
might break through to the carriers; no more would
survive.

And the infidel carriers were dying. He bared his
teeth, aware even through the fire of battle that he was
drunk with fatigue, reduced to the level of some prime-
val, red-fanged ancestor. It didn't matter. He watched
the first two carriers explode, and a roar from Tracking
echoed his own exultation.

He turned back to the main engagement as *Steadman*
closed to laser-range.

Mosquito staggered as missiles pounded her light
shields flat. More missiles streaked in, and damage signals screamed as fighter lasers added their fury to the
destruction.

Hannah's plot went out, and she looked up at a visual
display just like the holo tank. Like the holo tank with a
wrong assumption. Six of her ships were gone and more
were going, but the Theban strike had shot its bolt.

And then she saw the trio of kamikazes screaming
straight into the display's main pickup. A lone Terran

fighter was on their tails, firing desperately, and one of
the Thebans exploded. Then a second.

They weren't going to stop the third, Hannah thought
distantly.

The range fell, and the last battle-line of the Sword of
Terra engaged the infidels toe-to-toe. The Theban battleship *Lao-tze* blew up, and the Terran superdreadnought
Foraker followed. *Charles P. Steadman* shouldered
through the melee, rocking under the fire raining upon
her and smashing back savagely.

Angela Martens whipped her fighter up, wrenching it
around in a full-power turn, then cut power. The Theban
on her tail charged past before he could react, and her
fire tore him apart. She red-lined the drive, vision graying
despite her heroic life support, and nailed yet another
on what amounted to blind, trained instinct. Her number
two cartwheeled away in wreckage, and Lieutenant
Haynes closed on her wing to replace him. They dropped
into a two-element formation, trying to find the rest of
the squadron in the madness and killing as they went.

The bleeding remnants of Hannah Avram's strike lined
up on the Theban carriers, and if more were left than
Admiral Panhanal would have believed possible, there
still weren't enough. Lieutenant Commander Saboski was
strike leader now—the fourth since they'd launched—
and he made a snap decision. They couldn't nail them all,
but the barges were too slow and weak to escape Admiral
Berenson's strikegroups if the big carriers got in.

"Designate the *Wolfhounds!*" he snapped, and the
command fighter's tactical officer punched buttons and
brought the single-seat fighters sweeping around behind
it. The strike exploded into a dozen smaller formations,
converging on their targets from every possible direction.

Bearhound emerged from the disorientation of warp
transit, and the humans aboard her could do little but

sweat while her catapults stabilized and her scanners fought to sort out the chaos that was the Battle of Thebes.

Almost simultaneously, Primary Flight Control announced launch readiness and Plotting reported the location and vector of Hannah Avram's escort carriers. Berenson's orders crackled, and *Bearhound* lurched to the recoil of a full deck launch even as she turned directly away from the escort carriers with her escort, TFNS *Parang*. He stared at his plot, watching *Bearhound*'s sister ships fight around in her wake as they made transit, following their flagship through the insanity.

"ECM coming up!" Mendoza snapped, and the admiral grunted. They couldn't get into cloak this close to the enemy, but deception-mode ECM might help. He stared into his display and prayed it would.

"Fighters, Fifth Admiral!"

Panhanal looked up at the cry, and his heart was ice as fresh infidel fighters raced vengefully up the tails of his shattered squadrons and the stroboscopic viciousness of the nightmare visual display redoubled.

The infidel carriers vanished as the data codes of battle-cruisers replaced them. There was a moment of consternation in his tracking sections—only an instant, but long enough for the leading infidels to turn and run while the computers grappled with the deception. Yet warp transit's destabilizing effect on their ECM systems had had its way, and the electronic brains had kept track of them. The data codes flickered back, and the admiral bared his teeth.

"Ignore the battle-cruisers—go for the carriers!"

"Aye, Fifth Admiral!"

Captain Rene Dejardin had heard Winnifred Trevayne's briefings, yet he hadn't really believed it. It wasn't that he doubted her professional competence, but rather that he simply couldn't accept the notion that a race could travel in space, control thermonuclear fusion, and still be religious fanatics of the sort one read about in history books. It was too great an affront to his sense of the rightness of things.

Now, as he tried desperately to fight his carrier clear of the warp point after launching his fighters, he believed.

The Theban superdreadnought bearing down on *Bulldog* showed on visual—*without magnification*. The latest range read-out was something else Dejardin couldn't really believe. Five hundred kilometers wasn't even knife-range—it was the range of claws and teeth. At such a range, *Bulldog's* speed and maneuverability advantage meant nothing. There was no evading the colossus on the view screen. And there was no fighting it—a fleet carrier was armed for self-defense against missiles and fighters; her ship-to-ship armament was little more than a sop to tradition. And the superdreadnought's indifference to the frantic attacks of *Bulldog's* escorting battle-cruiser removed his last doubts as to the zealotry of the beings that crewed her.

Steadman's massed batteries of x-ray lasers fired as one, knifing through *Bulldog's* shields at a range which allowed for no attenuation, and mere metal meant nothing in that storm of invisible energy.

But even as *Bulldog* died, her sisters *Rottweiler*, *Direhound*, and *Malamute* emerged and began to launch their broods.

The wreckage of the anti-carrier strike fell back, fighting to reform, and Captain Martens cut her way through to them. The Thebans broke off, desperate to kill their attackers yet forced to retreat to rearm. They had to use the barges; none of the carriers remained.

Thirty-one of the one hundred forty-four attacking fighters escaped.

Hannah Avram dragged herself back to awareness and pain, to the sliminess of blood flowing from her nostrils and lungs filled with slivered glass, and knew someone had sealed her helmet barely in time.

She pawed at her shockframe. Her eyes weren't working very well—they, too, were full of blood—and she couldn't seem to find the release, and her foggy brain reported that her left arm wasn't working, either. In fact, nothing on her left side was. Someone loomed beside her, and she blinked, fighting to see. The vac suit bore a captain's insignia. Danny, she thought muzzily. It must be Danny.

A hand urged her back. Another found the med panel on her suit pack, and anesthetic washed her back into the darkness.

TFNS *Gosainthan* emerged into reality at the head of Second Fleet's last five superdreadnoughts. Ivan Antonov remained expressionless as he waited for communications to establish contact with Berenson. Preliminary reports allowed him to breathe again as he studied the plot while Tsuchevsky collated the flood of data. The Theban fighters still on the warp point were a broken, bewildered force, he saw grimly, vanishing with inexorable certainty as Berenson's pilots pursued them to destruction.

Gosainthan's heading suddenly altered, and he glanced at his tactical read-outs as Captain Chen took his ship and her squadron to meet the surviving Theban superdreadnoughts. The admiral nodded absently. Yes ... things could, indeed, be worse.

"The Wings are rearming, sir. They'll begin launching again in seven minutes."

Admiral Panhanal grunted approval, but deep inside he knew it was too late. Those cursed small carriers had diverted him, sucking his fighters off the warp point just in time for the fleet carriers to erupt into his face. Five of the newcomers had been destroyed, others damaged, but they'd gotten most of their fighters off first. And enough survived to rearm every infidel fighter in the system.

He'd lost. He'd failed Holy Terra, and he stared with burning, hate-filled eyes at the fleeing fleet carriers and the battle-cruisers guarding their flanks. He was so focused on them he never saw the trio of emerging infidel superdreadnoughts that locked their targeting systems on *Charles P. Steadman*'s broken hull.

For the first time in far too many hours, David Berenson had little enough to do—acknowledge the occasional report of another Theban straggler destroyed, keep Antonov apprised of the pursuit's progress—that he could sit on *Bearhound*'s flag bridge and look about him at the system that had been their goal for so long.

Astern lay the asteroid belt, with its awesomely regular cleared zone, where Antonov had wiped out the last of the Theban battle-line. *Must tell Commander Trevayne how accurate her holo simulation turned out to be*, he thought with a wry smile. Ahead gleamed the system's primary stellar component, a G0 star slightly brighter and hotter than Sol, whose fourth planet had been dubbed Thebes by that extraordinary son-of-a-bitch Alois Saint-Just. The red-dwarf stellar companion, nearing periastron but still over nine hundred light-minutes away, was visible only as a dim, ruddy star.

"Another report, Admiral." Mendoza was going on adrenalin and stim pills, but Berenson hadn't the heart to order him to get some rest. "A confirmed kill on the last fighter barge."

Berenson nodded, and a small sigh escaped him. The destruction of the remaining Theban mobile forces had been total. The TFN now owned Theban space. The beings who ran the planet that lay ahead now had no hope at all and would surely surrender. Wouldn't they?

CHAPTER TWENTY-EIGHT
A World at Bay

Fire wracked the skies of Thebes as the planet's orbital fortresses died.

Ivan Antonov had no intention of allowing those fortresses to figure in whatever action he finally took—or was required by his political masters to take—with respect to the planet. Nor did he have any intention of bringing his surviving capital ships within range of the weapons mounted by those forts and the planet they circled. Even assuming that the planetary defenses had not been strengthened since Lantu's fall from grace (and Antonov cherished no such fatuous assumption), Thebes was best thought of as a fortress itself—a world-sized fortress with gigatonnes of rock to armor it and oceans to cool the excess heat produced by its titanic batteries of weapons.

So Second Fleet stood off and smashed at the orbital forts with SBMs. Fighters also swooped in, their salvos of smaller missiles coordinated with the SBMs to saturate the Theban defenses. They took some losses from AFHAWKs, but the forts had no fighters with which to oppose them. The drifting wreckage to which Second Fleet had reduced the enormous Theban orbital ship-yards would build no more, and all of Thebes' limited number of pilots had been committed to the captured carriers and barges ... and died with them.

Everyone made a great production of stressing that point to Winnifred Trevayne: the Shellheads' fighter strength *had* been limited after all. It didn't help. She might sometimes fall into anguished indecision when lives were *immediately* at stake—her well-hidden but painfully intense empathy, Antonov had often reflected, would have made her hopeless as a line officer—but in the ideal realm of logic, with the actual killing still remote enough to admit of abstraction, her conclusions were al-most always flawless. It was a weakness, and a strength, of which she was fully cognizant. Yet this time a misas-sessment of a mentality utterly foreign to her own had led her to a conclusion as inaccurate as it was logical. No one blamed her for the lives which had been lost ... no one but herself.

It worried Antonov a little. Irritating as her certainty could sometimes be, she would be no use to him or anyone else if she lost confidence in her professional judgment. So it was with some relief that he granted her uncharacteristically diffident request for a meeting with him, Tsuchevsky, and Lantu.

"Admiral," she began, still more subdued than usual but with professional enthusiasm gradually gaining the upper hand, "as you may recall, the captured data base that gave us our first insights into Theban motivations contained statements suggesting that the flagship of the old colonization fleet had survived to the present day, and serves as the headquarters and central temple—the 'Vatican,' if you will—of the Church of Holy Terra."

"I seem to remember something of the sort, Com-mander. But it didn't seem very important at the time."

"No, sir, it didn't. That was one reason I didn't empha-size it; another was that I wasn't really sure, then, although it seemed a fairly short inference. But now Admiral Lantu has confirmed that that ship, TFS *Starwalker*, does indeed still rest where it made its emergency landing. It will never move under its own power again, but its computers are still functional." She paused, and Antonov gestured for her to continue. He wasn't sure where she was going, but she was clearly onto something, and she seemed more alive than she had since the battle.

"You may also recall that in the course of analyzing that data base, I sent back from QR-107 to Redwing for the records of the original colonization expeditions in this region. What I got was very complete—the old Bureau of Colonization clearly believed in recording *everything*. Including—" she leaned forward, all primness dissolving in a rush of excitement "—the access codes for *Starwalker*'s computers!"

Suddenly, Antonov understood.

"Let me be absolutely clear, Commander. Are you telling me it may be possible to access those computers from space?"

"But, Admiral," Tsuchevsky cut in, "surely the Thebans have changed the codes over all these generations. And even if they haven't . . . is such remote access really possible?"

"It wouldn't be possible if *Starwalker* were a warship, or even a modern colony ship, Commodore," Trevayne admitted, answering his second question first, "but BuCol built her class—and their computers—before we ever ran into the Orions, back when humanity believed the Galaxy was a safe place." She made a slight moue at Tsuchevsky's snort, dark eyes twinkling for the first time in much too long.

"I know. But because they believed that, they were more concerned with efficiency than security, and her computers don't have the security programming imperatives and hardware ours do. In fact, they were *designed* for remote access by other BuCol ships and base facilities. And as for the Thebans changing the codes . . . my technical people tell me it would be extremely difficult. We're talking about a combined hardware *and* software problem, which would require almost total reprograming. Assuming"—her eyes glowed—"that they'd ever even considered the possibility of its being necessary!"

"Even if it were possible," Lantu said slowly, "the Church won't have done it." He gave a brief Theban smile as they turned to him. "Everything about that ship is sacred; even the damage she suffered before setting down has been preserved unrepaired. The successive prophets have locked all the data pertaining to the Messenger's—to Saint-Just's—lifetime, but if they tried to change it in any way the entire Synod would rise up in revolt."

"So," Antonov mused in an even deeper voice, "we can steal all that data. . . ."

"Or wipe it," Tsuchevsky stated bluntly.

Antonov almost smiled at the looks on Trevayne's and Lantu's faces. He was learning to read Theban expressions—and Lantu was clearly still capable of being shocked by sufficiently gross sacrilege against a faith in which he no longer believed. And as for Winnie . . . Antonov had a shrewd notion of what was going on behind that suddenly stricken face.

Tsuchevsky saw it, too.

"Well," he said a bit defensively, "consider what a body blow it would be to Theban morale. Not to mention the confusion caused by the loss of all the information they may've added to those data bases more recently."

"No," Antonov said quietly. "I will not permit any attempt to wipe the data. Its historical value is simply too great. And the morale effect might be the opposite of what you suppose, Pavel Sergeyevich—sheer outrage might make them fight even harder." He turned to Trevayne. "Commander, you will coordinate with Operations and prepare a detailed plan for covertly accessing *Starwalker*'s computers."

"Aye, aye, sir." Her dark eyes glowed. "Now we'll

know—not merely be able to infer—what *really* happened on Thebes!"

And confirm that your analysis was right all along. This time Antonov did allow himself a small smile.

Father Trudan groaned, rubbing his cranial carapace and wishing the lights weren't quite so bright. He hated the late-night shift, and never more than now. Panic hung over Thebes like a vile miasma, creeping even into *Starwalker*'s sacred precincts, yet at this moment the priest was almost too tired to care. His own gnawing worry ate at his reserves of strength, and the Synod's insatiable demands for data searches robbed him of sleep he needed desperately, despite his nightmares.

He lowered his hands, cracking his knuckles loudly, and his expression was grim. Terra only knew what they hoped to find. They'd been back through every word the First Prophet had ever written, searching frantically for some bit of Holy Writ to answer their need. Indeed, he suspected they'd delved even deeper, into the locked files left by the Messenger himself, but he couldn't be certain. Only Synod members, and not many even of them, had access to *those* records, and—

Trudan's thoughts broke off, and he frowned at his panel. He'd never seen that particular prompt before. In fact—he rubbed his muzzle, cudgeling his weary brain— he didn't even know what it meant. How peculiar!

The prompt blinked a moment, then burned solid green, and bemusement became alarm. He was one of the Synod's senior computer techs; if *he* didn't know what it meant, it must be one of the functions restricted to Synod members. But what in Terra's name did it do? And why was it doing it *now*?

He checked his board, assuring himself none of the other computer stations were manned, and disquiet turned rapidly to fear. He scrabbled for the phone and punched in Archbishop Kirsal's number.

"Your Grace? Father Trudan. I realize it's late, but something strange is happening on my board." He lis-

tened, then shook his head. "No, Your Grace, I don't
know what it is." He listened again and nodded sharply.
"Yes, Your Grace. I definitely think you'd better come
see it for yourself."

He hung up, staring at his panel, and the mysterious
prompt continued to blaze. He watched it, praying the
archbishop would hurry and wondering what "RMT ACC
ENG" meant.

First Admiral Lantu looked physically ill. His eyes
were haunted, and his short, strong body hunched as he
rested his feet on the stool before his human-size chair.
Now he looked into Ivan Antonov's bedrock face as Winnifred Trevayne stopped speaking, and the pain in his
alien expression stirred a matching sympathy in the burly
admiral. He knew, as a Russian, too well how "history"
could be manipulated to serve the needs of a ruling
clique.

"I must agree with Commander Trevayne," Lantu said
quietly. He drew a deep breath. "The First Prophet was
either mad . . . or a tyrant who seized his chance. This"—
his four-fingered hand gestured to his own copy of the
report—"is no mere 'error'; it's a complete and utter
fabrication."

Antonov grunted agreement and looked back down at
the matching folder before him. Alois Saint-Just's soul
must be writhing in Hell over what had been wrought
in his name, and in a way, he almost hoped it was. Whatever the man's original intent, he'd contributed directly
to the creation of a monster almost beyond belief.

"So." His deep voice was a soft, sad rumble as he
touched the printed hard copy. "You and Commander
Trevayne are both convinced Saint-Just never mentioned
religion at all."

"Of course he didn't," Lantu said harshly. "His own
journal entries show he never claimed Terra was divine.
He emphasized the desperation of the Federation's plight
again and again, but every word he said made it perfectly
clear Terrans were mortal beings, despite the superiority

of their science." The Theban gave a short, bitter bark of laughter. "No wonder Sumash's fellow 'disciples' were horrified when he proclaimed Terra's divinity! They knew the truth as well as he did—*damn* his soul to *Hell!*"

His voice was raw with agony and hate, and more than one set of eyes turned away from his distress. Kthaara'-zarthan's did not. They rested enigmatically on his anguished face, and they were very still.

"The First Admiral is correct, sir," Trevayne said softly. "We can never know why Sumash did it, but he knowingly set about the construction of an entirely falsified religious edifice only after the last Terran died. There is absolutely no hint of divinity in any of the records predating Saint-Just's death, yet the fusion of so many different elements of Terran history into 'the Faith of Holy Terra' couldn't have been accidental. Someone clearly researched the historical sections of *Starwalker*'s data base to concoct it, and that someone could only have been Sumash. He'd eliminated all other access to the records . . . and anyone who might have disputed his version of what they held."

"But the Synod *must* know!" Lantu protested. "They have access to the forbidden sections. They have to know it's all a lie! They—" Angus MacRory's big hand squeezed his shoulder, and he bit off his outburst with visible effort.

"They do," Trevayne confirmed, "but not all of them. Only the current Prophet and those he designates have access to the original documentation. Those designations are made not on the basis of seniority but on the basis of who he trusts, and there's substantial evidence that on the occasions when his trust has been misplaced, the weak link has been quietly eliminated. I've analyzed the security lists. Eleven prelates have died of unspecified 'natural causes' within one week of gaining access."

Lantu was silent, but his teeth ground as he remembered Manak's death. The old man hadn't known. He must have known the Church edited the information it transmitted to its flock, but there'd been too much integrity in his soul for him to have lived such a lie. And that very integrity—that unshakable faith in the lie—had killed him.

"But why didn't they just wipe the original evidence?" David Berenson wondered aloud. "No matter how tight their security, they must have known there was a chance it would leak."

"Human history, Admiral Berenson," Antonov said flintily, "abounds with megalomaniacs who chose to preserve information they suppressed. I see no reason to assume a megalomaniacal Theban should act any more rationally."

"In a sense, they probably had no choice," Trevayne suggested. "Not after the first generation or so, anyway. This is the seminal holy writ, Admiral Berenson, the most sacred of all their texts. Even if no one's allowed to read it, their programmers know it's there—and they might know if it had been destroyed. If it were, and the news got out, it would do incalculable damage."

"Which suggests at least one interesting possibility," Tsuchevsky mused.

"It wouldn't work, Commodore," Lantu rasped. Tsuchevsky raised an eyebrow, and the first admiral shrugged. "I assume you're referring to the possibility of using the truth to discredit the Synod?" Tsuchevsky nodded. "Then I'm afraid you underestimate the problem. All of you are 'infidels' in the eyes of the Church and so of the entire Theban race—and I, of course, would be an even more detestable heretic. They know they can't win, yet they're still digging in to fight to the death. If we tell such 'faith-filled' people the truth, it will be seen only as clumsy propaganda inspired by the Satan-Khan. The sole effect would be to fill the People with an even greater hatred for us all as defilers of the Faith."

"Then you see no hope of convincing Thebes to accept the truth and surrender," Antonov said flatly.

"None," Lantu replied even more flatly. He rubbed his face with both hands, and his hopeless voice was inexpressibly bitter. "My entire race is prepared—almost eager—to die for a lie."

The medical shuttle hatch opened. It was summer on New Danzig, a day of dramatic clouds pierced by sunlight, and the moist scent of approaching rain blew over the attendants guiding the litter down the ramp.

The woman in it stared up at the clouds, brown eyes hazy, lying as still as the dead. As still as the many dead from this planet she had left behind her, she thought through the drugs which filled her system. Tears gleamed, and she tried to brush them away with her right hand. She couldn't use her left hand; she no longer had a left arm.

Her right arm stirred, clumsy and weak, and one of her attendants pressed it gently back and bent over her to dry them. She tried to thank him, but speech was almost impossible.

Hannah Avram closed her eyes and told herself she was lucky. She'd been a fool not to seal her helmet when the fighters came in, and she'd paid for it. The agony in her lungs before Danny drugged her unconscious had told her it had been close, but it had been closer than she'd known. She owed MaGuire her life, yet not even his speed had been enough. A fragment of her right lung remained; the left was entirely ruined. Only the respirator unit oxygenating her blood kept her alive.

A warm grip closed on her remaining hand, and she opened her eyes once more and blinked at Commodore Richard Hazelwood. His face was so drawn and worried she felt a twinge of bittersweet amusement. The medship's staff had gotten her stabilized, but they'd decided to leave the actual lung replacement to a fully-equipped dirtside hospital, and he'd apparently thought she was in even worse shape than she was.

Her litter moved around the base of the shuttle pad, and she twitched at a sudden roar. She stared up at Hazelwood, lips shaping the question she had too little breath to ask, and he said something to the medics. They hesitated a moment, then shrugged, and one of them bent over the end of the self-propelled unit. She touched a button and the litter rose at an angle, lifting Hannah until she could see.

She stared in disbelief. Hundreds of cheering people—thousands!—crowded the safety line about the pad, and the thunder of their voices battered her. There were Fleet personnel out there, but most were civilians. Civilians—cheering for the stupid bitch who'd gotten so many of their sons and daughters killed!

The sea of faces blurred and shimmered, and Dick was beaming like a fool and making it a thousand times worse. She tugged at his hand and forced her remaining fragment of lung to suck in air despite the pain as he bent.

"Wrong," she gasped. The word came out faint and thready, propelled by far too little breath, and she shook her head savagely. "*Wrong*. I . . . lost your . . . ships!" she panted, but his free hand covered her mouth.

"Hush, Hannah." His voice was gentle through the cheering that went on and on and on, and her mind twisted in anguish. Didn't he *understand*? She'd lost twelve of her carriers—*twelve* of them! "They know that—but you won the battle. *Their* people won it. They didn't die for nothing, and you're the one who made that possible."

She could no longer see through her tears, and her attendants lowered her back to the vertical, moving her toward the waiting ambulance vertol, but she refused to let go of his hand. He walked beside her, and when her lips moved again he bent back over her once more.

"Something . . . I never . . . told you," she got out, "when I . . . took com—"

His hand hushed her once more, and she blinked away enough tears to see his face. His own eyes glistened, and he shook his head.

"You mean the fact that you were only frocked to commodore?" he asked, and her eyes widened.

"You . . . know?"

He climbed into the vertol beside her, still holding her hand. The hatch closed, cutting off the surf-roar of voices, and he smiled down at her.

"Hannah, I always knew," he said softly.

The Legislative Assembly sat in dreadful silence. President Sakanami had come to the floor to make his report in person, and every eye stared at him in horror as he stood at Chantal Duval's podium. Second Fleet's losses had been so terrible even the announcement that Ivan Antonov now controlled Theban space seemed almost meaningless.

Howard Anderson hunched in his chair, cursing the weakness which had become perpetual, and tried not to weep. Better than any of these politicians, he knew—knew bone-deep, in his very marrow—what Second Fleet had paid. He had commanded in too many battles, seen too many splendid ships die. He closed his eyes, reliving another terrible day in the Lorelei System. The day he'd cut the line of communication of an Orion fleet which had driven deep into Terran space during ISW-2, sealing a third of the Khanate's battle-line in a pocket it could not escape. Ships had died that day, too—including the superdreadnought *Gorbachev*, the flagship of his dearest friend . . . and his only son's command.

Oh, yes, he knew what Second Fleet had paid.

". . . and so," Sakanami was saying heavily, "there is no indication of a Theban willingness to yield. Admiral Antonov has summoned the 'Prophet' to surrender, and been rebuffed. He has even threatened to disclose the contents of *Starwalker*'s secret records, but the Prophet rejects his threat. Apparently they realized those records had been accessed, for they have already begun a campaign to prepare their people for 'falsehoods and lies which may be spread by the Satan-Khan's slaves.'"

A grim, ominous rumble filled the chamber, and Anderson's hands tightened on his cane. Sakanami was being as noninflammatory as he could, but the hatred Waldeck's LibProgs had stoked for months hung in the air, thick enough to taste. However dispassionately the president might report, his every word only fed its poisonous strength.

"At present," Sakanami continued, "Admiral Antonov has invested the planet from beyond capital missile range. The planetary defenses, however, are so powerful that the collateral damage from any bombardment which might destroy them would render Thebes ... uninhabitable."

He drew a deep breath in the silence.

"That concludes my report, Madam Speaker," he said, and sat.

An attention bell chimed.

"The Chair recognizes the Honorable Assemblyman for Christophon," Chantal Duval said quietly, and Pericles Waldeck appeared on the huge screen.

"Madam Chairman, Ladies and Gentlemen of the Assembly," the deep voice was harsh, "our course is plain. We have made every effort to spare the Theban race. We have suffered thousands of casualties in fighting our way into their system. Their position is hopeless, and they know it. Worse, their own leaders know their so-called 'religion' is, in fact, a lie! Yet they refuse to surrender, and we cannot—*must* not—leave madmen such as they have proven themselves to be the power ever to threaten us again."

He paused, and Anderson heard the Assembly's hatred in its silence.

"There has been much debate in this chamber over the Prohibition of 2249," he resumed grimly. "Some have striven mightily to spare the Thebans from the consequences of their crimes against the civilized Galaxy. They are an immature race, it has been said. Their atrocities stem from a religious fervor they might outgrow with time. Whatever their crimes, they have been *sincere* in their beliefs. And now, ladies and gentlemen, now we see that it is no such thing. Now we see that their leadership has known from the outset that their 'jihad' was born in falsehood. Now we know their fanaticism, however real, has been forged by a cold and calculating conspiracy into a tool for interstellar conquest—not in the name of a 'god' but in the name of *ambition*.

"Ladies and Gentlemen of the Assembly, it is time to do what we know in our hearts we must! They themselves have forced our hand, for if their space industry has been destroyed, their planetary industry has not. We know they must now have sensor data on the strategic bombardment missile. With that data, it is only a matter of time before they develop that weapon themselves. Every day we hesitate increases the chance of that dire event, and when it comes to pass, ladies and gentlemen, when those massive defense centers are able to return fire with thousands upon thousands of launchers, the cost of crushing them will be inconceivable."

He paused again, and his voice went cold and flat.

"If this mad-dog regime is not destroyed, such battles as Second Fleet has fought may be forced upon us again and again and again. There cannot be—*must not be*— any compromise with that threat. A landing attempt against such powerful defenses would incur unthinkable casualties, and the bombardment required to cover it would effectively destroy the planet anyway. Invasion and occupation are not tenable options, but at this moment in time Second Fleet can bombard the planet from beyond the range of any weapon they possess. We must act *now*, while that advantage still exists, for we have no choice.

"Ladies and Gentlemen of the Assembly, I move for an immediate vote to override the Prohibition of 2249, and to direct Admiral Antonov to execute a saturation bombardment of the Theban surface!"

The delicate balance for which Anderson had fought, the tenuous restraint he had nursed so long, crumbled in a roar of furious seconds it took Chantal Duval ten minutes to calm, and Howard Anderson's heart was chill within him.

"Ladies and Gentlemen of the Assembly," the Speaker said when silence had finally been restored, "it has been

moved and seconded that this Assembly override the Prohibition of 2249 and direct Admiral Antonov to bombard
the planet of Thebes." She paused for a heartbeat to
let the words soak in. "Is there any debate?" she asked
softly.

Anderson prayed someone would speak, but not a single voice protested, and he cursed the fate which had let
him live this long. Yet the stubborn will which had driven
him for a century and a half drove him still, and he
pressed the button.

"The Chair," Duval said, "recognizes President Emeritus Howard Anderson."

Anderson tried to rise, but his legs betrayed him, and
he heard a soft ripple of dismay as a lictor appeared
magically at his elbow to catch his frail body and ease
him back into his chair. For once, the "grand old man
of the Federation" felt no anger. He was beyond that,
and he sat for a moment, gathering his slender store of
strength as the same lictor adjusted his pick-up so that
he need not stand.

Silence hovered endlessly until, at last, he began to
speak.

"Ladies and gentlemen." His strong old voice had
frayed in the past half year, quivering about the edges
as he forced it to serve his will.

"Ladies and gentlemen, I know what you are feeling
at this moment. The Federation has poured out its trea-
sure and the lives of its military protectors to defeat the
Thebans. Civilians have died in their millions. The price
we have paid is horrible beyond any mortal valuation,
and now, as Mister Waldeck says, we have come to the
final decision point."

He paused, hoping the assembly would think it was
for emphasis without recognizing his dizziness and fatigue. He was so tired. All he wanted was to rest, to pass
this burden to another. But there was no one else. There
was only one sick, tired old man who had seen too much
killing, too many deaths.

"Ladies and gentlemen, I can't tell you he's wrong

about the current Theban regime, for the truth is that it is every bit as fanatical, every bit as corrupt, as he would have you think. Not all of it, but enough. More than enough, for the portion which is those things controls the Church of Holy Terra and, through it, every Theban on their planet.

"Yet they control them through *lies*, ladies and gentlemen." Flecks of the old sapphire fire kindled in his eyes, and his wasted frame quivered with his desperate need to make them understand. "The mass of the Theban people *do* believe in 'Holy Terra,' and it is through that belief that the Prophet and his inner clique—a clique which is only a fraction of their entire Synod—drive and manipulate them. The people of Thebes haven't rejected surrender; their religious leader—their *dictator*—has rejected it in their name!"

He leaned into the pick-up, braced on his cane, and his lined face was cold. His strength slipped through his fingers, and he no longer sought to husband it. He poured it out like water, spending it like fire.

"Ladies and Gentlemen of the Assembly," his voice lashed out with the old power, "the human race does not murder people who have been duped and lied to! The Terran Federation does not murder entire worlds because a handful of madmen hold their populations in thrall!"

He struggled to his feet, shaking off the anxious lictor, glaring not into the pick-up but across the chamber at Pericles Waldeck as he threw all diplomatic fiction to the winds.

"Whatever the Thebans may be, *we* are neither mad nor fools, and this Assembly will be *no one's* dupe! We will remember who we are, and what this Federation stands for! If we do not extend justice to our foes, then we are no better than those foes, and the genocide of an entire race because of the twisted ambition of a handful of insane leaders is not *justice*. It is a crime more heinous than any the Thebans have committed. It is an abomination, an atrocity on a cosmic scale, and I will not see murder done in the name of my people!"

His knees began to crumble, but his voice cracked like a whip.

"Ladies and Gentlemen of the Assembly, Pericles Waldeck would have you stain your hands with the blood of an entire species. He may drape his despicable deed in the cloak of justice and the mantle of necessity, but that makes it no less vile." His vision began to blur, but he peered through the strange mist, watching fury crawl across Waldeck's strong, hating features, and hurled his own hate to meet it.

"Ladies and gentlemen, one man, more than any other, wrought this disaster. One man led his party into dispatching the Peace Fleet to Lorelei. One man crafted the secret orders which placed Victor Aurelli—*not Admiral Li*—in command of that fleet's dispositions!"

The fury on Waldeck's face became something beyond fury, deeper than hatred, as a chorus of astonished shouts went up. The younger man rose, glaring madly across the floor, and the lictor pressed the emergency button on his harness. He tried to force Anderson back into his seat, and a white-coated medic was running across the floor, but the wasted old man clung to the edge of his console and his voice thundered across the tumult.

"*One man*, ladies and gentlemen! And now that *same* one man calls on *you* to cover his stupidity! He calls upon you to destroy a planet not to save the Galaxy, not to preserve the lives of Second Fleet's personnel, but out of *ambition*! Out of his need to silence criticism for political gain! He—"

The thundering words stopped suddenly, and the fiery blue eyes widened. A trembling old hand rose, gripping the lictor's shoulder, and Howard Anderson swayed. A thousand delegates were on their feet, staring in horror at the Federation's greatest living hero, and his voice was a dying thread.

"Please," he gasped. "*Please*. Don't let him. *Stop* him." The old man sagged as the racing medic vaulted another delegate's console, scrabbling in his belt-pouch medkit as he came.

"I beg you," Howard Anderson whispered. "You're better than the Prophet—better than *him*. Don't let him make us murderers again!"

And he crumpled like a broken toy.

CHAPTER TWENTY-NINE

The Final Option

"Good Lord!" Winnifred Trevayne blinked at the technical read-outs on the screen. "What in heaven's name *is* that?"

Admiral Lantu was silent—he'd said very little for days—but Colonel Fraymak snorted at her other elbow. The colonel had read *Starwalker's* records for himself, and the stance he'd taken largely out of respect for Lantu had been transformed by an outrage all his own as he threw himself wholeheartedly into collaboration with his "captors."

"That, Commander," he said now, "is an *Archangel*-class strategic armored unit."

"The hell you say," General Shahinian grunted. "That's a modification of an old Mark Seven CBU." Trevayne looked blank. "Continental bombardment unit," Shahinian amplified, then frowned. "Wonder where they got the specs? Unless ..." He grunted again and nodded. "Probably from *Ericsson*. I think I remember reading something about BuCol giving colonial industrial units military downloads after ISW-1 broke out." He made a rude sound. "Can you see some bunch of farmers wasting time and resources on something that size?" He shook his head. "Just the sort of useless hardware some fat-headed bureaucrat would've forgotten to delete."

"I've never seen anything like it," Trevayne said.

"You wouldn't, outside a museum, and it's too damned *big* for a museum. That's why we scrapped the last one back in—oh, 2230, I think. Takes over a dozen shuttles to transport one, then you've got to assemble the thing inside a spacehead. If you need that kind of firepower, it's quicker and simpler to supply it from space."

"When you *can*, sir," Colonel Fraymak pointed out respectfully.

"When you *can't*, Colonel," Shahinian said frostily, "you've got no damned business poking your nose in in the first place!"

Trevayne nodded absently, keying notes into her memo pad. That monstrosity would laugh at a mega-tonne-range warhead, and that made it a sort of ultimate area denial system, assuming you planned to use the real estate it was guarding.

She sighed as she finished her notes and punched for the next display. The data they'd pirated from *Starwalker* was invaluable—the Synod had stored its most sensitive defense information in the old ship's computers—but the more of it she saw, the more hopeless she felt.

Thebes was the best textbook example she'd ever seen of the sort of target Marines should *never* be used against. The planet was one vast military base, garrisoned by over forty million troops with the heaviest weapons she'd ever seen. And while those weapons might be technical antiques, Marines were essentially assault troops. The armored units they could transport to the surface, however modern, were pygmies beside monsters like that CBU. Even worse, their assault shuttles would take thirty to forty percent casualties. Fleet and Marine doctrine stressed punching a hole in the defenses first, but not even Orions had ever fortified an inhabited planet *this* heavily. There was a fifty percent overlap in the PDCs' coverage zones. The suppressive fire to cover an assault into that kind of defense would sterilize a continent.

She glanced guiltily at the sealed hatch to the admiral's private briefing room. In all the years she'd known and served Ivan Antonov, she had never seen him so ... elementally enraged. It had gone beyond thunder and lightning to a cold, deadly silence, and her inability to find the answer he needed flayed her soul. But, damn it—she turned back to the display in despair—there *wasn't* an answer this time!

Antonov swiveled his chair slowly to face his staff, and his eyes were glacial. The doctors said Howard Anderson would live ... probably ... for a few more years, but the massive stroke had left half his body paralyzed. His century and more of service to the Federation was over, and the thought of that dauntless spirit chained in a broken, crippled body—

He chopped the thought off like an amputated limb. There was no time to think of the price his oldest friend had paid. No time to contemplate getting his own massive hands on that *svolochy*, that scum, Waldeck for just a few, brief moments. No time even to take bleak comfort in the ruin of Waldeck's political career and the rampant disorder of the LibProgs as the truth about the Peace Fleet massacre came out.

It was not, Antonov reminded himself bitterly, the first time fighting men and women had been betrayed to their deaths by the political swine they served. Nor would it be the last time the *vlasti* responsible escaped the firing squad they so amply deserved. That wouldn't be *civilized*, after all. For one moment he let himself dwell on the fate the *Zheeerlikou'valkhannaieee* reserved for such *chofaki*, then snorted bitterly. No wonder he liked Orions!

But in the meantime ...

"I have received final clarification from Admiral Brandenburg," he rumbled. "The Assembly has opted to seek 'expert guidance' in determining policy towards Thebes."

Those bleak, cold eyes swept his advisors. "Before voting to override the Prohibition of 2249, they wish my recommendation. I have been informed that they will act in whatever fashion I deem most prudent."

Winnifred Trevayne inhaled sharply; the others were silent, but he saw it in their faces. Especially in Kthaara's. The Orion had been unwontedly diplomatic over the Peace Fleet revelations and the Assembly's confusion, but now his contempt bared ivory fangs. And with good reason, Antonov thought. Whatever his decision, the politicos had managed in time-honored fashion to clear their own skirts with a pious appeal to "expert military opinion." What a shame they so seldom bothered to seek it *before* they created such a bitched-up shitball!

"With that in mind," he continued, "I need whatever insight any of you may offer. Commodore Tsuchevsky?"

"Sir," the chief of staff said somberly, "I don't have any. We're still examining the data—we know more about the enemy's defenses than any other staff in military history—but the only solution we can see is a massive application of firepower. There are no blind spots to exploit, no gaps. We can blow a hole in them from beyond their own range, but doing so will have essentially the same effect as applying Directive Eighteen. And—" he paused, visibly steeling himself "—much as I hate to admit it, Waldeck had a point. It's only a matter of time before the Thebans' planet-side industry produces their own SBMs and we lose even that advantage."

"I will not accept that." Antonov's voice was quietly fierce, the verbal pyrotechnics planed away by steely determination, and he turned his gaze upon Lantu. The first admiral looked shrunken and old in his over-large chair. The fire had leached out of his amber eyes, and his hands trembled visibly as he looked back up at Antonov from a pit of despair.

"You must." His voice was bitter. "Commodore Tsuchevsky is correct."

"No," Antonov said flatly. "There *is* an answer. There is no such thing as a perfect defense—not when the attacker has data this complete and the services of the enemy's best and most senior commander."

"Best commander?" Lantu repeated dully. He shook his head. "No, Admiral. You have the services of a fool. A pathetic simpleton who was asinine enough to think his people deserved to survive." He stared down at his hands, and his voice fell to a whisper. "I have become the greatest traitor in Theban history, betrayed all I ever believed, sacrificed my honor, conspired to kill thousands of men I trained and once commanded—all for a race so stupid it allowed five generations of charlatans to lead it to its death." His hands twisted in his lap.

"Do what you must, Admiral Antonov. Perhaps a handful of the People will live to curse me as I deserve."

The humans in the room were silenced by his agony, but Kthaara'zarthan leaned forward, eyes fixed on Lantu's face, and gestured to his interpreter.

"I would like to tell you a story, Admiral Laaantu," he said quietly, and Lantu looked up in astonishment sufficient to penetrate even his despair as, for the first time ever, Kthaara spoke directly to him

"Centuries ago, on Old Valkha, there was a *khanhar*— a war leader. His name was Cranaa'tolnatha, and his clan was sworn to the service of Clan Kirhaar. Cranaa was a great warrior, one who had never known defeat in war or on the square of honor, and his clan was *linkar'a ia' Kirhaar*, Shield-Bearer to Clan Kirhaar. Clan Tolnatha stood at Clan Kirhaar's right hand in battle, and Cranaa was Clan Kirhaar's *shartok khanhar*, first fang of all its warriors, as well as those of Clan Tolnatha.

"But the *Khanhaku'a'Kirhaar* was without honor, for he betrayed his allies and made himself *chofak*. None of his warriors knew it, for he hid his treachery, yet he spied on those who thought themselves his *farshatok*, selling their secrets to their enemies. And when those enemies moved against them, he called Cranaa aside and ordered him to hold back the warriors of Clan Tolnatha while he himself commanded Clan Kirhaar's. Clan Tolnatha was to lie hidden, he told Cranaa, saved until the last

moment to strike the enemy's rear when their allies—
including Clan Kirhaar—feigned flight."

He paused, and Lantu stared at him, muzzle wrinkled
as he tried to understand.

"Now, Cranaa had no reason to think his *khanhaku's*
orders were a lie, but he was a skilled warrior, and when
he considered them they made no sense. His forces
would be too far distant to intervene as ordered, for by
the time messengers reached him and he advanced, the
feigned flight would have carried the battle beyond his
reach. And as he studied his *khanhaku's* commands, he
realized that a 'feigned flight' was no part of their allies'
plans. The battle was to be fought in a mountain pass,
and if they yielded the pass they would be driven back
against a river and destroyed.

"All but Clan Kirhaar," Kthaara said softly, "for they
formed the reserve. They would be first across the river's
only bridge, and it was they who had been charged with
mining that bridge so that it might be blown up to prevent pursuit. And when Cranaa realized those things, he
knew his *khanhaku* had betrayed him and all his allies.
Clan Tolnatha would advance but arrive too late, and it
would be destroyed in isolation. Clan Kirhaar would fall
back, and his *khanhaku* would order the bridge destroyed
'to hold the enemy,' and thus deliver his allies to their
foes. And when the battle was over, there would be none
alive to know how his *khanhaku* had betrayed them.

"But Cranaa had sworn *hirikolus* to his *khanhaku*, and
to break that oath is unthinkable. He who does so is
worse than *chofak*—he is *dirguasha*, outcast and outlawed, stripped of clan, cut off from his clan fathers and
mothers as the prey of any who wish to slay him. There is
no greater punishment for the *Zheeerlikou'valkhannaieee*.
Before we suffer it, we will die at our own hand.

"Yet if he obeyed, Cranaa's clan would die, and its
allies, and the traitor would wax wealthy and powerful
upon their blood. And so Cranaa did not obey. He broke
his oath of *hirikolus*—broke it not with proof he could
show another, but on the truth he knew without proof.

He refused to lead his clan into battle as he was commanded, but chose his own position and his own time to attack, and so won the battle and saved his clan.

"And in doing so, he made himself *dirguasha*. He could not prove his *khanhaku's* treachery, though few doubted it. Yet even had he been able to do so, it would not have saved him, for he had thrown away his honor. He was cast out by his own litter mates, outlawed by the allies he had saved, deprived of his very name and driven into the waste without food, or shelter, or weapons. A lesser warrior would have slain himself, but to do so would be to admit he had lied and cleanse his *khanhaku's* name, so Cranaa grubbed for food, and shivered in the cold, and starved, and made his very life a curse upon his *khanhaku's* honor. And so, when he was sick and alone, too weak to defend himself, his traitor *khanhaku* sent assassins, and they slew him like an animal, dragging him to death with ropes, denying him even the right to die facing them upon his feet.

"Thus Cranaa'tolnatha died, alone and despised, and his bones were gnawed and scattered by *zhakleish*. Yet all these centuries later, the *Zheeerlikou'valkhannaieee* honor his courage . . . and not even Clan Kirhaar recalls his *khanhaku's* name, for they have stricken it in shame. He was a traitor, Admiral Laaantu—but our warriors pray to Hiranow'khanark that we, too, may find the courage to be such traitors if we must."

There was utter silence in the briefing room as Lantu stared deep into Kthaara'zarthan's slit-pupilled eyes, and the others almost held their breath, for something was changing in his own eyes. They narrowed, and an amber light flickered in their depths—a bright, intent light, divorced from despair.

"There might," First Admiral Lantu said softly, "be a way, after all."

It was, Ivan Antonov thought, an insane plan.

He stared out the view port of his quarters, trying to

convince himself it might work, trying not to think about the cost if it failed.

He turned from the port, pacing back and forth across his cramped cabin, wrestling with his fears. It was to risk all upon a single throw of the dice, yet hadn't he done precisely that at Redwing? Hadn't he done it again on New New Hebrides?

Of course he had, but then he'd had no choice. Here he had an option, one which he knew would work without risking a single Terran life. What possible logic could justify sending three full divisions of Marines to almost certain death when that was true?

But it wasn't true. He wheeled abruptly, staring back out at the silent stars. He could save sixty thousand Terran lives . . . but only by taking six *billion* Theban ones.

He drew a deep breath and nodded once.

"This, ladies and gentlemen," Winnifred Trevayne said, "is Planetary Defense Center Saint-Just on the Island of Arawk. It is, without doubt, the most powerful single fortification on the entire planet—and your objective."

The staff of the Third Corps, TMC, looked at the holographic schematic for one horrified moment, raised their eyes to her in total disbelief, then turned as one to stare at their commander. General Shahinian looked back silently, and more than one hard-bitten officer paled at the confirmation in his expression. Their gazes swiveled back to Commander Trevayne, and she moved in front of the holo and folded her hands behind her, masking her own dismay in crisp, decisive words.

"PDC Saint-Just is the central planetary command and control facility and the Prophet's personal HQ. The primary works are buried under two hundred meters of rock in Arawk's Turnol Mountains and protected by concentric rings of ground defenses forty kilometers deep. We believe that at least two and possibly four strikefighter squadrons based on Saint-Just have been held back to intercept incoming assault shuttles, but Second Fleet's fighter strength should be more than sufficient to cover you against their attack. Of greater concern are the aircraft also based inside Saint-Just's perimeter. Under the circumstances, it will be impossible for us to insert our own aircraft to engage them, nor can we neutralize them with a pre-attack bombardment. Any attempt to do so would only alert the defenders, and the ancillary damage would make the actual penetration of the facility even more difficult."

"*Penetration?*" That was too much, and Brigadier Shimon Johnson, Third Corps' ops officer, wheeled back to his CO in pure, unadulterated horror.

"Penetration." Shahinian's confirmation sounded like broken glass, and he gestured to Trevayne, who sat in unmistakable relief. The general's shoulder-boards of stars glittered as he stood in her place.

"We're going inside." There was dead silence. "This fortress contains the only Shellheads who *know* their religion is a lie. These are the people who refuse to surrender—the ones using our unwillingness to destroy their entire species against us. They're terrorists, holding their own race hostage while they sit under the most powerful defensive umbrella on the planet. If we can take *them* out, we may be able to find someone sane to negotiate a surrender with. By the same token, our ability to neutralize their most powerful defensive position should prove tremendously demoralizing to the Thebans as a whole. Finally, Arawk's island location limits the overlap in its neighboring PDCs' coverage to less than fifty percent. Destruction of Saint-Just's ground-to-space weapons will open a hole—a small one, I know, but a hole nonetheless—through which future assaults can be made without resorting to saturation bombardments."

"But, sir," Second Division's CO, Lieutenant General Sharon Manning, said quietly, "there won't be enough of us left to *make* any future assaults."

"I believe that may be a somewhat pessimistic estimate, General," Shahinian replied. "And, in any case, the decision has already been made."

Manning started to say something more, then cut herself off at her superior's bleak expression. Aram Shahinian had come up through the ranks; he knew precisely what he was sending his troops into. She closed her own mouth and sat back, black face grim, and Shahinian gestured to Trevayne once more.

She began punching buttons to manipulate the holo image and highlight features as she itemized Saint-Just's defensive capabilities, and the Marines went absolutely expressionless as battery after battery of weapons glowed crimson. Missile launchers, massed point defense stations that doubled as shuttle-killers, buried aircraft and strikefighter hangars, mutually supporting auto-cannon and artillery pillboxes, mortar pits, minefields, entanglements, subterranean barracks and armored vehicle parks. . . . It wasn't a fortress; it was one enormous weapon, designed to drown any attacker in his own blood.

Trevayne displayed the last weapon system and turned to the iron-faced officers. Most of these people knew her well, some were close friends, and they stared at her with hating faces. It wasn't her fault, and they saw the anguish in her own eyes, but they couldn't help it.

"General Shahinian will brief you on his general tactical objectives," she made herself say levelly, "but we do have one priceless advantage: Admiral Lantu is intimately familiar with Saint-Just and the network of secret tunnels radiating from the PDC. These serve two purposes: to provide an access route safe from radioactive contamination following any bombardment, and to evacuate the Prophet and Synod in the event Saint-Just is seriously threatened. We intend to use one of these tunnels to insert a small, picked force under cover of the main attack."

No one spoke, but she could hear them thinking very loudly indeed. *Secret passages? Only a Navy puke could come up with something that stupid!*

"These routes rely primarily on concealment for their security," she went on, "with computer-commanded anti-personnel weaponry. Although they're shown in the *Star-*

walker data base, the majority of Saint-Just's garrison knows nothing about them, and access is controlled entirely by security-locked computers. Admiral Lantu knows the access codes, and even though they were included in the data we extracted from *Starwalker*, there is no reason for the Synod to alter them, as there is a retinal-scan feature built into the security systems. No human eyes could activate them, but Admiral Lantu's retinal patterns are on the authorized list, and the Thebans, with no knowledge that he's come over to us, have no reason to delete them. They certainly haven't deleted them from any of the other security lists we recovered from *Starwalker*.

"We hope to accomplish two objectives via this penetration. Colonel Fraymak will lead one element of the assault party directly to Saint-Just's primary command center, where our Raiders will eliminate the PDC's command staff, central computers, and com net. A second element, led by Admiral Lantu, will be charged with the seizure and deactivation—" she paused and drew a deep breath "—of the two hundred-megatonne suicide charge under the base."

In the utter silence that followed, it was with some relief that Trevayne acknowledged the raised hand in the back row.

"Question, Commander," came the drawl. "What do we do *after* lunch?"

Ivan Antonov stood in *Gosainthan*'s boat bay and watched First Admiral Lantu and Colonel Fraymak exchange a few final words with General Shahinian before departing for the transport *Black Kettle*. There was no longer any distrust in the Marine's expression as he bent slightly to listen to the two Thebans, but there was pain . . . and envy. Shahinian was about to commit three of his four divisions to an attack which would gut them, even if everything went perfectly, and he could not accompany them. He would remain on his command ship, *Mangus Coloradas*, coordinating an elaborate deception maneuver with his staff, while General Manning took his troops in on the ground.

The conversation ended, and Lantu and Fraymak crossed to Antonov. Their hands rose in Theban salute, and he returned it, feeling Kthaara's bitter disappointment at his side. The two Thebans had to accompany the assault, despite their inability to wear combat zoots; Kthaara did not, and his skill in fighter operations might be invaluable to Shahinian if, in fact, the Thebans had managed to secret more fighters than they knew.

"Good luck, Admiral, Colonel." Antonov clasped their backward, too-narrow hands firmly. The colonel looked tense, anxious, and just a bit frightened even now of the sacrilege he proposed to commit; Lantu looked completely calm, and somehow that worried Antonov more than Fraymak's tension.

"Thank you, Admiral Antonov." Lantu looked deep into the human's eyes. "And thank you for running such risks to save my people."

The burly admiral made an uncomfortable gesture, and the Theban swallowed anything else he might have been about to say. He turned towards the waiting cutter, but an arm covered in night-black fur reached out and stopped him. He twitched in surprise and looked down at the clawed hand on his forearm, then looked up at Kthaara'zarthan.

The Orion's interpreter wasn't present. Antonov or Tsuchevsky could easily have translated for him, but Kthaara said nothing. He simply reached to his harness, and steel rasped as he drew his *defargo*. The bay lights gleamed on the honor dirk's razored edge as he nicked his own wrist. Crimson blood glittered amid sable fur as he gave the weapon a strange little flick, tossing it up to catch it by the guard and extend its hilt to the Theban.

Lantu stared at it for a moment, then reached out. He held it while Kthaara unhooked its scabbard one-handedly from his harness and extended it in turn. And then, though Antonov knew he could not possibly have been told of the significance of the act, the Theban raised his own wrist. The unbloodied edge of the blade snicked, drawing Theban blood to match that of the *Zheeerlikou'-valkhannaieee* already on it, and Kthaara'zarthan's eyes glowed. He drew a small square of silky fabric from a belt pouch and wiped the blade reverently, then watched as Lantu sheathed it and affixed it to his own belt.

Antonov wondered how many others present recognized the formal renunciation of *vilknarma*—and why he himself felt no shock. He only watched as his *vilkshatha* brother extended his right arm, gripping Lantu's too-long arm in a *farshatok's* clasp, and then stepped back beside him.

Lantu's eyes were unnaturally bright, and his hand caressed the *defargo* at his side. Then he drew himself up, nodded once, sharply, and followed Colonel Fraymak into the cutter.

CHAPTER THIRTY
Vengeance Is Mine

First Marshal Sekah stood in PDC Saint-Just's central command and frowned at the holo sphere. He was a son of the Church, prepared to die for Holy Terra, but the thought of all the deaths which would accompany his sickened him. *Yet better that than defilement*, he told himself fiercely. *Better death of the body than of the soul*.

Still, the infidels' quiescence had puzzled him. They'd destroyed his orbital works over a month ago, yet made no move against the planet itself. Was it possible they simply didn't know what to do with it? He grinned mirthlessly, recalling the utter lack of fortification on the captured infidel worlds and the infidel tactical manuals' insistence on keeping combat out in space "where it belonged." As if Holy Terra's People should fear to live or die with their defenders! But even such as they must realize the People would never yield, so why delay? They had the range to slay Thebes from a position of safety—surely they couldn't be so foolish as to think the Prophet might change his mind and surrender to the Satan-Khan as they had!

Now he watched the shifting patterns in the sphere and shivered. It seemed whatever had caused them to delay obtained no longer. Formations of infidel starships were sweeping into position, close to the edge of the capital missile envelope yet tauntingly beyond it, and Sekah's mind heard sirens howling in every city across the planet. Not that it would do any good.

"Summon the Prophet," he said quietly to an aide.

"All units in preliminary positions, Admiral," Tsuchevsky reported, and Antonov nodded his massive head.

"Get me *Mangus Coloradas*." Aram Shahinian looked out of the com screen at him, and Antonov gave him a thin, cold smile. "The Fleet is at your disposal, General," he said simply.

"Aye, aye, sir." Shahinian saluted, the screen blanked, and Antonov leaned back in his command chair and crossed his legs. He'd just become a passenger in his own fleet.

"Firing sequence locked in." TFNS *Dhaulagiri*'s gunnery officer acknowledged the report and watched her chronometer tick steadily down. Somebody down there was about to take an awful pasting—if not quite as bad as the one he probably expected.

Lantu looked up as a towering zoot paused beside him, then smiled in faint surprise as Angus MacRory grinned.

"I hadn't realized you were coming, Colonel."

"An' where else should I be? Ye're still my prisoner, in a manner o' speakin'."

"And you're coming along to make certain I don't escape. I see."

"Actually, First Admiral," Major M'boto said from Lantu's other side, "Colonel MacRory's in command. He'll be leading the element which accompanies you."

"Indeed? And why wasn't that mentioned to me sooner?"

"We weren't certain the colonel would complete his

zoot training in time." M'boto's teeth flashed in his ebon face. "That was before he shaved almost two weeks off the old record."

First Marshal Sekah folded his arms behind him as the first infidel missiles launched, then looked up as the Prophet and his entourage arrived.

"Your Holiness." He unlocked his arms and genuflected, but something about the Prophet's eyes—a bright, hard glitter too deep in their depths—bothered him. He brushed the thought aside. Even Holy Terra's Prophet might be excused a bit of tension at a moment like this.

The First Marshal returned his attention to the sphere and frowned. The infidels still appeared to be trying to limit collateral damage—perhaps they hoped despair might yet seduce the People into apostasy and surrender? No matter. What mattered was that they were flinging their missiles at the isolated PDCs crowning the northern ice cap. Well, that suited Sekah. He was in no hurry to see the People's women and children die, and those fortresses were eminently well equipped to look after themselves.

Immensely armored PDC silo covers flicked open and then closed, and the atmosphere above Thebes' pole blazed with kilotonne-range counter-missiles. The SBMs were intercepted in scores, but statistically a few had to get through, and fireballs marched across the sullen PDCs, vaporizing rock and ice, shaking the ice-crusted continental mass with their fury.

Shock waves quivered through flesh and bone, but the grim-faced Theban defenders watched their read-outs with slowly mounting hope. They were stopping more missiles than the most optimistic had projected, and those that got through were doing less damage than they'd feared. The megatonnes of concrete, rock, and steel armoring their weapons glowed and fused, yet the infidels seemed to have no deep-earth penetrators, and surface bursts lacked the power to punch through and disembowel the forts.

The atmospheric radiation count mounted ominously, yet it, too, was lower than they'd feared. The infidels were employing only nuclear warheads, without the antimatter explosions the defenders had dreaded.

First Marshal Sekah scanned the PDCs' reports and bared his teeth. They were hurting him, and even these lower radiation levels meant terrible contamination, but no fleet could match a planet's magazine capacity. Even if Theban missiles were too short-ranged to strike back, the infidels would have to do far better than they were to breach *those* defenses before they exhausted their ammunition.

General Aram Shahinian watched his own read-outs, glancing occasionally at the visual display and the glaring inferno blasting ice into hellish steam. His eyes were calm, his expression set. His worst fear was that someone down there would run an analysis and realize Second Fleet was deliberately throwing lighter salvos than it might have for the express purpose of *helping* their point defense, but there was nothing he could do about it if they did.

He glanced at his chronometer and keyed his com button.

"Execute phase two," he said.

"They're moving, First Marshal."

Sekah grunted and rubbed his cranial carapace. The infidels' fire had slackened, suggesting exhaustion of their longer-ranged missiles, and their ships were closing to the edge of the capital missile zone to maintain the engagement. Their ECM was far better than his, and they could dodge; his PDCs couldn't, but he would take any shot he could get. His weapons might be less accurate, but he had far more launchers than they.

"Infidel fighters launching," Tracking reported, and he chuckled mirthlessly.

"First Marshal?" He looked up at the Prophet's quiet voice.

"Strikefighters don't worry me, Your Holiness," he explained. "Their missile loads are meaningless beside what the infidels are already firing, and fighters themselves are useless in atmosphere. The infidels can't be certain we're not hoarding fighters they don't know about, so they're deploying a combat patrol to cover their ships." He bared his teeth again. "It won't help against what they *should* be worried about."

A huge, soft hand squeezed Lantu as *Black Kettle* launched her assault shuttles. He sealed his helmet, then realized just how pointless that reflex was. If anything hit a vessel as small as this one, its occupants would never know a thing about it.

He smothered a half-hysterical giggle at the thought. What in the name of whatever was truly holy was he doing here? He was an admiral, not a Marine! He glanced up at the face behind Angus MacRory's command zoot's armored visor, and Angus's set, tense expression made him feel oddly better.

Ivan Antonov's eyes gleamed coldly as he wondered what the Thebans made of the numbers. Over twelve hundred small spacecraft were jockeying into the positions Kthaara and Shahinian's staff had worked out with agonizing precision over the past two weeks, but only three hundred were truly fighters. The other nine hundred were the slightly modified assault shuttles of three Marine Raider divisions, each fitted with a fighter's transponder. Now if the enemy would only concentrate on killing starships and ignore any little anomalies their scanners might detect . . .

Sekah felt an edge of surprise. That was several times the People's best estimate of their fighter strength. Why hadn't they used more in their warp point attack, if they had so many? He shrugged the thought away. It scarcely mattered now, and he had more urgent concerns. The first infidel ships entered the range of the polar PDCs, and he nodded to his exec.

Stomachs clenched aboard the capital units of Second Fleet as hundreds of capital missiles lunged at them.

XO-mounted EDMs sped out to interpose their false drive fields between the enemy and their mother ships. Point defense crews tracked incoming warheads with professional calm while heat-lightning tension crackled through their nerves. Counter missiles raced outward. Laser clusters and auto-cannon slewed rapidly, and brilliant balls of flame began to pock the vacuum, reaching across the light-seconds towards the ships of Terra.

Gosainthan lurched as the first Theban missile eluded her defenses. Another got through. And another. But it was only a handful, Antonov told himself. A tiny fraction of that incredible storm of fire. His flagship's shields shrugged the damage aside—for now—and he tightened his shockframe.

Sekah smiled as the first infidel shields began to fail. It wasn't much—yet. But if the fools would only stay there a little longer . . .

"You will observe, Your Holiness," he said, "that we are spreading our fire widely at the moment. This confronts the infidels with smaller salvos and enhances the effectiveness of their point defense, but it also allows us time to further refine our tracking data while forcing them to expend their EDMs. After a few more salvos, we will have reduced their ability to deceive our missiles and greatly improved our fire control solutions." He smiled wickedly. "Which is when our PDCs will suddenly switch their firing patterns to concentrate on a handful of targets with everything they have."

The Prophet smiled in understanding, and Sekah glanced at the holo sphere once more. The infidel fighters were spreading out, clumping on the sunward side.

They were almost directly overhead, and Saint-Just's fire control officer asked for permission to engage with AFHAWKs.

"A little longer, Colonel. They're still closing; let them get all the way to the edge of atmosphere if they want to, then go to rapid fire."

Aram Shahinian checked his read-outs once more, and a drop of sweat trickled down his forehead. The Shellheads were playing it smart, whittling away Second Fleet's EDMs. If someone down there was keeping count, they'd know the capital ships were running dangerously low. Any minute now, they were going to change their targeting, and his brain screamed to rush the attack wave so he could get the fleet the hell out of it.

He made himself wait. Every second they didn't open up with AFHAWKs let his shuttles creep a little closer and meant a fraction of a percent more were going to get through. If the Shellies ran him out of EDMs first, the fleet was just going to have to take it.

He punched another com stud. "General Manning?"

"Aye, sir." Sharon Manning's taut voice was barely a shade higher than usual. There was, Shahinian reflected, a hefty pool awaiting someone the first time Sharon's voice actually broke.

"I doubt they're going to ignore you much longer, General. You are cleared to go when the first AFHAWK launches."

"Now, Your Holiness," Sekah murmured.

TFNS *Viper* bucked in agony as the first massed salvo saturated her point defense. The battleship writhed as brutal explosions killed her shields, ripped at her drive field, and gouged deep into her hull. Atmosphere gushed out despite slamming blast doors, and another salvo pounded her weakening defenses. A direct hit wiped away her bridge. Another smashed main missile defense, and her point defense faltered as it dropped into local control.

Viper's exec wiped blood from his forehead and cursed as he stared at the displays in after control.

"Condition Omega!" he snapped. "Abandon ship! All hands, abandon ship!"

His command crew jerked their feet in close to their chairs as escape pods slammed closed about them. Explosive charges blasted them out of their ship, but the exec clung to his console just a moment longer, repeating his bail-out command until he was certain everyone had heard.

He waited one moment too long.

Ivan Antonov's jaw tightened as Viper blew apart. It was the only change in his rock-hard expression.

Sharon Manning's dark face was expressionless, but she couldn't believe they'd gotten this close. Of course, no one had ever been insane enough to try such a maneuver before. Guile and deception were all very well, but a good, heavy bombardment beat hell out of either of them.

She checked her systems again. Dear God, they were less than two hundred klicks out of atmosphere! Didn't anybody down there have a brain? Even a Marine knew fighters avoided atmospheres like the plague!

She fought her impatience, trying to ignore the capital ships blazing behind her, and almost prayed someone would open fire on her.

"Very well, Colonel," Sekah said, smiling as Saint-Just's tactical officer almost danced with impatience. He could hardly believe the targets the infidel strikefighters were giving them, either, but it passed belief they would come still closer. "You may engage."

*   *   *

Another battleship exploded. The superdreadnoughts, with their greater external ordnance capacity, still had EDMs; the battlewagons did not.

"Order the battleships to open the range," Shahinian said. He hated to do it—but not as much as he hated watching them die.

"Aye, aye, sir." Janet Toomepuu passed his order, then stiffened. She started to speak, but Shahinian already saw it in his own display.

"Assault wave—*go!*" General Manning barked as the first AFHAWK exploded. More followed it, hundreds more, and the real fighters on the edges of her formation took the brunt. The Shellheads were firing clusters of the damned things at each target, bracketing its potential evasion maneuvers with merciless precision. A pilot might evade the first, even the second, but number three or number four was waiting for him when he did.

Yet they didn't have to take it for long. Nine hundred assault shuttles suddenly screamed forward—not away from the planet, but *towards* it—even as Kthaara'zarthan's fighters played his final trick. A thousand close attack missiles punched out, aimed not at the planet but at a point just beyond its atmosphere. The heavy warheads exploded as one in an intolerable flash of plasma . . . and an incredible pulse of radiation.

Three divisions of Terran Marine assault craft attacked out of the blinding fury of an artificial "sun."

First Marshal Sekah whipped around to the holo sphere in disbelief. *What in the name of Holy Terra—?!*

No amount of EMP could burn out his hardened sensors, but they'd never been intended to confront *that* massive a dose! For one priceless moment they were blind, and in that moment nine hundred assault shuttles slammed into atmosphere at reckless speed, shrieking downward like homesick meteors to close on a single island in the sunlit Sea of Arawk.

*   *   *

"*It worked, by God!*"

Aram Shahinian actually flinched from the high-pitched soprano scream, and then, despite everything, his face creased in an enormous grin. Sharon must have forgotten her mike was open—and someone had just come into a tidy little sum, indeed.

Lantu tried to tell himself this was a foolish moment to worry about his dignity, but he felt like an utter idiot as Angus snatched him up bodily. The admiral's armored vac suit didn't have a repulsor unit, and that meant—

He gasped as the shuttle rolled and its entire side opened. A corona of superheated air ripped past, lethally beautiful on the far side of a mono-permeable field of force. He stared at it in fascination, then closed his eyes in terror as MacRory gathered him to his chest in massively armored arms and hit his jump gear. A savage foot kicked Lantu in the belly, a fierce stab of heat clawed at him through the protection of MacRory's repulsor field, and then the two of them were falling through ten thousand meters of empty air.

"Sweet Terra, it was a trick." Sekah whispered as his scanners came back up. "They're not after the polar PDCs—they're after *Saint-Just!*"

The Prophet eyed him blankly, clearly not understanding, and Sekah seized his arm. He almost shook him before his staggering brain realized who he'd grabbed, but he turned the Prophet towards the sphere and pointed.

"Those aren't fighters, Your Holiness! They're assault shuttles! The infidels are landing Marines right on top of Saint-Just—and they're already inside our engagement range!"

The Prophet paled in understanding, staggering back a half pace as the first marshal released him and whirled to his staff. He began barking orders, and alarms screamed throughout the vast subterranean base.

*   *   *

Marine Raiders plummeted like lethal, ungainly hawks, and the totally surprised defenses of PDC Saint-Just roused to meet them. Stunned crews flung themselves at their targeting scopes as close-range missile launchers and cannon muzzles slewed crazily, but there wasn't enough time. Not enough to sort out target signatures as small as single repulsor fields. Not enough to track and lock. A few defensive emplacements got lucky, and almost a thousand Marines died before they grounded, but they came in fast and dirty. Getting down quickly was more important than a precise landing pattern, and they overrode their automatics ruthlessly, screaming down at velocities which would have seen any one of them busted back to doolie if they'd tried it in training.

Another few hundred died or broke limbs, despite their zoots, at the speed they hit, but three Raider divisions were down, and their total casualties were barely five percent of what a conventional assault into those defenses would have cost them.

Sharon Manning slammed into the ground, cursing as two bones broke in her right foot, but her zoot was in one piece and she hit her rally signal even as she reached for her own heavy flechette launcher.

This ain't no place for a general, she told herself as a totally astonished Shellhead sentry emptied his magazine at her and she blew him into bloody rags, *but it beats hell out of being dead!*

"Get them back—now!" Aram Shahinian snapped, and Second Fleet's capital ships hurled themselves towards the limits of capital missile range.

First Marshal Sekah cursed horribly, despite the Prophet's presence, as the infidel fleet retreated. It was all a *trick*—and he'd fallen for it!

More and more surface defense positions went into action, but the infidel assault shuttles had already made their drops. Heavy weapons and ammunition canisters still plummeted behind the Raiders, but the shuttles were streaking away, hugging the sea to stay below his heavy weapons, and he snarled in frustration at their speed. The cursed things were too fast for his aircraft to catch—and they were armed. One squadron of high performance jets managed to cut the angle and intercept, but it took everything they had in full afterburner, and they got one shuttle—*one!*—before the rest of the infidel formation blotted them from the heavens.

But those shuttles were still dead if Saint-Just held. They might run rings around atmospheric craft, but they couldn't get *out* of atmosphere without braving his defensive umbrella. Yet if they *did* manage to take Saint-Just, they'd have a gap. A narrow one, but wide enough for more assaults to break through and nibble away at his ground bases. . . .

But *why?* Why run the insane risk of coming in on the ground? They could have opened the same hole from space without putting thousands of people on the planet, cut off with no retreat if their assault failed! It made no sense, unless . . .

The Prophet! They knew where he was, and they were after the Prophet himself!

He crossed quickly to the Prophet's side, bending close to murmur into his ear.

"Your Holiness, I believe the infidels know you're here. They hope to capture or kill you with this insane assault! I urge you to evacuate immediately. Allow us to deal with them before you return."

"Evacuate?!" The Prophet stared at him. "Don't be preposterous, First Marshal! This is the strongest fortress on Thebes. They'll never take it with a few thousand infantry!"

Sekah stared at him, longing to argue, but the Prophet had spoken—and this was, indeed, Thebes' strongest fortress. But was it strong enough? If the infidels had known exactly where to strike, might the Satan-Khan also have told them *how* to strike?

His spine stiffened, and he returned to his staff with

a grim expression. Satan-Khan or no, the infidels would get to the Prophet only over his own dead body.

A Theban bunker vaporized as the HVM struck, and Sharon Manning popped her jump gear, hurling herself into the glowing crater. Her staff—what of it had managed to join her—tumbled into it about her, zoots ignoring the fiery heat. A heavy weapons section materialized out of the chaos, setting up to cover the hole, and Manning grunted. It wasn't much of a CP, but it didn't look like anyone could range on them—except for that damned mortar pit. She barked an order, and three Raiders swarmed out to deal with it.

They did, but only one of them came back.

Lantu grunted in anguish as they hit the ground and MacRory's unyielding armor bruised him viciously through his armored vac suit. But he was intact, more or less, and Angus set him instantly on his feet. More Raiders filtered out of the forest about them, zoots slimed with tree sap and broken greenery, but not a single weapon fired on them. They were over two hundred kilometers from the inferno raging atop Saint-Just, and Lantu swayed dizzily as he found his bearings. Major M'boto came bounding up in the effortless leaps of his jump gear, carrying Fraymak like a child.

"That way." Lantu raised an arm and pointed. "We're still about ten kilometers east of—*ullpppp!*"

He cut off in chagrin as Angus snatched him up again and the entire battalion went streaking off along the mountainside.

Ivan Antonov watched his display, clamping his jaw and wishing his scan sections could show him what was happening. But the range was simply too great. He could only watch the relayed data from *Mangus Coloradas* and pray.

He looked up as someone stopped beside his chair.

"Well, Kthaara," he said quietly, "your little trick worked."

"Indeed," the Orion replied softly, flexing his claws as he, too, stared at the display. One hand touched the empty spot where his *defargo* had hung, and he seemed to relax slightly.

Sekah sat before his console, taking personal command of Saint-Just's defense, and sweat rimmed his cranial carapace. Those weren't mortals—they were demons! He'd never dreamed of infantry weapons like the ones they were using against him, and that powered armor—! No wonder the Fleet's boarding attacks had been so persistently thwarted after the first few months!

But demons or not, his interlacing fields of fire were killing them. Not in hundreds as they should have, but still in dozens and scores.

His orders rolled out, diverting troops from unthreatened sectors to back up his fixed positions as the infidels blew them apart. They were coming in from the west, carving a wedge-shaped salient into Saint-Just's defenses, and they were through the outer ring and into the second in far too many places. But the deeper they came, the more they exposed their flanks.

A battalion commander led his men scuttling through the personnel tunnels and launched them into the rear of an infidel company advancing up a deep ravine.

"*Your six! Watch your s—!*" Major Oels' voice died suddenly, and Lieutenant Escalante spun to the rear. A screaming wave of Shellhead infantry rolled over Delta Company like a tsunami, rocket and grenade launchers flaming. A dozen Raiders went down in an instant, and then the rest of the company was on them. A tornado of flechettes and plasma bolts piled the attackers in heaps, but eight more Delta troopers went with them.

Escalante panted, turning in circles, flechette launcher ready, but there were no live Shellheads left. Then someone touched his arm, and he damned near screamed. He whirled to face Sergeant Major Abbot, and the sergeant's grim expression crushed his scathing rebuke stillborn.

"Skipper just bought it, Lieutenant," Abbot said harshly, and Escalante noticed the blood splashed all over his zoot. "Captain Sigourny, too."

Escalante stared at him in horror. Third Battalion had been spread all over the island in the drop. Murphy only knew where the other three companies were, and Delta had already lost Lieutenant Gardener and Lieutenant Matuchek. Dear God, that meant . . .

The big sergeant nodded grimly.

"Looks like you're it, sir."

Lantu hung onto his breakfast grimly as branches lashed at his armored body. The drunken swoops wouldn't have been so bad if he, like MacRory, had known when they were coming. The colonel's jump gear was a marvel, but it was like being trapped in a demented, sideways elevator, and just clutching his inertial guidance unit was—

"Stop!" he shouted, and five hundred Terran Marines slammed to a halt as one. He was too preoccupied to be impressed. "Put me down, Colonel!"

Angus deposited him gently on the forested mountainside, and the admiral peered about, wishing it hadn't been winter the one time he'd seen this spot with his own eyes. All these damned leaves and branches. . . .

"There." He pointed, and the Terrans craned their necks at the creeper-grown hillock. It didn't look like a heavy weapons emplacement—until they checked their zoot scan systems.

" 'Twould seem yer on yer ain, Admiral," Angus said, but Lantu was already scrambling up the slope.

General Manning nodded thanks without even looking up from her portable map display as Sergeant Young slapped a fresh power cell into her zoot. This was her third CP, if such it could be called, since landing, and she was amazed they'd gotten this far. The tangled mountainsides made beacon fixes hellishly difficult, but it looked like they were into the fourth defensive ring. She grinned humorlessly. Only four more to go, and then they'd hit the *hard* stuff.

Amleto Escalante couldn't believe it. Here the Shellheads went and bored these nice, big tunnels so they could shuttle infantry back and forth, and they didn't even bother to cover them with sensors!

Not that he had any intention of complaining.

His lead squad was a hundred meters ahead of him, probing cautiously. He could have wished for more spacious quarters—in fact, his skin crawled at the thought of wallowing around in here like a bunch of troglodytes—but if there wasn't enough room to use jump gear there was still enough for them to move two abreast. He only had sixty troopers left, but he had a sneaking suspicion Delta Company was deeper into the defenses than anyone else. Now if he only knew what he was doing. . . .

"Two branches, Lieutenant," Abbot reported. "One east, one west."

Escalante flipped a mental coin.

"We go east," he muttered back.

Lantu's heart hammered as he approached the entrance. He carried only captured Theban equipment, and the Terrans had stopped beyond the scanner zone, but if they'd guessed wrong about his retinal prints . . .

He drew a deep breath as no automated weapon system tore him apart. As long as nothing fired, no alarm had been tripped—now it was up to him to keep it that way, and he removed his helmet with clumsy fingers.

A push of a button opened an armored panel, and he leaned forward, presenting his eyes and wincing as brilliant light flashed into them. He held his breath, staring into the light, then exhaled convulsively as the blinding illumination turned to muted green. He cleared his throat.

"Alpha-Zulu-Delta-Four-Niner-One," he recited carefully, and then his mouth twisted. "Great is the Prophet."

Something grated, and a vast portal yawned. He stepped through quickly, reaching for a blinking panel of lights on the tunnel wall, stabbing buttons viciously. There was a moment of hesitation, and then he grinned savagely as the entire panel went blank.

First Marshal Sekah muttered to himself as reports flooded in. The infidels were cutting still deeper, but their rate of advance was slowing. He cursed himself for not having seeded the outer rings with nuclear mines. The infidels were bunching up, and sacrificing a few thousand of his own troops would have been a paltry price for taking them out. He'd already tried air strikes, but their damned kinetic missile launchers had an impossible range. None of the nuclear strike aircraft from his other bases had lived to get close enough, and Saint-Just's own air fields were closed by heavy fire.

But even without nuclear weapons, he was grinding them down. It was only a matter of time, he thought, and tried not to think about the Satan-Khan's malign influence.

The first twenty Raiders crowded into the lead monorail car as Lantu clambered into its control chair. He'd been more than half afraid to summon the vehicles lest he trigger someone's suspicions, but they needed the speed. And the system was fully automated. With so much else to worry about, he doubted anyone had the spare attention to monitor it.

"Ready?" He looked back at MacRory, and Angus nodded sharply. The first admiral breathed a silent prayer to Whoever might really be listening, and five hundred Terran Marines—and two traitorous Thebans—went streaking into the heart of PDC Saint-Just at two hundred kilometers per hour.

"Oh, *shit!*"
Escalante hugged the wall in reflex action as the sudden roar of combat rolled down the tunnel. He punched

an armored fist into the stone, then jerked back up and
bounded forward. Sergeant Major Abbot grabbed for
him, missed, and went streaking after him, cursing all
wet-nosed officers who didn't have the sense Mithra gave
a Rigelian.

"Sweet Terra!"
Sekah jerked as fresh alarms shrieked, and his eyes
turned in horror to the illuminated schematic of Saint-
Just's personnel tunnels. A crimson light glared—*and it
was inside the final defensive perimeter!*

Escalante rounded a bend into a huge, brilliantly lit
cavern just as his point finished off the last astonished
Shellhead missile tech. He looked around him in disbelief, staring at the sequoia-sized trunks of capital missile
launchers. Sweet Jesus—they were inside *the main base!*
"Sar'major Abbot!"
"Aye, sir!" Abbot appeared almost as if he'd been chasing him, and Escalante pointed across the cavern.
"Cover that tunnel! Mine it and drop it. Then I want
blastpacks on that hatch over there—move it, Sar'major!"
"Aye, aye, sir!" Abbot barked. Mithra! Maybe this idiot
knew what he was doing after all!

"Brigadier Ho is pinned down, sir."
Sharon Manning grimaced and tried to think. Ho's brigade was her point now, and he'd been shot to hell. She
stared at her map display, scrolling through the terrain
and thanking God Commander Trevayne had managed
to get them such detailed maps. Now where—?
It had to be coming from that bunker complex. And
that meant . . .
"Hook Fourth Brigade around to the north." A burst
of rifle fire battered her zoot, and she curled around,
automatically protecting the display board without even
looking up. The cough of a flechette launcher from behind her silenced the fire, but she hardly noticed. "While
the Fourth moves up," she went on without a break, "get

Second Battalion of the Nineteenth out on their flank. Tell them to watch out for rocket fire from—"

She went on snapping orders, and tried not to think of how many of her people were already dead.

A company of Theban infantry pounded down the tunnel to Missile Bay Sixty-Four, unable to believe their orders. There was no way—*no way*—infidels could be *inside* Saint-Just! It *had* to be a mistake!

The captain at their head raced around a turn and sighed in relief as he saw the closed hatch. *False alarm*, he thought, waving for his troops to slow their headlong pace. *If it weren't, that hatch*—

Fifty kilos of high explosive turned the hatch into shrieking shrapnel and killed him where he stood.

Escalante started to wave his troopers forward, then stopped dead. Fuck! Maybe Sergeant Grogan had been right about what lieutenants used for brains! Here he was deep inside the enemy position, and he hadn't even bothered to tell anyone about it! But none of their coms would punch through this much rock, so . . .

His eye lit on Private Lutwell. Something big and nasty had wrecked the exoskeleton of her zoot's right arm, and the useless limb was clipped to her side while she managed her flechette launcher with an awkward left hand.

"Lutwell!"

"Sir?"

"Shag ass back down that tunnel. Tell 'em we're inside and that I'm advancing, sealing branch corridors with demo charges to cover my flanks."

"But, sir, I—"

"Don't fucking argue!" Escalante snarled "*Do* it, Trooper, or I'll have your guts for breakfast!"

Lutwell popped into the tunnel like a scalded rabbit, and Escalante swung back to his front. He paused for just an instant as he saw the grin on Abbot's face, and then his people were moving forward once more.

*   *   *

The monorail braked in a dimly-lit tunnel, and the battalion spilled out, looming like chlorophyll-daubed trolls in the semi-dark. Lantu scuttled out behind Angus as Fraymak pelted up with M'boto.

"That shaft, Fraymak." Lantu pointed. "Remember the security point just before Tunnel Fourteen." Fraymak nodded. He could handle the standard security systems on the way, but his retinal patterns couldn't access the classified security point; he and M'boto would have to blow their way through.

"Remember," Lantu said, "give us ten minutes—at least *ten* minutes—before you blow it."

"Yes, sir." Fraymak saluted, then held out his hand. Lantu took it. "Good luck, sir."

"And to you." The admiral squeezed the armored gauntlet and stepped back. "This way, Colonel Mac-Rory," he said. Angus scooped him up once more, and the battalion vanished into the darkness down two different shafts.

"Your Holiness," Sekah's face was pale, "the infidels are inside our inner ring."

The Prophet inhaled sharply and raised one hand to grip the sphere of Holy Terra hanging on his chest. Sekah swallowed and cursed himself viciously. He didn't know how they'd gotten so deep, but he should have stopped them. It was his *job* to stop them—and he'd failed.

"I don't know how big a force it is," he continued flatly. "It may be only a patrol—but it may be the lead elements of an entire regiment. I've diverted reinforcements, but it will take them fifteen minutes to get there." He drew a ragged breath. "Your Holiness, I implore you to evacuate. You can escape to safety in one of the nearby towns until we've dealt with the threat or . . . or—" He broke off, and the Prophet's eyes narrowed. But then he smoothed his expression and touched Sekah's shoulder carapace gently.

"As you say, my son. Doubtless you will fight better

without us to worry over, anyway." He raised his hand and signed Holy Terra's circle. "The blessings of Holy Terra be upon you, First Marshal. She will give you victory, and I shall return to see your triumph."

"Thank you, Your Holiness." Sekah's eyes glowed with gratitude, and the Prophet turned away. He beckoned to Archbishop Kirsal, and the prelate leaned close as they hurried from the control center.

"That fool will never hold," the Prophet murmured.

"Agreed," Kirsal returned equally quietly.

"We'll swing by my chambers. The suicide charge will cover our absence long enough to escape the island."

Private Sinead Lutwell stuck her head out of the tunnel—and jerked back as a blast of powered flechettes blew rock dust over her.

"*Hold your fire, you dip-shit, motherless bastard!*" she screamed, and the trooper who'd fired reared back in astonishment. She squirmed forward on her belly and glared up into the business end of a flechette launcher that was lowered with a sheepish grin.

"Delta Company's *what?*" This time General Manning did look up from her display, and her jaw dropped at her aide's asinine grin.

She bent back to the display unit, punching buttons madly, and an unholy smile lit her own face. She didn't know who the hell Lieutenant Escalante was, but he was damned well going to be *Captain* Escalante by sunset!

"Contact Fifth Brigade!" Fifth Brigade was Fourth Division's reserve, and this was just why The Book insisted on reserves. "I want at least a regiment—two, if they've got 'em loose—up that tunnel yesterday!"

"Aye, *aye*, sir!"

Lantu gestured abruptly, and Angus set him down as the final security panel came into sight. The admiral scuttled over and presented his eye, then pressed a careful sequence of buttons. The panel flashed bright for an instant until he punched two more and it went dead. A hatch slid wide.

Lantu stepped through, looked both ways down the tunnel, then waved, and two hundred and fifty Raiders filed out as quietly as their zoots would permit. He started down the passage, but an armored hand stopped him.

"Wait," Angus said quietly, and held him motionless until twenty Raiders had put their zooted bodies between him and anyone they might meet.

Escalante swore as the auto-cannon blew his point man into mangled gruel, then ducked as grenade launchers coughed. Echoing thunder rolled over him like a fist, and his dwindling force moved forward once more, slipping in bits of entrails and less mentionable things which had once been a Shellhead gun crew.

Colonel Fraymak checked his watch, then nodded to Major M'boto. Four blastpacks went off as one, blowing the armored hatch clear across Tunnel Fourteen, and four zooted troopers followed before it bounced. Two spun in each direction, hosing the passage with fire, and a dozen hapless technicians died before they realized what the concussion was.

Angus MacRory stopped, and Lantu pushed his way quickly through the Terrans. This circular chamber was the meeting point of all the escape routes, and Marines were already spreading out to cover all twelve of them. Lantu ignored them as he hurried past the elevators from above toward the coffin-shaped steel box against one wall. He stripped off his gauntlets—this one required finger-prints and retinal prints alike—and bent over it.

First Marshal Sekah whirled as a fist of thunder battered its way through the command center hatch. What—?

*   *   *

Major M'boto swore savagely as a flail of rocket fire smashed down the tunnel. They'd gotten in clean only to run into what sounded like a fucking regiment! What the hell were they doing running around this deep inside—?

He glanced at a mangled Theban body and froze, then grabbed the corpse, jerking it up to see better. His eyes widened as he saw the episcopal purple collar tabs and the golden sphere of Terra. God, no wonder they were taking such heavy fire! They'd just collided with the Prophet's personal guard!

More rockets streaked in, but his people were hugging the walls for cover and pouring back an inferno all their own. He eased forward behind them, keeping himself between the incoming and Colonel Fraymak.

The Prophet stepped into his personal chambers, ignoring the priceless artwork and tapestries. He crossed to a utilitarian computer station and brought the system on line with flying fingers, then frowned in concentration as he slowly and carefully keyed the complex code he needed.

Lantu threw back the cover of the bomb and stepped quickly aside as Angus reached in past him. His armored fist closed on the junction box the admiral had described in the planning stages. Exo-skeletal "muscles" jerked.

The Prophet punched the last key and stood back with a smile—a smile that turned into a frozen rictus as a scarlet light code flashed. He bent forward once more, pounding the keyboard in a frenzy.

Nothing happened.

He wheeled with a venomous curse, wondering what freak of damage had disabled the arming circuit. Well, no matter! He could set the charge by hand as they went by it.

M'boto's Raiders inched forward, driving the Prophet's

Guard before them. It wasn't easy. The fanatical Thebans contested every meter, and casualties were mounting. Even zoots couldn't bull through such close quarters against people who could hardly wait to die as long as they took you with them.

Colonel Ezra Montoya led his regiment down the tunnel as quickly as they could move. To think a grass-green little first lieutenant had stumbled onto something like this and known what to do with it when he did! It only proved, the colonel told himself firmly, that there really was a God.

First Marshal Sekah coughed as smoke drifted down the tunnel. The Guard were fighting like heroes, but the bellow of combat was coming closer. He turned his back on the hatch, trying to decide from his displays where the other infidel penetration had gotten to.

He didn't know, but *this* one couldn't be them . . . could it? Yet how could *two* infidel forces have pierced Saint-Just's heart?

No matter. He had to deal with the one he knew about, and he snapped fresh orders. Two battalions which had been feeling their way towards the other penetration wheeled and converged upon the Guard.

M'boto crouched with Fraymak behind a shattered blast door. But for the Prophet's Guard, they'd already have been inside the command center, but the bastards had slowed them just long enough to get help, and reinforcements were springing up like ragweed.

He looked at the colonel, and Fraymak's eyes were bitter. They weren't going to break through, but if they stayed where they were, someone was going to take them in the rear, and then—

The two officers froze as a roar of weapons erupted behind them.

Sekah bared his teeth at the report. The infidels had

gotten within two hundred meters of his CP, but they were done for now. He had them trapped between the surviving Guard, reinforced by a fresh battalion, and a second battalion coming in behind them. Powered armor or not, they could never survive that concentration of firepower.

Amleto Escalante had never been so tired, so scared, or so alive. They'd moved the better part of a klick in the last ten minutes without seeing a soul, and he was just as happy. His people were out of demo charges, and their flanks were hanging wide open with no way to seal the side passages, but so what? They should all be dead already, right? And the deeper they got before they had to fort up, the better.

He looked around at his remaining thirty troopers and saw the same "what the hell" grins looking back at him. He waved them forward.

Major M'boto squirmed around and headed down tunnel, then stopped as he saw his rear-guard falling back toward him. Whatever was coming must be nasty, and he reached out and grabbed the nearest demolition man.

"Charges!" he snapped. "There, there, and there. When the last of our people come by, blow the whole fucking thing in their faces!"

"Aye, aye, sir!"

M'boto headed back up front. That took care of the back door. Unfortunately, it also meant the only way out was forward.

The Prophet shoved past Kirsal into the elevator and waited impatiently for the others. They crowded the large car uncomfortably, but his thoughts were on other things as he punched the "down" button.

Lantu sat on the disarmed bomb, holding his Theban-made assault rifle across his lap. Terra, he was tired!

He realized what he'd thought and grinned, but he

was really too weary to think up a fresh oath. He watched Angus deploying one company to hold the tunnels while the other headed back to link up with M'boto before a pincer up the elevator shafts opened a second avenue to the control center.

He inhaled deeply and marveled at the sheer, sensual joy of doing so. He'd never expected to be alive this long—hadn't, he finally admitted, *wanted* to be alive—but he was. And it felt remarkably good.

He grinned again and reached for his armored gauntlets, then froze as a light blinked above the elevator doors.

Escalante's tiny force stiffened as they heard the thunder ahead of them, and the lieutenant grinned fiercely.

"Well, Sar'major, sounds like some more of our people've dropped by."

"Can't hardly be anything else, Skipper," Abbot agreed with an answering grin.

"Let's go crash the party."

Sekah cringed as a fresh explosion sent rock dust eddying into the command center. Frantic voices in his headphones told him the infidels had dropped the tunnel roof on the rear battalion's lead platoon, but his people between them and the control room were still holding. Barely.

He punched commands into his console, looking desperately for troops to divert to the fire fight. If he could just bring in a few more—

Something made him look up, and he gawked in horror at the troll which had suddenly appeared in the unguarded hatch across the control room.

He was still lunging to his feet and clawing for his machine-pistol when Lieutenant Amleto Escalante, TFMC, blew him into bloody meat.

The Prophet swore with satisfaction as the elevator

came to a halt. The doors slid open, and he stepped out, already turning towards the bomb.

The last thing he ever saw was the muzzle flash of First Admiral Lantu's assault rifle.

General Manning limped slowly along the tunnel, unable even now to believe they'd done it. Casualty reports were still coming in, and they sounded bad. So far, she had at least nine thousand confirmed dead—fifteen percent of her total force—plus God only knew how many wounded, and she knew damned well they were going to find lots more of both.

But for the moment she pushed the thought aside and opened the visor of her bullet-spalled combat zoot. Even the smoke inside PDC Saint-Just smelled better than *she* did after nineteen hours of combat.

She was on her last set of power cells, like almost all of her people, but the destruction of the command center had been decisive. The defenders' coordination had vanished, and when Montoya brought an entire regiment right into the middle of their position, the Shellheads had nowhere to go but Hell.

Which, she thought grimly, was precisely where most of them had gone.

She stepped over a heap of Theban bodies into what had been the command center, and her eyebrows rose as she saw both of their Theban allies. Incredible. She'd never expected any of that forlorn hope to survive.

People saluted, and she returned their salutes wearily. MacRory, she saw—and what asshole ever let a sergeant with his potential slip away without re-upping?—and M'boto. And somebody else.

"General," MacRory said, " 'tis a fine thing tae see ye."

"And you, Colonel." She nodded to Colonel Fraymak and Admiral Lantu, filing away the latter's strange, deeply satisfied expression for later consideration, then turned her attention to the young man sitting on the computer console between MacRory and M'boto. A big, grim-faced sergeant hovered protectively behind him, and he was no longer wearing his zoot—for obvious reasons, given the blood-soaked splints on his left leg and arm. There were more bandages strapped around his torso, and his face was pasty gray. Nasty, Manning thought, but all the bits and pieces still seemed to be attached. That was all the medics really needed these days.

"And who might this be?" she asked, for the youngster had lost his shirt in the first-aid process, and she saw no rank insignia.

"Och, 'tis the lad who saved M'boto's arse!" MacRory grinned, and M'boto nodded firmly. "Lieutenant Escalante, General."

"I'm afraid you're wrong, Colonel," Manning said. The injured young officer looked up at her in more confusion than pain-killers alone could explain, and she held out her right hand. He extended his own automatically, and she clasped it firmly, ignoring the baffled expressions all around her.

"This, gentlemen," she announced, "is *Captain* Escalante, the newest recipient of the Golden Lion of Terra."

It was really too bad, she always thought later, that she hadn't had a camera with her.

CHAPTER THIRTY-ONE
The Terms of Terra

Ivan Antonov glowered at the recorded image on his screen and tuned out the long, impassioned diatribe. Sooner or later the Theban would run down and get to the heart of his reply. And, unless the Theban race truly was insane, Antonov knew what that reply would be. Of course, he was beginning to wonder if, with the exception of a few individuals like Lantu and Fraymak, there might not be something to the theory of racial insanity.

PDC Saint-Just had cost less than he'd feared, if far more than he would find easy to live with, and if there were any justice in the universe its loss would have finished the Church of Holy Terra. But no. The surviving Synod had gotten together, canonized its dead Prophet, anointed a new Prophet in his stead, and announced its determination to pursue the jihad even unto martyrdom.

Personally, Antonov was about ready to oblige the *svolochy*.

Vanya, Vanya that's the nasty side of you talking! And so it was, but if he could contrive to hang just the Synod, perhaps the rest of the population might learn from example?

Of course, the best way to encourage fanaticism was to provide it with fresh martyr-fodder, yet he couldn't quite suppress the wistful temptation. It was really too bad he couldn't even voice it aloud, but he shuddered to think how Kthaara would react after all his lectures. And it didn't help his mood to find the Synod reacting to the truth about the First Prophet exactly as Lantu had predicted. The new Prophet stubbornly insisted that if infidels could extract data from *Starwalker's* computers they could also *insert* data, and his fire-and-brimstone denunciation of monsters vile enough to defile sacred scripture had brought Antonov to the point of apoplexy. And the worst of it—the absolute worst—was that the old bastard actually *believed* the *polneyshaya* he was spouting. They'd gotten rid of a clique of self-serving, lying charlatans only to replace it with a crop of true believers!

Religious fervor! The only thing it's good for is turning brains to oatmeal! And if there's one thing in this galaxy worse than Terran *politicians, it's theocratic politicians!*

The Prophet's latest fulmination reached its peroration, and Antonov's eyes sharpened as the Theban who had once been Archbishop Ganhad of the Ministry of Production glared at him.

"And so, infidel," the Prophet said bitterly, "we have no choice but to hear your words. Yet be warned! Your accursed master the Satan-Khan will not pervert our Faith as he has your own! The true People of Holy Terra will never abandon their Holy Mother, and the day shall come when you and all of your apostate race will pay the price for your sins against Her! We—"

Antonov grunted and killed the message before the old fart got himself back up to speed. That was all he really needed to know—now he could let Winnie wade through the rest of this drivel and summarize any unlikely tidbits of importance. He felt a tiny qualm of conscience at passing the task to her, but rank, after all, had its privileges.

Thank God.

"Actually," Lantu said, "I must confess to a bit of hope."

The first admiral's almost whimsical smile was a far cry from the tortured expression he'd worn before his personal extermination of the Prophet and his entourage, and Antonov envied him. Kthaara'zarthan envied him even more, but he was content. His *defargo* had been present if he couldn't be, and he'd almost purred as he made Lantu relive every moment of the encounter. The bared-fang grin of total approval he'd bestowed on his one-time mortal enemy had surprised even Antonov; the rest of Second Fleet's senior officers were still in shock. And when Tsuchevsky had caught the Orion initiating the Theban into the pleasures of vodka—!

"You must?" Antonov asked, suppressing yet another ignoble urge to twit his *vilkshatha* brother.

"Indeed. Aside from his religious fervor, Ganhad is no fool. Once you get past his ranting and raving, it looks as if he recognizes the reality of his helplessness, and unlike his predecessor, he truly cares about the People. That should make some sort of settlement possible."

Antonov grunted and turned his glass in his hands. Delighted as he was by Pericles Waldeck's fall from power, the chaos on Old Terra had dumped yet another pile of manure in his lap. President Sakanami's administration had been devastated by Howard's Assembly revelations. One or two LibProgs were actually muttering about impeachment in the apparent hope of saving themselves by poleaxing their own party's president, and his cabinet was a shambles. Of all the pre-war ministers, only Hamid O'Rourke remained. Waldeck and Sakanami had gone behind his back to transmit Aurelli's pre-Lorelei orders via the minister for foreign affairs, and his work since the Peace Fleet massacre, especially as Howard's ally within the cabinet, had won widespread approval.

There was even—Antonov grinned at the thought—talk of running him for president. One thing was certain; no one would be renominating Sakanami Hideoshi!

Meanwhile, however, the confusion left the foreign affairs ministry a total, demoralized wreck, too busy defending the careers of its survivors and fending off Assembly "fact-finding" committees to worry about diplomacy. And since he'd done so well fighting the war, the politicos had decided to let Ivan Antonov *end* the war. After everything else they'd saddled him with in the last two and a half years, the *vlasti* had decided to make him a peace envoy!

"No, really." Lantu's improbably long arm stretched out to refill his own vodka glass. "You're not going to get him to accept unconditional surrender, and if you show a single sign of weakness or wavering he may be able to convince himself 'Holy Terra' is intervening on his side and turn stubborn, but otherwise I think he'll accept the terms you actually plan to offer."

"The terms *you* plan to offer," Antonov corrected for, in a sense, that was no more than literal truth. Lantu's personal familiarity with the Synod's members had guided the careful crafting of a package both sides might be able to live with, though the prelates' reaction, had any of them suspected who the infidels' advisor was, scarcely bore thinking on.

Lantu gave him a small, Theban smile and shrugged.

"Actually, Admiral, I believe the first admiral is correct." Winnifred Trevayne's diffidence couldn't quite hide her delight. She was in her element analyzing the Theban responses—which, Antonov reflected, probably said something unhealthy about her intellect. "The new Prophet will undoubtedly rant and rave, but he has no realistic option. He knows that. If he didn't, he wouldn't have agreed even to meet with you, and I think he's afraid you're going to demand something far worse. No doubt he's screwed himself up to accept martyrdom rather than that something worse, and when you start turning the screws, he's going to be certain that's what's

coming. Which means that when you offer him the rest
of the terms Admiral Lantu's suggested they'll seem so
much better than his expectations he'll jump at them."
She smiled slightly. "In fact, he'll probably think you're
a fool for letting him off so lightly."

"You do great things for my self-esteem, Commander,"
Antonov growled, but his eyes gleamed appreciatively.

"Well, sir, it's not really that different from a military
operation, is it?" she replied. "We don't care what they
think of us. We only have to worry about what they do."

The Prophet of Holy Terra's nostrils flared as he entered the conference room. His stiff face was expressionless, but his eyes flitted about as if he expected the Satan-
Khan himself to materialize in a puff of smoke. Antonov
rose on the far side of the table, flanked by his staff
and senior officers (with the conspicuous exception of his
special deputy for fighter operations) as the Prophet's
delegation of bishops and archbishops followed him.
Their yellow eyes flared with contempt for the heretics
before them, but contempt was a frail shield for the terror which lurked behind it.

Antonov waited as they took their waiting chairs stiffly,
then sank into his own chair, followed a fraction of a
second later by his subordinates. He faced the Prophet
across the table and cleared his throat.

"This is only a preliminary meeting," he rumbled, "and
there will be no discussion. You may debate among yourselves at your leisure; I do not intend to do so."

The Prophet stiffened even further, but Antonov's
flinty eyes stopped him before he spoke. They held the
Theban's gaze unwaveringly, and the Prophet closed his
lips firmly.

"I will say only this," Antonov resumed when he was
certain the other had yielded. "Were we indeed the 'infidels' you term us, your planet would be dead. You have
no weapon which can prevent us from destroying your
species. We have not done so solely because we *choose*
not to do so. Our continued restraint is contingent upon

your ability to convince us that we can allow you to live
without endangering ourselves or our allies, and the only
way in which you can convince us is to accept the terms
I am about to announce."

Two pairs of eyes locked anew, and Antonov felt a stir
of satisfaction at the desperation in the Prophet's. Lantu
and Winnie were right. The Theban was terrified of what
he was about to hear, yet knew he had no choice but to
hear it.

"First," he said coldly, "Thebes shall disarm, totally
and completely. All planetary defense centers will be
razed. All heavy planetary combat equipment will be destroyed. No armed starships will be permitted."

He watched the dismay in the Thebans' faces and continued unflinchingly.

"Second, the Terran Federation Navy shall maintain
asteroidal forts and OWPs, in strength sufficient to satisfy
its own security determinations, within the Thebes System. These fortifications will command a radius of ten
light-minutes from the system's warp point.

"Third, the Federation government shall retain possession of the planetary defense center on the Island of
Arawk and shall maintain there a garrison of up to one
Terran Marine division plus support troops. A spaceport
facility shall be built within the enclave so established
and shall be under the exclusive control of the Terran
Federation."

Dismay became horror at the thought of an infidel
presence actually profaning the surface of Thebes, and
he paused, letting their revulsion work upon them. As
Lantu had predicted, they were clearly gathering their
courage to reject the still worse demands to come, and
he cleared his throat.

"Fourth," he said quietly, "there shall be no general
occupation of Thebes." The Prophet's eyes widened in
astonishment, but Antonov maintained his stony expression. "The Terran presence on Thebes beyond the Arawk
enclave shall be limited to inspection parties whose sole
purpose shall be to determine that the conditions of the

peace settlement are fully observed. Said inspections shall have complete, unlimited access to any point on Thebes, but Theban inspectors shall be free to accompany our own.

"Fifth, any Theban citizen who desires to emigrate shall have the right to do so. If the Theban government chooses not to support such emigration, the Terran Federation will do so through its facilities on Arawk Island.

"Sixth, the Terran Federation shall be free to present its interpretation of the history of Terra to the Theban people via electronic media." Breath hissed across the table at the thought of such spiritual contamination, but he continued unhurriedly. "We are aware that you reject the truthfulness of your own computer files. We do not share your doubts as to their veracity, but the Terran Federation will declare that the events described in that data occurred on the planet of Thebes and, as such, constitute a portion of the history of Thebes, and not of Terra. We will, therefore, undertake to make no reference to any events which occurred within the Theban System prior to the present war."

The Prophet sank back, his eyes more astonished than ever. Surely the agents of the Satan-Khan couldn't resist the opportunity to attack the very foundations of the Faith! Antonov noted his expression, and this time he permitted himself a thin smile.

"Seventh, the government of Thebes shall have sole and unchallenged control over its own immigration policy, with the exception of movements within the Arawk enclave."

More of the Synod gawked at him. No general occupation? No use of the locked files against them? Not even an insistence on infiltrating agents of heresy in the guise of "tourists"?!

"Eighth, the Terran Federation, which honors a tradition of freedom of conscience and guarantees a legal right to freedom of religion, shall neither forcibly suppress the Faith of Holy Terra on Thebes, nor restrict the right of Theban missionaries to move freely among Federation planets and their populations."

The Thebans verged on a state of shock. Had they been even a little less experienced in the Synod's political infighting, jaws would have hung slackly.

"Ninth, although Thebes will be permitted no armed starships, a Theban merchant marine may be established if the people of Thebes so desire, with the sole restriction that all starships departing the Thebes System shall do so subject to boarding by Federation inspectors from the fortifications to be maintained therein. Said inspections shall be limited to a determination that the inspected vessels are indeed unarmed. Theban trade shall not be restricted in any way, and Thebes shall be free to trade with the Federation should it so desire.

"Tenth, in light of the fact that Thebes will be allowed no military forces, the Terran Federation shall guarantee the security of the System of Thebes against external enemies.

"Eleventh, Thebes shall not be required to pay indemnities or reparations to any star nation. *However*"—Antonov's voice hardened—"the government of Thebes *shall* be required to acknowledge, formally and for the record, that the attack by its armed forces on the Tenth Destroyer Squadron, Khanate of Orion Space Navy, was made without provocation under the guise of an offer to parley. And the government of Thebes shall further acknowledge that this attack was made on the express orders of the then Prophet."

Ivan Antonov leaned forward and spoke very quietly.

"Twelfth, Theban personnel responsible for atrocities on planets of the Terran Federation shall be held personally accountable by the Federation."

He met the Prophet's eyes coldly.

"I do not care why this war was launched, Prophet, but there will be no question, now or ever, of who fired the first shot and under what circumstances, nor will we permit criminals to escape punishment. The Federation will return its Theban prisoners of war as rapidly as possible, but individuals who, while in occupation of Terran-populated worlds, committed acts which constitute criminal offenses under the laws of those worlds, will be tried and, if convicted, sentenced by Terran courts. We did not attack you. We have suffered far higher civilian casualties than you. Our legal system will deal with those who have committed atrocities against our people."

He held the Theban's gaze unwaveringly, his face carved from granite, and it was the Prophet's eyes which wavered.

"The terms I have just enunciated are those of the Terran Federation. They are not negotiable. You have one standard week to accept or reject them. If you choose not to accept them by the end of that time, my forces will move against Thebes in whatever strength I deem appropriate."

He rose, his staff standing behind him, and his voice was frozen helium.

"This meeting is adjourned."

CHAPTER THIRTY-TWO

Khimhok za'Fanak

This time Francis Mulrooney felt no surprise when the *kholokhanzir's* herald led him into the guarded apartment, yet tension more than compensated for its absence. The aged Orion on the dais seemed not even to have moved in the thirty-two standard months since their last meeting, and his bright eyes watched the Terran ambassador's approach.

Mulrooney stopped and bowed, then straightened. Liharnow'hirtalkin's hand rose. It held the formal parchment document, signed by the Prophet of Holy Terra and sealed with the sigil of his faith.

"I have received your message and your document, Ambassador," the *Khan'a'khanaaeee* said. "Your Admiral Aantaahnaav is to be commended upon his understanding of the *Zheeerlikou'valkhannaieee* and the demands of our code of honor." The Khan's ears twitched. "Perhaps he had also some small assistance from Kthaara'aantaahnaav," he added dryly, and Mulrooney felt an icicle of relief at his tone. Then Liharnow's ears straightened more seriously, and he sat fully erect.

418

"Neither the *Zheeerlikou'valkhannaieee* nor the Federation read the original events in Lorelei aright, Ambassador. Had we done so, much suffering on the part of your people might have been averted. Yet even after the truth was known, the Federation honored its responsibilities. This"—he twitched the parchment—"shall be placed among the state records of my people and of my clan to serve the *Zheeerlikou'valkhannaieee* forever as an example of a *khimhok's* fidelity. We have received *shirnowkashaik* from the oath-breakers who slew our warriors, and in the name of the *Zheeerlikou'valkhannaieee* I now renounce all reparations. There has been *khiinarma*. I am content, and I declare before Hiranow'khanark and my clan fathers that the Federation is *khimhok za'fanak*."

Despite decades of diplomatic experience, Mulrooney exhaled a tremendous sigh of relief and bent his head with profound gratitude.

"In the name of my people, I thank you, *Hia'khan*," he said softly.

"Your thanks are welcomed, but they are not necessary," the khan replied just as softly. "The *Zheeerlikou'-valkhannaieee* themselves could not have more honorably acquitted themselves. There will be no more talk of *cho-faki* among my fangs. You are not *Zheeerlikou'valkhannaieee*, yet we learned to respect your warriors' courage as allies against the Rigelians; now their honor makes the differences between us seem as nothing. And that, Ambassador, is what truly matters to us all."

Mulrooney bowed once more, touching his fist to his chest in silence, and the Khan rose with fragile, aged grace. The Terran's eyes widened as the *Khan'a'kha-naaeee* stepped down from his dais and performed an unthinkable act. He extended his hand and touched an alien ambassador.

"It is time to present this *shirnowkashaik* to my fangs," Liharnow said, leaning upon the human's arm for support, "and I would have you present when they receive it." He smiled a wry, fang-hidden smile as the Terran moved with exquisite care, supporting his weight as if it were the most important task in the Galaxy. "For today, you shall be Fraaanciiis'muuulroooneeee, a *hirikrinzi* of the *Zheeerlikou'valkhannaieee*, and not the Ambassador of the Terran Federation, for ambassadors are not required between warriors who have bled for one another's honor."

All the other farewells were over—but for one—and for now Antonov and Kthaara had the small lounge in Old Terra's Orbit Port Nineteen to themselves. They stood side by side, human and Orion silhouetted against the transparent bulkhead as they gazed at the breathtaking blue curve of the world they had left only hours before.

Kthaara had accompanied Antonov back to the home world that was, in part, now his. He had wanted to see it . . . and he had stoically endured the ceremonies in which humanity loaded him down with decorations and promoted him to captain, a rank he would now hold for life. And now he awaited the liner that would take him on the long voyage back to *Valkha'zeeranda* to become again a small claw of the Khan and resume the life he would never again see through quite the same eyes.

He finally broke the companionable silence. "Well," he said mischievously, "has the new Sky Marshal settled into his duties?"

Antonov snorted explosively. "They couldn't give me more rank," he rumbled, "so they created a new rank. And they've decided they need a clearly defined military commander in chief . . . especially now that they won't have Howard Anderson to tickle their tummies and wipe their butts for them! Of course," he smiled thinly, "they don't *really* believe they'll ever need the position—or the military—again. Every war is always the last war!" His smile grew even thinner. "Well, the politicians may *think* they've put me in a gilded dust bin, but until I finally take Pavel Sergeyevich's advice and retire to Novaya Rodina, those *vlasti* aren't going to forget I'm here! I'm going to use the position to make sure the Navy is ready when it's needed again—as it will be!" He sighed deeply. "There is much we can learn from the Orions, Kthaara . . . such as seeing the universe as it is."

"There is much the *Zheeerlikou'valkhannaieee* can learn from your race, as well," Kthaara replied quietly. "And before you depart for Novaya Rodina—where I expect you will be terribly frustrated, since a young colony cannot afford a surplus of politicians for you to growl about!—I plan to hold you to your promise to visit *Valkha'zeeranda* and meet the other members of your clan." He grew serious. "You are right, of course. Dangers which we cannot foresee will threaten our two races in the future. But whatever happens, the Federation will always have a friendly voice in the councils of the *Khan'a'Khanaaeee*. Clan Zarthan is now linked to your people by bonds of blood, for we are *vilkshatha*." He gave a carnivore's smile in which Antonov could recognize sadness. "My ship departs soon, so let us say our farewells now . . . Vanya."

He had never heard anyone call Antonov that (in fact, the mind boggled at the thought), but he'd looked up the familiar form of Ivan and practiced until he could produce a sound very close to it. Now he waited expectantly . . . and saw an expression he'd never seen on his friend's muscular face. He even—incredibly—saw one droplet of that saline solution Human eyes produced for any number of oddly contradictory reasons.

"You know," Antonov said finally, "no one has called me that since Lydochka . . ." He couldn't continue.

"You never speak of your wife. Why is that?"

Antonov tried to explain, yet could not. In the decades since Lydia Alekseyevna Antonova had died with her infant daughter in a freak, senseless traffic accident, her widower had gradually become the elemental force, without a personal life, the Navy now knew as Ivan the Terrible . . . but there were some pains even Ivan the Terrible could not endure explaining—even to himself.

Now he gave one of the broad grins only those who knew him well were ever allowed to see. "Never mind.

Farewell, Kthaara," he said, and took the Orion in a bear hug that would have squeezed the wind from a weaker being.

"Well, isn't this cozy!"

Howard Anderson's powered wheelchair hummed into the lounge. The right corner of his mouth drooped, and his right hand was a useless claw in his lap, but the old blue eyes were bright, and if his speech was slurred it was no less pungent than of yore.

"My ship leaves soon, and I only just gave my nursemaid the slip. And unlike some people—" he gestured at the remains of the bar "—I'm about to dry up and blow away! So for God's sake pour before the doctors catch up with me, Ivan! Two bourbons—right, Kthaara?"

"Actually, Admiral Aandersaahn, I believe I will have vodka." Anderson's eyebrows rose, but worse was yet to come. Kthaara tossed off his drink with what sounded awfully like an attempt at a Russian toast, then addressed Antonov. "Oh, yes, Ivaan Nikolaaayevicch, that reminds me. Thank you for the translations—and I hope you can manage to send more." He turned to Anderson. "Although I admit to some trouble with the names—a problem, I understand, not entirely unknown even among Humans—I find I have acquired a taste for Russian literature. Indeed," he continued with the enthusiasm of the neophyte, "I regard it as a unique ornament of your race's cultural heritage. Do you not agree, Admiral Aandersaahn?"

Anderson turned, horrified, to face Antonov's beaming countenance.

"You Red bastard!" he gasped. "You've corrupted him!"

Old Terra receded in Anderson's cabin view port, and the left side of his mouth twitched in a tiny smile as he contemplated the chaos he was leaving behind on that world. Just over a year of Sakanami Hideoshi's presidency remained, and if he was very lucky he might be able to fix a traffic fine before leaving office; he certainly wasn't going to achieve any more than that. Anderson was a little sorry for him, but only a little. The man had done a workman-like job of actually fighting the war, but if he'd done his duty properly, there never would have *been* a war. If he was as astute a politician as Anderson thought, he knew that only his resignation might let him end on a note of dignity.

Nothing, on the other hand, was going to save Pericles Waldeck from history—or his fellows. He was guilty of two crimes too terrible for political pardon: he'd lied to the Assembly and provoked a war ... and he'd been caught at it. That was a source of unalloyed satisfaction to Howard Anderson. The LibProgs would recover—probably by denouncing Waldeck and Sakanami more vociferously than anyone else—and the Corporate Worlds' political power would continue to grow, but he'd taken them down a peg. He'd slowed them, and the planet of Christophon would require decades to regain the prestige it had lost.

Yet the fates of politicos, however satisfying, were as nothing beside his pride in the Terran Federation and its Navy. With all its warts—and God knew they were legion—humanity had risen to its responsibilities once more. He wouldn't be here to see its next great challenge, but as long as there were Ivan Antonovs, Angus MacRorys, Caitrin MacDougalls, Andy Mallorys, Hannah Avrams, and, yes, Hamid O'Rourkes, the human race would be in good hands.

And for now, he had one last task to perform.

He looked down at the document folder in his lap, and his left hand stroked the embossed starships and planet and moon of the Terran Federation Navy on its cover. He had promised Chien-lu he would visit Hang-chow, and so he would—to deliver personally to Chien-lu's son the official verdict of the Court of Inquiry on the Battle of Lorelei.

His fingers stilled on the folder and he leaned back against his cushions to watch the stars.

* * *

Hannah Avram walked slowly out into the sunlight and brushed back her hair with her right hand. She was becoming accustomed to her robotic arm, but even under her therapists' tyranny, it would be months yet before she trusted its fingers for any delicate task. She stood leaning against the hospital balcony's rail, reveling in the sheer joy of breathing as her grafted lungs filled with New Danzig's autumn air. The ghosts of her dead had retreated, especially after the crushing defeat the New Danzig electorate had handed Josef Wyszynski and his entire Tokarov-backed slate of candidates.

The door opened behind her, and she turned as Dick Hazelwood joined her on the balcony. He, too, wore an admiral's uniform, and he squeezed her right shoulder gently, then leaned on the rail beside her, staring out over the city of Gdansk.

"It's official," he said quietly. "Admiral Timoshenko wants me for The Yard."

"Good. You deserve it."

"Maybe, but . . ." His voice trailed off and he turned to frown at her. She met his gaze innocently, and his frown deepened. "Damn it, Hannah," he sighed finally, "I know it's a great opportunity—better than I ever thought I'd see—but I don't want to leave New Danzig."

"Why not?"

"You *know* why," he said uncomfortably, looking back out over the city.

"I do?"

"Yes, you do!" He wheeled back to her with a glare. "Damn it, woman, are you going to make me say it? All right, then, I love you and I don't want to leave you behind! There! Are you satisfied now?"

She met his eyes levelly, and her lips slowly blossomed in a smile.

"Do you know, I think I am," she murmured, reaching up to touch the side of his face. "But I'm not going to be in therapy here forever, you know. In fact—" her smile turned wicked "—they're transferring me to Galloway's World to finish my convalescence before I take over Sky Watch there."

Lantu—no longer First Admiral Lantu, but simply Lantu—stood with his arm about his wife and watched Sean David Andrew Tulloch Angus MacDougall Mac-Rory scuttle across the floor towards his mother. The infant's speed astounded Lantu, for Theban children were much slower than that before they learned to walk. And, he thought with a small smile, he would have expected the sheer weight of his name to slow him down considerably!

The commander in chief of the New New Hebrides Peaceforce stood beside Caitrin, craggy face beaming as he watched his son, and he chuckled as Caitrin scooped him up.

"Och, Katie! 'Tis a gae good thing he takes after yer side o' the family, lass!"

"Oh, I don't know." Caitrin ruffled the boy's red-gold hair, cooing to him enthusiastically, then smiled wickedly at her husband. "He's got your eyes—and I haven't heard him say a word yet, either!"

Angus grinned hugely, and Lantu laughed out loud. He and Hanat crossed to their hosts, Hanat moving a bit more slowly and carefully than was her wont. Her slender figure had altered drastically in the last two months, for Theban gestation periods were short and multiple births were the norm, but her smile was absolutely stunning.

Angus waved them into Theban-style chairs on the shady verandah, and the four of them sat, looking out through the green-gold shadow of the towering banner oaks at the sparkling ocean of New Hebrides.

"Sae, then, Lantu," Angus said, breaking the companionable silence at last. "Is it an official New Hebridan ye are the noo?"

"Yes." Lantu leaned further back, still holding Hanat's hand. "The Synod knows about Fraymak and me, and we've both been anathematized and excommunicated." He grimaced. "It hurts—not because either of us cares about their religious claptrap but because we can never go home again."

"Ah, but hame is where yer loved, lad," Angus said gently, and Caitrin nodded beside him. " 'Tis no what I expected when I was scheming how t' kill ye, ye ken, but 'tis true enow fer that."

"I know," Lantu looked over at his hosts and smiled with a trace of sadness, "and I imagine the Synod's been a bit surprised by how many of our people refused repatriation. I suspect they're going to be even more surprised by what happens to their religion once younger generations start comparing humanity's version of Terran history to theirs, too. Fraymak and I may even get a decent mention in Theban history books, someday."

"Aye t' that," Angus agreed, holding his friend's eyes warmly. "Any race needs a Cranaa'tolnatha of its ain," he said softly.